TATTOOED HEARTS

by Mika Jolie

DEDICATION

To my husband, thank you so much for all of your support and for taking over our happy chaos when I need to write. A toast to our lifetime of dating. You are my biggest fan and that makes you even sexier than you already are. Je t'aime.

My wonderful group of writers—WWLR and the ladies at Three Chicas and a Book. What can I say? You ROCK!

A big awesome hooray to my beta readers Bonnie Messinger and Lucy Gage. What can I say? We make a great team. You continue to push me and make me better. I love you bro'

Last but not least, to all the readers—without you this wouldn't be as much fun. Thank you so much for all you've helped me to accomplish.

Anyone else I may have missed. Fear not, there are more books to come.

Love you all!!!

CHAPTER ONE

*"One of the hardest things in life is having
words in your heart that you can't utter."*
~ James Earl Jones

Vineyard Haven, Martha's Vineyard, thirteen years ago . . .

CLAIRE RAN HER tongue over her lips, checking their current state. A soft, smooth, and slightly-moist mouth was ideal for kissing. Hers didn't feel chapped or dry, but to be on the safe side, she swiped the shea butter pomegranate chapstick over her lips, pressed them together then blew into her hands for a breath check.

Minty fresh.

Perfect.

The girls she knew were experts in the art of kissing. It embarrassed her to admit at fifteen, she hadn't kissed anyone. But they didn't pass judgment. Rather, her friends had given her pointers and informed her fresh breath was essential for a French kiss. For that reason, she managed to avoid garlic, onions, milk, and her favorite, corn. The tasty grain was on the *Cosmopolitan* list of "What Not to Eat" before a kiss. Last thing she wanted was Forrest pushing her away because of corn residue in her mouth.

Her gaze swept over Herring Creek Farm. The August sun shone on green everywhere. The edge of woodland sloped down gently to a bramble-filled ditch, overgrown with cow parsley. Beech trees lined the fence to the north. Their overhanging boughs provided dapple shade for the horses that stood idle, flicking away flies with their tails. Chirping birds and humming bees filled the air with the sounds of their daily duties.

Male laughter rose as Jason, Adam, and Blake tossed a football between them in the yard. They rarely let her wander away from their view, not that she had a wild streak or anything, but they were Alphas and they hovered. Always uncertain of what the band of brothers might throw at her, she didn't dare get too close to the boys. They loved to throw questions at her or worse, ask her to participate in their football tossing game, just so they could play the big brother role.

Big brothers tended to be overbearing.

Phooey! She wasn't even related to any of them.

Her gaze swiveled to Forrest. He stood not too far away in cargo Khakis and a fading Transformers T-shirt, throwing tennis balls to his father's two black Labs.

Warmth spread inside her chest, a sensation that was now synonymous with Forrest. The sight of him held an intriguing allure. Tall, athletic, with tousled dark brown hair that flopped over his eyes. Woven leather bracelets encircled his left wrist, drawing attention to the lean, hard muscles of his arms. All that football and skiing had done wonders for his amazing frame. His face wasn't too shabby either—sharp, angled jaw, full, firm lips that curved into a proud yet pleasant smile, and a nose that was just a little too big. The slight imperfection only made him more appealing.

Women often stopped in their tracks and stared at him. Claire noticed the admirers every time, but Forrest seemed oblivious to the sudden pauses and clandestine stares. When he did bestow them with a glance, his fans overcompensated with a weak smile or a blush, a dead giveaway of their admiration. He always took it in stride, never flaunted, and without a trace of arrogance. He was modest and unaware of the chaos he caused; this made the girls fall for him all the more.

According to the few conversations she overheard between Jason and the others, teenage boys were horny all the time. They thought about sex every second of the day. If the wind hit them just right, they would get excited.

Not Forrest.

He thought with the head on his shoulders, not the one south of his waist. He was different that way and stood apart from the others. Despite the opportunities that came his way, he dated very little. She once over-heard him telling the other guys he was a one-woman man who prized genuineness and thoughtful conversation above lipstick and high heels.

He was handsome, breathtaking. Her racing pulse and breathless-ness proved it. However, what she really loved about him was his in-ner beauty. From the way he cared for the animals on the farm, to his warmth with everyone on the island, and his commitment to his family and friends. He was eighteen–if a day older–and he stole her heart with-out even knowing it was in his pocket.

For the last two years, these new and strange feelings often left her befuddled. They were too strong, too intense. Physically and mentally, she reacted to him in a way she never had with any boy. The slightest touch, whether it was tugging on her hair or fixing her backpack, sent her heart spiraling out of control. On days they weren't around each other, she missed him. When she saw him, heard his name, happiness filled her. At night, his face was always the last thing she'd see; her stom-ach would backflip and she'd tingle all over before drifting into a dream where they held hands and kissed.

Now in a few days he'd leave the island and head to Boston for col-lege. Her heart screeched in anguish, its flesh lay bare in the raucous col-lision between reality and fantasy.

She had to kiss him. And for that she needed complete privacy.

She studied the stoned-faced, two story red barn with an old, worn-down tractor collecting dust next to it. She glanced at the boys, still lost in whatever they were talking about. Probably all the college girls they would be meeting when they arrived on campus. Which meant Forrest would be meeting college girls, too—knowledgeable, sophisticated girls living away from their parents, who no doubt would be on him as quick as lightning.

Panic set in. Fear. Her chance with Forrest was slipping through her fingers. She needed to kiss him and let him feel everything in her heart.

Here goes nothing.

Stealthily she moved around the farm and hauled open the unwieldy door, tired hinges creaking like a testy old man. She paused and waited for one of the boys to call after her. When they didn't, she rushed inside, closed the door behind her, and sucked in a deep breath, calming her nerves. A puff of the sweet, musty summer's straw odor pressed into her nose.

The barn had recently undergone extensive renovations by Luc and Marjorie, Forrest's parents. Old flooring was removed and replaced with a new tongue and groove floor. Claire walked passed the stalls with rubber mats and hay racks to the corner away from the windows in case the boys peeked around. She dug inside her second-hand hobo bag for the ripe plum carefully picked from her mother's kitchen. Her friends had told her to find a nice piece of soft fruit that tasted good.

Tilting her head to one side, she bit a mouth-sized hole into the plum. The taut skin of the fruit was tangy, a complete contrast to the sweet juice that rolled down the side of her mouth. With a flick of her tongue at the corner of her lip, she licked away the sweet nectar.

It was delicious, just like how she'd imagined Forrest would taste.

She went in for another bite. Her eyes lulled shut as she drowned in the fantasy of kissing Forrest. She pushed her tongue into the flesh of the plum a little more and surrendered to the sheer pleasure of experimenting.

"Claire."

Startled, she jumped back and almost toppled over. The plum slipped from her hands onto the ground. *Oh. My. God.* Utter humiliation. Forrest saw her kissing a freakin' plum. She stood frozen, silently praying he'd turn and walk out of the barn, instead she listened to his steps closing in on her until they stood facing each other, barely inches apart.

He picked up the plum, brushed off the collected dirt, and examined it for a second or two. His eyebrows knitted close together. "Were you kissing a plum?"

"No." She tried to grab the fruit from him, but the big goof was already six feet tall and built like a quarterback compared to her small, five-feet-two-inch frame. He lifted his arm out of her reach.

"Then what were you doing?"

Pretending I'm kissing you. Pathetic. "Um . . . nothing."

His gaze searched her face. Claire's first reaction was to make a run for it, but then Jason would think one of his best buds did something to her. Mortified, she lowered her head and focused on the floor.

"Claire, look at me." His voice was low, with a trace of huskiness and authority.

There was no rescue from this embarrassment. Pure absolute torture. She coughed and pushed her hair back behind her ear, even though it was already there. He caught her chin and raised her face, forcing her to look at him. His eyes were gray, not a dull, unremarkable gray like that of concrete or stone, but a combination of misty gray and blue like the ocean at dusk. They were sensual, alluring, and warm. They beckoned her to reveal her deepest secrets, and to lose herself in their warmth.

"Who is the guy?"

A thick fog dampened her ability to think. "What?"

"The guy you want to kiss. Your crush." His eyes searched hers for answers. "Who is he?"

You. She wanted to scream. Instead her heart tripped and stalled.

"Claire, who's the guy?" His voice racked her brain as she scrambled for a name of any fifteen-year-old boy from her class. But they lived on an island where everyone knew everyone's business. If she was brave enough to lie—for the record she wasn't—the boy would have to live his life in fear with her four protectors breathing down his throat.

"I don't have a crush."

He smiled. "So I didn't just catch you making out with a plum?"

She turned hastily and tried to run off, but mortification followed. Forrest stepped in front of her, blocking her escape.

"Have you kissed your crush?"

"No." She tried to walk past him. He inched closer to the door. "I need to go," she said and hoped she sounded annoyed and angry. Unfazed, he made no attempt to move.

"Have you kissed anyone?"

Something in his voice grabbed her attention. It was low and gravelly as if he cared whether or not she'd been kissed before. Chin up, she stared into the eyes that had captured her heart, caught the twinkle of amusement, and her stomach flopped in disappointment.

Silly of her to think Forrest might actually look at her and see an actual girl with feelings instead of Jason's shadow. As if that wasn't bad enough, he was one of the Vineyard's elite. She was the half African-American, half-Japanese, flat-chested girl who lived in the same house with his best friend. Not that he was ever rude just . . . indifferent. Unlike the others, he never went out of his way for her. Once or twice, she'd caught him looking her way, brows knitted, an annoyed look on his face. No, never rude. But his opinion of her was clear; she was the little girl who followed his best friend everywhere. A nuisance, plain and simple.

Humiliation quickly turned to anger. She planted her legs wide and crossed her arms over chest. "How did you know I was in here?"

He shrugged. "You weren't outside."

"I could have been by the lake."

The corners of his mouth lifted up, then his smile widened into a grin "I saw you come in."

"You were watching me."

His eyes narrowed. "We all watch over you. That's what we do."

Not exactly what she'd hoped to hear. Realizing she stood no chance to win this banter, she quickly opted for plan B. The truth. What she wanted most in the world. To be kissed by him. She edged further into the room and leaned her elbows on the window sill, her denim shorts brushing against the dusty wall.

"Fine. You were right," she started in a low voice, her back to him. "I was practicing kissing because I've never been kissed."

"Go on."

"*Cosmopolitan* has a step-by-step guide on how to practice kissing and I was following the instructions." She paused and inspected her battered red Converse, building courage to spill everything. "But it also says the best practice is with another person." She turned to look at him. "Will you kiss me, Forrest?"

"No," he answered without a beat.

The swift blow of rejection knocked every wisp of air from her lungs. Claire struggled to inhale, to exhale, to do anything. Stunned and disoriented, she swiftly turned her attention back to the window. The sun stung her eyes, they watered. She quickly batted away escaped tears.

"Claire," he said, his voice a bit more soothing. "You're so young."

"I'm fifteen," she said in a desperate voice caught between frustration and crying.

"And I'm eighteen."

She whipped around and looked straight at him. "We're only three years apart."

He smiled. "Right now, it feels like ten."

They stood, staring at each other in a companionable silence, broken only when Forrest let out a deep breath.

"I'm leaving for college in a few days."

Although it was summer, the words chilled her spine. She needed to kiss him and let him see, feel everything she felt inside but could find no words to express. "What if I wasn't fifteen?"

"Still no."

The rejection, although gentler this time, still cut deep into her heart.

"Am I that unappealing to you?"

He dragged his fingers through his hair. "Claire."

She held up a hand. "It doesn't matter. Most of the boys here are trying to figure out what to make of me. An African-American-Asian girl. Is she pretty or just weird-looking?" She shrugged with indifference, but deep down the quick glances here and there bothered her.

"What do you care what others think? You're beautiful."

An equal mixture of pure ecstasy and excruciating pain made her heart go pit-a-pat. "You think I'm beautiful?"

He nodded. "Definitely."

"So why won't you kiss me?"

With quick strides, he came to stand next to her and gently stroked her cheek with the pad of his thumb. "You should be kissing boys your own age."

She looked into his eyes and her heart swelled from the emotion bottled inside. Feelings even she didn't understand, let alone try to express. He gave her a quick smile then walked back to the door. The bitter taste of regret stung her tongue like a rusty razor blade. The moment she had planned, spent so many sleepless nights imagining, had slipped from her hands.

He opened the door and turned to look at her once more. "When you do kiss your crush, I hope it's everything you imagined it to be." He smiled—a sweet, sexy smile that got her all flustered—and then he walked out of the barn.

* * *

RAIN LASHED DOWN on Claire in cold, icy pellets bit into her skin. Wet grass and dirt mushed under her shoes, slashing up her legs and staining the skirt of her dress. Focusing on Forrest, she quickened her pace. She had fallen asleep watching her favorite soap opera.

Stupid. Stupid. Stupid.

She'd almost missed him.

"Forrest," she called after him, heart in her throat, fearful he would enter his parents' waiting pick-up truck and drive away forever. "Forrest," she screamed his name again, a dozen needles dancing in her stomach. She stopped, her breathing stuttered in her lungs, exhausted from fear.

Please look at me.

He slowed his steps and after a second or two he turned. "Claire," he said, squinting.

Her heart leaped with joy. She caught him just before his parents drove away to catch the ferry to Falmouth. Smiling, she ran forward, closing the distance between them, and said through ragged breaths, "You're leaving."

"I know." He looked over his shoulder at his parents' truck. "What are you doing? It's pouring."

She launched herself at him, strong arms clamped around her waist. "I love you," she whispered and squeezed her eyes shut.

For a minute neither moved. Time stopped. They stood still, holding on to each other, their bodies drenched from the downpour. She shivered, not from the coldness of the rain but the string of electricity shooting through her veins. Her heart, like a fly in a cobweb with nothing to do, waited for his laughter to confirm how ridiculous she sounded. But it didn't come. Sucking in a breath, she waited a little longer. Except for the huge raindrops splattering with charged energy, there was absolute silence.

Slowly, she opened her eyes and looked into the depth of his gray ones. A fluttery feeling took over her body. "Forrest."

He swept back her matted hair, and his lips cracked into a smile. "I'm your crush."

She shook her head. A crush was the lowest level of romance. Her feelings ran beyond that. "It's not a crush."

"Claire, you're fifteen."

The world around her started collapsing. "I'm in love with you," she said emphatically.

"It's an infatuation."

No. No. This was bigger than an intense, naïve, adolescent admiration. She searched his face for any hint that just maybe deep down he believed her, only to come up short. Empty. Nothing. Feeling weak and hopeless, her shoulders slumped. She was losing this battle. "You're going to have sex in college."

He let out a heavy sigh. "Claire."

"I know about sex."

"Jesus, Claire, if you're having sex with some douchebag."

"I'm not having sex," she cried, fighting back the tears threatening to spill. "But I know what it is. I don't want you doing it with girls in college." She grabbed his arms. "Please wait for me."

"What makes you think I haven't had sex?"

Raindrops, hard and thick, hit her face like bullets. With a quick brush of her hand, she swept a handful of hair away from her face. "I overheard you telling the guys you were waiting for that person." She was making a fool of herself but at this point what did it matter. "You want it to be special . . . your first time." She swallowed the panic choking her. "I want to be your first, Forrest, and you mine. I love you."

He looked at her for a long moment. His eyes became shadowed. Hope bubbled in her stomach. And then he sighed, took a step back and broke their connection. Her heart dropped all the way to her toes.

"This is a crush. It will pass," he said quietly.

"No." He owned her heart. Forever. It didn't matter she was only fifteen. Some things only happened once in a lifetime and had nothing to do with age. "Promise me, you'll at least try to wait for me."

"I have to go. I'm sorry, Claire." He touched her face and stared at her for a long beat. "One day you'll look back at this and laugh."

"No," she choked.

"Yes."

Their gazes locked. The pitiless rain continued thrashing her skin.

Forrest took her hand in his and brought it to his lips. "I have to go." He released his grip and walked to his parents' truck. For a brief moment, he hesitated and looked back. Hope stirred low in her belly, then he tossed his backpack in the truck and shut the door.

Nausea pained her stomach, heart and chest. She had waited for this moment to come forward with her deepest feelings and bring to life those three words she'd been harboring.

She fought and lost.

Her world collapsed.

Emotionally bankrupt, she stood in dazed isolation and took the onslaught of the chilled rain. Her wet dress hugged her, its weight heavy and oppressing. With blind eyes to the world, she stared at the shadow of the pick-up taillights until they faded. It was hard to tell when she started crying and even more difficult to discern between her tears and the rain as she turned her face to the sky above. Her eyelids fluttered to deflect the water, she wanted to move, to run, but her legs were weak and incapable of doing anything. So she stood in the pelting rain and let her body and mind drown in the cold, wet afternoon.

CHAPTER TWO

"All my life, my heart has yearned for a thing I cannot name."
~ Andre Breton

Chappaquiddick, Martha's Vineyard, Eleven years ago . . .

TWO YEARS AFTER Forrest left her broken, Claire was still his puppet. Technically she was single, but her heart was hooked, taken by someone she couldn't call her own. Sure, she'd managed to establish a little distance between them whenever he visited the island, but only out of embarrassment. A sanity check.

She even dated here and there, kept up appearances, but nothing that could be construed as boyfriend-girlfriend status. As the Wolf Pack's adopted sister, the major cock block, she was untouchable. Threats of major bodily harm came with a promise to be inflicted on anyone who dared toy with her heart. Since she had no interest in dating anyone other than Forrest, the beyond reach pedestal suited her fine.

Those who were brave enough to ask her on a date were either too clingy or after one thing. She didn't like the band geeks she sang with. The boys from the debate club always wanted to discuss the variances between the Japanese and American culture. Yeah, no thanks. She didn't even know her father. And the jocks—they barely looked at her and she barely looked at them. Besides who could hit a fastball the farthest, topic of conversation was zilch. Well, Forrest was a jock, but he was also smart. Brains and brawn, the perfect combination to make her heart do that pitter-patter dance.

On her bed, lying flat on her stomach, with her body stretched out long, Claire clicked on the mouse. The note reappeared on her computer screen and her heart went crazy.

Dear Claire,

I just sent my last final to my professor. It's late and I'm sitting in the library . . . thinking about you. Us. Our friendship. Two years ago, it broke my heart to walk away from you crying in the rain. That image is tattooed in my heart. Like an old movie reel, I've replayed that scene at will . . . over and over. I've searched for words to apologize, to explain, but the words never seemed right. I hope you don't hate me.

Our relationship has been a bit strained since that moment, and I hope we can get past it and continue as we used to be. You mean a lot to me, much more than you will ever understand.

Anyhow, I'm coming home for Christmas break. Charles has asked my parents if I can spend a day or two in Chappy. I hope you and I will be able to hang out.

By the way, I wear glasses now. I sent you a picture, not sure if you received it as I never heard back from you. I thought I'd hate them and feel like a nerd, but let's be real—I'm the smartest out of the bunch.

Well, I won't write a journal, although I could go on and on. I guess I don't want to say goodbye. I miss you. I miss your smile, your laughter, and all that you are.

Forrest

In the last week, she must have read the note a thousand times and had yet to grow tired of it. She held on to each word, analyzing them for hidden meaning. She clicked open the photo folder, a picture of Forrest with his new glasses filled her computer screen. Dressed in a dark gray hoodie and cargo pants, he looked smart and so damn sexy.

Did he regret not kissing her?

He said he missed her, surely that meant . . .

She pushed the thought–hope–aside and walked across her room to retrieve her jeans and the Northeastern sweatshirt he'd given to her. She slipped her socked feet into her tennis shoes and scrunched her hair into a ponytail.

Ready. Set. Go!

Forrest was in Chappy until tomorrow. He said he wanted to *hang out* and she knew where he'd be. She'd waited, timed it perfectly until she knew he'd be alone.

She tiptoed past her mother's bedroom, down the stairs as quietly as possible, holding her breath the whole time until the door closed behind her. Claire stepped into the blackness of the winter night and scurried across the backyard to the large oak tree. She looked up. At the very tippy top, the tree house sat with magnificence. A miniature home Charles had custom designed and built for the boys.

Forrest was up there.

A sharp twist rattled her gut. Under the inky sky, she pressed a hand to the nervous spot in her stomach and looked around until she found what she'd been looking for. A small swing hung at the bottom, rocking with the whistling wind. Charles added it for her later after the boys nailed a sign to the tree. The big, red letters still read *Girls Not Allowed. This means YOU Claire!*

From the base of the tree, she looked up at the house. The deck was built high in the trees with no stairs, halfway to the top a short ladder hung precariously a few feet off the ground. If she wanted to go up, she had to climb up.

Well, she was about to break their rule. Not for the first time, since she'd been practicing whenever possible.

Claire positioned herself on the rock underneath the tree, jumped and grasped onto an overhanging branch. Her body swung, her legs flailed beneath her as she grappled for leverage. With a push, she hoisted herself up. Step by step, grab by grab, she clambered up and moved closer, ignoring the scuff marks and scratches on her hands from the rough bark. Adrenaline coursed unchecked, urging her to go forward. Fight or flight. Stand or run. Halfway up the tree, she eased her body onto the small ledge and braced herself for the look on Forrest's face when he realized she'd broken the protocol. Had Jason been there, he'd probably shove her down. Good thing he was out with his latest flavor of the month.

After a few more steps, she reached her destination. Thoughts scattered, too excited to think, she pushed the door open, stepped inside, and froze. Forrest stood by the pool table with a beer in his hand. He wore a pair of loose black sweats with the Northeastern University logo, battered sneakers, and a T-shirt plastered to his flat abs and broad chest. Though his hair was rumpled and black glasses framed his eyes, he'd grown into his already-striking features, with bone structure now well-defined and perfectly symmetrical. He looked strong, muscular, and more beautiful than ever.

He was . . . manly.

At twenty, his groupies had expanded beyond teenage girls. Older women flirted more openly now whenever he returned to the island. The few times she'd been around Forrest, his adherent followers' eyes would flick from her to him and back again. Cool and composed, she'd gladly returned their contemptuous stares.

Forrest's head jerked up and their gazes locked. He placed the pool cue on the table and took a swig of his beer; his eyes never wavered from where she stood.

"In your email." She shifted her weight from one foot to the next. "You said you wanted to um . . . spend time together."

His hooded gaze swept over her. Feeling a bit self-conscious under his searching eyes, she brushed loose strands of hair from her face. She peered at her appearance–her sweatshirt hung haphazardly on her frame, her denims now frayed. She bit her lower lip and frowned at the worn edge of her sneakers. She looked ragged and unkempt, definitely not the way to go when attempting to seduce your crush.

"You broke a tree house rule," he said, voice low and rough.

Claire gulped. Time to say hello to her good buddy, rejection. She was all too familiar with that uninvited houseguest. "Should I leave?"

His lips twitched. "Close the door, Claire. It's cold outside."

She focused on the beer bottle dangling from his hand. "You're drinking."

It wasn't a question, but for confirmation, he swallowed another large gulp.

"You're not twenty-one yet." Damn it! She sounded like a scared virgin. Let's add that to the list of *what not to say when trying to seduce the love of your life.*

He smiled. "Don't tell anyone and I won't tell your mother you snuck out of the house to come up here to be with me."

There was something in his expression, the way he spoke, that sent a rush of heat along her spine. "I . . ."

He placed the beer on the edge of the table, picked up the pool cue and aimed. Complete focus and accuracy. "Don't worry, I'm not drunk and I promise not to touch you," he said after making the shot.

Too bad. She wanted to be touched. Claire closed the door behind her.

"We sneak beer up here." He pressed one finger over his lips. "Charles and Victoria can't know, or your mom."

"What else do you sneak up here?"

He tore his attention from the pool table and looked at her. "You mean who. You want to know if we bring girls up here."

She didn't care about what Jason, Blake, or Adam did. As good looking as they were, she didn't want them. "Do you?"

"Girls are not allowed, remember?"

Something loosened in her chest. Relief.

"Do you play pool?"

"I played once." She'd been terrible, but no need to divulge inconsequential little tidbits of information.

He came to stand next to her. "On a date?"

He was so close to her, all six feet plus inches of masculine strength, making it impossible to breathe, much less think. So she nodded. He was silent for a moment, then to her surprise a faint smile curved his lips as he handed her the pool cue.

"Play with me."

"I'm not very good."

"I'll teach you." He tipped his head forward. "Come on, let's play and talk."

Excitement bubbled up inside Claire's stomach, her champagne cork ready to burst. She took the pool cue from him and moved to the other side of the table. "Do we need to break?"

"Let's finish this round as a warm-up for you. You can have–" He examined the table. "Solids."

Claire leaned over the table and tried to focus on the red solid ball. Problem was Forrest was standing on the opposite side and her eyes kept landing on that bulge in his sweatpants. Crazy thoughts zipped through her head.

Was he wearing boxers or briefs?

What if she slipped her hand beneath the waistband of his pants and touched?

A sensation that surfaced whenever she thought of Forrest, shot between her thighs. Groaning, she took her shot, and missed.

"Your aim was wrong."

Truer words had never been spoken. "Um . . . yeah."

"Here, let me show you."

He came to stand behind her. "Follow my lead," he said, way too close to her neck, so close the heat of his breath tickled her skin. "You have to focus on your target. Which ball do you want to hit?"

"What?" Her voice came out husky. She cleared her throat.

He chuckled. "Pick a ball and I'll show you how to aim. Let's go for the red ball again. I think that's the one you tried for before, right?"

Oh, God, she was hot. The last thing she needed was to start sweating. Mouth dried, she nodded. Finely sculpted muscles of his chest pressed down on her back. She sucked in a breath, in an attempt to control the tremors inside.

"There are physical and mental aspects of playing pool," he said quietly.

Umm . . . right. Rife and powerful desire spread through her. She nodded again.

"If you want to hit that ball, you need to forget about the others and give all of your attention to the one you're aiming for. Turn your body a little to the left." His hands guided her hip right against his hard male heat. "Don't move. Now pull your shoulder back and swing forward . . . gently. Move with me."

Mesmerized by everything Forrest, from the way his mouth was so close to her ear, to the feel of what made him male pressing on her back, she followed the instructions and watched the red ball sink into the corner pocket.

"I did it." Excited, she tried to spin and face him, hug him, anything to have her hands on him. But he tightened his grip and held her steady.

"Don't move."

She stood stock-still. More like bent over. Her bottom pressed against the front of his sweatpants. A rush of heat pooled in her stomach. For the record, he was going commando.

"Focus," he said in a thick voice. "Aim for the orange ball. Here turn your body this way." He shifted her hip. His iron-hard body with that thing poking at her, moved along with her. "Remember what I told you, forget about everything else and go with the flow."

The torture continued for about ten minutes until Claire somehow managed to focus enough to clear all the solid balls from the table. Her palms were damp. Her body was damp too, yearning and aching for him. She turned, leaned on the table and looked into his eyes, watching every slight flicker take a dark, stormy shade. For a beat, she thought he was going to let her go but instead he cupped her face. Warm breath caressed her lips as he leaned ever closer, his nose brushing against hers.

"That day inside the barn and that afternoon in the rain, I wanted to kiss you."

Her heart leaped, going a mile a minute. He was so close, so real, and she'd dreamed of this moment for so long.

"I want to kiss you now."

"Kiss me," she mouthed.

He hesitated. Then slowly, so slowly it hurt, he brought his lips down to hers for one too-short second. Claire's body trembled. Her heart missed a beat. And then he jerked away, stepping back.

Her fingers went to her bottom lip, feeling the imprint of his mouth. She wanted more. "Forrest."

"I promised I wouldn't touch you."

"Are you drunk?"

"No."

"Will you regret kissing me?"

"Maybe." He raked a hand through his hair. "I don't know. I can't think straight." He took another step, furthering the distance between them. "I know you kissed Tyler."

Her first kiss. The weak attempt to mend her broken heart by kissing a boy one grade ahead of her. Part of her had done it because she knew word would get back to Forrest, and she'd hoped to get a rise out of him. There'd been rumors Jason, Blake, and Adam had threatened to tear Tyler apart limb by limb if he mustered the courage to get close to her again. But Forrest had done absolutely nothing.

"To forget you," she whispered. "I was hurt."

"Did it work?" His voice was low and grainy.

While the kiss had been nice, pleasant, it failed to ignite the flame in her bonfire heart. She moved closer, homing in on his lips. "No. If anything I want you more than ever."

Forrest pressed his forehead to hers and swore beneath his breath. "Claire."

"Please, Forrest, I'm beg . . ."

And then he kissed her again. It was magic, the way his lips connected with hers. Among all the dizziness, heat, and clinging to him like a lifeline, something inside her changed, never to be reversed. This new feeling could be dwelled upon later, because, for now, she was exhilarated to feel his breath come and go with hers.

She closed her eyes to better enjoy the sensation as his tongue lightly swept across and between her slightly parted lips. The hardness of his body pressed into hers as the kiss went even deeper. His tongue, filled with the spicy beer flavor, becoming a substitute for all the other parts of his body she'd like to absorb into her own. A rough groan escaped the back of his throat as his lips became more fervent and rougher until they broke for air.

"God, Claire." He walked over to the large couch, this time putting enough distance that she couldn't touch him. "We can't do this."

"Why not?"

"You're practically my best friend's sister." He reached for his beer.

"But I'm not." She took slow, calculated steps to where he stood with beer in hand. She took the bottle, gulped down a mouthful and nearly spit it out. The shit tasted disgusting.

"You shouldn't be drinking," he warned, watching her.

"Technically, neither should you."

"How often do you drink alcohol?" he asked, ignoring her countering.

There was that one time she had a glass of wine with one of her friends. "Here and there."

He looked at her for a beat. Obviously not buying her bullshit, then the last thing she expected happened. He grabbed another bottle. "First, let me say, I know you've never had beer before."

"I've had beer."

"Right."

His tone confirmed she was a terrible liar. *Whatever.* She was on a mission and took another swig. Yep. Still disgusting.

"Second, let's make a toast."

She met his eyes. "A toast?"

He clinked his bottle to hers. "To you and me and all this tension between us."

"I'm not mad at you. I was just embarrassed."

"Not that kind of tension."

Her heart kicked up a notch as realization sank in. "Oh." Throat suddenly dry, she took another swig of the beer, nearly choking with a hiccup. "And you like this because?"

"It's an acquired taste." He quaffed down the alcohol. "Up for another game of pool?"

"Can we talk about the um . . . tension?" She took another mouthful of the alcoholic drink. Still tasted awful but she needed strength and something to boost her confidence.

"I'm listening."

"You feel it too?"

"Yes."

The admission did something funny to her stomach. And lower. She took another swallow of the beer.

"You're drinking too fast."

She ignored the warning and gulped down another mouthful. "I thought you didn't want me. Why are you telling me this now? Unless . . ."

"There's no unless. I just thought you should know the feeling is not one-sided."

They stood in silence, face to face, his beautiful slate gray eyes glinting with lust and desire. He wanted her. He was fighting it.

"I want you, Forrest." Her fingers skated across the bulge of his pants. "Looks like you want me just as much."

"Don't go there." His voice was rough, his hands gentle as he caught hers and held them still.

"Why?"

"You're not even legal. You're seventeen."

"The legal age for consensual sex is sixteen. I checked."

"It's more than that. You should be dating."

"I don't want to date. I want you. My heart belongs to you."

"You're too young to know that."

The room moved and Claire squeezed her eyes shut for a second or two to regain her composure, "I know what I feel." They stood facing each other, gazes locked, neither daring to break the silence. Sexual tension hung thick in the air. Tilting the beer bottle to her mouth, she swallowed the last drops. She inched closer, tiptoed, and removed his glasses. "What will your excuse be next year when I'm eighteen?"

He squinted, stared at her, then scrubbed a hand over his face. "I won't have any. But your feelings might change."

"They won't."

He looked at her long and hard. "If you still feel the same way on your eighteenth birthday then I'm yours, Claire. For as long as you want me."

Something fluttered crazy low in her stomach. Hope. Excitement. Happiness. "Forever. I'll want you forever."

He smiled. "Tell me that next year."

"You'll wait for me?"

One hand went to her ponytail, pulled it loose and tangled his fingers in her hair. "I'll wait for you."

His lips found hers again, warm in contrast to the cold outside. Everything faded away, and all Claire heard was her breath and their heartbeats.

CHAPTER THREE

"Only the united beat of sex and heart together can create ecstasy."
~ Anaïs Nin, *Delta of Venus*

Herring Creek Farm, Martha's Vineyard ten years ago . . .

FINALLY, THE MOMENT Claire had been wishing for was here. Giddy with excitement, she wanted to run, to shout, and tell everyone what was going to happen. The day had been the longest of her almost eighteen years. She boiled the kettle for the fifth time that morning. Filled to the brim with tea and wired with caffeine, she busied herself with a book.

A romance novel, her fave.

It failed to divert her attention from thoughts of Forrest. Instead her mind kept running wild with scenarios—Forrest's lips on her breasts, his fingers between her thighs. Romance novel. Bad choice.

Unable to sit down, let alone read, she walked back to the kitchen and stopped. Another quick glance at the luminous digital clock of the oven made her wonder if time had slowed down, her stomach knotted. Every distraction she chose for herself–much like a butterfly would flutter toward the possibilities of tonight. Then she'd get that tingly feeling all over again.

But try as hard as it might, the day couldn't last forever. The afternoon heat reluctantly faded and Claire found herself behind the wheel of her Volkswagen Cabriolet. *Wait for me,* the words replayed in her head. She shifted the gear of the convertible to park and looked at her watch. Eleven fifty-eight p.m. Two more minutes and she'd officially be eighteen.

Humming to the tune of *Feel Good* by The Gorillaz and De La Soul, she sat back and stared at the dappled moonlight surrounded by little stars. There was something beautiful about nighttime, magical, when the world's asleep. The minute hand moved forward, nearing midnight.

Eleven fifty-nine p.m. As Claire stepped onto the grounds of Herring Creek Farm, the light breeze brushed the skirt of her dress. A nervous kind of energy crept through her body. She tugged at the new dress the store assistant swore accentuated her curves in the most flattering way. But she knew better; willowy and without a large bust, she barely had any curves. Now she wondered if Forrest would think she looked beautiful or find the mini wrap dress too short. With each tug, the front went lower and lower, so she stopped and glanced up at the corner window of the Victorian estate.

Forrest.

Her heart pounded like the thundering hooves of a thousand wild stallions.

Three hundred and sixty-five days unable to think of anything except this moment. She'd written and circled the date on every notebook. It felt like an eternity, waiting and wanting to transcend the stolen kisses whenever he'd visited the island. But Forrest had insisted they wait, and now . . .

Midnight and officially eighteen. Every fiber of her body vibrated.

She looked up at his bedroom window again. Pitch black. Probably sleeping, he had no idea she'd be coming tonight. His last words to her were, *See you at your party.* But she'd been desperate with longing. Grateful Charles had suggested they stay in town for the weekend, so all of her friends could easily attend her birthday party, Claire had gone to bed fully dressed and watched the clock until all the lights were out, before grabbing her car keys and making her way to the farm.

Her fingers twitched, she paced back and forth on the grass yard, found a small rock and picked it up. She aimed at Forrest's bedroom window, held her breath at the little *tlock* sound against the window pane.

Swallowing a hard lump in her throat, she waited. Her palms were sweaty and her knees were shaking. Just when she thought she'd go crazy from waiting, the window slid open and Forrest stuck his head out.

She watched as he donned his glasses and brought her into focus.

"Claire." His voice was low, filled with questions.

"I'm eighteen," she said in a whispery voice.

Absolute stillness. No air stirred the grass or leaves. No clouds drifted in the sky. No water dripped or flowed. Not a sound could be heard either close at hand or in the distance. Even her own breath died as soon as it left her mouth. It was an eerie sort of tranquility, instead of being soothed, her senses heightened.

She glanced at her watch again, now a few minutes past midnight. Shit, did he change his mind?

"In the tree house, you said . . ." she started softly, her heart thudding.

"Don't move. I'm coming down."

And then he disappeared. Nerves now on edge, Claire sunk her teeth into her bottom lip in order to keep her knees from buckling under the weight of her wobbly body. Within minutes the front door opened and Forrest came into view, wearing a pair of low-slung black pajama pants and nothing else. Sheer male perfection.

"I'm eighteen and I thought . . ." She squeezed her hands together. "I mean, I want, we said–"

He peeled his body from the doorway and started toward her. "You're rambling."

As he closed the distance between them, she let her gaze go south to well-defined abs, to the trail of dark hair that disappeared beneath those deliciously indecent low pajamas. He was beautiful and she was in love with every inch of him.

"It's my birthday."

A smile crept across Forrest's face. His eyes sparkled in the moonlight. The air grew thick, forcing her to breathe slower, deeper.

"Happy birthday." His lips brushed over hers, then his mouth moved to the tender area at the base of her neck. Claire's eyes fluttered shut and light exploded behind her closed lids. When he drew back, she quickly searched his face, panic ready to take over.

"Claire, we don't have to–"

"I want to." She cut him off. "You said when I turn eighteen . . ."

"I know what I said." He ran the pad of his thumb over her lips. His eyes hooded behind his glasses. "I want you to be sure."

"I'm on the pill." She was prepared. "I couldn't be surer."

"Let's go inside," he said after a beat.

"I brought a blanket." She had a picnic basket in the trunk of the Cabriolet with a blanket and everything. "I figure we can go by the lake."

"My bedroom."

"What about your parents?"

"They're in Nantucket 'til tomorrow." He smiled. "You could have knocked."

"You didn't tell me they were gone." He scratched the back of his head. And Claire's eyes narrowed. "You knew I'd come over if you told me."

He gave her a sheepish smile. "It crossed my mind."

Was he having doubts? The idea chilled her. She ran a nervous hand over her dress and let her face fall with gravity, focusing her attention on nothing in particular. "Did you change your mind?" she asked, heart in her throat.

"No." He exhaled. "God, Claire, I can't stop thinking about you." He clutched her hand. "Let's go inside. I have a gift for you."

A sigh of relief streamed through her lungs. Her gaze went back to his face. So handsome. "I've been waiting."

He chuckled and shook his head. "Not my penis. I bought you something."

Forrest wrapped one arm over her shoulder and pulled her closer. She inched her nose toward his neck. His scent was intoxicating, not of cologne but of freshly cut timber, like the damp forest on a rainy day. With her body pressed against his side, they walked inside the house. In comfortable silence, they headed down the hall to his bedroom, her pinky hooked into his. He didn't let go until they entered his room to turn on the lamp.

She glanced around the place she'd visited many times in the past and could never get enough of. In here she was surrounded by everything that represented Forrest. Deep azure walls with white slat board added a classic balance to the otherwise sports fanatic decorated room. A wall decal of his all-time favorite quarterback, Joe Montana, one of his skateboards casually thrown against the red dorm trunk next to a football. His favorite Ronix surfboard leaned on the wall next to his headboard. She peered at the bed. Butterflies fluttered in her stomach, her head buzzing with possibilities.

"Sorry, room's a bit messy." He grabbed a balled-up royal blue tee and a black rash guard from the floor, then walked over to the closet and tossed the shirts inside. Their eyes met for a split second and she gave him a quick smile. "Right now," he said in a grainy voice, "my heart is beating really fast."

Good to know she wasn't the only one with nervous knots in her stomach. "I'm worried that . . ." Her voice dropped until it was practically inaudible. "I'm not going to live up to your past experience."

"I don't have any other experience to compare you to."

Certain she misheard, Claire blinked, lips parting on a gasp of disbelief. He grinned, an almost shy grin. Forrest removed his glasses, walked past her and placed them on the desk. He rubbed his eyes, then looked at her. Absolute stillness in the room.

"You asked me to wait for you." He scraped a hand through his hair. "And so I did."

His words caressed her soul, smoothing it out and removing the jagged edges. The magnitude of the moment seeped through. That afternoon, doused with rain she had declared her love and begged him to wait for her. He had walked away with barely a glimpse back, but not only had he heard her, he'd listened.

He'd waited.

She'd be his first just as he'd be hers. Her hands shook. Her pulse thumped erratically. The edges of her eyelashes blurred with tears.

He was quick by her side, cupped her face in his hand and wiped the tears away. "Some people are worth the wait, and you're one of them."

"You love me." It wasn't a question, but a realization.

He stared into her eyes, his own as hot as liquid steel. "I love you."

Her heart flipped, desire spiked. Just as the longing became unbearable, Forrest tilted his head and kissed her until all insecurities and fear stopped in their tracks, replaced by this moment. His hands roamed over her dress, fiddled with the small knot around her waist and unsnapped the buttons. With a slight brush of his hands the cotton material fell to the floor.

After all these years of the crushing yearning, she stood in Forrest's arms, covered only by a purple lace push-up bra with matching panties. Panic set in. What if she was too skinny? Without the extra padding of her bra, her breasts were only a handful. But he loved and wanted her. This much she knew.

Trepidation and excitement coiled in her stomach. He stepped back, eyes hooded, taking in her every curve. His face flushed with lust and love easing her feeling of self-consciousness.

"You're so beautiful." His lips were on hers again. There was an edge of urgency about his kiss, a hunger that might suddenly rage out of control, yet strangely tender and sensuous, setting her entire body aflame with desire. His hands explored, becoming acquainted with every inch of her body. Her hands drifted to the waist of his pants, undoing the button. So hot in the kiss, they stumbled on the bed as he stepped out of his pajama pants.

On top of her, he mouthed against her lips. "Tell me if I do anything you don't like."

She nodded, although she'd bet her whole wee-bit savings that she wouldn't have any complaints.

His touch became firmer, more dangerous, going places he'd never gone before. With heated kisses, his mouth journeyed over her shoulders and breasts, sending electric shivers straight to her core. Her eyes watered when his tongue traveled the line of her flat stomach and finished with a little seductive suction action on her hip. She cried his name, her breath coming short and fast. He settled between her thighs, his straining erection pressed against the spot she needed him. Every muscle in her body tensed with expectation.

Their fingers laced. His eyes, dark with desire, locked with hers as he slowly pushed himself inside her. Claire sucked in her breath. The slight pressure and pain was expected, but still startled her.

Forrest swallowed and stilled, bracing himself on his elbows. "Good?"

The soft expression of concern was a pure benediction of his love. She knotted her hands around his neck and pressed closer to him. "Don't stop."

After a slight hesitation, he stroked her cheek and kissed her lips.

Then slowly, he pushed deeper inside her, pausing once more to search her face for any discomfort. She leaned into him and kissed his tanned chest. He let out a low groan, rocking slowly into her over and over, breaking her barrier, inch by inch, until her body was taken by an overwhelming feeling of pleasure. It lasted only moments, but when he shuddered in her arms as he gripped her hips, she knew nothing would ever be the same between them. They had crossed that line they'd been teetering for the last year and now they were forever connected, body and soul.

Breathless excitement pounded in her heart as he showered her face, neck, and collarbone with gentle, soft kisses before rolling onto his back. She moved along with him, wrapped her arms around his torso and hugged him close. "That was . . ." Her voice trailed as she searched for the right word. Perfect just wouldn't do.

"It'll get better," he said in a promising tone.

She just had to take his word for it. She had no complaints. For first timers, the experience had left her breathless and wanting more. "It was beyond perfect," she said, circling his chest with her index finger. "I feel complete."

"It was you, Claire." His voice had an unfamiliar tightness to it. "You made the experience perfect."

Euphoric warmth flowed through her, causing her heart to expand. *Not gonna cry. Not gonna cry,* Claire willed herself as they lay in a sweetheart's cradle position.

"This is for you." He handed her a small velvet box.

"Where did that come from?" she asked as he handed her the box.

"My nightstand. It's been here the whole time." He smiled. "I told you I bought you a gift."

She pulled herself to a sitting position and almost forgot she was naked until she followed Forrest's gaze to her breasts. Heat seared through her cheeks under his scrutiny, and for a minute Claire thought her face was on fire. Feeling a bit awkward and coy, she reached for the navy-orange Rugby stripe duvet.

"Open your gift."

With a slight nod, she opened the box and gasped. A white gold necklace with an infinity pendant gleamed at her. She held up the delicate metal with trembling fingers. "The infinity symbol." She looked back at him, and her heart fluttered inside her chest. "I love it. I love you . . . forever."

He yanked her to him and covered her mouth in a hungry kiss. "At this moment, we are infinite." He stroked a finger over her temple, pushing back a loose strand of hair behind her ear.

"We should get infinity tattoos."

His brows went up. "You and me?"

Smiling, she nodded.

He let out a short laugh. "That's so permanent."

"Like us, forever," she said breathlessly.

"All right then, we can go to Boston tomorrow and get tattoos before your birthday party." His voice was firm. Decision made. No hesitation. For as long as she'd known Forrest he'd always been sure of the things he wanted and the people he surrounded himself with. And now he had given her the most precious gift, his love. "Tonight," he continued, a faint smile on his lips, "we make love again, and again, and again."

"I have to go back to the house." But really she wanted to stay right here, in his arms, forever.

He grinned back and she could feel the excitement radiating out from him stronger than a hundred watt bulb. Pure energy. One of the many reasons she loved him.

"No chance. You're staying with me."

"But . . ."

"We'll sneak you back in before anyone can notice. I've done it for Jason a few times. Then we can meet and go to Boston together for our tattoos." He tilted her head to the side and kissed her, his lips demanding. Smoldering heat ran deep within Claire as his grip tightened. With a sweeping movement, he rolled her under him, crushing her body to his, gentle yet firm. He slanted her head further, deepening the kiss.

He was right. The second time the exquisite friction sent her flying.

CHAPTER FOUR

"You only hear the music when your heart begins to break."
~ My Chemical Romance—*The Kids from Yesterday*

Edgartown, Martha's Vineyard, Ten Years Ago . . .

"HAPPY BIRTHDAY!" SMILING faces chanted.

Claire raised a hand to cover her beating heart as she took in the scene in front of her. Colorful balloons swayed in the soft breeze. A cupcake tower sat on a table at the far end of the yard along with other treats. Streamers covered everything. Her mother, Jason's parents, Charles and Victoria, held a big banner that read *Happy 18th Birthday Sweetie*!

With quick steps, she crossed the well-manicured lawn into her mother's arms. "Thank you." She hugged her mother, then Jason's parents.

"Anything for you, love," Jason's mother chimed in. Her pale, petite hands massaged Claire's shoulder. "Nice tattoo, by the way." She turned Claire's wrist to examine the fresh ink. "I have one as well."

"Thank you." Feeling her mother's inquisitive gaze, she glanced nervously at the newly acquired black ink. The infinity tattoo–a simple, yet elegant loop with a twist through its center mirrored the number eight on its side, curved seductively inside her left wrist. The permanent mark of her eternal love for Forrest gleamed from the A&D ointment she applied after treating the sensitive area.

Her mother took her hand and examined the ink. "So permanent."

"It's the infinity symbol, Rosa." Victoria chuckled. "Our little girl is in love."

"Who's the lucky guy?" Charles asked, his blue eyes fixated on where Jason and Forrest stood talking.

Claire followed Charles' gaze and rested on Forrest. He was laughing, probably over some lame story from Jason. She ached to wrap around his muscular form and nestle against him, as she'd done all night. But they were still new, still processing everything between them, and Forrest had insisted to be the one to break the news to his best friend that the two of them were officially dating. While the others had relented a bit on their big brother mode, Jason's had heightened.

Forrest's eyes wavered from his friend and locked into hers. Images of their naked bodies discovering each other flamed her brain, making her private thoughts roasting hot. Feeling her mother's and Victoria's watching her; Claire turned her head to the side, averting their curious stares.

"Let's not interrogate Claire," her mother chimed in. "Go enjoy your celebration with your friends. We can talk about the tattoo later." She smiled, a silent message telling her daughter she could care less about the permanent ink.

Summertime, the go-to summer jam by Will Smith and DJ Jazzy Jeff, blasted from the speakers in its exuberant beat, wooing the ears of the crowd. Boyfriends grabbed the waists of their girlfriends as everyone started to sway to the tune. Boyfriend, she officially had one of those. Not just any boyfriend–Forrest Montgomery Desvareaux, one of the Vineyard's favorites, a hunk with a capital H. The one she'd always wanted. He was hers.

Emotion coiled tight in her stomach. She turned to her mother and Jason's parents again. "Thank you for all of this."

Charles hugged her. "We love you. Have fun."

Hours later, Claire scanned the crowd. A feeling of joy filled the air. Twinkling lights hung from tree limbs. Booming sound from the oversized speakers thumped in time with her heartbeat as though they were one. Chatter of voices and people moving around drowned out by the music.

Her entire senior class was here. Actually except for Blake and Adam, the whole island was here. Blake had chosen to start law school early and Adam was busy making a name for himself as a Formula One driver.

Claire pressed through the horde of people in search of Forrest. Through all the chaos and mingling, other than a wayward glance and short conversations surrounded by friends, they hadn't been alone. She wanted to touch him, kiss him, breathe him. Anything. She wanted Forrest.

Her feet came to a screeching halt. A short distance away, Forrest stood smiling, chatting with two curvy and sharply defined college girls in very short shorts. With lust in their eyes, his admirers stared as if he were a god. The blonde's head fell back in laughter; she pressed her chest a little closer to Forrest. He didn't appear affected by either of the sex-pots, but he didn't push them away either.

Claire's skin crawled. Forrest was hers.

She had bruises on her body as proof. Heart hammering in her chest, she swallowed the lump in her throat and tried not to think of the worst case scenario. But the thoughts nagged her mind. What if she hadn't been good enough in bed?

Umph!

She stroked the infinity tattoo inside her left wrist and tried to ignore the jealousy burning her chest.

"Smoke is coming out of your head."

Startled, she turned to Jason. "What?"

He looked at Forrest then back at her. His blond hair, similar to his mother's, was as wild as the jungle, untamable and unruly. "No need to be jealous. He's in love with you."

Her brother-sister relationship with Jason was strong. At times overwhelming so, but she loved him. She opened her mouth to deny she'd been secretly hooking up with his friend, but Jason's eyes, crystal blue, so much like his father's, twinkled with a mixture of arrogance and ba-dass, told her not to bother. She should have known he'd be onto her. He didn't graduate top of his class, heading to Harvard Law, based on his looks and the Montgomery name alone.

"He's flirting with them," she mumbled.

Jason chuckled. "No, he's not. He's being polite. There's a differ-ence. He's into you." He slung one arm over her shoulder and squeezed her into a tight embrace. "Even when I told him you were a scrawny pain in the ass, it was all about you."

Claire smiled a little. "How long have you known?"

"That he's in love with you?" He chuckled. "Definitely before you started sneaking up to the tree house."

"I've never snuck . . ."

"Yeah, you did. Still doing it."

She tried to push him off, but he tightened his grip and planted a kiss on the top of her head.

"Happy birthday, punk ass."

"So loving," she muttered; the usual banter between her and Jason relaxed her a bit.

"You snuck out of the house last night."

She looked at him. Her plan had been foolproof . . . unless. "You weren't in the house."

"I left right after you."

His voice had a solemn tone that pulled her heartstrings. Jason was more than the son of her mother's boss. As much as she annoyed him, he always looked after her. Siblings didn't always have to be by blood.

"Why do you sneak out?" she asked with concern.

"I don't. I walk out."

Again, she noted tightness in his voice. She turned her head and focused her attention on the man she loved like a brother. "Jason, what's wrong?"

"Let's just say, you're lucky to live in the guesthouse." It happened quickly, but for a brief moment anguish flickered through his eyes. Claire followed his gaze to his parents talking to Forrest's parents. From the outside looking in, his parents looked happy and loving, but perception was not always reality. "You don't have to listen to the constant bickering," Jason continued.

Besides Forrest's parents, Charles and Victoria, beautiful, rich, and loving, were Claire's epitome of a happy, loving relationship. "Your parents love each other."

Jason shrugged. "Probably, but there's deep-rooted anger." He caught her wrist, dismissing the topic as quickly as it was brought up. "Come on, let's go chat with that boyfriend of yours. Cool tat, by the way."

"Thanks. I like your eagle." She often admired the eagle tattoo covering Jason's left shoulder to bicep.

"Thanks. Dad hates it." He peered at Forrest again. "I never thought he'd get one. He's not really into body art."

She knew that and the fact Forrest had chosen to be permanently inked for her made her love him even more. "Are you mad about me and Forrest?"

He shook his head. "You're the sister I've never had, and he's the brother I wish I had." He squeezed her hand. "He loves you. There's no one else for him. It's always been you." He flashed her one of his charming smiles. "Forrest is the type of guy who loves forever. You're in good hands."

CLAIRE SAID GOODBYE to the few lingering stragglers. Dusk had fallen, the mosquitoes were out, and goosebumps of anticipation spread across her arms. She stifled a yawn. She was tired, but also excited.

She focused on her boyfriend leaning on his Jeep, arms crossed over his chest. Her skin tingled with happiness. Their relationship was officially public, when she and Jason had walked to him and the two overly enthusiastic girls, Forrest had pulled her to him and planted a possessive kiss on her lips, claiming her in front of his best friend and everyone else on the island. His two admirers got the message. Good thing too, because she'd been ready to go toe-to- toe with them.

"I never thought I'd want my own party to end." Claire twisted frizzy hair from the blistering heat into a knot. "Forrest."

"Hmm . . ."

"You're going to Dartmouth for medical school."

"And you're going to NYU."

Moving away from the island, adjusting to college, the workload, the changes, all brought on different emotions. Excitement, fear, and now melancholy, over the distance that would exist between them. "What will become of us?"

He pulled back a bit and searched her face. "What do you mean?"

"I thought about it and I don't know . . . you're going to be in New Hampshire and I'm going to be in New York."

He caught a strand of her hair between his fingers and gently stroked it. "Not a big deal."

He sounded so confident, it was almost reassuring. But now that they were official, the distance presented a new obstacle.

Claire pressed on. "We're going to be even further apart. What if . . ."

"There are no 'what ifs,' Claire." His eyes moved to her face in a slow perusal. "Stop worrying. You're it for me. You have to trust us, or else we won't work."

"I trust us." But her voice cracked on the words, and her stomach tensed with angst. Not that Forrest had given her cause to mistrust him. Her skepticism was an acquisition gained from birth. A gift bestowed on her since the day her mother gently explained to her why she didn't have a father. Something her boyfriend would never understand; he was the epitome of a well-balanced life with loving parents.

"I'm not saying it's going to be easy being so far away from each other," he continued, his brows knitted. "But we are worth it." Thrusting a hand in her hair, he exhaled and a muscle in his jaw ticked. "Forever, Claire. I'll wait for you forever." He kissed her neck; a wave of pure pleasure ran through her entire body. "I have to go. I'll be waiting for you tonight."

"Your parents are home."

He shrugged. "They're on the other side of the house. They won't hear us. Call my cell when you get to the farm and I'll let you in." He leaned in for one last kiss before jumping into his Jeep. "I brought a shit-load of condoms in case you want to get off the pill."

"I liked how you felt," she whispered, feeling just a little bit shy.

"I love how you felt." He stuck his head out of the car window and brushed his lips over her forehead. "When should I expect you over?"

"One hour."

"See you then. I love you."

She reached into the car and kissed him once more. "Forever."

With a final wave, he was gone. She didn't move until the soft rumble of the Jeep faded. Smiling, Claire practically skipped her way to the house, happy as a dog in a dinosaur dig. Her steps slowed when her mother's and Victoria's voices echoed from the kitchen.

"I'm just saying Rosa, you need to talk to Claire."

Victoria's voice, while calm, carried a level of warning. Claire stopped dead, her stomach shifted uneasily. This had to be about her sneaking out. Shit. She promised Forrest she'd be over. Hell, she wanted nothing more than to be with him again tonight. She caught a fleeting stiffening of her mother's shoulders and quickly withdrew out of sight. In the shadow, back pressed against the wall, she inched a little closer.

"Talk to her about what exactly, Victoria?"

Claire held her breath.

"You can't let Claire believe there's a future between her and Forrest. I mean, he's a . . ." Victoria paused. "His parents are millionaires."

The sound of dishes being dropped in the dishwasher was deafening in the tense silence.

"Your point?" her mother asked.

"In the Vineyard, we have the *haves* and the *have-nots*," Victoria answered.

A sharp stabbing sensation ran through Claire. "So you're saying Claire falls in the have-nots?"

Claire stood knee-deep in silence, hoping this was all a dream. Water dripped from the faucet into the sink, reverberating around the room like a cymbal, yet no one moved to stop it.

"I never thought you saw Claire that way. Me perhaps, but never my daughter," her mother continued, her voice tight and controlled.

"Oh, I don't. But the reality is this is how things are. When Forrest is ready to settle down, it will be with someone of similar background, not with a sub-par singer."

Victoria's words flew from her mouth like vapor but landed in Claire's guts as shrapnel, tearing her insides.

She absently stroked the tattoo on the inside of her wrist. The memory of the needles moving in and out, up and down, pushing the ink below the surface of the skin made her wince. Unlike earlier, when it brought life to her soul, and gave her a sense of longing and hope, it now stung like a hot razor blade carving her skin.

A pair of heels clicked across the room. Her mother said in a tight voice, "I see."

"Rosa, he's going to medical school. When Claire goes to New York, she'll drown among all the big fish."

"Why are you so invested in what Forrest does?"

"He and Jason are basically brothers," Victoria said in a matter-of-fact voice, "and no matter how close we are, or how we put it, Claire is the daughter of a housekeeper. That will never be good enough for any of the boys. Forrest will realize that one day and turn to someone within his circle."

Victoria's words slashed Claire with betrayal.

"That's enough, Victoria," Charles ordered in a stern tone.

"Darling . . ."

Claire heard the surprise in Victoria's voice and cringed. Charles, while approachable and giving, was not one to fuck with. Born with a silver spoon in his mouth, he was accustomed to have things done his way and could be ruthless when crossed. In the world of lawyers, business negotiations, he was known as shrewd and callous.

"I was just telling Rosa . . ."

"I heard what you told Rosa," Charles interjected, his voice carefully quiet, but edged with steel. "You should apologize."

"Her daughter sneaks out of the house whenever he's here to be with him." Frustration evident in Victoria's voice. "We all thought it would end, but now they are probably having sex."

"How do you know they are sexually active?" her mother asked.

Victoria laughed. "She didn't come home until what time this morning?" She paused, waiting for an answer. When none came, she continued. "I doubt they are even using protection. Heaven! She might end up pregnant."

"Victoria," Charles warned again.

"I'm just warning Rosa what will become of Claire if she thinks Forrest will marry her," she continued, ignoring Charles' cautioning tone. "As her mother, it's your job to save her from being heartbroken or worse." She huffed. "Would you rather hear the warning from Forrest's parents themselves? I'm the one they discuss this with."

Anguish swelled in Claire's chest, tears clogged her eyes and filled her vision. She slapped a hand over her mouth to keep in a bitter cry. The distorted view she had of the people who became the bedrock of her life slowly came into focus, killing her self-esteem and trust. She should walk away, run to Forrest, but she sucked in a breath and held it. If only for a moment, she willed herself to be strong and continue seeking shelter in the shadow.

"Victoria, I said that's enough." Charles heavy footsteps ran out in the stillness. "Rosa, I apologize for Victoria's behavior tonight. Please disregard her words and do not mention this conversation to Claire." He exhaled deeply. "I'm sorry you had to be the recipient of this."

The apology from Charles made Claire's heart squeeze. All her life, he'd been the father figure she never had. He never made her feel any less than Jason. At times, she had forgotten she wasn't his biological daughter. He taught her to swim, drive, and even attended all of her father-daughter dances. She loved him and in her heart of hearts believed his apology was sincere, still she couldn't help wondering if he'd be as accepting had she been dating Jason. No matter what, she was the daughter of the housekeeper. The charity case.

She listened to partnered steps until they left the room. Her mind started to fail, like an engine that turned over and over, never kicking into action. She glanced at the door. Her eyes went to the walls, then back to the door.

Life had suddenly become a roller coaster; everything too fast to comprehend. Her stomach lurched in her throat, choking her and making a huge tangle of devastation.

Claire's head pounded, every cell in her body screamed for oxygen. She had to take a breath. She had to get out. Leave this house, the island, Forrest. Her mother would be frantic, but she'd call her in a day or two. Grabbing her purse and key to the Cabriolet, she pulled the doorknob and embraced the night.

Outside was nothing but moon speckled darkness. She inhaled, but her lungs were filled with betrayal and hurt, leaving less space for air. She sucked in the cool night air as if it were the remedy to her heartache. It failed to lessen the pain. She was still dizzy and worse, all her nerves were alive as ever and her senses heightened. She needed clothes, but that meant returning to the house, and she couldn't do that, couldn't face them.

Thankful for Charles' regular allowances, she had enough to get her started with the basics. She wouldn't need much; two shirts, two pants, intimates, toiletries, and enough to pay rent for a month or two. Everything else could wait until she found a job.

She rushed into the car, started the engine, and drove onto Main Street. Her mind screamed out as pain pierced through her heart. Confusion, hatred, hurt, and agony stifled her throat. Tears made wet tracks down her face and dripped to her wobbling chin. She swiped them away, but they stubbornly continued to flow until she surrendered and let the sadness surge through her veins and deaden her mind.

On Main Street, she steered the Cabriolet and made a left turn, away from Edgartown, toward Oak Bluffs, to catch the last ferry leaving the island.

About twenty minutes later, the captain's voice shrieked in the night. "All aboard!"

Heart in shreds, she sat in the car and listened to the engine of the ferry as it sailed away from the place she called home. Her phone buzzed in her purse.

Forrest.

Her heart skipped.

She patted the hobo bag until she located the vibration and quickly retrieved her cell. She flipped it open and studied the text message.

You're not here. What's going on? It's been one hour. I'm waiting.

Her heart contracted in pain. Forrest was out of her league, the son of millionaires, on his way to one of the best medical schools in the country. Long distance relationships never worked out anyway. He'd be tempted by other girls and the flesh was weak. But more importantly, he deserved to marry his equal, one of those perfect college girls. Not the daughter of a housekeeper.

Nausea swirled unrestrained in her stomach. Her head swam with half-formed regrets. Air, love, life, and warmth sucked out of her inner core and left her empty. She shut off her phone and dropped it in her purse, leaving the text unanswered.

Claire stepped out of the parked car and made her way up the stairs to the deck. The night breeze whisked her ebony hair and she let out a little quiver. Stretching out in front of her like a map, the unknown studied her fears, her courage and her knowledge. Blackness engulfed her thoughts. She glanced back at the island where she grew up. There was no life here, at least not for her. Not anymore.

Her eyes settled on the narrow and elegant infinity symbol inside her wrist. Her love for Forrest permanently etched on her flesh. A part of him—of them—would never come off, imprinted on her skin until the day she died to remind her of how beautiful he was and how clueless she'd been for allowing herself to fall in love with him.

The African-American, Japanese daughter of the housekeeper shacking up with the son of millionaires. What was she thinking?

The joke was on her for listening to her heart. It was a freakin' muscle for Pete's sake; its job was to pump blood, nothing else. Last time she'd let a stupid muscle guide her. The ferry left the Vineyard, promising a new beginning. She entombed her memories of Forrest in thick-walled ice, closed her eyes and took in a deep breath of the salty air, steeling herself to only think of her future. A future she would mold, build, and direct without Forrest.

She was in charge, in command of her own mind, body, and soul. She now walked into her own destiny, a destiny that lay squarely in her own hands.

CHAPTER FIVE

"The heart takes and gives life."
~ Luc Desvareaux

Martha's Vineyard, Present day . . .

THE SOLES OF Forrest's running shoes hit the ground. Calves burning, breath forming clouds in the air, he settled into the rhythm of his daily run. *You're temporary, I don't want temporary.* Exactly four months ago, he uttered those words to Claire the night of Jason and Minka's wedding. They hadn't spoken since. In the past, they always kept a rapport, no matter where her singing career took her; he always received a text, an email, even if it only contained her typical two words: Saying hello.

He'd respond with the same or similar words and that would be enough for them. But even that stopped. For years, they managed to ignore the strain that existed between them, mostly for the sake of keeping the Wolf Pack intact. They even trained themselves to be friendly with one another, like the time he gathered the whole gang at his house for an impromptu dinner. No matter what, they were friends, their circle ran small and tight. Being raised as an only child compelled each of them to seek companionship with one another.

So what Claire ripped his heart apart ten years ago; like any love-struck young man driven by anger and a crazy libido, he'd gone on a quest to forget and heal his heart. It worked for the most part. Time eventually petered out the anger, and he'd gotten his heart back. Well, half of his heart anyway. Frozen memories thawed and seeped into his consciousness, but he paid no heed to his tormentors.

An icy blast of February air congealed the last of his thoughts. He glanced over at his jogging partner. Even in the frigid weather, sweat soaked his hoodie. "Still trying to make babies?" he asked between ragged breaths.

Blake chuckled. "No success yet, but having fun trying. You're the last man standing in the group."

And Claire. Her existence in his life wasn't an option he could choose to pass on. The unofficial sister of his longtime friend Jason, by default, she held a rightful place in his circle. Besides him, the Wolf Pack as Adam labeled them, contained four others–Jason, Blake, Adam, and Claire. Now that all three of the other guys were married, their knit had expanded to welcome wives and soon children. He did a quick mental calculation; Adam's wife, Lily, was about six months pregnant. In spite of all the additions, their circle managed to stay whole. The bond between him and the others was as strong as ever.

Except for Claire.

The relationship nowadays was a matter of necessity to not rock the boat. It hadn't always been that way. Morphed from friends to lovers, everything had been fine. Perfect. Until that summer night when she uprooted and hightailed out of town. From that moment, a whole lot between them changed. Now their communication had come to a halt. He told himself it was for the best. He needed to let her go. She was temporary, a wildflower.

He inhaled. Cold winter air rushed in and out of his lungs in a mild burn, forcing him to keep his breathing in tune with his steps. Forrest's running shoes pounded across muddy ground and patches of gray snow. Stark, bare trees with outstretched arms gave them a full view of Lake Tashmoo, the body of water where he often went sailing, and the view from his kitchen–now nothing but a blanket of ice. Typically, he'd admire the calmness of the lake, but today fighting the unrest feeling inside, he kept his gaze straight ahead.

The path drenched in glutinous muck for miles, an indication it still hadn't recovered from the couple inches of snow that touched the island two days ago. Wet dirt squelched beneath his feet like the tentacles of an angry beast, spitting out mud.

"Hey, what's the problem?" Blake hollered, speeding up to Forrest on their midday run.

"No problem," he bellowed.

"Looks to me like you got some demons chasing you. Good thing I can keep up."

Forrest continued in silence. Puffs of moisture left his mouth. Blake chuckled.

"When was the last time you spoke to Claire?"

"Four months ago," he answered, his breath hitched.

They rounded the bend in the path, and the afternoon sun beat down on his forehead. With the back of his hand, he wiped the sweat of his brow. Sex, he told himself; he needed sex. Quickly he flipped through his mental list of available women and groaned. His jogging pace accelerated to a full sprint.

"Still dating . . ." Blake's voice trailed. "What's her name?"

"Kerry, and no."

"What was wrong with this one?"

She wasn't Claire. He'd dated a fair amount, but those women did nothing for him. Not one could ever live up to the time he spent with Claire. Lord knew he'd tried to move on, and hoped the memories would fade. They hadn't. It didn't matter that their time together had been a fleeting couple of months. She still managed to brand his heart, just like that stupid infinity tattoo they'd gotten together a decade ago, forever marking them.

When the small wooden pedestrian bridge and his orange Jeep came into view, Forrest and Blake slowed their pace to a jog, cooling down from the vigorous run, until they came to a stop.

"Nice run," Blake said, barely out of breath.

"How did we do?" Forrest referred to the app they usually used to track their miles. His calves burned, that should mean something.

Blake checked his phone and smiled. "You ran like a maniac today." He shoved the phone in Forrest's face. "See for yourself."

Forrest eyed the screen. They averaged a mile every six minutes, a total of ten miles in one hour. "Good stuff."

"Do we have time for a few pull-ups?"

Blake was the king of pull-ups, an excruciating core exercise Forrest long concluded he hated but loved the result.

"Let me check." He opened the driver door of his Jeep and grabbed his phone sitting by the drink holder for a quick time check. Immediately, he noticed the three missed calls from his mother, and a text message from Peter, a fellow doctor who worked the ER.

Report to the hospital. STAT.

His gut tightened. Mrs. Kane, one of the island's favorite senior citizens, was battling Lyme disease. She was due at his office for a checkup. He wondered if she had taken a turn for the worse.

"What's going on?" Blake asked in the background.

Forrest held up a finger. Brows creased, he hit the code to retrieve his messages and froze.

Forrest, your father's been in an accident. Come quick.

Similar words were repeated two other times. In each voice mail his mother's speech became more and more urgent.

"Gotta go." He was already sliding in the car, his heart thudding in his chest.

"What's going on?" Blake reached for the door, concern in his voice.

"Dad was in a car accident. Peter sent a text to get there ASAP." He checked the text message again for a timestamp. That was twenty minutes ago. As a doctor, he knew a person's condition could quickly deteriorate in the span of five minutes. Shit.

"I'll meet you there."

He shook his head. "Not necessary."

Blake's phone beeped. He peeked at the screen and smiled. "Ovulating time."

"Go home."

"All right, but send me a text as soon as you get there."

FORREST SWERVED THE Jeep into an empty parking space, jumped out and bolted toward the entrance. His heart pounded to the beat of his feet racing against the pavement, only one thought swarming through his mind. *Please let Dad be okay.*

He avoided the revolving door and shoved through the manual entryway, taking the flight of stairs by two, three even, until he reached the reception area. An older woman probably in her early seventies sat behind the desk. Damn it, she must be new, as he didn't recognize her. Her eyes grazed up, and grew wide at his untamed appearance.

"Forrest Montgomery Desvareaux, my father, Luc, is here." He jotted down the French names, first and last for her to avoid any spelling confusion. He knew the process. She'd ask him to spell his last name at least two times before looking it up on the computer. Writing his name down took away at least two minutes.

She scanned the paper where he'd just written his father's name. As she typed, each click scraped across his raw nerves. He bit back the anxiety swimming through his veins, willing himself to be patient. After a few attempts at what he guessed was typing his name properly, she looked up, pity on her face.

"ICU," she said in a low tone. "Third . . ."

Her voice faded behind him. He already knew which floor. He might have his own practice but he worked closely with the only hospital on the island. Within seconds he was by the elevator, punching the UP arrow again and again until the door slid open. Mind racing, he hit the number three with a trembling hand. As the door closed, he grabbed his phone and thumbed *ICU* to Blake. Intensive Care Units catered to patients with the most severe and life-threatening illnesses and injuries.

After what felt like hours, the hollow ping announced he'd reached his destination. The elevator door opened and he stepped onto the quiet floor. For a minute he stilled, letting the strange feeling that he was here this time not as a doctor but as a son settle in before walking to the nurse's station.

"Hey."

He turned to Gwen, the pretty nurse who'd dated Adam once upon a time. She touched his shoulder, a compassionate touch. He recognized it. As a doctor, he was all too familiar with the bedside manner reserved for people losing a loved one soon. He'd done the same on a few occasions.

"Is it too late for surgery?" he asked, needing to know.

Gwen cleared her throat, a sign of nervousness. His heart clenched.

"Has the neurosurgeon seen him?"

"Yes."

A deafening silence settled between them for a beat. But the doctor in him got the message; it was too late.

"Third room on your right. Your mother and Charles are there."

Charles Montgomery was Jason's father, his parents' best friend.

"Thanks, Gwen."

He walked down the hall to the room, dazed in an almost dreamlike state. For the first time in a long time, the antiseptic smell sickened his stomach. It smelled clean–overly clean to the point of nothing, but there was so much nothing that the nothing was something. Dead germs, he concluded, hospitals carried the scent of faintly dead germs, like a hotel room for souls in purgatory.

He entered the room, sounds and beeps of the machines greeted him. Trained eyes immediately checked his father's vital signs and heart rhythm. Luc's heart was beating alarmingly slow. Forrest clung onto hope. His gaze moved to his mother, her usual rosy complexion now pale and sunken. Charles stood on the other side of the bed, tall and powerfully built like his son. He nodded at Forrest, his face grim.

"A tourist was on a scooter, drunk as a bat." His mother spoke softly into the silence. "Your father sw-werved to avoid him . . . and . . . w-went head-on into a tree." Her voice cracked on the words.

He didn't have to ask, no seatbelt. They've had many arguments over the use of the safety device. Wrapping his arms around his mother, Forrest looked down at his father on the hospital bed and his breath caught. Fifty-nine years young, his father was the poster child for health. Having worked on the farm for so long, he was naturally big and sturdy, but at this moment, he looked frail, sickly and gray. Tubes and IV inserted in his pale skin, the only thing connecting him to earth.

Forrest glanced around the room; everything was expectedly sterile, and yet a faint smell of death hung in the air.

"Intracerebral hemorrhage we were told," Charles' said in a low muffled tone. "Luc had a stroke as he was transported here."

He nodded at Jason's father. Forrest was all too familiar with the medical term. Intracerebral hemorrhage was caused by an artery in the brain bursting and creating localized bleeding in the surrounding tissues. This bleeding killed brain cells and could lead to coma and death. His eyes went to the slow blip of his father's heart on the monitor. The mortality rate for this type of injury was over forty percent.

Heart hammering painfully in his chest, Forrest's breathing went from quick to next to nothing. He dropped his gaze to the linoleum tiles. Even though the floor was scrubbed spotlessly, he could see all the tears that were ever shed on it.

"Forrest." His father's voice split on his name.

He quickly moved closer. "I'm here, Dad."

He watched his father fight to open his eyes, when he finally succeeded, he smiled. A weak smile. Hope slipped.

"I waited for you."

Forrest grasped his father's hand in his. "Don't talk. Relax, we're here." A doctor until the very end, his voice sounded deceptively calm, no hint of the panic and fear eating him up.

"We?"

He nodded. "Mom and Charles are here as well."

Charles peeled himself away from the wall and came to stand next to Forrest. His mother followed. His father's gaze slowly floated from each of them, a smile on his face.

"Thank you." His father said to his wife and Charles. "Thank you for giving me my son." He focused on Forrest. "I love you." He smiled once more, took one last jagged breath and slipped away into an endless sleep.

Forrest stood absolutely still, silent and frozen, as if his brain short-circuited and needed to be rebooted. Around him, everything was in fast-forward while he remained motionless in the middle of it all. The monitor continued with the loud buzzing sound.

Code blue! Code blue! The hospital code used to indicate a patient requiring immediate resuscitation echoed in the speaker. Soon the door swung open, fast, high-pitched voices spitting out medical terms: Push epi, pupils blown, intubation. The words flew around him; he recognized each one of the terms. He'd spent countless hours with his nose buried in medical books. But suddenly he understood why people called it medical jargon because none of the words made any sense. Until the doctor spoke, "Time of death, three-fifteen p.m."

Forrest's soul shriveled.

He stepped back. An arm filled with life and strength dropped on his shoulder. "I'm okay," he told Charles, but his voice trembled.

"Let's go to the waiting room."

He nodded. Standing next to his father's best friend, he clutched his mother's hand and the three of them walked out to the waiting room where the rest of the Wolf Pack sat, waiting.

TEN LONG YEARS and nothing had changed. Forrest was everywhere. He occupied every space in Claire's mind and heart. That explained why she was on the ferry this cold winter evening, crossing the Atlantic Ocean back to Martha's Vineyard. A wild wind whipped a mass of ebony hair, prodding her face. With a hot cup of cocoa wrapped in black fingerless gloves, she lifted her chin, eyes closed, and relished the fierce, frigid air rushing around her.

"Oh, my gosh, you're Claire Peters! Can we take a picture?"

Her day had started at three a.m. in her Los Angeles apartment, quickly eating a mix of fruit and yogurt and drinking a cup of coffee before heading to her first television appearance of the day. After she completed the taping, stuck in a bumper-to-bumper limo ride to a meeting, she had leaned over and changed her destination.

Six hours later, after a flight from L.A. to Boston, this ferry ride, and an anxious heart, she was exhausted. But she didn't get where she was alone, and for that she would never complain when people recognized her.

"Absolutely," she said with a smile to the two excited girls. They looked to be of college age. "Are you from the island?" She didn't recognize them. Not that she knew everyone; she wasn't there enough anymore for the closeness.

"No," the brunette answered. "We're here for the weekend. We go to Northeastern University."

Forrest's alma mater. Her heart fluttered like a butterfly learning to fly.

"We don't want to bother you," the other girl with a ponytail said, cell phone ready for the picture. "By the way, I love your middle name. What does it mean?"

"Yasō," she said the middle name she rarely used. "It means wildflower." She squeezed between the two girls and smiled for the selfie.

After a couple rounds of thank you and names were exchanged, the two girls stayed true to their words and retreated back to their chairs. Claire leaned on the rail and exhaled, her breath forming clouds.

Few passengers stood nearby, their voices simmering with excitement, completely oblivious to the Massachusetts bitter winter. The same college girls now giddily discussed the possibility of hooking up with a Kennedy or any other local, now that the only Montgomery was married. She didn't have the heart to tell them this time of year the island was like Stephen King's *The Shining* with a population of barely fifteen-thousand people scattered over six towns.

Claire on the other hand was reminded of why she'd stayed away the last four months. In the cold months, once all the tourists were gone, the island became dismal and desolate. And, oh yes, she had thrown herself at Forrest but he hadn't taken the bait. Instead he reminded her why Martha's Vineyard was no longer her home. She was temporary. So she'd stayed away.

Until now.

Four months ago, caught up in the magic of Jason and Minka's wedding, she gave in to her deepest desires and kissed Forrest. The audacious move got her nowhere. He walked away, but not fast enough. With just a kiss, he had crushed down all the walls and freed her heart. The fist-sized powerhouse had expanded and contracted with life.

Treacherous, unreliable heart.

That's why she was on this ferry. Time to let Forrest go or surrender to her heart. Either way, she craved closure and a much-needed break. Her choice. Probably not the smartest career move to walk away in the middle of a promotional tour, but she needed the break. After years of touring, filming a movie, and designing countless wedding gowns, she was burned out. Her creativity had dried up and she couldn't write a song to save her life. More importantly, her career felt like a chore of late. The happiness it once provided had dissipated.

Two weeks she told James, her manager of the last ten years. Two weeks without anything to do. Two weeks to be Claire Yasō Peters. Two weeks to figure out no matter how hard she tried to remove all traces of Forrest out of her mind's eye, he stubbornly kept hanging to her heart. When the captain announced they had docked safely, a sudden panic washed over her. A myriad of wild scenarios raced through her head.

What if Forrest wasn't home alone?

She kept tabs on him, sort of. Here and there he'd posted a picture of Lake Tashmoo on his Twitter or Facebook account. Once upon a time, she'd commented, not anymore. Now she received her updates through their mutual friends. Well the girls anyway. From them, she discovered until recently he was still seeing Kerry, the redhead who had him for lunch four months ago.

Jealousy poked its ugly head and Claire reminded herself she no longer had any rights to him. She stroked the infinity tattoo inside her left wrist. Now or never, she reminded herself and made her way down the stairs to her black Audi sedan.

The car glided quietly along the streets. After a short time, she turned onto State Road. At six o'clock in the evening the streets were dark, mystifying, and empty, a sharp contrast to the summer months. By spring, they would start arriving–the tourists, the homeowners who migrated to Florida, Canada, or somewhere in the West during the winter. Come summer, the population would hit its typical one-hundred fifty thousand plus and bustle with visitors, shoppers, scientists, residents, and passengers. But until then, only the locals were here, the fishermen, the teachers, the students, the policemen, her friends. And let's not forget the Vineyard's most eligible doctor.

The car slid onto Herring Creek Road, location of the farm owned and operated by Forrest's parents. There were no street lights, no traffic lights, yet, in the dark she remembered every turn, every Yield or Stop sign.

Her heart picked up speed as she erased the distance between her and Forrest. Logic told her she could wait until the morning to see him, she'd be calmer.

And do what tonight?

No one knew she had returned to the island, not even her BFF Keely. There was the Montgomery compound her mother managed, but that would mean she'd have to catch a boat to Chappy. For that, she'd have to contact Jason. She didn't want to do that. Not tonight.

From Herring Creek Road, she made a left on Tisbury Lane and continued to drive about a mile. She cruised along the winding road through acres of what she knew comprised of picturesque, open pastures and arrived on Meadow Lane. Her fingers gripped the steering wheel, she blew out a deep breath, and made a right onto the well-trodden path that led to Forrest's waterfront home on Lake Tashmoo.

She spotted the orange Jeep right away. Her heart leaped with anticipation and nerves. Stepping out of the car, Claire rushed across the lawn, avoiding any patches of snow, all along convincing herself a phone call hadn't been necessary. Once a friend, always a friend. *But now he's an ex- lover,* reason whispered.

Well, too late now. She knocked on the door and waited. Nothing.

She knocked again, a little firmer this time. Still nothing.

Claire reached in her purse and grabbed her phone. Damn, no signal. Another perk of living on the island. Phone signals were capricious. She turned on her heel to the back of the house where she knew he kept the emergency key, then headed back to the front. The night wind penetrated the wool coat with absurd ease, making her shiver. She drew her shawl around herself more tightly to keep out the cold as she fumbled with the key.

The door slowly creaked open. She stepped inside and was greeted by a muted house, not typical of Forrest. She headed down the hall to the family room, the click of her heels amplified with each step on the wooden floor. In here, ESPN always blared in the background. Tonight, there was nothing but an eerie, hollow silence.

A bad feeling slithered up the back of her neck.

She dug in her purse for her phone again. One finger dragged along the screen, it lit up. Still no signal. A knot of fear twisted in her gut.

"Claire."

Forrest's voice, infused with a question mark, caused her heart to jump and fill with joy, relief. She whipped around and faced the main reason she came back to Martha's Vineyard.

CHAPTER SIX

"How to save your heart . . . Should: never demand"
~ Anonymous

HE STOOD STILL, barefoot and casually dressed in an unbuttoned white shirt that appeared to have been thrown on at the last minute and worn jeans that hung low to his lean hips. The hard muscles he earned from hours of manual labor on his parents' farm on full display. Try as she might, Claire couldn't tear her gaze from the exposed skin—the broad expanse of his chest, his toned, sculpted stomach and narrow waist.

He slid his hands in the pockets of his unsnapped jeans, giving her a peek of black and red waist boxer briefs.

"Claire." Forrest's voice cut through the air, forcing her to look at him.

Through black-rimmed glasses, smoldering slate gray eyes with slight azure tinge jolted through her, his facial expression taut with tension.

At a loss for words, she stared.

"Did you speak to Jason? Keely?" he asked when it became obvious she'd lost all ability to speak.

His voice sounded cracked and strained. Something was definitely wrong.

Claire shook her head. "No one knows I'm on the island." She took a few steps closer, erasing the space between them. One hand rose to caress his face. He didn't move, but she caught the slight clench of his jaw and pulled her hand back at the last moment. "What's wrong, Forrest?"

Faces inches apart, eyes locked on one another, the air between them charged with static electricity. For a beat neither spoke, her question hung in the air. His jaw flexed and his eyes wavered, breaking their connection. He walked past her into the room. His movement pulled her to him like a lion being turned into a hunter's spear.

She glanced around, rich leather furnishings and a shaggy rug grounded the airy room, giving it a relaxed coziness that balanced the panoramic view of the ocean. The natural world outside echoed inside with wildlife-embroidered pillows. A *Twelve Monkeys* poster hung over the fireplace adding a pop of color. Polished, yet welcoming and casual, a perfect representation of the man standing before her. Everything was the same, except for the dispirited feeling in the room.

"Something is wrong, I can feel it."

"Aren't you supposed to be on a promotional tour or something?" he asked while stacking the books on the reclaimed-wood coffee table as if she had not spoken at all, quietly closing the door that led to his emotions in her face.

His aloof manner showed how distant they'd become. Her heart wobbled like a train on a rickety track. She was unequipped to deal with this detached man speaking to her as if they were strangers, instead of two people who'd known each other all of their lives, had been friends, ex-lovers.

She hadn't expected an enthusiastic welcome but his chilly composure knocked her off her axis. "Yes."

"Then what are you doing here?"

If I must, to let you go. Claire let out a long breath. Coming to him was a mistake. Instinct told her to run. She was after all the queen of running away, a total passive aggressive, at least when it came to Forrest. But for once, her feet didn't give in to the will of her insecurities.

He continued to watch her with those intense eyes of his as if he was pondering her existence. She felt naked, vulnerable. Exposed.

"I needed a break." she answered. That was partially true.

"How long is your break?"

A dead, cold silence settled between them. *You're temporary, Claire, I don't want temporary.* He didn't need to say them this time, through the indifference in his stare each word pricked into her heart and stung her.

"Two weeks." Her voice sliced through the silence.

"And you came to my house for your break."

Well, when he put it that way, she sounded pretty selfish. She walked away from him a decade ago without an explanation, and never looked back until four months ago. Not that she hadn't wanted to. The temptation, the desire never slipped away but deep down Claire knew any chance to regain Forrest's trust was slim.

For one there was her career, which consisted of long months away from everyone, flying all over the world, often jet-lagged. And loneliness. Along with the success came that too. As much as she loved and appreciated her fans, no amount of unrecognizable faces screaming *I love you* or sold out concerts could fulfill that empty spot in her heart.

Ten years ago, hurt, and shattered into a million little pieces, she made a choice. Leave the island, make something of herself and prove the naysayers wrong. The decision had been an easy one to make because in her heart of hearts, even at the tender age of eighteen, she knew nothing was permanent. Especially a relationship between a wide-eyed teenager and one of Martha's Vineyard's elite, one who was on his way to medical school in New Hampshire. The son of millionaires and she . . . well, she belonged in the have-nots. Even now, a decade later, the phrase still had a bite.

She learned from her African-American mother, who'd been foolish and given her heart unconditionally to a Japanese heir. In the end, he walked away without a glance back, the fact her mother had been pregnant didn't convince him to change positions. He left and married his equal. Happily Ever After only existed in fairy tales, at least for the Peters women. Some things were best left untouched, that included a relationship with Forrest. But she'd touched. She couldn't resist the temptation and gave in to her heart. Now a decade later, no longer trapped under fear of being deserted like her mother and accomplished in her own right, her heart still burned for him.

"Claire," he said her name again, snapping her out of the hypnotic trance.

He continued to watch her, the vibes clear and loud he wasn't particularly pleased to see her.

What did she expect coming to his house unannounced?

A welcoming parade. Yeah deep down, she had wished for warmth, or maybe even a tepid reception. She would have taken that, anything but the cold air that slapped her face.

She pinched the inside of her mouth with her teeth. Her mind fogged with uncertainty. The well-laid out plan . . . Wait. There was no plan. Nothing had been thought out. Everything she'd done had been on impulse and governed by her heart.

Stupid heart.

"I'll leave." She turned on her heels and started toward the long corridor when Forrest caught a hold of her wrist. At the slight touch, her skin tingled and her body swelled with longing. Claire turned and their gazes locked until he slowly released his grip on her.

"Stay," he said in a low voice. "Stay the night. You can go to Chappy tomorrow."

By Chappy, he meant Chappaquiddick, the small island off the eastern end of the larger island of Martha's Vineyard and part of Edgartown. About a decade ago, a storm breached the beach and the two islands became separated. That's where the Montgomery compound resided and where she grew up.

"Take any room you want. I'll get your bag from the car."

Not until he disappeared into the night, did she dare move and make her way up the stairs. She paused behind the master bedroom, the one room she'd never been in. Unpolished fingernails brushed over the door, all she had to do was push it open and take a peek. Bad idea. Shaking off the temptation, Claire walked down the hall until she reached the room the farthest away from Forrest's.

THE BUZZING SOUND of her phone on the nightstand pulled Claire from sleep. Lids half shut, she reached for the phone and peered at the screen—an incoming text from Keely, along with a slew of messages and missed calls from her friends, her mother and Charles.

Urgency screamed at her. The gnawing sensation from last night resurfaced. Pulling her weight to a sitting position, she read the text.

Why aren't you answering your phone? Is everything okay? You need to come back to the island ASAP. Call me. Luv, Keely.

She skimmed through the other text messages, missed calls, from Blake, Jason, Minka, Adam and Lily. None from Forrest. All of the messages carried the same pressing tone, asking her to call them back as soon as possible. Her gut tightened, whatever happened had serious and grave written all over it. Shit!

She tapped in Keely's name and pressed *TALK*.

"Where are you?" Keely asked, answering the phone at the first ring.

With anyone else she would have hesitated on revealing her location, but not with her BFF. Outside of Jason, Keely was the only other from the group who knew all the ins and outs of her brittle relationship with Forrest. "At Forrest's."

"Oh."

Claire picked up the surprise in her friend's voice. "I arrived last night and came straight here." She sighed. "I don't think that was a good idea."

"Claire, you don't know."

The wretchedness in Keely's voice made Claire cringe. "What don't I know? What happened, Keely? I can tell something is wrong but Forrest didn't really say much."

There was a long beat of silence, then Keely spoke. "His father was in an accident." Her friend paused and sniffed. "Luc . . . passed away yesterday."

Claire winced. A chill turned the pit of her stomach to ice as sadness seeped into her bones. Luc was dead. She shut her eyes, but a vision of Forrest from last night burned her mind. She should have pushed, forced him to open up. Everything in her had sensed something was wrong. She'd felt his pain. Some connections never died.

"Claire?"

"I have to go, Keely. I'll stop by later." Claire dropped the phone on the bed and sat in a fog.

It hit her then, Forrest had managed to shut her out and sever their connection. Her heart mangled beyond recognition, her mind numb, racing in circles. Once upon a time they used to spend hours talking, teasing, and laughing with each other. Now he chose to keep her in the dark, silently telling her she wasn't needed or wanted.

She should understand that, at least that's what her logical side said. After all, she'd been the one who left the day after they chose to brand themselves with the infinity tattoo, a symbol of their love. Unlike most restless teenagers who sought to leave the island and move to Boston after high school, she had run all the way to a shitty apartment in New York, busied herself with two waitressing jobs, and ignored all of his text messages and phone calls.

Eventually he stopped trying. It wasn't until she learned from Jason that Forrest had left for medical school did she dare go back to the island. By then, she had moved to campus and started school herself. As she made friends and attended parties, she managed to convince herself this was the time for Forrest to explore. Not be tied down to her. Over the years their paths continued to cross. At times, they'd been friendly, but the static electricity continued to trigger sparks between them.

None of that mattered now. Forrest was in pain. Claire kicked the covers off, rubbed her knuckles onto her eyes, and jumped out of bed. She swiftly made her way down the hall, the cold plank floor creaking under her bare feet. Unlike last night she didn't hesitate and pushed the bedroom door open. Her eyes quickly scanned the room.

No Forrest.

The door leading to the shower was cracked open, she listened. Silence greeted her.

He was gone.

Streaks of sunlight penetrated the unadorned window, tapping her face. She stepped inside and walked over to the unmade button-tufted bed. Her hand brushed over the brownstone quilted comforter. A vision of Forrest in bed, dealing with the loss of his father, flashed before her. Once upon a time, he would have reached out to her. The unwillingness to share his anguish with her further solidified the emotional distance between them. A gut-wrenching plunge of regret crashed in her heart.

She exhaled and skimmed through the room, cream colored walls bare, with the exception of an airy abstract piece of artwork hung over a mahogany-stained dresser. A brass photo frame lay face down on the drawer. She walked over and fixed her gaze on the picture, but her attention was drawn to the small collection of treasures scattered across.

Among the assortment loomed the talisman silver bracelet she gave him as a good luck charm the day before he took his MCAT. He no longer wore it, so naturally she assumed it had been discarded or lost. She'd been wrong. It was simply tucked away, like the infinity necklace she no longer wore and now sat on her nightstand as a reminder of something she once had.

She picked up the picture and her heart crumbled. Forrest had his arm slung over his father's shoulder, both men laughing, looking happy, stared back at her. "Oh, Forrest," she whispered.

"What are you doing?"

Startled, Claire jumped and almost dropped the picture. Turning quickly, her eyes locked with Forrest's probing gaze. He was dressed in a medium weight pebbled sweater and low-slung denim. His hair wildly tousled. He looked tormented, worn, and filled with anguish. She wanted to run to him, fling her arms around his big body and protect him. Instead, she crossed her arms beneath her breasts.

"I spoke with Keely."

Silence.

Irritation swelled up inside her. The death of his father was bigger than the two of them. "Why didn't you tell me? I felt something was wrong. I asked you last night."

Another empty silence. His gaze shifted to the frame in her hand, back to her face and ate her up with cold, steady eyes.

Frustrated, Claire drew in a deep breath and slowly released before speaking. "God, Forrest, do you hate me that much?"

In a few quick strides, he stood in front of her. Without a word, he removed the picture from her grasp, and put it back on the drawer. This time it wasn't faced down.

"I don't hate you, Claire," he said in a spectral voice.

"Then what is it?"

WHISKEY-COLORED EYES GLISTENED, one slow tear slipped out running down her high cheekbones. She tried to wipe it away as quickly as possible, but the evidence of her shock and grief were now permanent in Forrest's heart. His gaze roamed over her appearance. Black hair scrunched up and secure, but thick strands escaped and touched the nape of her neck, her lips full and rosy, trembling with shock. Cotton black shorts revealed creamy, smooth nutmeg skin and toned, shapely legs. The white tee hugged her petite frame, emphasizing every curve and angle of her petite frame.

He removed his glasses and rubbed his eyes. His initial reaction was to take her in his arms and kiss her until he ceased to exist. Only that wouldn't solve anything between them. No, it would only ignite all the things he had finally tucked away in the Claire compartment.

"It doesn't mean I hate you." The emotional distance was for self-preservation. He chose not to open up to her last night. Not because of some macho stance but the grief that swept through his system, leaving him with nothing left him vulnerable. They would have made love. Hell even now he fought the urge to touch her. She had that effect on him. Neither sickness, heartbreak, nor death would allow him to take or give anything out of pity. Because of that he'd kept the searing pain in his heart buried deep until he collapsed on his bed.

"You've shut me out." Her voice came out low and cracked. "Everyone called me but you. Why didn't you call me? Why didn't you tell me?"

"What would that have done?"

She eyed him for a beat. "I would have come to you." Her voice seemed caught in her throat as she struggled to form the words. Tears streamed unchecked down her face. "I would have dropped everything and come to you."

His heart rolled. He was equipped to handle lots of things in his life. Claire had never been one of them. "It's not necessary."

"We're not strangers. Once upon a time we were friends." She looked at him through damp eyes. "We were more than friends."

He looked into her grief-stricken face and felt a stab of pain deep in his gut. Shit. He didn't need this. They've played this yo-yo game long enough. Forrest exhaled and raked a hand through his hair. "That was the past, Claire."

"You and I grew up together." Her voice thundered between sobs. She stopped and inhaled. "You're still my friend. We . . ."

"Don't make this about us," he interjected.

Her eyes were on him, absorbing his words. She took a step closer to him. "You made it about us," she said, chest heaving under her white tank. "You, me, Jason, Adam, and Blake, we are a family. We've always been."

He let out a low growl of annoyance. "You walked away from us, Claire, do I need to remind you of that?"

She glared at him and her lips curled in anger. "I didn't walk away from our group."

She'd been to every wedding, every major event. Saying she walked away wasn't entirely true. She only walked away from him.

They stood there in silence for a moment, gazes intertwined. Memories cascaded like a waterfall, their first kiss, the first time they made love, and getting that damn tattoo together. Forrest took a step back and turned toward the window.

"I loved your father," she said in a low voice, tears brimming her eyes. "I deserved to know."

His gut tightened at the past tense reference. No matter how many ways he sliced it, his father was dead. Gone forever, leaving a void no one could fill, not even Claire. He turned to face her once more. She swiped her hand across her face.

"My father died yesterday," he muttered, eyes fixed on her. "My entire body is overwhelmed with sadness. I feel weak and tired and all you can think about is why the fuck I didn't call you."

She flinched at his words and a small breathless whisper escaped her lips. Her hands tightened into fists and crashed on his chest. He caught her wrists and held her still. For a moment time stood still between them.

"I would have come to you," she said again.

She continued to stare into his eyes. Layer by layer, she stripped away his shield.

The right thing to do here was to walk away, let her go back wherever she came from. But he was too lost to be logical and do the right thing, not even to save himself.

"You're here now." Lowering his head, he kissed her long and deep and silenced that little voice in his head that told him nothing good would come out of this.

CHAPTER SEVEN

"The heart knows what the heart wants."
~ Keely Greene Alexander

THE KISS WAS firm and gentle as Forrest pulled her in, burning her lips with his mouth. Claire closed her eyes and became lost in a sea of lust. He nibbled, stroked, and teased her; a spicy, powerful combination that sent waves of passion crashing over her and garnered a low helpless murmur of arousal. She gripped his sweater for support as the kiss grew more urgent, rushed. Sparks flew and Claire's heart lit up like fireworks on the Fourth of July.

She missed Forrest, everything about him–his smile, his easy nature, and this. She missed kissing him the most. Of course she knew this wasn't the right time. He was using her as a Band-Aid to cover a deeper pain. She dismissed the nagging thoughts biting her brain and gave in to the sheer pleasure and kissed him senseless, making up for the last decade spent dreaming of doing exactly that. When he pulled back, she automatically met his gaze. His eyes appeared more blue than gray, filled with lust and something else.

Regret maybe?

She couldn't tell. But whatever it was, it made her stomach tighten with discomfort. He licked his lips and turned his large frame toward the door, blocking her from view. It was then, she realized they weren't alone. Jason stood in the doorway in a black pea coat with matching colored gloves palmed in his hands. Inquisitive eyes met hers briefly, questions in his.

She already knew what he was thinking. *Stay away, Claire, you're not ready to commit.* The four men were close, but there was this bond between Forrest and Jason. Maybe it was the fact that their parents were close friends, or the many years Jason spent working on the farm with Forrest. It didn't matter, she always admired their closeness.

"You didn't show up so the guys sent a search party. That'd be me," Jason said to Forrest. He tilted his head and met Claire's gaze once more, then back to Forrest. "I'll be downstairs."

Once alone, Forrest turned to her, a deep furrow knitting his brow. He was back in charge and yeah, his hooded eyes were definitely drenched with regret. The kiss had been a momentary lapse of self-control, something he'd always been good at, until their first kiss.

The sight of his remorse washed over her with the vengeance of a crashing wave. It was time to make her exit. Catch the ferry to Chappy or ask Jason to have the Montgomery boat take her to the other side of the island. She took a step forward to retreat, grab her overnight bag, and make a run for it, but he caught her wrist and closed down her escape.

"Where are you going?"

"To Chappy."

Silence engulfed the space between them. Claire adjusted her weight from one foot to another. Typically she welcomed the soothing sound, let it smooth her soul and take away her jagged edges from days on the road, but the quietness magnified the line of disconnect between them.

"The funeral is in two days," Forrest said at last and released her hand. "If you choose to stay, I'll see you then."

Without another look in her direction, he walked out of the room. She watched him, the rippling muscles of his back taut, straining his sweater. He'd shut her out for good. And just like that her world came crashing down, piece by piece, all she could do was watch.

On auto-mode, she took urgent steps out of the room, down the hall, ready to go after him, but came to an abrupt halt at Jason's voice.

"Arrangements made?" Jason asked.

"Yeah," Forrest's voice was solemn. "Mom is pretty bad. I'll have to stop by there later."

Footfalls echoed from downstairs. Claire envisioned the two men standing side by side. Jason, fair with steel blue eyes to Forrest's dark hair and gray eyes. Such contrast in appearance, personality, yet so similar in their mannerisms.

"All right, man, wish you had let us come with you."

"Some things are best done alone," Forrest responded. His voice held a dark sad edge that made Claire shiver.

"Holding up okay?" Jason continued.

"Yeah." The word came out flat and dull.

A lie, of course. Men were like that. They never shared their pain. But even from out of view, the sorrow in Forrest's voice cut her. Claire remained standing in the same spot and listened, yearning to comfort him.

"Come on," Forrest said a few seconds later. "Let's go meet the others."

"Is Claire staying with you?"

"No." His definitive tone left no room for argument. "She's going to Chappy today to her mom." Then the door closed behind them.

For a few minutes, Claire remained in hallway, lost in the silence of the house, overwhelmed with emotion, pain, sadness, decisions made, and a loneliness that couldn't be described.

Once upon a time she'd been welcome in his house. Not anymore.

The realization slipped down her throat, stealing her breath. It spilled into her heart like a cold shot, sending chills throughout her body. She stood there, frozen with sadness, left with no choice but to accept the wedge between them. A wedge built as high as possible, a result of her actions.

Claire stroked the permanent ink inside her wrist. She needed to promote *Tattooed Hearts*, her first movie, write and record the theme song. Instead here she was back on the Vineyard in the middle of winter, putting the career she spent years building on hold to run to someone who no longer wanted her.

Her life was a mess.

Releasing a deep breath, she headed to the room where she'd spent the night. She grabbed her phone and sent a group text to the three women she was closest to.

Lunch?

Lily response came first.

Most definitely. Vapor? Only place open in town.

But that meant she'd run into Forrest again. The town's favorite bar, owned by Jason and Adam, was their usual meeting spot. She typed back.

Another option?

Her phone chirped. Lily texted back.

The boys are meeting at our house. I need to get away from Adam. He's driving me crazy over this pregnancy.

Claire smiled. A doting Adam, now that she had to see. She typed back

Okay, Vapor it is.

Keely and Minka's response came almost simultaneously.

See you at noon.

✳ ✳ ✳

AT EXACTLY NOON, Claire pulled the Audi sedan into the empty parking spot one block down from Vapor, stepped onto the street and was greeted by an ominous silence. Not a soul on the street, no bird song typical on the island during warmer months could be heard. Instead, the harsh winter air prickled her skin with its ice-cold touch. Definitely different from her life in Los Angeles where temperatures in the fifties and sixties were considered freezing.

She tightened the wool scarf around her neck and headed in the direction of her friends' bar. Her footsteps, the only sound to be heard, tapped away on the sidewalk of Main Street. She passed familiar shops; Boneyard, one of the many surf shops on the Vineyard, the independent bookstore, restaurants, wine and coffee shops, all closed for the winter. Everything was still, as if a magic spell had been cast over the island.

Pulling the door open, she stepped inside the town's favorite tavern. A mixture of rustic and contemporary décor greeted her–brick, glass, and reclaimed hemlock wood throughout, vaulted ceiling exposing beautiful beams adorned by suspended lightbulb fixtures illuminating the space with a warm inviting glow, giving the eatery an upscale yet casual vibe. She scanned around the boisterous room, voices over one another, beer mugs clinking. Someone shouted, "To Luc."

Goosebumps popped along her skin. The whole island was here celebrating the life of one of their own. She should have known. Vapor was one of the few places that stayed open year round, not because Adam and Jason needed to work, but the bar, centrally located in Edgartown, was the heart of the island. People gathered at Vapor for comfort.

On the Vineyard, comfort was key.

She moved farther into the room, toward the bar when she spotted her friends sitting at a corner table. Minka waved at her. Smiling, Claire switched direction.

"Well, look who the cat dragged back to the Vineyard and in the winter months too," Lily said as the three women rose to their feet.

They staggered together for a big group hug, linking arms around their shoulders like a team huddle. For a minute, Claire closed her eyes and let the familiarity of her friends seep in. Although she spoke to them on a regular basis, nothing beat the good feeling of being surrounded by some of the people she trusted the most.

She stepped back and appraised each one of them. Underneath the sadness over Luc's death, their faces flooded with euphoria. After a year-plus of marriage, Keely still had that blissful gleam, Minka radiated with happiness and quiet confidence, and Lily seemed to be glowing all over. They looked happy, in love, and at peace. Something pulled every string of Claire's heart, not envy or jealousy but a yearning, an ache.

She was elated for each one of them, their road to happiness had not been easy but they got there. Forrest's unemotional and stolidly calm disposition after their kiss flashed in her mind's eye. Sadness panged from somewhere below her ribs. Yeah, that ship sailed. Once upon a time he'd been there, ready to give her everything her friends had. She walked away, actually she ran away.

Here and there, she managed to convince herself she left the island to chase her dream of becoming a singer, but in reality she'd been driven by insecurities. She was a chicken, a coward.

She brushed aside the little voice trying to tell her she wanted what her friends had—to wake up next to the same person every morning, the feet touching, the secret smiles. She turned to Lily and focused on her friend's round belly. "Every pregnant woman should look like you."

Lily stroked her belly, a joyous smile lighting her face. "Almost seven months."

"I still wish I had designed your wedding dress," Claire said with regret. Lily and Adam's wedding had been spontaneous with the two of them and their parents.

"We'll have a big party after we give birth." Lily patted her stomach again. "You can design a kick-ass dress for me then."

"It's a deal." Claire slid into the vacant seat. The other women followed. "How's Adam doing?"

"A total pita," Lily answered.

"Adam is a soft flatbread," Claire teased her friend, knowing how much Lily loved Adam.

"Pain. In. The. Ass." For added flair, Lily let out a heavy sigh. "He hovers and now . . ."

"Don't tell us. No sex," the three women said together.

Lily wrinkled her nose and laughter broke around the table. Claire welcomed the silliness.

"He's hinting we might come to a halt. Something about the baby's head and his you know what." Lily grimaced.

"That's scientifically impossible," Keely said between giggles.

"Try telling him that." Lily brushed her bangs away from her eyes. "He's lucky I'm in love with him."

"And your parents love him," Minka added.

Lily rolled her eyes and picked up the menu. "Oh, yeah, that too."

"Your brothers still haven't come around?" Keely asked while scanning the menu.

"I think deep down they like him, but they get a kick out of giving him a hard time."

The other three women nodded in agreement. Claire was acquainted with Max, one of Lily's three brothers. From the few times their paths had crossed and discussed his sister's marriage to one of her closest friends, she knew Adam had gained their trust. That of course didn't mean he was free of Lily's brothers putting him through the ringer.

"Good to see you ladies again." Maxie, Vapor's favorite waitress, greeted them with a warm smile. "What can I get for you?"

"Hi Maxie, aren't you supposed to be in college?" Claire had practically watched Maxie grow up on the island. From what she remembered she was attending Boston College.

"I came to help out for the weekend." She cleared her throat. "And to attend the funeral."

Just as Maxie said that, a man in plaid shirt held his beer and shouted. "To Luc."

Everyone rose their glasses and repeated the chant in Luc's honor. Forrest's father had been such an integral part in the community, in her life. On the farm, Luc had always been patient with her, showing her the ropes. Raw grief swept through Claire's system. She loved Forrest's father and now he was gone. Just like that. Death often came unannounced.

"Jason appreciates you doing this, Maxie," Minka said in a solemn voice.

"So does Adam." Lily added with a subdued sorrow in her voice.

"I love those guys." Maxie smiled sadly at them. "I'm not missing a day of class. I'll leave first thing Monday. What should I get for you? The French onion soup is tasty."

"Well," Claire said, handing the menu back to Maxie, "French onion soup it is, and that great warm butternut squash salad Vapor is known for."

Once Maxie left, Lily took a sip of her decaffeinated tea and twisted her face in disgust. "This no caffeine thing is going to be the end of me." She turned and hit Claire with that Lily stare that sees right through you. "Word on the street you and Forrest were kissing . . . again," she added, a reminder Lily had witnessed the kiss Claire shared with Forrest the night of the wedding.

Keely placed her menu down and gave the conversation her full attention. Minka shot Lily an I'm-going-to-kill-you look, solidifying her role as the CEO of the rumor mill. Actually her good-looking husband Jason must have started the gossip. Not that it mattered. Self-deprivation was the only reason she never confided in Lily and Minka about Forrest. She'd convinced herself their fleeting romance was locked in the past vault, to be glanced upon only as a point of reference. Except she returned to face her demon and he'd shut her down.

She waved a dismissive hand. Nothing to dwell on. Only lately, actually always, her heart told her differently. No matter how many times she chided her heart that feelings were impermanent, nothing lasted forever, everything was temporary, even emotions; it never faltered.

"When I was seventeen and Forrest was twenty, we got drunk together," she said softly. "I kissed him. I wanted more, but he was sober enough to stop me. He promised if I still wanted him when I turned eighteen, we could . . ." Her voice trailed. This stroll down Memory Lane and recalling some of the happiest time of her life sucked big time.

"The heart knows what the heart wants," Keely said thoughtfully.

"A year later," Claire continued. "On my eighteenth birthday, we made love." She smiled, the night still so vivid in her mind. "We were both virgins."

"No way," Lily exclaimed. "Totally swoon worthy."

"So romantic," Minka added.

"He was on his way to medical school and here I was an eighteen-year-old virgin confessing my love."

"But the two of you made love," Minka whispered, "he had to feel something. Forrest is not the love them and leave them type. At least based on what I've seen so far."

Claire knew that. He'd never been the casual type. "Once upon a time he used to be in love with me."

"He's still in love with you," Keely said.

A smile touched Claire's lips. She knew better. The physical desire might still be there, but the emotional connection they once shared no longer existed. "That summer, we were together. Only Jason was aware of our relationship."

"Where were Adam and Blake?" Lily asked.

"Adam was in Italy with his parents and Blake didn't come back that summer. He started law school."

Lily and Minka nodded. They'd been undergrads at Yale while Blake was in law school.

"A summer fling. Did Forrest break it off?" Minka asked with a slight frown.

"No," Claire answered without a beat. "The day after we got tattoos in Boston, I left without saying goodbye. I went to New York first then L.A. He thought we were forever, but I left. I broke the deal."

"Oh," Minka and Lily whispered at the same time.

"There's more to the story," Keely added gently. She glanced at Claire, seeming to ask for permission. When her friend didn't stop her, she continued. "The night of her eighteenth birthday, Claire overheard a conversation between Jason's mother, Victoria, and her mother." She stopped and looked at Claire again. "It's your story, you should tell it."

And so she did. It took her less than five minutes to summarize the conversation that changed her life forever. In the end, she chuckled, a sad sound from the back of her throat. "Yeah, I fucked up." She lowered her gaze to her drink. "I hurt him, I know." Her voice choked with emotion. God, she wanted a good cry.

"Does Jason know this about his mother?" Minka asked, a look of concern clouded her eyes.

Claire shook her head. She never held Victoria's words against Jason or Charles. Actually, with time she even learned to forgive his mother. "Jason's gone through enough dealing with Victoria's mental health and everything." The *everything* eventually led to self-destruction.

Minka chewed her lower lip in a way Claire knew to be an indication she was troubled by what she'd learned.

Claire shook her head again, this time more vehemently. "No need to tell him."

Minka sighed and looked down at her hands. "He still struggles with her death."

"And I don't want to mar whatever good he has left of her," Claire said gently. "He's that big brother I never had."

Minka nodded. "One day, you should tell him. But I'll leave it at that for now."

Maxie returned with their soups on a large tray. She placed the bowls on the table along with their drinks and disappeared.

"But you still want him. I saw that kiss the night of Minka's wedding." Lily studied her. "Is that why you're back?"

They all knew she was supposed to be on a promotional tour. "I don't know why I came back. I guess to either say goodbye or figure out where we go from here." Not entirely true, her heart whispered. She took a break from her career and headed straight to his house. She had some kind of expectations. Hopes.

"Crappy timing though," Keely suggested. "I mean, his father passed away yesterday. He's vulnerable."

The words from her friend almost sounded protective of Forrest, but Claire knew better. After years of friendship she knew Keely well enough to admit the woman had never been anything less than fair. She had a valid point, the timing couldn't be more inconvenient. "I didn't know about Luc."

"Your heart knew," Lily the forever romantic, said gently. "You came back because you felt he needed you. Emotions are diet of the heart."

Claire smiled. Lily and her grand idea of love. It might have worked for her and Adam, but . . . Claire shook her head. "I came back for my own selfish reasons." She sighed. "Reasons that aren't even clear to me anymore."

Minka squeezed her hand. "You'll figure it out."

"He kissed you," Lily pointed out. "He has to still feel something."

"A momentary slip. Lust."

Lily nodded with a knowing look. For a while her relationship with Adam had been purely physical. "I've been there, but look at me and Adam now."

"You've never hurt Adam. If anything you saved him."

"Are you still staying at his place?" Keely asked after a short silence.

"No, I'm going back to Chappy today." Claire picked up her spoon and gave the squash soup a stir. "Last night wasn't the most welcome reception, which is understandable now I know what he was going through. I'll stay for the funeral."

"Well, we're glad you're here," Keely said warmly. "No matter for how long."

She shared a connection with these women that transcended time and distance. Her career brought many people into her life; some genuine and some out for their best interest. But her friendship with Lily, Minka, and Keely kept her grounded. They understood she was a frayed knot. Jason, Blake and Adam still resided in that place labeled for family in her life, but lately, she found herself gravitating more toward the women in their lives. "I'm glad to be back too."

No matter for how long.

CHAPTER EIGHT

"Love-Once rooted in the heart, it never dies."
~ Marjorie Desvareaux

TO ENTER THE cemetery Claire had to skirt around a pile of brown, frosted leaves. Small white ice crystals covering the ground crunched with every footstep, echoing every person's pain. Today, the island had come to a halt to mourn one of their own. Even those who escaped the grim winter had return to bid farewell before being permanently separated with their friend by six feet of earth.

Grief covered the entire congregation like a black shroud. Claire blew out a breath and slipped one hand in the crook of her mother's arm, a desperate attempt to stabilize the wobbly nerves roiling in the pit of her stomach. Instead a fresh chill ran along her spine. Shadows of ghosts lurked in the open space, watching, whispering. She shivered. Cemeteries were places to keep the dead, held them prisoners, entombed in cement and dirt. The last time she stepped foot on this barren and shallow place was six years ago to bid farewell to Jason's mother. It felt like yesterday.

"You okay?" Her mother asked as they headed toward the site where Luc was to be buried.

Under the wintry air, her breath rose in visible puffs. She glanced at her mother. Long braids sprinkled with gray streaks pulled back into a bun away from her barely wrinkled face. As always, her mother's skin had a glow, despite the heartbreak from her first love, left alone pregnant at twenty-four, the financial hardship she faced growing up dirt-poor, she'd always maintained a positive outlook on life. And for that, Claire always found herself in awe of her mother.

"I'm fine." She looked up to the sky. Overhead, dark clouds blotted out the sun, hanging over the stones of the dead like a heavy, suffocating sheath. Yet, the air smelled clean and crisp, nothing at all like rain.

Snow. A storm was brewing. The gods were either happy to welcome Luc home or upset over their tragic error.

She scanned the graveyard, hundreds of tombstones around her, each one bearing the name of someone who once lived on the island. Now, as the myth said, their souls roamed these lands, right where she stood. "I feel like I'm being watched by thousands of restless souls."

"We think graveyards are spooky because we fear death," her mother said in a reflective voice. "Why not think of it as a resting place?" She glanced at Claire and smiled. "A peaceful place to recall good memories."

"Everything here screams final."

"You think so?"

"I do." Her gaze stayed on the six men carrying the mahogany coffin–Forrest; his lifelong friends, his godfather, Charles; and Adam's father, Christiano–all dressed in black. Six strong men, yet, from time to time they had to stop and garner their strengths.

Claire's gaze followed the multitude of mourners turned out to bid adieu to Luc. All around were tear-stained faces, shoulders slumped under the weight of death's hand. Some chatted in a hushed tone, nodding with a smile over words spoken amongst them.

Once the coffin was placed by the dug-up soil, Charles and Forrest trudged over to Marjorie. Claire's heart clenched at the sight of Forrest's mother. Her eyes swollen with saturated grief, acknowledging the finality of death, never to look upon her husband's face again, feel his embrace, or surrounded by his love. Charles said something to Forrest then wrapped Marjorie in the comfort of his arm. Pain etched the older man's face. He'd been down this road before; this was his second time burying a loved one. His wife and now his best friend.

Claire peeked at Forrest–shoulders squared, face still and serious as he stared straight ahead into nothingness. The only thing that gave a hint of his agony was the few days old scruff he neglected to shave. Still, he looked perfectly put together. He always had a way of maintaining full control of any situation. She'd known him all of her life and could count on one hand the few times he'd lost control, most of them with her.

Along with her mother, Claire huddled by the tombstone next to Adam, Jason, Blake, and their wives. Greetings and hugs were already exchanged at the church, now as they stood by the cold earth where Luc was to be laid, silence prevailed.

"Would anyone like to say something before the final farewell?" the pastor asked.

Without a word, Charles released Marjorie to Forrest and walked up to the coffin. His fingers lingered on the casket. After a short pause, he looked up at the noiseless crowd. "Over thirty years ago while touring France with my beautiful fiancée, I met a big, goofy, French-American man who would become my best friend, my brother. I loved him." He chuckled, a painful sound really and rubbed his temple. "Correction, I love him. Luc will always be the brother I never had. Today I say to you, *a bientôt*." Charles paused and looked up into the heavens. "I'll see you soon." He touched the coffin one last time then walked over where Forrest and Marjorie stood.

"Forrest?" the pastor called.

Claire watched Forrest as he took steps on the hallowed ground and walked over to the coffin. He abruptly turned his face in her direction. Gray eyes locked onto hers and for a moment the whole world ceased to move. She wanted to touch him, caress his face, look into his eyes and tell him time had a way of healing all wounds. Eventually, even this great pain would become bearable, but she knew that was not entirely true. All she had to do was look deep into her heart, time failed to dim her memory. Lost under his spell, she smiled a little, to reassure him she was here, would always be here for him, no matter the distance.

With a slight nod her direction, as if he heard her unspoken words, Forrest squared his shoulders and addressed the crowd. "My father taught me everything I know. Everything I am is because of my parents. I love them." He exhaled, gulped down his sorrow as his fingers skimmed along the coffin, his attention solely for the man who shaped him. "For the rest of my life, I will search for moments of you." His breath came in a gasp and his lips tightened, then he spoke again. "Goodbye, Dad."

Claire continued to stare up at Forrest. His chin trembled as he low-ered his lips to the casket and bid his father a safe journey. Her chest constricted. Sadness welled in her throat, ready to overcome its wall.

"Today," the pastor said, "we bid farewell to our dear friend Luc; father, husband, and friend."

That's when the empty heartache seeped in. Forrest's mother screamed her husband's name as the coffin slowly lowered in the ground; the mouth of Mother Earth swallowing her child. Through blurred vision, she watched Forrest. He clenched his jaw, struggling to hold back his grief, but hot torrents of grief coursed down his immobile face.

Her stomach twisted at the sight.

A piece of Forrest's life was gone forever.

Sick in the gut and unable to continue looking at him, so hurt and broken, a feeling of helplessness washed over her. Knowing she couldn't take away his pain, she gave him the only thing within her grasp. She stepped away from her mother, walked up to Forrest and squeezed his hand tightly in hers.

ABOUT ONE HOUR later, Forrest stood in the large but cozy sitting room in Martha's Way. He scanned the many faces in the crowd, voices talking over one another. Some carried a note of sorrow, while others filled with joy as they shared fond memories of his father.

His heart rankled and filled with emptiness. Needing an escape, he strode over to the large fireplace and gazed out of the window. Snowflakes floated from the heavens, covering bare branches and sticking to the remaining oak and beech leaves still clinging to the trees.

"Four months ago, I stood at this exact spot and couldn't tell Liliana I loved her."

Forrest pulled his gaze away from the window and glanced at Adam. "You were a fool."

"But I was in love with her, you know. I was too arrogant and overwhelmed with fear."

Claire walked by. She stopped to talk to Adam's parents, then Charles before walking over to join Keely and Blake. Adam followed her movement. Forrest had no choice. Her presence—in the room, in his life—was a tornado swallowing him whole. His eyes swept over her, taking in every detail. She looked classically elegant in a form-fitting black dress, her thick hair pulled back in a bun, giving him full view of her face. She looked beautiful.

"When is she leaving?" Adam asked.

Forrest peeled his gaze away and shrugged. "Who knows."

"I watched the two of you today and realized something."

"What's that?"

"The two of you slept together at some point."

Forrest lifted his glasses from his nose, and rubbed his eyes. "Dude, this is not the time."

"I'm trying to make a point."

"You should get to it. This is a repass."

"You have a thing for her and she has a thing for you."

Forrest peered at Claire again. She had moved and was talking to his mother and hers. "What's your point?"

"Ever thought about giving in to whatever you two had once more?"

He stared at his friend.

Adam raked a hand through his hair. "We are family. Whatever the outcome is, nothing will break us."

Forrest glanced at Claire talking to his mother. Charles walked over and joined them, said something to his mother and the two walked out of the room together. For the first time in the evening, Claire stood alone. Across the room, she looked up and held his gaze for a beat. Her eyes flickered in silent interrogation, then she treaded to where Jason, Minka, and Lily stood talking.

Disappointment rattled through him. What did he expect? Deep down, he knew the answer–for her to come to him. Dismissing the thought, he turned his attention back to the fallen snow. The last person he wanted to think about was Claire. Although if he cared to admit, truth was, she'd been occupying his mind all his life.

"What do you have to lose?" Adam pushed.

His heart. "My sanity."

"I hate to tell you this but I think when it comes to Claire, you lost your sanity a long time ago." He slapped Forrest back. "Think about it."

"Are you singing the love song too?"

Adam laughed. "I'm in love with my wife, but I know it's not for everyone. I'm saying I don't want you to get all fucking depressed and internalize everything like I did."

"And Claire somehow is the answer to my pain."

"You'll always have the memories of your father." Adam exhaled. "Mine still haunts me. Bad or good, they stay with you."

Adam had come a long way facing his past, but Forrest knew the road to get there had not been easy. He nodded, understanding his friend's reference. In his heart of hearts, he knew memories never die, but right now the thought failed to bring him comfort.

"Life doesn't stop," Adam continued. "From where I'm looking, looks like she's here for you."

"She's here because she's tired and needs a break."

"That may be partially true." Adam shrugged. "But you're the reason she's back on the island." He paused, glanced at Claire then back at Forrest. "Look, it's obvious something is still there between you two lovebirds. See what happens. I have to get back to my pregnant wife. We're gonna head out before the snow gets too heavy. See you at the potluck."

The actual event was called a musical potluck. Music performed by local singers, lots of food, and mulled wine. It all started the Sunday before Thanksgiving for those who dared to stay behind on the island during the winter months. They danced, ate too much, drank, and laughed. With the exception of when Forrest was away for school, he'd never missed the get-together held at Chilmark Community Center. "Yeah, I'll be there."

Adam nodded. "Remember, we're family. Whatever you need, we got your back."

He watched Adam walk over to Lily. His friend placed a kiss on his wife's lips and led her to where Blake and Jason were engaged in a conversation. The men shook hands, then hugged Lily goodbye.

Forrest examined the men who had become an extension of his family. His friendship with Jason came first, they grew up together. Their parents had been inseparable. Even after the death of Victoria, his parents still stayed close to Charles.

Somewhere along the way, he and Jason befriended Blake, later Adam. Expanding their circle, or Wolf Pack as Adam affectionately referred to them. Since Claire grew up in the same house with Jason, she'd always been around, whether they wanted her there or not. They often teased her because, well, she'd been a pain in the ass, always tagging along. Even when they just wanted to do boys things, such as sneaking beer, getting drunk, or playing a random sport shirtless on those lazy hot summer days, Claire had always wanted to play with the boys. The worst was when they played basketball; she couldn't make a basket to save her life.

Once in a while they did let her play football, because she'd been a good distraction. The opposing team would jump at the opportunity to end up on top or under her after a strategic tackle. Jason used to complain the most for being stuck with her. Not only she followed him around, she also lived with him. In a way, she became the surrogate sister to them all.

Except for him. He never viewed her as a sister. As a scraggly little girl, she'd been a burden, a party pooper who eventually became a friend. Other than that, she'd always been a girl, and through the years she became a woman. A gorgeous one at that.

As hard as he tried to resist her, he broke the *Do-Not-Touch Claire* rule. The first time, he'd been twenty, she seventeen. Underage drinking with a sexy teenager had trouble written all over it. He'd known better. He did it anyway. On the night of her eighteenth birthday he eventually gave in to the sweet temptation that was Claire. Those incidents ignited the tension that still existed between them today.

Forrest took in a deep breath. Needing a diversion from thoughts of the one woman who continued to haunt him, he slipped out of the room and headed down the hall, toward the door. From there he'd escaped without being noticed. He needed air.

He walked by Jason's office, Charles' voice caught his attention. There was something in the older man's tone, an urgency. Forrest slowed his steps and edged a little closer.

"You need to tell him, Marjorie."

"Charles, not today."

Forrest noted pain in his mother's voice. He frowned, debating if he should walk in there and rescue his mother from whatever Charles was demanding. As much as he respected and loved Jason's father, he knew Charles could be a slayer when necessary.

"Soon. Promise me that." Charles persisted.

Silence.

"Marjorie."

"I don't know."

"There is no reason to lie anymore. Forrest needs to know. If you don't tell him, I will."

"You can't do that." His mother's voice rose with a determination he didn't know she possessed.

Okay, so he was the reason for this conversation. Forrest grabbed the doorknob and pushed it open. "Tell me what?"

CHAPTER NINE

"The human heart has hidden treasures, in secret kept, in silence sealed."
~ Charlotte Brontë

HIS MOTHER FLINCHED and quickly met Forrest's gaze before looking away. In the split second that they made eye contact, a pained expression crossed her face. She looked over at Charles, his crystal blue eyes glued to her. The air was thick with tension. No one moved. No one spoke. A sacred, deathlike silence fell upon the room.

"Tell me what?" he repeated. The question lingered in the silence. He glanced at his mother, then Charles then back at his mother.

Charles walked over to Jason's weathered black desk and picked up a silver framed picture. Forrest's gaze followed the older man as he studied the photograph for a bit before placing it back then walked over to the window and buried his hands in his pockets. His strong, prominent jaw tight, his broad shoulders stiff.

As Jason's friend, Forrest knew the frame contained one of the last pictures Jason took with his parents before Victoria passed away. Jason's mother, while in a frail mental state, had discovered her husband's infidelity. That had been the icing on the cake and drove her over the edge.

Forrest swallowed the bitter taste of the memory, closed the door behind him and stepped further into the room. "What is so urgent that I need to know?"

His mother tugged on her brown hair and walked across the room to where Forrest stood. He watched her moving with extreme uneasiness, as if she was defenseless and powerless to deal with a danger that seemed vague but imminent.

"Forrest." She took his hand in hers. "Your father just died. Whatever it is can wait." She glanced at Charles. "Right, Charles?"

Dead, cold silence filled the room.

His mother sighed at Charles' lack of cooperation. Her eyes drooped down and appeared to have no focus, staring at nothing specific. "I'm sorry," she said in a flat voice. "I'm so sorry, Forrest."

His gut clenched, but Forrest shook it off. Unable to watch his mother in so much distress, he wrapped an arm around her shoulder. She turned and buried her face in his chest.

"I think that's enough for today, Charles," he said over his mother's shoulder.

"I made a . . . m-mistake." His mother choked on the words.

Forrest glanced down, her head still buried in his chest. He looked over at Charles, the other man's expression grim. "Mom." He stroked her arm, silently urging her to stop. The last few days had been tough on her. Whatever her mistake was, it could wait.

But she straightened herself and stepped out of his grip. She swiped her cheeks with the back of her hands and sucked in a breath. "Over thirty years ago, from a momentary lapse, I made a mistake." She smiled and touched his face. "It was the best mistake I've ever made."

His mind went blank. Forrest shook his head in confusion. "I'm not following." But inside, the beat of his heart hammered erratically.

"And Charles is right. He deserves to be a part of his son's life."

Time slowed. His gaze darted between the two conspirators. Like an unsteady Jenga tower with someone tugging at a crucial brick, Forrest could feel his foundation crumbling. "Am I hearing this right?"

A low sigh escaped his mother's lips. Charles' jaw bunched.

"I can't ask him to keep our secret anymore."

Time stood still. Suddenly reality was an endless nightmare and Forrest was trying to claw his way out. The image of the coffin being lowered into the cold, hard earth, replayed itself over and over in his mind.

"For thirty-one years Luc and I were pretty selfish and kept you to ourselves."

Shock froze Forrest's limbs.

"Forrest," she pleaded.

Delicate hands brushed over his arm, without a word he gripped his mother's wrist and freed himself of her touch. "What are you saying?"

His mother's chin quivered. A thundering silence echoed far and wide in the room. Every still second that passed, the more his expanding lungs burned for air and even though he knew he wouldn't get any, he still took a breath.

"Say it," he pushed in a low voice. The edges of reason blurred, angry waves crashed against each other, as if fighting over which would drown him.

"That's enough." Charles ran a hand through flecks of gray hair.

"Say it," Forrest demanded again, ignoring Charles' command.

"Luc isn't." She shook her head, her gray eyes blurred with tears. "Wasn't," she corrected, "your father. Charles is. I'm sorry."

Forrest's heart caved in and crumbled away. Pain surged through his body as if he'd been stabbed with a branding iron. Even though he saw it coming, the words hit him like a metal baseball bat slamming into his muscles. His blood vessels burst and his diaphragm collapsed under the force of his mother's words. Disgust rippled through every fiber of his muscles and he tasted bile.

"Forrest." She reached for him again but he put his palms up, closing his mother off and her arms fell limp at her sides.

He waved one arm toward where Charles stood. "You fucked him."

"Watch your mouth," Charles ordered.

"Stay out of this," Forrest spat without looking at Charles.

"I'm afraid I can't." Charles' gaze swept over him. "You've always been my business and you can't speak to your mother that way."

He did a quick calculation between his birthday and Jason's. About three months apart. From what he knew, Charles had been engaged to Jason's mother and his parents had been newlyweds. "You slept with him while he was engaged."

"It was . . ."

"You're still sleeping with him." The accusation made his mother flinch. Forrest took a deep breath, but it hurt his ribcage. He exhaled, inhaled again. No relief. Instead his head felt as though it would split in two.

Charles stepped away from the window and came to stand next to

Marjorie. Everything about the older man told Forrest whatever happened between them took two and had been mutual.

The hinges of the door squeaked open, Jason shoved into the room with Minka by his side. He turned to his father, his eyes alight with fury. "Tell me what I thought I heard isn't true."

Father and son's gazes clashed across the room. Minka grabbed onto Jason's arm.

"Looks like we're brothers in every sense of the word." Forrest turned to Charles. "Go ahead." His voice boomed across the room. "Tell him about you and my mother. How you fucked your best friend's wife."

"Tell me it's not true." Jason said, his tone calm and patient, completely unfazed by his surroundings.

"I can't do that," Charles replied, looking Jason directly in the eye.

"Jesus, Dad," Jason said after a beat. He released Minka's hand and took another step forward. "Do you have any limits?" He shook his head. "I didn't think you could sink any lower."

"We were together once," Charles responded, his voice indicating he was in full control. "It shouldn't have happened, but it did. I don't regret that Marjorie and I made a son out of it."

"You betrayed your best friend by sleeping with his wife," Jason said, his voice echoed his disbelief, his disappointment. "I thought you said you only cheated on Mom once."

"It's true."

Jason raked a hand through his blond hair. "Either I'm terrible at math or your version of once doesn't add up."

"Marjorie and I happened before I married your mother." Charles let out a breath. "Three months before."

"You were engaged," Jason said with disgust. He glanced over at Marjorie. "She was married to your friend."

"I went to Charles," his mother said, and slouched slowly in a chair.

Forrest hissed. "Dad wasn't good enough?"

"Enough, Forrest," Charles shouted.

"Why now?" Jason asked. "After thirty-one years. Why now?"

Charles' blue eyes swept over Jason. "Because he's my son just like you are."

"My father is dead." Revulsion burned Forrest's gut. Unable to withstand any more of the madness and desperately needing to relieve the pressure building inside his chest, he opened the door and almost slammed into Claire. The horrid look on her face told him she'd heard everything.

He hurtled past her, brushing her shoulder in the process.

"Forrest." He heard her call after him, but didn't look back. He struck the door open and stepped into the snowstorm. He shook. Not from the cold, but rather the thrashing inside him and the feeling he'd lost not just his father but himself today.

CLAIRE BOLTED TOWARD Forrest's front door. Gut-wrenching. Heart pumping. A swirling storm of screaming silver continued to fall from the sky. The soft crystals she would have found so bewitching from the other side of a pane glass, found their way into her jacket in every possible way. She slogged through the snow. The leather soles of her heels had terrible traction in the snow, causing her to stumble and almost fall.

She looked downward and kicked some of the powder off her black pumps. Had she given herself a moment to think things through, she would have changed into her Adirondack boots before running out of Martha's Way. But after Forrest charged past her, she'd only had one thing in mind–go to him and be the friend he desperately needed right now.

She knocked on the door, blew into her bare hands, and pulled tight on her coat. She waited, her mind whirring. Flashes of the conversation between Marjorie, Charles, and Forrest whipped through her mind.

She had to help Forrest.

She needed to be here for him.

They were connected, no matter what time had done.

She knocked again, this time her hand formed into a fist, then turned her attention to the night. Flakes pelted against her frozen cheeks, clinging to eyelashes and hair. A marked hush pervaded the earth and the sky. Her gaze stayed on Forrest's orange crush Jeep. It stood alone in the driveway, rugged and impressive under the storm, just like its owner.

She turned, ready to knock again, when the door opened. Forrest stood before her, without his signature glasses and still dressed in the

custom fit black wool gabardine suit. The solid white shirt was unbuttoned, giving her a glimpse of the finely sculpted muscles of his chest.

She dragged her gaze to his face—clouded brow, pained mouth.
Intense rage stared back at her. Hurt and anger etched across his face.
His vibe screamed *I'm really pissed off.*

There was something frighteningly sexy about the way he looked.

For ten years she'd tried to deny the desire, the emptiness, and
the hole in her heart. But standing in the doorway, she became lost in
Forrest, in the feeling of wanting to connect with him. Comfort him.
Electricity sparked every cell in her body. She stood frozen and wanting
nothing more than to kiss him.

He stepped back. She walked past him into the entryway. His familiar scent teased her senses. Fresh and woodsy tones mixed with citrus,
pine, cashmere wood, and leather that screamed athletic. Sexy. Her body
drummed with emotions buried for way too long.

Lust.

Longing.

Need.

A need to ease his grief, give him all that she could and never be the
cause of his pain again.

His graphite eyes swept over her with unabashed lust. "Claire, don't
test me. I'm not that strong right now." His voice was raw and sensual, a
perfect combination of passion and pent-up anger.

She pushed aside any doubts and closed the space between them.
Under normal circumstances, he probably would have walked away
from her. She was temporary after all. Tonight none of that mattered.
She touched his face, the stubble on his jaw scraping her palm.

"Forrest," she started but he caught her wrist and pulled her to him.
Silence floated around them, everything frozen in mid-air. She met the
smoky steel of his gray eyes. For a beat, they stayed like that, looking at
each other with mutual intensity, until he cupped her chin in his hands.

With a tortured sound, his lips crashed onto hers, burning her with
his mouth. The kiss was demanding, urgent, with no hint of that deep
heady emotional connection he once freely gave her. She was in his arms
for one purpose only, to be used as a shock absorber, a cushion. That
much was clear. But because her heart was tattooed with his name,

Claire wrapped her arms around his neck and pressed full length against him, giving all of herself to the man who forever owned her.

"I'm not going to be gentle," he said thickly against her lips, leaving no room to mistake where his mind was going.

"I don't care." She found his mouth once again, desperate to give him the one thing she could. . . . herself.

They devoured each other with lips and hands. Their tongues dueled. Passion flared. She moaned against his mouth, wanting more. Claire wasn't sure for how long they kissed or touched, until Forrest pulled away. She held on to his jacket, not wanting him to stop. Not ever. Slowly she opened her eyes, ready to beg if need be. "Don't stop."

He lowered himself to his knees, her gaze followed. Her heart stuttered at the sight of Forrest kneeling in front of her.

"Taking off your shoes."

He didn't have to. She kicked them off and stepped onto the plank wood floor.

"And tights."

Claire's hands immediately went to her dress; all she had to do was scoot up the hem and wriggle out of the thick black tights.

Forrest caught her hands. "Let me."

Steady hands caught the skirt of her dress and bunched it to her thighs. Forrest smoothly striped off her stockings and black lacy underwear. All the while his fathomless eyes held hers captive. She sucked in a breath. No turning back now. When he came back to his feet, he gently spun her around so that she was facing the foyer desk. Taking her hands in his, he pinned them out on the table, forcing her to bend over.

"Don't move," he said in a thrillingly rough voice and gently squeezed her hand. Not that she had any intention of moving. She was here for him—to do as he pleased. She closed her eyes and let herself go.

"Watch." His voice was quiet and gruff against her ear, leaving her no choice but to surrender to his demand.

Claire opened her eyes and saw herself in the oversized natural wood mirror on the wall above the table. The sight of her bent over the table, dress pushed up to her thighs, hair spilling from its rhinestone ponytail holder, lips parted, sent a thrill through her middle. She looked rumpled, conquered.

She met his gaze in the mirror. He stripped off his jacket, undid his belt, and unzipped. They were both half-dressed and there was something so sexy about the way he stood behind her like a caged tiger—big, silently angry with contained rage ready to pounce on an overconfident attacker.

They looked . . . hot.

They stood like that for a long moment, staring at each other in the mirror. Slow burn of desire crackled. Then he leaned forward and cupped her breasts over the cotton material of her dress, gently squeezing. Hunger flamed in his eyes. Hunger for her. The thought made her head spin and scorch her body from the inside out. He glided one hand lower, between her legs. A tremor ran through her as he dipped one finger between her thighs.

"Oh . . ." she whispered then spread her legs for him.

From behind her, Forrest let out a very low, sexy male sound, and then he was exploring her most sensitive spot for the first time in a decade. His fingers trailed her own moisture over her, exploring every dip and crevice, until she was ebbing and flowing. Claire gripped the desk edges for support, eyes closed, and her head back against his chest, she gave in to the wave of ecstasy sweeping over her.

"Watch, Claire," he reminded her again.

He slid another finger deep inside her, filling her, and she let out an incomprehensible little cry. "Please, now," she begged.

"Look at me." He cupped her ass tightly in his hands and spread her open, exposing her most guarded place. One long finger glided across her swollen clit, making her buck forward. Her eyes flew open and locked with his.

"Tonight we fuck." His voice carried a cool, even authority of command.

This was the first time she was seeing this side of him. Ten years ago, they'd been inexperienced and blindly in love. Tonight Forrest was in complete control. Excitement coursed through her veins. Her heart beat faster, blood rushed to her face, and ah, down there. Pulsating with need, she longed to pull him toward her, to put some part of him between her—in her—and fill that unfilled space. With his thighs, he nudged her legs apart a little more then plunged inches of perfection into her, causing a split second of pain. She gasped and let out a little whimper.

He stopped. Hot, hard flesh buried deep inside her core.

"Good?" he murmured.

Oh God, yes. So good. She nodded and writhed against him, silently letting him know she was up for whatever he was willing to give. Then he was thrusting inside her, deep and borderline rough, burying his suffering in her with every tumultuous stroke. His gaze, dark and hooded, never wavered from hers as he hammered away his pain, crushing down walls of her body until she was able to accommodate every inch of his hard perfection.

Her shoulders dropped back. Her lips parted. She took each thrust, arching her back for more, letting him use her. And so he did. He continued to pummel, sinking deeper and deeper. With each stroke, Claire got another jolt, another zap. Their bodies became reacquainted with the perfection of their chemistry. Together they fell into a rhythm and began to move simultaneously.

"Forrest," she cried out his name, her muscles constricting.

"Right there with you."

Their bodies collided, powered only by the need to get off, to have it rough and hard and fast while reaching for the pinnacle. One hand moved to her hair and dug into her scalp as they fell in the abyss of their desire until she shuddered and her legs buckled.

Strong arms were quick around her waist. He pressed her back against the wall of his chest, holding her steady. "I got you."

She wanted to tell him how much of her he got, possessed. But his breath was hot in her ear, making her shake and clouding her mind.

"Okay?" His voice carried a tenderness she hadn't felt from him in a long time.

"Yes."

He slipped out of her, breaking their connection. "Come on, you're staying the night."

CHAPTER TEN

"There are many things in life that will catch your eye,
but only a few will catch your heart . . . pursue those."
~ Michael Nolan

CLAIRE SLOWLY ROSE from the depths of oblivion and became aware of three things. One, her neck and the muscles between her legs ached. Two, the reason for the soreness, she'd slept with Forrest–okay, they had wild animal sex, over and over again. And three, she was alone on his sofa, where they eventually collapsed and fell asleep.

Images from last night trundled through her brain. Forrest bending her over in the entryway and once more in the living room, until his legs had been the ones to give way to the madness. The fiery chemistry had not waned with the years. Last night had been . . . intense. She went to him and he took—a lot of deep penetration, in and out, super-fast and hard. A total act of lust without a drop of any emotional connection. Pure, uncontrolled sex. Nothing more. Sure, he held her in his arms and kissed her goodnight but through it all, something had been missing.

Love.

That wonderful, powerful bond where the heart and soul connected and the emotions were so heightened that they could fly. They had that once before and she wasn't surprised to realize she missed the feeling. Truth was she'd been in denial all along, running away from what her heart craved.

The sex had been invigorating. But now in his living room alone, emptiness swallowed her. They hadn't made it to his bedroom, the reason was obvious. He hadn't wanted that intimacy from her. Not that she blamed him. He'd been hurt and grieving. But deep down, she wished she had woken up in his arms. Groaning, she lifted the mocha knit thrown casually over her and assessed her current state. Still in her dress. Another barrier. No need to get completely naked. She offered. He took. End of story. Shame flooded her veins from head to toe. With a sigh, she pulled herself to a sitting position and looked out of the window. Outside was picturesque, a bright, sunny day with white covering the yard.

The snow had stopped, which meant she could totally escape and deal with facing Forrest later. Tossing the throw aside, she rose from the sofa. All she had to do was find her shoes and quietly slip out. Her gaze toured the living room floor. No shoes. The foyer. She'd kicked them off there by the door. Perfect.

"Looking for these?"

He caught her right smack in the middle of her exit strategy. Biting her lip, she gave herself one of those silent pep talks similar to the ones she'd done before facing thousands of screaming faces, then turned to face her tormentor. Her breath caught.

He stood by the doorway with her shoes dangling in one hand and her purse in another, looking so handsome she had to suck in a breath. Freshly showered with his hair slicked back from the water so his features were more prominent—icy gray eyes tinted to classic light blue, stubble accentuating soft, kissable lips, chiseled jaw, and a hint of a frown on his face. He was the epitome of masculine strength and beauty. The faded jeans hanging low on his hips and the olive cashmere Henley hoodie didn't help either. Her first instinct was to touch him or maybe drag him back to the sofa . . . this time they'd be naked. Instead, Claire crossed her arms beneath her breasts.

"Why are you always looking to run, Claire?" he asked as he closed the space between them and handing her the shoes.

Because that's what I do. I run because your hold on me is too firm. Illicit images of Forrest standing behind her in the entryway scrambled themselves to the surface. Panic set in. The shoes slipped through her fingers as he passed them over and clunked to the floor. She bent down to pick them up just as he did and their heads bumped.

She released a sudden sigh and tried to speak. But no words came.

Gulp. Then with a little more strength she said, "Sorry." But it came out hoarse, barely audible.

After placing her purse on the coffee table by his phone, he walked over to the fireplace and propped her shoes next to the stack of firewood. His eyes met hers. "We should talk."

Claire always prided herself for being strong and able to deal with pretty much anything . . . well, except for the man standing here with her. He was a mighty force. He haunted her. But other than that one little weakness, she was an impregnable fort. She did after all manage to achieve her goal as a singer. Oh, and let's not forget a pretty well-known wedding gown designer. She was tenacious, determined, focused. But the one thing she couldn't take, especially from Forrest, was regret. And right now, she could smell it a mile away. "I came to you last night. I knew what I was getting into."

He continued to look through her. "I wasn't going to apologize for having sex with you."

Oh, okay. What then? She waited.

Forrest's phone chirped, the modern day cricket. She lowered her gaze to the glowing screen. "It's Jason."

"Let it go to voice mail."

The coolness in his voice drew her attention back to his face. He rolled the sleeves of the Henley to his elbows, muscles flexing during the act. For the first time in her twenty-eight years, she caught a hint of familiarity between Forrest, Charles, and Jason. Proud and stubborn just like his father and brother. Even the blue flecks in his eyes were like theirs.

He ran a hand over his face. "We didn't use any protection."

Claire rubbed the inside of her left wrist. She had been caught up in the rapturous moment and forgot caution.

His eyes were fixed on hers, brows bunched into a line across his forehead. "I wasn't thinking straight."

She was smart enough to read between the lines. What he didn't say was the last thing he needed was an unwanted pregnancy.

"Don't worry, I'm on the pill. And I'm not on antibiotics," she added since that's how Lily and Adam's mishap happened. "So we're good."

"Good to know." He continued to watch her with those mesmerizing eyes of his. "I think you should know the last time I had unprotected sex was with you ten years ago." He rubbed the back of his neck. "And it's been awhile, so we're good on my part."

Awhile as in ten years. She wanted to ask but didn't dare. It was silly of her to hope he actually had been abstinent until last night. She knew he dated and probably had his share of fun while in medical school. On the island, while he was discreet and private, four months ago she witnessed one of his dates at West Chop.

Reality dawned. His concern ran beyond pregnancy. Of course the Vineyard's favorite doctor would be thinking about STDs and all. Well, he had nothing to worry about there. Considering the last time she had sex with an actual person, her deluxe silicone boyfriend not included, was two years ago. Any past lovers had been failed attempts to replace Forrest, including the only two other men who could be labeled as boyfriends. In the end, no one measured up, so she stopped trying. "Same here."

He continued to hold her gaze as if he was processing her admission. "Your car won't make it out."

Forever polite, but the message was loud and clear. Time to leave. Her presence was no longer needed. "I'm sure I can manage. I got here last night."

"Your panties are in your purse."

She nodded. Both of their gazes went to the purse then back to each other. Neither made an attempt to move. Another vision of sexed-up Forrest standing behind her popped in her mind's eye, she pursed her lips. His jaw ticked. Something flickered in his eyes. Heat. His mind had gone there too.

"I'll drive you to Martha's Way." He started to walk past her, stopped, and gave her a once-over. "Thank you for staying till the funeral. As it turned out I needed you after all."

ABOUT TWO HOURS later from a drive that typically took twenty minutes, Forrest pulled his Jeep in front of Martha's Way, tucked away amidst seven acres of lawn, garden and woods. The drive had been eerily silent. With his eyes hidden behind the black-rimmed aviator glasses, his expression etched in stone, Claire had nearly run out of the Jeep into the sanctuary of the inn. Not that he made any attempt to stop her. The word goodbye had barely slipped out of her mouth, when he drove off. Tires peeling through the snow, powder flying as he hit the banks.

Once inside, she gave her body a little shake and tried to snap herself out of her fog. What better place to relax than Martha's Way?

No matter how many times she stayed there, the simplicity and elegance always held her attention. Artfully blending the hushed privacy of a boutique hotel with the intimacy of a romantic bed and breakfast, Jason had managed to create a haven of tranquility with an emphasis on guest comfort.

For three consecutive years, it was voted by the *Massachusetts Gazette* as the number one place to stay when on the island. Since going back to work with his father, he'd relinquished the everyday managerial duties to Nora, but he still stayed close enough. This place was his baby. A smile touched Claire's lips as she made her way down to hall to one of the sitting rooms. The familiar feel of the inn slowly began to sink into her bones.

She entered the smaller of the sitting rooms and was not surprised to find Minka, Lily, and Keely sitting at the nearby table eating what appeared to be a late breakfast. She had spotted their respective cars in the parking area when Forrest dropped her off.

Claire groaned. She didn't want to think about Forrest, especially how hurt or sexy he was. He'd literally kicked her out of his house. Not with words, of course, he was too polite for that. The emotional distance spoke volumes.

The three women focused on her. Keely, fork in hand, signaled for her to join them.

"It's all right, I'll just sit here." She waved at the walnut-colored armchair by the fireplace. She was in a crappy mood and wanted to sulk alone.

Minka shook her head. "We'll invade your space either way, so might as well join us."

The power of friendship. By the sound of her voice they were able to detect her mood. Knowing she had lost this battle, Claire made her way to the round table and flopped into the empty chair between Lily and Keely.

She looked them over, noticing they were in their dresses from yesterday. "What happened?" she asked looking at Lily. "I thought you guys left before the storm hit."

Lily rolled her eyes. "Had we been driving a car equipped for this weather, we probably would have made it home."

Minka chuckled. "Your little Mercedes isn't any better in the snow."

"Adam turned around because he was worried about your safety," Keely said while filling her plate with freshly cut kiwi, blood orange, and pomegranate seeds.

"Why do you guys always stick up for Adam?" the soon-to-be mother asked without a hint of anger in her voice.

"I don't know." Minka shrugged, a dreamy look on her face. "He's one of the good guys and he's so in love with you."

Claire nodded in agreement. "Is my mom here?"

Keely shook her head. "She left with Charles. My guess is they are in Edgartown at his house. No way was the boat going to make it to the other side of the island last night."

Claire made a mental note to call her mother later. "And Marjorie?"

"She went home with Adam's parents," Minka answered. "How's Forrest? He didn't answer any of Jason's calls."

Claire shrugged. "Hurt and angry."

"You look like you had a crazy night," Keely noted and the other women gave Claire a once-over. "A terrible morning and now you're ready to have the earth swallow you."

Claire offered a faint smile. She'd never been good at one-night stands. Hell, let's be real, she'd never had one and now she went there with Forrest. "That pretty much sums it up."

Keely chuckled. "So you and Forrest went there after ten years?"

By there, Claire was sure her BFF meant doing the wild thing with the Vineyard's favorite doctor. She could deny it of course. But, she'd never been good at lying and these women were her partners in crime.

"Yup," she admitted. "You'd think I'd be smarter than that." Shaking her head, she picked up a freshly baked biscuit from the basket. Forrest had offered to make breakfast but knowing it had been out of politeness, she had declined and chose not to overstay her welcome.

"You're pretty smart," Minka offered gently.

She'd argue otherwise, because what she did was the complete opposite. She had fed the beast known as *heart* and even though she felt like shit, the stupid muscle wanted more. "I'm actually not smart at all."

"Honey, you're in love," the forever logical Keely chimed in. "Quit running and face the big l-o-v-e monster. You did come back here for him."

Technically, she hadn't been running away from Forrest. Their paths crossed on many occasions and would continue to do so. It was inevitable. Their worlds were forever connected by family and friends. At every moment their lives intersected, her heart took the opportunity to remind her it was branded with the island's favorite doctor. She needed him there. She loved him. Infinitely.

"Last night was just sex," she muttered.

Lily pulled her iPhone from her purse and tapped on the screen, drawing Claire's attention.

"Is everything okay?" she asked her friend. Lily's brother Zander was a Navy SEAL and her friend constantly worried over his safety.

Lily nodded, her eyes never leaving the screen of her phone as she typed away. When she finally looked up, she had a satisfying grin on her face. "I just added you to the bidding war on the most eligible doctor on the Vineyard."

Claire frowned. "I'm lost."

The twin sisters chuckled, but it was Minka who spoke. "The guys are doing a fundraiser to help raise money to move Gay Head Lighthouse back from the cliff's edge. A lucky bidder will win a date with Forrest."

From the few articles she'd read in the *Vineyard Gazette*, Claire knew the iconic landmark was in danger of falling into the sea as the nearby cliffs continued to erode.

"The first day of spring, they will announce the winners," Lily added. "Now you have a reason to stick around, especially after you and sexy doctor had out of this world sex."

Claire's heart twisted at the idea of Forrest on a romantic date with someone. Last fall, she caught a glimpse of one of his dates. Kerry had been all over him, but Forrest hadn't seemed to mind. Ugh! "I'm not bidding on Forrest."

"Why not?" Keely asked. "What better way to show him you still want him?"

She stared at Keely. "And how would that help other than making a fool of myself?"

Minka leaned in. "Maybe you can just tell him you're in love with him and want him back."

Lay all of her cards on the table and be honest about her feelings with Forrest. Under normal circumstances that would be the most reasonable approach, but after ten years? She stood no chance. So why did she walk out of her promotional tour and back on the island again?

All right, she was a bit lost and confused. Sue her. "Nope. Never gonna happen."

Lily slid her phone in front of Claire. "Your screen name is Tattooed Hearts. Password is foreverectomy. All one word and lowercase." She wrinkled her nose. "I'm going for the whole Gray's Anatomy thingy."

"Isn't that ominous, considering?" Keely's expression said she thought so.

"Hence why that's not the password." Lily beamed.

Minka and Keely stifled a laugh. Claire exhaled.

"Foreverectomy," Minka said.

Lily nodded, her face glowing with pride. "It means a surgical procedure that lasts a very long time." She glanced at Claire. "Like the hold Forrest has on you."

Keely arched a brow then nodded in agreement. Claire sighed.

"Your account is ready for you to bid whenever your heart desires," Lily continued.

Claire glanced down at the phone. "I won't be here by then. As soon as I can catch the ferry I'm leaving."

While at it, she'd gladly sell off her heart. The creative part of her brain already had a catchy phrase to get rid of the damn thing. *For sale— One heart. Condition—Horrible. Asking Price—Will take anything for it. Just cut it out of my chest and end this suffering.*

CHAPTER ELEVEN

"I am proud of my heart. It's been played, stabbed,
burned, and broken. But somehow it still works."
~ Anonymous

AFTER A SNOWBOUND day in his house and filled with pent-up energy, Forrest sprang from the mat and was immediately greeted by another body shot from Blake. This one to his ribs sent fresh ripples of pain through his torso. He didn't fall–he made absolutely sure that didn't happen. Ignoring the excruciating pressure with promises to be sore later, he covered the distance between them, threw three quick jabs. Left-right-left. Each one landing on his sparring partner's headgear.

Blake seemed immune to the blows and counterattacked.

Punches flew. Forrest retaliated. He swung his leg around in a semi-circular motion into a roundhouse kick. Blake dodged and threw a haymaker. Forrest ducked but didn't parry the blow. It landed on the side of his head.

He stumbled to the side, recovered, and responded with an uppercut. The blow landed, forcing Blake to step back. With full force, Forrest charged forward. A clean shoulder-to-shoulder hit arched Blake's spine and the two men came down hard on the mat. They tumbled over each other, arms and legs entangled, grappling as they brawled to pin each other to the ground. Eventually they fell on their backs with arms splattered on their sides and a whimper of exhaustion left their lips.

"You tapped out," Blake said between short gasps of breath.

Forrest lay on the mat, eyes closed, sweat dripping down the side of his face. "In your dreams." He rolled to his side, bruised ribs protested in pain. A vision of Claire's lips kissing his aching muscles burned his brain.

Shit.

Shaking his head, he hauled his weight to his hands and knees, head hanging low, like a winded horse.

"I almost broke your arm," Blake insisted.

Forrest laughed for the first time since his father's death, but the act hurt his ribcage. He hoisted himself to his feet and extended a hand to Blake. "We can go at it again."

"I can't let you take all of your anger out on me. Beside, you owe me a drink for picking you up at the inn."

Right. He did drag Blake on his mission to return Claire's car.

Blake wiped his forearm across the sweat trickling in his eyes. "And for driving your ass back to get your car."

Forrest grabbed his bottled water, twisted off the cap and gulped down a few mouthfuls, quenching his thirst.

"And by the way," Blake continued, "you're chicken shit for not facing her."

Forrest couldn't argue there. Especially after she unselfishly gave herself to him to be done with as he pleased. The bastard in him had done exactly that, until they collapsed half-delirious with pleasure. In the morning he toyed with the idea of asking her to stay for one more day, but the sight of her looking for an escape brought back bitter memories and forced him to automatically shut down.

Once upon a time she was all he wanted.

His heart, safely tucked in a steel cage, banged against its rigid barrier.

He ignored the protest. Claire was the last person on earth he should be involved with on any level.

Still, he probably could have been–scratch that, he definitely could have been more appreciative. After burying his pain in her, he'd made his body fit on the crammed sofa with Claire basically on top of him so that they didn't share his bed. A desperate attempt to guard his heart.

He was a cad.

Regret emerged and tried to consume him, but Forrest shoved it down. He would not analyze every action or word from every angle and writhe in the agony of paths untaken. He'd been down that road before.

When she first left, pangs of woe, remorse, and nostalgia would come to him in quiet moments, during sleep or with his nose buried in a medical book. Regret for not chasing her and demand an explanation would seep to the foreground of his mind and commanded to be re-examined again.

No amount of analysis was going to turn back the clock. He had to get on with the here and now. Tired of thinking about Claire, he vowed a long time ago he'd make better choices next time around. That included sex, especially with Claire. No matter how perfectly suited they were or that he wanted a replay of last night as badly as his next breath.

He had to stay away.

For that reason, he hadn't gone inside Martha's Way to return the car key. "I'm not running from Claire."

"Could have fooled me."

Forrest grabbed his workout bag and threw it over his shoulder. The movement burned his shoulder blade. He hissed over the self-inflicted pain. "Thanks for the free counseling session. Meet me later and I'll buy you a beer."

"See you at Vapor."

"Pick another spot."

"Avoiding Jason too?" Blake shook his head. "He didn't ask to be a Montgomery any more than you did."

"I'm not a Montgomery."

Blake opened his mouth to say otherwise, but seemed to think better of it.

"Gotta go. I have snow to shovel."

"Wait, you're the lucky speed dial this time and not me?" Blake said in a dejected tone.

All four of them were on Mrs. Kane's speed dial for emergencies. They loved it. She was Maxie's grandmother, one of the island's oldest locals, proud member of the town's gossip crew, his favorite Lyme disease patient, and she made the best damn S'mores cookies in the world. Today luck was on his side. "I'm the lucky one. And she will probably make . . ."

"S'mores chocolate chip cookies," Blake finished.

Forrest chuckled. "Send me a text with a location for drinks later," he said over his shoulder before walking out of the gym.

A little over an hour later, Forrest absently massaged the stabbing pain in his left shoulder, and kicked off his snow boots before entering the colonial home. The aroma of freshly baked S'mores chocolate chip cookies, full of heaven, filled his nostrils. He walked into Mrs. Kane's TV room. Murmurs of undying love filled his ears. Mrs. Kane's daily soap opera droned out any other sound in the house and turned back time. His mother and Claire had been soap opera addicts.

Memories flickered like a blazing bushfire. While his mother used to openly dedicate at least one hour of the day to her favorite show, Claire had been a closet addict. One day he'd walked away from a volleyball match at East Beach to bike back to the Montgomery compound with her, only to watch her drool over some actor.

He'd teased her, over and over, but like a true sap struck by Cupid's arrow, he eventually started watching with her. He could care less about the half-naked women walking around, although the view had been an added perk for his young adult hormones. But most importantly, sitting there with Claire, for one or two hours, just the two of them, had been the best part of his days. The last time he'd watched any daytime television other than sports-related news had been the day of her eighteenth birthday, lying in bed beside her with General Hospital as backdrop to their lovemaking.

Memories were the worst kind of monsters.

He shoved them to the back of his subconscious and focused his attention on his patient. Earlier this morning Mrs. Kane had called for some assistance with her driveway. Fatigue and body aches were two common side effects from someone fighting Lyme disease. Since diagnosed the older woman was well on her way to recovery, but Forrest always feared a chance of relapse.

"Forrest, I mean Doctor Desvareaux," The seventy-plus-year-old woman greeted him with a bright smile. Her armchair perfectly positioned to face the television. "Come sit down." She gestured toward the antique wooden chair across from her. "I baked some cookies. Would you like some?"

Forrest watched her pick up the plate of freshly baked cookies from the small lamp table. He smiled and ran a hand over his abdomen, but reached for the cookies anyway. He and his friends had a mutual understanding with the older woman. She baked cookies and they shoveled her snow. "You're trying to fatten me up, Anne."

She winked at him with eyelashes matted down with mascara. "Son, if I were twenty years younger, I'd make a play for you."

Twenty years would put her at exactly fifty-four. Close to his mother's age. But no need to go there. "Your driveway is spotless."

Mrs. Kane stretched her neck for a better view of the television screen. "I meant to call Jason or Blake. Last thing you need right now is me bothering you."

"You could never bother me." He took a bite of the cookie and savored the combination of chocolate, marshmallow, and graham crackers. A total healthy lifestyle buster, but so worth it. "What's in these things? So delicious."

"Did you check on your mother?"

"My mother is fine." He ignored the tightness in his gut.

"You spoke to her? She's all alone on that farm of yours."

"It's not my farm. And she has help." He reached in the leather bag for his stethoscope and thermometer. "Let's do a quick physical."

Less than two minutes later, Mrs. Kane had the pleasure of hearing she had no fever. Forrest tapped her knee and checked her reflexes, then her breathing.

"Looks like you're healthy as a fifty–year-old." He picked up his phone and typed in a reminder to check on her doxycycline prescription. "Everything looks good. Next time call me and I'll come shovel your snow or anything else you need done around the house."

She smiled. "You're a good boy, Forrest. We need to find you a good woman."

A vision of Claire sleeping in his arms popped into his head. He tapped another reminder. *Claire: Poison. Stay away.* "Anything you need done before I leave?"

The Lyme disease, a rampant curse on the island, had left Mrs. Kane with some physical limitations. Since she tired easily, he tried to keep her from any strenuous physical activity.

"I think I'll be okay. Have you checked on the auction?"

Truthfully, he'd forgotten all about it. Late last summer, the guys decided to help raise money to move Gay Head Lighthouse by having an auction. Each had agreed to put something of theirs up for bids, but since they were all married, happily so, he'd been coerced into a date with the highest bidder. "No, I haven't."

She pulled out her cell phone from somewhere in the sofa's cushion and scrolled through. She studied whatever she was looking at then smiled. "Well, Adam is leading the bidding." She grimaced. "But you're a strong second."

"Adam has the best prize," he said after another bite.

"What's his prize again?" Memory loss and confusion were side effects of the disease that plagued the island.

"An all-expense paid trip to one of his races overseas."

"That is a great prize. And as sexy as Adam is, I'd bet on it too. Just to be on the sideline. And that beautiful wife of his, I like her," she said once the show went into commercial. "What's her name again?"

"Lily," he responded, although he'd bet all of his savings, Lyme disease or not, Mrs. Kane knew everyone's name on the island.

She waved a hand. "What does he call her?"

"Liliana."

"Yes." She beamed. "I love that he calls her by her full name in that sexy accent of his. You're sexy too, but you know . . . the bookish kind."

"Thanks."

She wrinkled her nose. "Maxie calls you guys the four hotties."

He made a mental note to beg Maxie, their favorite waitress at Vapor, to stop referring to him as a hottie. While at it, drop the "sexy," "hottie," or whatever.

"Well, you don't have an accent."

Forrest picked up his bag. He always enjoyed a visit with Anne, but damn it his shoulder blade was officially burning. Ice pack and ESPN should do the trick. Something deep in his heart whispered Claire's name and tried to tell him to call her, but he ignored it. "I should leave before my ego is fully deflated."

"Oh, don't be silly." She laughed and Forrest couldn't help but smile. "I love you. You're my favorite doctor out of your crew."

"I'm the only doctor."

"Technicality." She handed him the phone. "Anyhow, it appears you made the news."

Frowning Forrest took the phone from Anne and looked at the screen. A picture of Claire standing next to him with her hand encased in his, both of them looking solemn. He glanced over the words.

The reason for Claire Peters walking away from her career seems to be to comfort her longtime friend and apparent first love. I think there's still something there between those two. They are burning the pages. H-O-T! What say you, readers? Word on the streets . . . he's a long lost Montgomery. More to come.

Forrest groaned over the invasion of privacy. Not that he was surprised by it. A lot of people probably overheard the shouting match between him, his mother, Jason, and Charles at the repass. While the people on the Vineyard were guarded and protective of their own, the funeral had attracted outsiders. One of them probably took that damn picture and went straight to the media.

His stomach churned.

Adam and Jason both had had their share dealing with the media. Jason had to deal with his mother's death with photographers in his face. For years Adam had a reporter breathing down his throat, digging into his past. They both managed not to feed the beast. Claire as well, she lived under a microscope. It was probably worse for her. He'd seen a few of the magazines she headlined. The tabloids described even the most salacious details of the private lives of the rich and famous. But Claire seemed to understand and accepted it. Forrest wanted none of the flash or notoriety that came with being a star or with the Montgomery name.

Montgomery. The name slashed at him with betrayal.

"We won't go into you being a Montgomery and all. But for the record, my friends and I always suspected."

"I see." His tone came out much more bitter than he'd intended.

"Oh, darling, I never thought I'd see you so angry. You'll have to let it go sooner or later. Holding on to pain is not good for the heart." She handed him the tray of cookies again. "Speaking of matters of the heart, how are things between you and our town superstar?" Anne's voice rose with interest. "I mean, she's the love of your life. Everyone knows that."

The admission didn't surprise him. One of the perks of living on an island was everyone knew everyone's business. Good or bad. "There's nothing between me and Claire. We are friends."

Those words made him a liar and in denial for refusing to accept the obvious reality of his situation. First, they were not friends. They hadn't been in a long time. Second, no way in hell was he over Claire. Not one bit. Never mind he hadn't been able to get her out of his mind for the last decade.

No matter how carefully he tried to compartmentalize their relationship, she still coursed through his veins. The other night had been the icing on the cake, the light that lit his bonfire heart. He wanted more. He'd take it slow this time and touch, kiss every inch of that wicked body of hers.

He raked a hand through his hair. She got through to him once before, even when common sense told him to stay away. She'd been too young, too impressionable, too naïve. He'd gone ahead and defied logic; followed his heart and took the plunge.

In the end she walked away with no explanation. Not even a goodbye.

He wanted none of that.

He'd be foolish to go down that slippery road again.

CHAPTER TWELVE

"How to save your heart—Don't get affected."
~ Forrest Montgomery Desvareaux

RUSTIC BARN PENDANT light cords hung from the beams on the high ceiling, giving the recreation center a warm and intimate feel. Tables stretched from one end of the room to the other, layered with trays of wood-fired pizza from Flatbread, lobster rolls, tapas style plates from Vapor. Grilled trout with lemon prepared by Adam and Lily sat among mounds of fragrant wild rice, potatoes, and diced pumpkin smeared with butter and spices. Countless cheeses with baskets of crackers, bread rolls shaped as seashells, and various salads and side dishes.

Claire placed her mother's smoked sausages and the pineapple-glazed ham on the table, then scanned the packed room. Adam had one arm around Lily's shoulder while talking to Blake, Jason and Tyler, the owner of Flatbread Pizzeria and her first kiss. Familiar faces–old, young, former classmates, hugging, laughing, and talking the night away. The world and his wife were here tonight.

"I'm going to go talk to a friend." Her mother leaned in a little closer. "No one here would ever contact the tabloids," she said, referring to the picture of Claire and Forrest from the funeral currently making the rounds. "We don't do that to one of our own. So relax and enjoy being home tonight. It feels good, doesn't it?"

It didn't. Regardless of the warm greetings she always received from everyone, she wasn't one of them. Not anymore. Not since she learned she'd never be good enough because she was the maid's daughter.

Her mother squeezed her hand then walked away. Claire watched her. Shoulders squared. Chin up. Her mother stood no taller than she did, yet she carried an air of confidence and seemed to own the room as she sauntered through the happy, chattering crowd. Within seconds, her mother fell into an effortless conversation with a few women from one of her social clubs. She might not have the financial wealth as the others in her circle, but her mother belonged here. The island and the people were as much a part of her as she was a part of them. Her home.

The familiar empty feeling reared up in her. Arms crossed over her chest, Claire stood rooted to the spot.

The aroma, the sea of faces, like pebbles on the beach, drone-like chatter of best friends, laughter of children, lovers holding hands, The Killers' *Mr. Brightside* blaring out of the subwoofers, conjured up memories of a time gone and a place she no longer called home. For a moment, she became lost in a transitory evocation of her childhood—Mickey Mouse every Saturday morning, watching a storm come in on the beach, riding her bike with the sparkling streamers while the boys chased behind. But she'd been away too long, and now it all felt like a half-forgotten dream. But not the hold Forrest had on her—that part of her past continued to gnaw at her heart. She used to force herself to believe their time was never that significant, maybe even a figment of her imagination. But like tonight, the ache of longing to be with him echoed through the very marrow of her bones.

"Come on, Miss Sunshine." Keely nudged her elbow on Claire's side and smiled. "You look like you're a stranger to everyone here."

She smiled at her friend. "In a way I am."

"Not any more than me. I didn't grow up here."

"Where's Minka? I don't see her anywhere."

"She's not feeling well. Jason said something about a stomach virus."

"Is Forrest here?" Quickly she gave the room another once-over. No sign of the island's favorite doctor. Was he avoiding her or everyone in general?

"I haven't seen him." Hazel eyes studied Claire. "Happy or sad over that?"

She exhaled. "I don't know. Last encounter wasn't the greatest."

"I can't imagine Forrest being blah in bed." Keely wrinkled her nose. "Not that my mind goes there, but if it were . . ."

"You're starting to sound like Lily." A little chuckle escaped Claire's mouth. "I mean the morning after."

"I have a feeling he caught you trying to run away again," Keely said with no judgment at all. "Maybe you should stop doing that."

"I'm not running. I'm here."

Keely looked her friend over. "You have uncertainty written all over your face." She slid an arm in the crook of Claire's. "Come on, let's go have some fun."

Sometime in the night, the happiness around the room became infectious. It started as a tingle in her fingers and toes, much like the feeling she had when she was anxious, but instead of worrisome, it was warm. Most of the food had been eaten and everyone was lively. Loud, thumping music played in the background making it impossible for Claire to hear her voice or anyone else's for that matter. It didn't matter. Tyler caught her hand and dragged her onto the dance floor.

For a split second, she hesitated, the picture of Forrest holding her hand while mourning his father still fresh in the headline. Ava, head of her public relations team, had called to see if damage control was needed. None necessary had been her response. The act had been intrusive, but to address it would fuel the fire and bring unwanted attention to Forrest. She could count on one hand the many times he'd been photographed with Jason or Adam. None with her—at least never alone.

"You're with friends, Claire," Tyler said, smiling. "Come on, let's dance. Maybe I'll get Forrest jealous for old time's sake." He grinned and pulled her into him.

"He's not here," she pointed out to her friend.

Tyler chuckled. "Ten bucks he'll show up. He can't stay away, not from you."

If only that were true. Ignoring the way her heart fluttered over the possibility, she looked around the room. A contemporary tune enticed guests to the dance floor. Dancing bodies tangled together. Among them, was her mother, laughing with a tall, slender man with ebony skin. With everyone being carefree, she decided to drop her guard and thrust herself into the writhing mass of sweating bodies. Random fun was something she used to be good at and needed at times.

In a matter of minutes, she was swaying to *Renegades* by X

Ambassadors. The alternative-soulful beat spun her around, lifting away gravity. It felt good. She became one with the beat, releasing the day's stress. A pair of strong hands grabbed her waist from behind, and she jumped at the sensation. Gooseflesh bloomed, making her skin tingle with desire. Only one person affected her that way.

She frowned at Tyler. He shrugged, nodded at the person behind her. "Looks like I got to him again." He smiled and gave her the I-told-you-so look. "You owe me ten dollars." And then he was gone.

Claire spun around to face Forrest, his hair tousled from the cold wind, annoyance on his face.

"I need to talk to you." His voice was like the magma chamber of a volcano, deep but filled with molten rock. Claire's bones vibrated.

"What about?"

"You and me. Come on." Large masculine hands pressed to the center of her back as he guided her through the room.

"Leaving the party?" Jason said by the door, a chilled bottle of beer dangling between his fingers. His blue eyes panned Forrest's face. "You don't take calls anymore."

"You sound like a wounded girlfriend," Forrest bit back.

Jason shrugged, as if he could care less. But Claire knew better. The two men had a long-standing friendship. "And you're acting like something crawled up your ass and died." He took a chug of his beer. "What the fuck is your problem?"

Silence hung in the air, suspended like the moment before a falling glass shatters on the ground.

"You're a Montgomery."

Jason stood a little straighter, the Montgomery pride and arrogance in full effect. "So are you."

Absolute stillness. The two men stared at each other. Alpha against Alpha. Chests lifted then expanded. Claire's stomach twisted. Seeing them at odds made her nauseous.

She looked at Forrest. "You wanted to talk."

With his hand still on her lower back, they walked outside of the room and down the hall. They stood with barely an inch between them, eyes locked. Neither spoke. "You're with Tyler?" he asked after a long beat of silence.

She blinked. "What?"

"He's a nice guy and all, but . . ."

"I kissed Tyler when I was sixteen."

His gray eyes darkened. "Only then."

Claire held her breath behind pursed lips to steel herself against the burst of laughter to come. It always came. Especially when she was feeling excited or nervous, in this case, it was a combination. Forrest was jealous. "Only then," she repeated.

"Claire, about the other day . . . ," he said after another long silence.

Her heart skipped. She waited.

"I apologize if I came off a bit . . ."

"Cold," she finished for him.

He let out a slow deep breath. "Distant."

She smiled tightly at him. "It's okay, Forrest. I'm a big girl."

"Are you okay then?" He removed his glasses and stared at her.

She hated when he did that. It made her feel naked and vulnerable. Claire brushed her hands over her sweater and peered at the window, focusing her attention on the blackness outside. "I'm fine."

He closed the distant between them in one stride and touched the pad of his thumb against her cheek, drawing her eyes to his. "Once upon a time I would have done anything for you. For us."

"And now?"

"That was ten years ago. A lot has changed."

His words splintered her, smashing her heart. Tears threatened to spill. She swallowed them down. "You don't love me anymore."

He straightened himself, took several steps away from her, and shoved his hands in his pockets. Every muscle in his face was tense and without a word he communicated a deep mistrust, anger, and a time lost. "You left without saying goodbye." There was a beat of accusatory silence. "Without telling me why."

"I wasn't good enough for you."

"You should have let me decide that."

"Forrest."

His jaw ticked.

"You're over me?" she asked, holding his gaze.

He squinted at her through hardened eyes that once gleamed with love and devotion. But now, as his gaze dissected her bit by bit with the least bit of care, Claire was struck by their coldness.

"Go back to L.A., Claire. That's your home." He pulled his coat tight and walked out of the center.

Her heart contracted then shrunk from Forrest's blow. She couldn't move, couldn't breathe. The hairs on her arms stood at attention as a militia of chills marched down her spine.

"You all right?"

She glanced over at Jason and gave him a tight smile. "Yeah."

He came to stand next to her and wrapped one arm around her shoulder as he'd always done. He was in big brother mode. She'd always loved that about him.

"No, you're not. You're still in love with the big goof. Why did you leave, Claire?"

"I wasn't good enough," she whispered.

"Says who?"

"Your mom." The words leaked out of her lips. "Jason . . ." She aimed for damage control, but his hands gripped her shoulders and turned her to face him, crystal blue eyes crashing into hers.

"What are you saying?"

She shook her head. "I didn't mean to say that."

"What did my mother say to you?" he persisted.

"Nothing." But her voice shook a little. More importantly, Jason knew her better than anyone else in her life. "I'm sorry, Jason, there's no need to talk about it. It's been ten years."

He scrubbed a hand over his face. "You left that night over something my mother said."

She could deny it, but what would be the point. Claire stepped out of his hold to the other side of the hallway. "Yes," she whispered. "I overheard her telling my mother I wasn't good enough for Forrest or any of you."

"What?" His voice resonated her shock a decade ago.

"How are things between you and your dad?" she asked, changing direction of the conversation. "The night of the funeral you were pretty upset with him."

"We spoke. We are fine." His blue eyes stared straight through her.

"Let's talk about you and the night you hightailed out of town."

"It hurt then." She rubbed a hand over her arm. "It still hurts."

"My mother was sick."

Something they all later found out after the sickness took her life. Perhaps that explained why she held no grudge toward Victoria. "I didn't know that then. I don't think you knew."

"I didn't realize she was sick until it was too late." Jason leaned against the wall, head hung to the floor, eyes fixed on his shoes. Neither spoke, silence lay between them as they wallowed in a valley of despair. "How come you don't hate me or my father?" he asked into the silence.

"I never hated your mom. I admit for a while I was angry, but never hate." She swallowed back some of the hurt. "As for you and your dad, neither of you ever made me feel inferior." She let out a soft laugh over the memories. "Your dad never wanted me to find out what your mother thought of me."

"She was sick," he said again.

"I know."

He exhaled. "I'm sorry you went through that."

"I'm fine."

He came to stand next to her again. "No, you're not. You're broken just like me and I never knew."

"I'm fine," she said again, but her inside was damp with uncried tears.

He pulled her into his arms once more, and placed a kiss on top of her head. "Are you going to fight for him?"

Claire blinked the tears away. "He doesn't love me anymore."

Jason chuckled. "He still loves you, Claire. You shredded him to pieces, but Forrest has never gotten over you. The question is do you have it in you to fight for him."

"His dad just died. He's hurt and angry right now."

"Fight or flight, Claire. I have to go home to my wife." He gave her arm one final squeeze. "I hope you stay and fight."

THE BITTER COLD bit Claire's face, seeped through her woolen hat, and crept under her clothes. Chill spread across her skin like the delicate tide on the frigid desolate beach. She wrapped the thick coat around her tighter and continued her walk. Other than the howling wind, a frozen puddle here and there cracking under her winter boots, the beach was empty, barren, yet still with beauty. She exhaled, puffs of white vapor floated in the air. A blustery beach walk was a great way for her to combat post-Forrest comedown.

Two weeks had come and gone, her heart was still empty. Something throbbed in her guts, deep and warm, but not in a good way. She inhaled and exhaled again, time to pack up and leave.

Fight or flight. Jason's words replayed in her head.

Regret was never sweet. It washed over her like the long slow waves on the beach–icy and cold, sending shivers down her spine. She longed to go back and take a different path, but now that was impossible. There was no way back, no way to make things right between her and Forrest. He even told her to go back home.

Home. A home was where the heart felt the most at peace, where one was surrounded by friends, family, traditions, and safety. A place where one hung their hat.

She hadn't had a home in years. As much as she enjoyed living in Los Angeles, it was semi-permanent, a short-term accommodation. It always felt that way. Claire kicked a small rock with the tip of her boots and sent it flying. Remorse ate at her the way it had every day since she left. She'd lost her chance at love, her one chance to truly be happy. She surveyed the pebbles with envy, hard and lifeless, unable to feel the torments of life.

She walked off the private beach, crossed the rolling meadows of the Montgomery compound to the tucked away cottage sitting distance away from the main house. From the large farmer's porch, she peered across the nearly fifty-acres where she grew up. Visions of Jason and his parents playing croquet came to her. Charles would always wave at her and insist she joined them. Her heart squeezed over the memories.

Home.

She was homesick for a place which may no longer exist, or able to return to. A place where her heart was full and her soul was understood. Once upon a time the island had been her sanctuary, her home sweet home. Until that night. Shoving the bitter memories to the back of her mind, she pushed the cottage door open. A smile crept in as soon as Claire stepped inside the open design two-bedroom house. Like any other day, she was greeted by her mother's morning coffee. Claire inhaled the strong, smooth aromatic scent.

"How was your walk?" her mother asked.

"Good." She removed her hat and tossed it on the sofa.

"Two weeks went by so fast."

She couldn't agree more. "I guess it's true what they said. Time flies when you're having fun."

Her mother looked her over and for a moment Claire thought she saw pity in her eyes.

"Are you having fun, honey?"

Yeah, definitely pity in those deep brown eyes. Claire's throat tightened. Her heart was tight too. "I have to go finish packing."

"Sure, love. I'll bring up coffee."

Claire made her way to the open staircase leading to the second floor, down the hall to her bedroom. The black leather overnight bag, firm and upright on the bed, hailed at her.

Go back to L.A., Claire, that's your home. Forrest's harsh words replayed like an echo. She snatched her favorite cable knit pullover from the wicker chair and jammed it into the bag. The tote fought the pressure and spit out the intrusion. Why was it always easier to pack when going somewhere and never on the return trip? Hands knotted into fists, she pressed the sweater into the little space left.

"So you're really leaving," her mother said at the door.

"Of course, Mom. I have a life back in L.A." She examined the pile of clothes on the bed, skirts, sweaters, pants, jackets. One day she'd learned to pack light. "I'll be back in the spring or something."

Stepping further into the room, her mother handed Claire the coffee "You're running." She picked up a sweater from the pile on and started folding. "When will you stop running, darling?"

"I have a song to write."

"How's that going? Did you make any progress?"

Well, the last few days, she'd written *Tattooed Hearts* at least twenty times a day. The title was important. One word at a time, she'd written two. That was an accomplishment. Eventually, Forrest would stop taking every space in her brain and let her creativity flow. "I've made great progress."

"You've always been a terrible liar."

Claire took a sip of the coffee. "It sucks that you know me so well."

Her mother folded the sweater and looked at the overnight bag. "Did you just throw things in there?"

As a matter of fact, last night after returning from the potluck, she had done just that. Claire swatted at the air. Her mother chuckled and pulled the stuffed clothes out of the bag.

"You're so emotionally stunted, darling." Her mother's voice was low and without daggers. "I can't believe I raised you to be a coward."

As calmly as the words were spoken, they still cut Claire and numbed her circulation. "I'm not a coward." Or sub-par. Or a little fish in the sea. All she had to do was look at her bank account, her investments, the charities she supported, all the chart-topping hits she'd written, co-produced and sang. The shiny awards on the mantel in Los Angeles were proof of her accomplishments. Cowards didn't leave all they'd ever known to pursue a dream.

Her mother glanced at her. "You're in love with Forrest. Have been forever, but you're blinded by the fact that I manage this place." Her mother folded another sweater. "And because of that you've convinced yourself you're not good enough for him."

"I didn't convince myself of that. It was pointed out to me, remember?" The day after she left the island, Claire had called and revealed to her mother she'd overheard her conversation with Victoria.

"So you let the words of a sick woman dictate who you are." She picked up a camisole and folded the delicate fabric. "You think Forrest will abandon you like your father did to me."

Silence filled the room. Claire scratched the inside of her wrist where colorful corded bracelets strategically covered the tattoo. She'd been the one to leave. Not Forrest.

Her mother picked up another sweater and held it before her. "I like this one."

"Then it's yours, or I can buy you one."

Her mother smiled and placed the sweater to the side. "I'll use it this winter." She examined one of Claire's favorite pair of skinny jeans. "You're so tiny. Do you eat in L.A.?"

In spite of herself, Claire smiled. "I've always been small. It's a curse."

"Forrest towers over you." Her mother observed while folding another pair of jeans. "Honey, don't think I'm not aware of what's in your heart. I've watched you run away from him. He's loved you all of his life. Don't you think it's time you allow yourself to be happy? Both of you deserve to be happy."

Claire sat on the bed and took another sip of her coffee. "It doesn't matter anymore. It's too late."

"Why do you say that?"

"He told me to go back to L.A."

"So you're leaving because Forrest said so." Her mother arched a brow. She sat beside her daughter and pressed a hand against Claire's. "You left him without an explanation. I don't think you ever told him what drove you to leave. The only father he's ever known just died. To further complicate things he now has to deal with knowing that wasn't his real father." Her mother exhaled. "So let's see, he's hurt, angry, and betrayed. And now you're running again when he needs you the most."

Without another word, her mother walked out of the room, leaving Claire alone with her bag packed and ready to go. She pushed a handful of beads up her wrist and the bracelets jangled in protest. Wretched memories swirled in her head.

'Go back to L.A., Claire, that's your home.' Forrest's words haunted her. She peered at her bag. A string of images, emotions buried, but never truly died breathed life in her heart. Ten years fell into the distance.

Time to fight.

Tugging at the bracelets, she removed the layers long used to cloak the memories, shielding her heart. The only one left was a silver feather bangle bracelet because Forrest had given her that one. But it didn't conceal the black ink, and it'd always been her favorite.

Reaching for her phone, she found Jason's number and texted.

I'm staying.

Jason's response came quickly.

Good. I'm proud of you.

CHAPTER THIRTEEN

"Sometimes you have to follow your heart, no matter the consequences."
~ Minka Greene Montgomery

TWO WEEKS LATER, Claire sat at a corner table at Vapor with her eyes glued to the crisp blank page in the spiral-bound journal. Clear-polished fingers tapped the pen on the table to Jack Savoretti's gritty soul-soaked vocals crooning *Breaking the Rules*. Not one freakin' word. She wasn't dubbed the queen of heart-wrenching lyrics for nothing, although the empty spaces in her notebook dared to argue otherwise. She peeped at the silver clock on the brick wall. She'd only been sitting here for ninety minutes, pocket change in songwriting land. In some instances, it'd take her two to three hours to write a sentence. But on most days, she could write a song in a day. After one month on the island, she was still where she started two months ago. *Nada. Nichts.*

She blamed her creative crisis on none other than sexy Doctor Forrest Montgomery Desvareaux or maybe he'd dropped his middle name and was now only Forrest Desvareaux.

Whatever!

He was the culprit. To rub salt in her already wounded heart, he'd gone and left the island. He ran all the way to New Hampshire for the last fourteen days, and no one had any clue when he'd return. Her life was a beautiful irony.

Her phone vibrated on the table. Claire glanced at the glowing screen. James Harrison. Her manager's name made her stomach twist with jitters. She picked up the phone and answered the call. "How is it going in Tinseltown?"

"Tinseltown is wondering when you're coming back." His voice was warm on the other end, but she knew her manager well enough to know he had his business hat on.

She had asked James for an additional two weeks. Well, two weeks had come and gone. "I need more time."

"It's been a month," he said, a hint of exasperation in his voice.

She didn't blame him. How much longer could he give Ava vague statements explaining her abrupt disappearance?

"You have a full calendar that you keep pushing off," James continued.

"I know." She stirred in her chair. "I just need . . ."

"Two more weeks." He exhaled on the other end. "He's that important?"

"Yes," she answered without a beat. James discovered her in New York at a karaoke night. He'd been by her side since, not just as a business partner, but also a trusted friend. "I need to close this chapter in my life."

"Have you made any progress?"

"He's not here."

"So why are you still on the island?" he asked after a short silence.

"He has to come back eventually. Martha's Vineyard is his home."

"And yours," James said gently. "Are you thinking about moving back?"

She opened her mouth to say no and stopped. "I haven't given that much thought."

"Then why are you going after a man whose heart belongs to a place you no longer call home?"

There was that word again. Home. "I need more time."

"All right, but I can't stop Hollywood from coming to you. The inquiring minds want to know why you've vanished."

The last thing she needed was paparazzi taking over the island. "We can ask Ava to release a statement. Something about me needing to be with my mother."

"Then everyone will want to know what's wrong with your mother. I can see the headline now. Claire Peters' mother in rehab or better yet,

Claire Peters' secret addiction to cocaine," he teased.

Claire shook her head. She always admired James' sense of humor. Not today. Vapor's door opened, her heart skipped with anticipation and Claire quickly looked up to see a gleaming Lily, a sick-looking Minka and a very quiet Keely entering the bar. She waved at them. "I have to go James. Two more weeks."

"That's the first day of spring."

Perfect. *That's when the island would start coming back to life.* More importantly, if things went accordingly, she'd be in Forrest's bed the next morning. "Okay the day after."

"How about that Monday?" he proposed. "Since we're talking about a Saturday."

"All right, Monday works." Her stomach twisted at the thought of leaving. She ignored the pang, ended the call and turned her attention to the fraternal twins. Lily was at the bar making out with her husband. "Why such gloomy faces? Weren't you supposed to be in Falmouth shopping for baby furniture?"

Minka groaned.

"Minka got sick on the boat," a very subdued Keely replied. "She threw up on my shoes."

"Sorry," Minka mumbled.

Claire studied Minka, her friend looked tired and a little run down. "Good thing you had your personal Montgomery boat at your service and not the ferry. So did you take a test? We need to find out if you're pregnant or not."

Lily pulled a chair and joined them. "We can get some pregnancy tests."

"Some?" Keely raised a brow.

"Well, yeah," Lily answered.

"She took ten tests," Minka informed the other women.

Claire chuckled. "Two wasn't enough to confirm you were carrying Adam's baby?"

Lily rubbed her protruding belly. "Minka doesn't even have to take a test. I am now an expert on when a woman is pregnant. And she's pregnant."

"I did take a test. Well, three to be sure," Minka said faintly.

Claire and Lily gasped then smiled. Keely reached for her phone and started tapping away.

"So," Lily said with a grin. "You're going to make us suffer."

Minka brushed a strand of curls away from her face. "Well, Jason and I wanted to wait until we get the ultrasound before making the big announcement."

Claire pulled Minka into a hug. "Shit Minka. I'm so happy for you and that husband of yours."

Keely dropped her phone in her purse and hugged her sister. "Sis, that's wonderful."

"Well, we don't know for sure yet. I mean . . . the heartbeat and . . ."

"I understand where you are," Lily said gently. "I've been there. Everything will be fine."

"When is Jason coming home?" Claire asked with concern. She could always go back to the house with Minka and keep her company if needed. It wasn't like the words were flowing anyway.

"Later tonight." Minka answered. "I'm going to head home and sleep until he gets here."

"I'll drive you. Adam is preparing a salad for me, then we can leave." Lily looked at the blank sheet of paper in front of Claire. "Making progress?"

"Lots," Claire replied dryly. "Has Adam spoken to Forrest?"

Lily shook her head.

"He hasn't called Blake either," Keely announced.

"And definitely not Jason." Minka picked up a glass of water, seemed to contemplate if it was a good idea to gulp down the liquid, and decided against it.

"Your salad, beautiful." Adam placed the to-go container in front of Lily.

Lily beamed, turned, and planted a passionate kiss on Adam's lips.

"Seriously, get a room," Keely mumbled.

"It's a slow day today." Adam's gold eyes flickered with mischief. "I'll be home early. I love you."

They watched him walk away. Tall, dark, edgy, and sexy with a capital S. Even now happily married, women still let their gazes linger a second or two too long. Like Forrest, Jason, and Blake, Adam never seemed to care or notice.

"God, he's pulchritudinous," Lily exclaimed.

"Pulchritudinous?" Claire asked.

"Beautiful," Minka translated, her face still colorless.

"Magnificent, charming," Lily continued.

"Sounds like an awful disease," Keely said with a smile, appearing a bit more relaxed.

Minka and Claire chuckled.

"Whatever. All of them are," Lily continued. She pushed her chair back and stood up. "Come on, ladies, I'll drop you home."

"Keely," Claire called after her friend, as the others walked ahead.

"What's up?" Her friend asked back at the table.

"Is everything okay?" Keely smiled, but Claire noticed the usual *joie de vivre* was missing. "What's going on?"

"Nothing."

Claire didn't buy the answer, but chose not to push. After ten years of friendship, one knew when to take a back seat and let the other come to you when ready.

"Have you bid on Forrest yet?" Keely asked.

"No."

Keely smiled and squeezed her shoulder. "You should. The auction ends this week. I gotta go. Text you later."

After Keely joined the others and left, Claire sat in silence for a beat. Her mind drifted to the theme of *Tattooed Hearts*–feelings, unrestrained passion, the heart and the head constantly at war. Nothing about the plot was foreign, she just needed to capture all those emotions in beautiful words.

She picked up the pen again and stared at the white sheet of paper.

Nothing. Writer's block in full effect.

"Hey, Claire."

She looked up at Tyler as he pulled a chair and made himself comfortable. Sandy brown hair and warm, friendly blue eyes, he was handsome and her first kiss. He didn't shake her world then and still didn't. A nice guy though, a sweetheart. Not her type, but as far as friends went, he was a keeper. "Collecting your ten dollars?" she teased and was glad to get a chuckle out of him.

"Not today," he answered in his good-natured way. "Would you headline a show for me this Friday?"

Claire's mouth gaped open. She'd toured the world, but never sang on the island.

"It's a charity event to raise some money for the boys and girls club on the island," he added. "Adam and Jason have been working on it with me. Your name as headline would bring a huge audience."

"I'll do it." She'd always been a sucker for a charity event and always supported any effort to give back to the island.

Tyler sat back, appearing a little more relaxed. "Awesome." He clapped his hands. "I'll tell Adam. The event will be here at Vapor." He stood up and examined her for a moment. "He'll come back eventually. The island is a part of him. He can't stay away."

She watched Tyler walk to the bar, her thoughts back on Forrest. Martha's Vineyard was his home. Tyler was right. In her heart of hearts she already knew it, but the reassurance from another local removed any doubts she might have had. She picked up her phone, swiped on the screen, and scrolled to Lily's last text. Brows furrowed, she examined the link to the auction.

Did she dare?

Every fiber of her being was vibrating with anticipation. Gathering her scattered impulses into one single passionate act of courage, Claire clicked on the URL. Her heart skipped. Adrenaline fueling her system, she glanced over the fine print and selected the bidding option. Not giving herself any time to think things through, she keyed in a thousand dollars, doubling the last bid amount for a date with Forrest.

FORREST CHECKED MRS. Kane's IV filled with antibiotic. After checking her heart rate and temperature, he updated her chart. Mentally, he let out a huge breath, releasing the tightening in his stomach since the hospital called to tell him Mrs. Kane was admitted. "I will prescribe something for your muscle ache."

"Nothing a shot of bourbon can't help."

Forrest smiled. "You are responding well to the IV. I'm going to keep you here until tomorrow."

Anne looked him over, a contemplative look on her face. "I had to get sick to get you back to the island."

"Anything for you, Anne."

Leaving the island had been spontaneous, a desperate need for solitude to escape everything and everyone. After leaving the potluck, he had gone straight home, packed his bag and left. A move that was completely out of character. Typically he faced his problems head-on. But late in the night, he'd found himself driving to the event he decided to skip, for one reason only—to see Claire.

Seeing her there, dancing with Tyler, laughing and looking like she had no worries in the world. Tyler's face lit up brighter than a toothpaste commercial. It took all of Forrest's strength not to punch his friend.

In a jealous rage, he told her to go back to Los Angeles, when he really wanted to pin her against the wall and kiss her until she begged to be taken. Instead, he'd gone to New Hampshire and skied until his muscles burned. A last-ditch effort to block Claire out of his mind, and put all the crap going on his life on a temporary hold.

"What about your mother?" Anne asked. "You can't just get up and leave her all alone."

A sick feeling settled in his gut. "I'm here to make sure you're okay."

"And that beautiful girl of yours?" she continued, "She's still here, you know."

Forrest ignored the way his heart nearly stopped at the mention of Claire. He hadn't expected her to still be on the island. Deep down, he'd hoped she had returned to L.A. "I don't have a girlfriend."

"I'm talking about Claire."

"I know who you are talking about."

"Still in denial." Anne reached for her phone. "Oh by the way, someone just bid a thousand dollars on you."

"I don't really follow the auction. It's just a date."

"Username Tattooed Hearts. Sounds like a hidden message."

He thought of the permanent artwork on his forearm, a constant reminder of how devoted he'd been to Claire. He ignored the familiar pain in his chest. "It's interesting."

"Don't you have a tattoo?"

"Drop it, Anne. Time for me to head home. I'll be back tomorrow."

"Forrest, I mean Dr. Desvareaux, welcome home."

He smiled. "Thanks."

"We missed you. Don't ever run away from us again."

"I needed a break."

She nodded. "You're back for good?"

"I'm back." He gave her shoulder a gentle squeeze. "See you first thing tomorrow."

About twenty minutes later, Forrest steered his Jeep onto State Road. Today had been his first time back at the hospital since Luc's death. He scrubbed a hand over his face and tried to eradicate the memory, but this one was forever branded in his mind. Face pale, lips bloodless, chest weakly rising and falling, struggling for breath, eventually laying still form.

Sickness bubbled in his stomach. In his profession, he'd seen many cadavers, worked on a few during medical school. He should be immune to this part of life. Through experience of having patients die, he'd learn not to dwell on what might go wrong and not to experience the full sense of pain and loss of a death. But, he'd never taken the class that taught people in his profession to handle the emotions when the loss was one of your own. In this instance, his father.

Father. His stomach churned. Charles and his mother–their big secret, her infidelity, her face frozen in apology, the words on her lips he'd never be able to erase. His head hammered.

He once read that brains were hardwired from caveman times to remember the bad stuff more, to help keep them alive. Which was ironic. What he needed was the good stuff, the fun days, the uplifting and hopeful. He wanted his father back.

His eye twitched as he let out a yawn. Rolling his head from side to side, he tried to stretch out the fatigue. Two hours and forty minutes, driving from New Hampshire to Woods Hole, with his mind on edge the whole time had sucked all the energy out of him. If he stopped moving, he'd probably fall asleep. Just what he needed. Once home, he'd take a long hot shower, then fall asleep to ESPN.

ESPN or Claire? The devil in him taunted.

His hands moved of their own accord turning the wheel toward Edgartown, the opposite direction to his home in Vineyard Haven. Claire would be nice to have in his bed too, naked, riding him until the room shifted and hazed. He shook the fantasy out of his mind.

He didn't want her.

He didn't need her.

He drove past Vapor and caught a glimpse of the black Audi. His heart kicked into high gear. Half of his brain told him to keep driving. The other half, the one owned by the devil, took over and hypnotized him. He steered the car into the empty space three cars ahead and before he knew it, exactly one month later, he was back inside Vapor.

As usual, it seemed whoever dared to venture out in the cold was here. Beer, wine, food, and the jangle of voices greeted him. He spotted Adam at the bar, talking to Tyler. At the far corner, Claire sat with her face buried in a notebook. As if she felt him watching her, her head lifted and their eyes locked. All the noise in the room fizzled out. He looked her over–skinny jeans, oversized blush sweater, winter boots. Her hair pulled back in a ponytail, lips bare, with the touch of clear lip gloss. She looked innocent, vulnerable, and very much like the young girl he fell in love with. Forrest groaned and headed to the bar.

"Look who decided to bless us with his presence," Tyler nodded at him.

"What are you doing here?" Forrest leaned on the edge of the barrel wood bar top, his eyes fixed firmly on the island's favorite superstar. He'd bet his money Tyler was here to make a move on her. Not that he cared, she was free to date whomever she wanted.

"Having a beer." He followed Forrest's gaze. "You left her all alone for two weeks." Tyler shrugged. "Fair game."

"Aren't you dating Gwen?"

"Relax, big guy. I wanted to ask her for a favor. Oh, and she said yes." He grinned and placed a bill on the bar. "Good to have you back on the island. I missed making you jealous."

"I'm not jealous."

Tyler smirked. "Must be tough knowing you'll never be the first guy she kissed."

Adam chuckled. "You have a death wish, man."

Tyler laughed. Forrest mentally counted to fifty while reminding himself he actually liked the asshole.

"What's your poison?" Adam asked once Tyler left.

Forrest's gaze skated over Claire.

Adam snorted. "A month later, she's still here. Even after you got up and left."

"I'm aware."

"Tell me again she's not here for you."

"She's not here for me." He continued to look in her direction again. Their eyes met once more. Just for a second, a small tight smile curled up the corners of her mouth before looking away. In his pocket, his phone vibrated, he ignored it and turned his attention back to the bar.

"Look man, you have the right to be pissed off, but you're treating Claire and Jason like shit." Adam poured a shot of gold tequila and pushed the salt-rimmed glass in front of Forrest. "This one's on me. I'd have a shot with you, but I'm working." He reached for another glass. "But then again, I own half this place." He poured himself a two-finger shot of his favorite Scotch and raised the glass. "To us and the women we love."

Forrest lifted the glass and threw the liquor down his throat. He welcomed the burn.

"By the way," Adam continued, "Lily mentioned you're catching up with me in the auction."

Forrest glanced at Claire again. She picked up her phone and scrunched her brows at the screen, seeming to contemplate whatever she was looking at, then quickly typed something in response. The powerful pull she had on him took over once more. "I'll be back," he said to Adam and headed to the corner table.

She didn't look up, didn't need to. Her body movement, especially the one tucking imaginary loose strands of hair behind her ears, told him she was aware of him just as he was of her. He pulled out a chair and sat facing her across the table. Claire looked up from her phone again, smiling in that tense way she did when she was uncomfortable.

"You're back," she said, in an even voice.

"Mrs. Kane is in the hospital."

She nodded. Of course she knew. This was Martha's Vineyard, the island where everyone knew everyone else's business.

"How is she feeling?"

"Better."

She picked up her glass of water and drank in the silence between them. His eyes shifted to the open notebook. "How's the songwriting?" he asked, filling the void with a noncommittal question.

"Great. I wrote down the title five times." She pushed out her lips just a little, and flashed him a big fake smile that didn't reach her eyes.

He dragged the open notebook away from her and examined the two words written several times on the paper. "Tattooed Hearts," he said as realization seeped into him.

"That's the name of the movie."

She twiddled her hair in a seemingly absent-minded way, drawing his attention to the exquisite length of her neck. Easily, he could close the space between them and kiss her collarbone.

Forrest cleared his throat. "You bid on me."

She ran her tongue over her bottom lip before tucking it back between glossed lips. Then she cocked her head to one side and stared at him. "I did."

"Why?" he asked, eyes locked unwaveringly on hers.

"It's for charity."

"That's it?"

She licked her lips again, drawing his gaze back to her mouth. He looked, wanting nothing more than to slam his mouth to hers and knock all the wind out of her lungs.

"No," she whispered.

She was quiet for a moment, then eyes like sunlight shining through whiskey met his. "I can't let you go."

CHAPTER FOURTEEN

"Every heart sings a song incomplete until another heart whispers back."
~ Plato

FORREST'S LIPS TWITCHED. Claire stared. She couldn't help it—they were full, firm and wickedly sensual. He had a great mouth and she wanted to lean over and latch on to his lower lip.

"You let me go ten years ago," Forrest said, snapping Claire out of her fantasy.

"Not by choice." But she knew better than to think such a simple explanation would be enough. Fight or flight, right?

She'd run enough. Time to come forward and put everything on the table.

His brows knitted. "What do you mean by that?"

"I needed to make something of myself first." Her eyes drifted to the blank sheet of paper. She wrote hurriedly–*It was always you. Can't fight these feelings for you.*

"Claire?" He pushed her to continue.

She placed the pen in the center of the journal and gave him her full attention. "Ten years ago, I was nothing but the daughter of a house-keeper." Her stomach twisted, no matter how many times she'd said the words, they were still sharp and cut through her every time.

"What?" he asked, confusion clear in his voice.

She smiled, but her heart felt sad, shredded. The world faded away, drained of all color except for the man sitting across the table. "The night of my party, I overheard Victoria telling my mother I wasn't good enough for you and that your parents hated the idea of us together." The painful memories, as raw as a howling winter wind, blew right through her.

He shook his head. "My parents loved us. They love you."

"I know, but . . ."

"Why would you believe her?" he persisted.

Claire shrugged. She floundered for words, something to express the regret that coursed through her, but nothing came.

"She wasn't well," Forrest reminded her.

"We didn't know that then."

He nodded. "For a long time I racked my brain for answers. I thought it came down to your father leaving your mother while pregnant."

"My father deserting my mother always messed me up," she admitted. "But that night was the catalyst of me being a broken mess." She inhaled and exhaled. "Now you know the truth."

"Why didn't you come to me instead of running that night?" Gray eyes, a shadow of agony, darkened behind his glasses. "I was waiting for you," he said in a roughened voice.

Sharp sadness stabbed her heart. At eighteen, she had been vulnerable and Victoria's words fed to her weakness and insecurities. In the process, she'd hurt the one person she never wanted to cause any pain. Guilt sat heavy and acrid in her belly.

Her eyes suddenly swam with tears. Claire hurried to scrub them from her face. Tears lead to sympathy, and sympathy always lead to more tears. "I'm sorry," she said in a strained voice. "I should have talked to you, but I was young and in shock." Quickly the feeling of security from her decision to stay and fight died away, shame and confusion filled in its absence. "Her words broke me that night."

He pushed his chair back and slid closer into the empty chair beside her. He caught her hand in his, their fingers becoming locked together similar to puzzle pieces. "No longer hiding your tattoo." It wasn't a question but an indication that he noticed.

"It's permanent." *Like my love for you.*

Forrest's jaw ticked. His expression, quiet and steady. The space between them slowly faded. As he leaned forward, her pulse raced, lips parted with anticipation. Looking into his eyes, she became lost in the deep pools of gray that displayed his soul.

His lips brushed upon her tear-stained cheek. Claire's heart came to a halt, breath caught in her throat. As the soft skin of his mouth left the side of her face, the exact spot where they came into contact burned and tingled. A hot, blazing fire pulsed through her. Forrest pulled away silently, but their eyes locked, having a private conversation on their own in a long muted moment.

"I'm sorry you went through that," he said quietly. "I can't even say I understand how you felt that night."

Claire lowered her gaze to their hands still knotted together.

"But that was ten years ago," he continued.

After a light squeeze, he released her hands. Sadness flowed through her veins, cold and unending. Any illusion of possibly mending their relationship fell away.

"Victoria died six years ago," he said, his voice perfectly even. "Why did you wait so long to tell me all this?"

"I thought you hated me."

He exhaled, placed his elbows on the table. "I was angry for a long time, but I never hated you."

Neither spoke for a beat. The silence seeped into Claire's pores, drowning her mind in its thick toxicity. "I should have come to you sooner," she said in a low voice. "But, I never felt good enough."

"You were always good enough."

She let out a low chuckle. "Hence all the additional things I do. The designing, the acting." Her eyes, filled with unshed tears, glazed over the two sentences she'd finally written down. "And now I'm tired."

"You'll write the song. Stop trying so hard. Take a break."

"I was referring to us." She met his gaze and held. "I'm tired of running from you."

"Claire." He sighed. "It's been ten years."

"Too long?" she asked in a tone she hoped was light.

"I gave you my heart freely." He smiled at her, not the warm, heart-melting smile, but one of regret and opportunity lost. "That shouldn't have made it worthless." He removed his glasses and dug the heel of his hands in his eyes then opened them again and stared at her. "That made it priceless."

"Your love was never worthless."

"I wish you trusted me enough then or came to me sooner." He raked a hand through his hair. "Ten years is a long time."

"We were supposed to be forever."

"You broke the deal," he responded after a beat, his voice thick with regret.

She searched his face, trying to find if they were really hopeless. His eyes held all the longing in her heart. "You still love me."

"This isn't about what I feel, but what I can give. I can't give you love." He released a deep breath. "It's time for both of us to let go."

She blinked. "Let go."

"You have a life in L.A. I live here. We'd never work." He shook his head. "Our time has passed." Slowly he lifted his weight from the chair. "Let's try to be friends again."

Their gazes intertwined once more, then he walked out of Vapor without even a last look in her direction. The wall clock ticked like the timer on a bomb. She couldn't stop it, reverse it or slow it down. Each tick dragged her forward to the here and now. Her phone pinged. She snatched it and skimmed through the notification. Someone had increased the wager on Forrest by five hundred dollars.

With nervous energy sitting in her stomach, she tapped her fingers on the table, contemplating whether to continue the bidding war or stop. He hadn't denied loving her still. Had he done so, it would have made it easier to let him go. She increased her bid, doubling the last bidder and raising her stake on Forrest to three thousand dollars.

Picking up the pen, she focused her attention on the last word written and scribbled.

In the arithmetic of love, one plus one equals infinity, and two minus one equals nothing. It is a cruelty of life that a heart can keep on beating even after it has been broken in two. It can feel as though it is being gripped in an ice-cold vice and ache as if it will implode in your chest, but still the boom-boom continues. I never said what I wanted to say, but I fell for you harder than a slip on black ice.

FORREST'S THROAT TIGHTENED the minute he pulled the Jeep into Herring Creek Farm. The place looked somber and deserted. He glanced at the yellow tractor by the barn and could almost see his father working the land. His heart clenched. He exhaled some of the pain from his system and continued driving to the Victorian house. His foot lifted off the accelerator, the Jeep slowed, passed one of the Herring Creek delivery trucks. Returning to the farm forced him to swim once more in the tide waters of the past, his childhood, who he thought he was, and was no longer.

He entered the house and was greeted by total hush. No sign of his mother. A combination of relief and sorrow tugged at him as he made his way down the hall. Photographs on the wall, cataloging some of the best moments in their lives followed him. A few were sun-bleached and a little damaged, but each was a conduit of his best memories.

His mother took pride in framing them, and was meticulous with the way they were hung. She measured the space between the frames so each celluloid could be properly aligned and exact in distance. She used to tell him these pictures encouraged her to visit these moments and kept them from fading, vanish from her mind, as if none of it ever happened. Forrest stopped to examine a particular picture of him with his parents. His mind's eye darted to that specific period in time when Victoria captured his father turning the hose on him and his mother. The love in his mother's eyes, the mischievous smile on his father's lip stared back at him.

"Forrest."

His mother's voice snatched him from the promenade down Memory Lane and forced him into the chaos his life had become. He turned and took in her appearance. She stood, tall and strikingly beautiful, with his father's two beloved black Labs at her side. The dogs ran to him, tails wagging. Forrest crouched down and scratched their ears.

She removed the woolen hat, sandy brown hair fell down to her shoulders in waves. Big, bright gray eyes that typically glittered looked washed out, like an old white shirt that had been washed with dark colors a few times too often.

"I didn't think you were here," he said, straightening to his full height.

"I was by the lake."

He nodded. They continued to stare at each other. Bright, vivid thoughts of him racing down the hall with his parents at his heels trundled through his brain with no intention of stopping.

"I'm glad you're here." A shaky smile settled on her lips. "Coffee? Tea?"

He shoved his hands in his coat pockets. "No thanks."

"Forrest . . ."

"I don't know why I came here." He glanced over her shoulder to the wall, specifically to the spot his mother had repainted after he and Claire went on a crayon coloring frenzy. Relentless memories continued their destruction.

"This is your home. It will always be." Eyes similar to his focused on a picture of his late father. "Regrets are moral residue," his mother's voice was low as she spoke. "I was hurt and angry and I did something out of character. Now it's stuck with me. I can't undo it." She looked at him. "I will never regret having you."

"I'm not here to discuss you and Charles." He ignored the gripping pain deep in his stomach and asked, "Did you or Dad ever tell Victoria that Claire wasn't good enough for me?"

His mother waved a dismissive hand. "That's absurd. We never thought that. Why do you ask?"

The answer didn't surprise him. "It's not important." He glanced around the hallway. Everything was as tidy as he could remember, not in a cold, detached way. Growing up in the house, as big as it was, had been the exact opposite–animated and full of life. His father, his mother, and he had been a team. "Do you need help with anything?"

"I was making some pies for a delivery tomorrow."

"All right." He removed his jacket, hooked it on the edge of the stairs, and started toward the kitchen. His mother always insisted he hang his jacket in the closet. Forrest waited for the scolding, but it didn't come. "I'll deliver them tomorrow," he offered.

"I'd like that. I can come with you."

He shook his head. "No need." In his peripheral vision, he caught her nodding, seeming to understand he wasn't ready for all of that mother-son relationship they once had.

"Have you seen Claire?" his mother asked as they walked down the corridor.

"Yes."

"She's here for you."

"It's too late for me and Claire."

She glanced at him. Forrest kept his focus straight ahead.

"She loves you."

"Maybe."

"She does."

"Okay."

He pushed open the cognac oak slab door and entered the well-equipped kitchen. A beautiful toned modern table stood in the middle. Handy wall hatches to keep appliances close at hand. Dried flowers hung from beams. Mixed style chairs provided tone and balance in the country setting. Nothing superfluous–minimalist and uncluttered. He walked by the fresh fruit on a cutting board to the sink, rolled up his sleeves and washed his hands. The kitchen, the heart of the house, always exuded a warm and welcoming spirit. How many nights had he sat there talking to his parents? Nostalgia washed over him once again. Forrest put up a mental hand to stop the onslaught of memories.

"Why are you shutting her out?" his mother asked while pulling out ingredients from the cupboard.

He turned off the running water and wiped his hands dry. "I don't trust her."

"You're too hard on yourself and everyone around you. We all make mistakes. Even you are capable of those."

"I'm not here for a lecture, Mom."

His mother placed several already prepared crusts on the counter. A busy silence fell between them. It wasn't the comfortable kind, more like tension-filled, but he stayed and baked pies.

Late into the night, one fresh-baked pie in hand, Forrest entered his house. After placing the sweet dessert in the fridge, he made his way to the sitting room, found the TV remote, and turned on ESPN for the latest sports news. But once again, his mind went to Claire. When she first left, his heartache had been an insatiable fire that burnt all the oxygen in his body, leaving him lifeless and empty. Years had reduced the pain to a thin layer of ice, cooling his insides, a gentle reminder of what came before and a warning not to stoke that fire again. They said once bitten, twice shy, but for him, it was more like forever shy. He wouldn't take that chance, however tempting it was, because his heart couldn't survive another inferno.

Still, he picked up his phone and checked on the auction for the first time. Claire's bid was now up to three thousand dollars. Despite all the internal warnings, he was eighteen again and Claire soaked right into his bones. Only this time, she wasn't fifteen and he didn't have to ignore the burning desire coursing through him. He scrolled through his contact list to her name and typed.

Tell me you made some progress with the song.

And pressed *SEND* before he could change his mind and erase the text. Forrest threw the phone on the sofa, telling himself she wouldn't answer. It was late, well past midnight. Besides, he didn't care if she answered or not. Within seconds, the ping of his phone announced her response.

Some.

He texted back.

You bid on me again.

She answered.

Someone tried to outbid me.

A reporter talking about Tom Brady and the New England Patriots blared in the background. While he was everything Boston, from the Red Sox to the Bruins, when it came to football, he was all about The Niners. He continued typing.

You should stop.

Her response came quickly.

Tell me you don't love me, and I'll stop.

Forrest studied her words. Definitely a bad idea to go there again. He texted back.

Goodnight, Claire.

He fixed his attention on the television screen. His phone vibrated. Forrest glanced at the glowing screen then looked away. The conversation was over. Neither of them had anything left to say. It was pointless to drag it out any longer. The buzzing sound came again, taunting his resolution. One peek wouldn't hurt. He didn't have to respond. But it was rude to ignore someone and he was never rude. He read the text.

Any call after midnight is considered a booty call. Is that what this is?

CHAPTER FIFTEEN

"How to save your heart—Know your limits."
~Claire Yasō Peters

THIS WASN'T GOOD. Claire frowned at the now-silent phone. No response. The after-midnight conversation with Forrest ended just as quickly as it had started. Disappointment filled her chest. What did she expect?

Well, he could have played along. He did initiate the back and forth texting. The minute she flirted a little, pushed his buttons a bit, he stopped. A reminder no matter how deep his feelings ran for her, Forrest had no desire to go down that path again. At least not without a fight. He was protecting his heart, she couldn't blame him, she'd do the same had the situation been reversed, but he wanted her, his eyes couldn't hide that.

She placed the journal on the nightstand. No point spending another minute staring at the words she'd written or waiting for another text. Progress often came one baby step at a time. Overall, the day had been a good one. She drafted a whole verse, and finally found the strength to tell Forrest the truth. Two big accomplishments. Maybe tomorrow she'd convince Keely to take the ferry off the island and spend the day shopping in Boston. Earlier at Vapor, her friend looked like she could use some distraction.

The ringtone on her phone snapped Claire out of her daze. Without checking, she knew it was Forrest. Her heart lurched and a host of butterflies swarmed in the pit of her stomach. "I didn't expect a phone call," she greeted her favorite doctor.

"This is not a booty call," he said on the other end of the phone. His tone, although dour, still made her belly go mushy.

Claire couldn't help but smile. "What is it then?"

He exhaled and she could envision him lounging in worn jeans, flipping through a book, with the TV on in the background.

"I spent the evening baking pies."

"Oh." Yikes, did he have a date? She could almost see Forrest in the kitchen, relaxed with a half day's stubble tilted in a wry grin while baking pies and raising some lucky girl's temperature at the same time. Ugh! Claire curled her fingers around the fabric of her cotton tank. "Um . . ."

"With my mother."

Her heart did a little happy dance. Relief. "How did that go?" From what she knew, this was the first time in a month Forrest had made any attempt to see his mother. As for Charles and Jason—well, that was another battle he probably wasn't ready to face.

"Awkward."

She nodded to herself on the other end, understanding how hard it must have been for him. "Sounds like you need a friend."

"I could use one," he admitted after a short silence.

"There's no way to get off Chappy right now," she said mostly to herself because if there were, she'd be on the ferry right away. Besides being late, the water was partially frozen due to the dip in the temperature. Not even the Montgomery boat could cross Norton Point Beach and the nine hundred feet that separated them.

"Good thing." There was a strange note in his voice that made her warm all over.

"Why?"

"We'd probably end up in bed," he said on a groan. "Not probably, definitely."

The admission caught her off guard. Every nerve ending in her body jumped to attention. "That would make us friends with benefits."

"Not a good idea."

"Would that be such a bad thing?" Oh, she was playing with fire. But the heady desire she'd kept buried for so long flared and if she couldn't be next to him then why not improvise and go for a little phone sex.

"Yes," he answered without a beat.

"We already had sex." For the first time in ten years, and she wanted more. "Would it be so bad if we were to do it again?"

"Claire . . ."

His tone was full of warning, but it caressed her goose-bumped skin. What she wouldn't give to see his face right now. His expression controlled and brooding. "Send me a picture." She pushed.

"Of?"

"You." She giggled when he released a breath. "You thought I meant . . ."

"Drop it."

But she couldn't. If anything, she wanted to whoop it up. "I meant a selfie. But . . . ." She purposely let her voice trail off. "If you prefer to send a pic of—"

"No," he cut her off.

She blew out a breath. He could be such a tough nut to crack at times. "Can I ask you a question?" She bit her lower lip and waited for Forrest to shut her down.

"Ask," he replied, giving her the green light instead.

"Do you ever touch yourself and think of me?" she whispered into the phone.

"Friends," he reminded her while managing to avoid answering the question.

Pretty clever, Doc. Not that it mattered. She took his evasive response as a yes. Heat rushed between her thighs over the thought. "You want me."

He groaned.

"I want you too, but you already know that."

"Where is this going?" His voice was hoarse and tortured on the other end of the line.

She shrugged, not that Forrest could see her, and went for the jugular. "Every time I touch myself, it's always you I think about. Goodnight, Doc." Claire pressed the *END* button, disconnecting their call. That was one of the most brazen things she'd ever done, planting an image of herself touching, and stroking, her most intimate spots into Forrest's mind.

Heart racing, she lay in the dark, eyes fixed on the ceiling. Apparently torture wasn't discriminatory. Her body felt restless and was way too hot. Swearing, she rolled onto her side.

She wanted Forrest.

She loved Forrest.

She wanted Forrest and his love. Even though ten years had passed, she'd never been able to let him go.

He told her to let go. Let's try to be friends, he'd said.

Phooey!

He wanted her.

He still loved her.

And damn the weather for making a trip to the other side of the island impossible. Mother Nature was definitely a morbid force. If only there was a way to get off Chappy. Whether or not he wanted to love her, they'd be going at it like two hormone-driven, angst-ridden teenagers, kissing, touching, and . . . Claire shifted. The ultra-delicate spot between her thighs ached.

A vision of Forrest standing behind her, burying deep inside, made her quiver. She wanted more of him. Flopping onto her back, she shoved off the comforter. Even though the house was well heated, cool air washed over her bare arms and across her chest. Underneath the cotton tank top, her nipples swelled, sending a stinging sensation to her flesh, to the point she captured one breast in her hand and squeezed. A little whimper escaped her lips as the pressure vibrated from between her breasts to her thighs. She clenched the comforter as thoughts of Forrest continued to tease her. Their first kiss to the first time they made love a month ago in his house. She could still taste him, could still feel his muscles flexing against her, in her.

Her breath caught at the phantom of Forrest's touch. After ten years, he'd awakened what she'd tried to keep dormant, and now she wanted more.

If only the ocean wasn't covered with ice.

If only it wasn't dawn.

If only she hadn't waited a decade.

Along her throat, her pulse picked up speed, her heart stuttered. Between her thighs, the ache became more forceful. In the darkness, her hand fluttered to her stomach, and slid down under the loose band of her sleeping shorts. She closed her eyes. The muscles in her belly tightened, her breath quickened.

The edges of her fingers slowly drifted over her thighs and slid between them. Shots of electricity seared through her veins. Catching her lower lip between her teeth to stop the cry building in her throat, her fingers slid through the wetness.

Images of Forrest continued its pillaging, gray eyes on fire with heat and his mouth against hers, coaxing her open. She moaned and stroked the swollen area. That felt so good. Her finger moved in quick jerky movements back and forth before Claire drew in a deep breath, and pushed in. A gasp escaped her throat as tension coiled.

She pushed a little deeper. The pressure sent another jolt and the burning in her core spread. Her hips jerked, rocked, as tension built deeper and deeper. In the darkness of her room, she grew hotter, wanting more. Visions of Forrest became even clearer–his mouth on hers, his eyes full of the love he withheld, his lips speaking the words he denied her, his hand, his fingers. The thoughts amplified the longing, and that was it. A moan erupted from deep inside her body as she unraveled.

Brain scattering of all thoughts, she collapsed against the pillows, arms and legs shaking. Claire wasn't sure how long it took for the tremors to subside, but eventually she rolled onto her side, the warm and fuzzy feeling reserved just for Forrest wrapped around her. She smiled and let the languid feeling invade her body, carrying her into sleep.

AT THE HARBOR, Claire's shoes clacked over the various hues of the wooden boards. Some newer planks with their bright unworn look, covered with patches of snow, sparkled under the sunlight, others dull and beaten by the countless freeze-thaw cycles and the salty air, perfectly balanced the upgrades and reflected the shabby chic look of the island.

Martha's Vineyard was a village of the past.

An escape to the present.

A sea explorer's dream.

Hands tucked in her pockets, she walked down by the Shanty, still feeling blissful from last night's conversation with Forrest and after. Ghosts of yesteryear strutted by her side and kept her company.

While the air was chilly, it was a beautiful day on the Vineyard, bringing out a slew of activities in downtown Edgartown. People flowed around her. They waved, stopped to make small talk, but no one was looking for her to sing, perform, sign papers, or design clothes. Nothing. She was simply one of them.

Such an exposed place, with nothing to hide behind, and yet, on the island she wasn't Claire Yasō Peters the singer, designer, and now actress. She was one of them. A local in the scenic vistas.

"Hey!"

Smiling, she turned to Keely. As always, her friend looked breath-taking. Under her winter hat and bone-straight brown hair, peeked eyes of hazel and honey. Unlike yesterday, when they were dim, today they sparkled with mirth.

"Ready for our shopping spree?" she asked, sliding a hand through the crook of Keely's arm.

Another good thing from being on the island for the last month, she met with her friends almost every day. First thing this morning she had sent a text to Keely suggesting a shopping trip to Boston and had been delighted when her friend had quickly agreed.

Keely laughed. "Are we really going to spend the whole time shopping for Lily and Adam's baby? No offense, but . . ."

Claire laughed. "Since there's no baby shower, we have to spoil the little bundle. Any accidental slip on the baby's gender?"

"Nope. They claim they don't know." She ran her hands over her coat. "This winter has been brutal."

"True."

Keely laughed. "Between Adam's parents and Lily's the baby is already spoiled rotten."

Claire laughed as they made their way in the ferry. Funny, the weather hadn't bothered her as much as she convinced herself in the past. "Better for us, we have carte blanche to buy whatever we want."

"Minka did speak to Lily and Adam's parents," Keely said, "In the spring, after the baby is born, we are throwing them a big party. Everyone is coming."

"Including her brothers?"

"I think so. I know Max confirmed. We have to check with Minka."

"That only means another battle of testosterone between the

Serrano brothers and the Wolf Pack."

Keely snickered. "It was good visual."

They walked up the ferry's deck. Turning her back to the water, Claire breathed in the cool crisp air and let the wind blow her ebony hair away from her face. "Oh, yes, the football game." They both sighed, looked at each other and burst into laughter.

"Any progress with Forrest?"

Claire thought of the late night conversation. Although Forrest hadn't taken the bait, it had been friendly enough. "He wants to put us in the friend zone."

Keely wrinkled her nose at the thought. "Men."

Claire couldn't help but chuckle. "But then he texted me late last night."

Keely arched a brow, clearly intrigued. "Like a booty call. Did you go?"

"Not a booty call, much to my disappointment. He needed a friend to talk to."

"Poor guy. He's going through a lot."

"He saw his mother for the first time yesterday."

"That's progress."

Claire nodded in agreement. "During our little sexting or texting." She shrugged. "He also told me if I had been there with him, we'd have had sex."

"Not very friend-like."

"Tell me about it. So of course I pushed and flirted a little. He shut down immediately. And then he called and we almost had phone sex."

"No fucking way!" Ripples of laughter passed between them again.

"He didn't take the bait," Claire added, still a tad disappointed over Forrest's lack of response. "But I could tell he was considering it."

"He still loves you."

"Maybe." Leaning on the rail, she focused on the slow waves of the ocean. "But he doesn't want to go there with me anymore."

"You told him everything. So give it some time."

She had no other choice.

Three hours later, Keely and Claire's arms were filled with shopping bags and they were starving. Arms linked, they walked along a narrow cobblestone with houses built in the late 1820s to a trendy Vietnamese restaurant.

After a slight hesitation from recognizing Claire, the maître d' led them to a table. As they sat down, Claire's phone dinged, announcing an incoming message. Knowing she hadn't responded to any of James' emails from this morning, she yanked the phone out of her purse and was surprised to see Forrest's name.

"Everything okay?" Keely asked across the table.

"It's Forrest." She studied the text.

> *A selfie as you requested. Thanks for the company last night and hope you slept well.*

The picture seemed to have been taken earlier in the day. He was outside standing by one of the Herring Creek Farm delivery trucks. A few days old stubble, glasses, Baltic Sea color shirt under a heavy full-zipped sweater. His short, dark waves casually blown from the cool morning breeze into a sexy mess. Something about the candid shot set her heart racing almost too fast. Claire blamed her reaction on the ruggedness. Major hotness.

"I asked him for a picture last night. He ignored me but he just sent one," she said to Keely.

"Oh." Keely smiled. "I hope there's a sexy text along with it."

"Not really." She read the text to her friend. "Very controlled. Very Forrest."

"Well, I'm going to make a phone call. Why don't you do a little sexting while I'm gone."

"Should I order you a drink?"

"Water is enough for now. Be right back."

After ordering a glass of dark and stormy for herself and water for Keely, she picked up the phone, started to compose a text then decided to call Forrest instead. He answered on the second ring. At the sound of his voice, butterflies fluttered crazy low in her belly.

"Thanks for the pic. You're a hottie. By the way, I slept great. You?"

He chuckled, clearly amused by her comment. So sexy.

"No to the word hottie and I'm glad you slept well. I won't ask," he said smoothly. The baritone of his voice reverberating through her bones.

Too bad. She wanted to play again. "Not even a bit curious?"

He made a low noise in his throat, then said, "I'm a man, so natural-ly I'm curious."

Heat coursed through her body and settled in that spot between her thighs.

"Where are you, Claire?"

She blinked, shifted in her seat and cleared her throat. "In Boston, having lunch with Keely. We spent the day shopping. You?"

"In my office staring at my computer screen and talking to you."

Her immediate reaction was to ask him if he'd been thinking of her as much as she'd been of him, but decided against the direct approach and tried another tactic. "Are you going to the farm later?"

"No."

"Dinner?" she asked and held her breath.

"How's six o'clock?"

A wide grin settled on Claire's lips. Her heartbeat raged out of con-trol, wanting out of her chest. She held back the urge to jump up and do the happy dance–only because she was in public. Thank goodness for that. "Your place?"

"No."

Oh well, she tried. "Why?"

"You know why."

"Remind me."

"Friends," he said in a tight voice. "We're working on that."

"Friends visit each other."

"True, but we're not there yet."

A ball of ice formed on her chest over the thought of ever being just *friends* with Forrest.

"Do you mind getting off the island again?" he continued. "I know a spot."

For Forrest, *anything*. "I'll meet you by Shanty at six and we can fer-ry over."

"See you then."

"It's a date," she said with a heavy heart.

She was still looking at her phone when Keely returned. The waiter quickly approached their table and took their order of Pho and Cha Ca. Claire dropped the phone in her purse and focused her attention on her friend. "You look sad again."

Keely shrugged, right before her shoulders slumped. "That was my obstetrician."

Claire held her breath. Well aware her friend had been trying to get pregnant for some time now.

"She wants to run some tests," Keely continued. "I'm tired of this pregnancy business. I need a break."

"It will happen."

"As of today, I'm not thinking about it anymore. I need wine." Keely laughed, no evidence of tension in her voice. "So what did our favorite doctor have to say?"

"We're going out to dinner tonight."

Across the table, Keely examined her. "So why don't you look happy?"

"He was all logic with that infernal, typical Forrest cool detachment." She wrinkled her nose. "He's really trying to put us in the friend zone. Forrest and I have never been friends. I've always been in love with him."

Keely sat back and took a gulp of her water. "You're a sexy superstar. Men jerk off to the idea of you."

Claire groaned. That image wasn't actually an ego-booster. "Not your greatest compliment."

"Sorry. But you have a date with Forrest that he initiated."

"Technically, I initiated."

"Whatever." Keely dismissed her rebuttal with a dainty wave. "The way I see it, he can't stay away. He's fighting the love, but losing the battle with the lust part. I say let's go buy you something sexy for tonight."

Her friend had a point. Love and lust were identical twins, similar on the outside and often mistaken for one another. But having experienced both, Claire knew on the inside, there was a world of difference between the two. She let out a breath. "I could use a nice, sexy outfit."

CHAPTER SIXTEEN

"Half of my heart takes time."
~ John Mayer—*Half of My Heart*

FOR THE SECOND time, Claire stepped off the ferry. This time the light of day had slipped away, and a thin mist oozed across the pink-and-gold sky. She was on her way to dinner with the love of her life in Woods Hole, the strolling village in Falmouth.

"Here, hold on to me." Forrest extended his arm as they stepped into a patch of snow.

Without a word, she slipped a hand in the crook of his arm. They walked off the harbor in close silence. Similar to life on the Vineyard in the winter, the town was embraced by quiet calmness. Even the rumble of traffic was absent. Unlike the many occasions in the last decade she'd been around Forrest, tonight the silence between them was comfortable, down to their footfalls clip-clopping in a rhythmic echo on the street.

"This is a new restaurant," he informed her, "Like the Wharf's Side, it's a part of the farm to table movement. Everything is sourced from local farms and fishermen."

"Do they work with Herring Creek?"

He nodded. "As a matter of fact, yes. I was here earlier delivering pies."

Claire smiled, envisioning Forrest on the farm's truck, making the morning's delivery. "I'm glad you and your mom are working together." She felt him stiffen. Once again, her heart twisted in pain for him and the complete disorder and confusion his life had become.

"I came alone," he said, his voice emotionless. "After that I went to the hospital to process Mrs. Kane's release forms, then my office."

"You had a long day."

"It wasn't too bad. Saw a few patients, nothing too heavy." He shrugged. "It gets a little crazy in the summer, otherwise, my workload is pretty manageable."

They ambled through the streets, the ambience comfortable, relaxed. There was something very natural with them like this, arms linked and walking side by side on a date. As friends, her conscience interjected for the hundredth time.

Two friends having dinner. Nothing more.

Just because they were of the opposite sex and had crazy animal sex recently meant nothing. They were friends. Longtime friends, who were once lovers. *Briefly.* That logical side of her brain pointed out. She had a shot at his heart and blew it. No need for the butterflies nesting in her stomach to start flapping their wings. No need to look forward to the goodnight kiss, and all the things that might come after.

Which meant there was no need for that beautiful, off the shoulder, ruffled chambray dress under her coat. Definitely no need for the lacy matching underwear or the ungodly amount of time she spent on her hair. A total waste of time. She'd looked in the mirror at her sexed-up hair. A full-bodied mess that said *take me*—up against the counter, in the women's bathroom, and again on the ride back to my place. Totally not a friend-zone hairdo. So she'd flattened the tangled curls into a wispy ponytail. Safe and pragmatic friend hair. Nothing sexy or *super-starrish.*

As for the four-inch, stunning, knee-length leather boots. Well, it was cold and at five-feet four inches tall, the additional height came in handy standing next to Forrest. At six feet three inches tall, he towered over her. The disparity in their height was almost laughable and sexy. Tall, rugged doctor-farmer next to her small, petite frame. The dapper gentleman whether in a tailored suit or in jeans, a shirt and leather jacket as he was now.

Yeah, definitely a turn-on for her in that *I'm big and strong and I protect you* kind of way.

She nestled a little closer, latching on to his muscular forearm as they walked off the harbor to their dining destination. Not that she needed his support. Aside from a few snow patches, the roads were manageable, and the restaurant was right across the street. But then his bicep flexed under the black leather jacket, and she couldn't help but tighten her grip.

Friend zone. She was reminded for the hundredth and one time.

Right.

With an imaginary flick of her middle finger, she told her conscience to shut the fuck up and grabbed tighter onto Forrest's arm on the chilly evening. She didn't pull away from his warmth until they entered the bright, nautical setting restaurant, a short stone's throw from the Steamship Authority Ferry Terminal with views of the ocean and ferry. Within seconds they were greeted by a young, attractive couple.

"Miss Peters, what an honor!" The pretty brunette beamed. "I'm Valerie and this is my husband, Richard." She smiled at her husband. "I'll take your coat and Richard will take you to your table."

Forrest helped her out of her coat before slipping out of his hip-length burnished black leather jacket. He removed the wool beanie and slid his fingers through his hair. Her heart went pitter-patter in her chest at the simple gesture. So very sexy. In dark jeans and slim fitted tattersall indigo shirt, he looked more like a fashion model than a doctor.

"When you told us you were coming for dinner, Forrest, we reserved the best table," Richard said with a smile after their coats were hung. "Please follow me."

Forrest reached for her hand, clasping it as he led her through the restaurant. Claire took in the layout of the tavern. The front half was seating for the café, with a relaxed, open feel, perfect for reading and spending time watching the boats sail by. As they walked toward the dining room, they drew a few glances, but no one seemed to care the famous Claire Peters was dining at a local tavern. If anything, it was Forrest the women's gazes lingered on a little too long. For as long as she'd known him, he seemed oblivious to the attention channeled his way. The dining room, decorated with simple elegance, gave a relaxed ambience with lighting perfect for a candlelight dinner. While the tables were close, wine crate stacks helped to keep a little privacy. Richard led them to table by the window with a stunning view of the ocean and sunset.

"I'm impressed, Dr. Desvareaux," Claire said once they were alone. "Great view."

"Great menu too."

"Do you come here often?" She tried to make her tone as indifferent as possible, but a poker face she'd never had. The idea of Forrest here on a date with another woman, laughing, talking. Ugh!

Friends, her conscience whispered.

"I've eaten here a few times since they opened."

Her stomach flopped.

"But not the way you're thinking," he continued. "I'm usually at the bar."

Bounded on a spree of sheer relief, she asked, "To what do I owe this honor then?"

"What do you mean?"

Claire turned her attention to the pinkish-orange hue casting over the sea, reflecting off the ocean waves rolling in slush due to the frigid winter, then back to Forrest. His eyes were on her and very serious, waiting for her to answer his question. She licked her lips, a nervous gesture. "I know this isn't a date."

He sat back and continued to watch her, looking calm and relaxed while she was squirming inside. Claire touched one of her ears. His eyes followed her movement then back to her face. Shit! She was beyond nervous.

The waiter came just in time to take their drink order. After Forrest ordered a bottle of wine, and they were alone once again, he said, "You were saying this isn't a date."

His eyes met hers once more. Claire absently brushed at the ruffles of her dress. It was hard to maintain that stare. The blue in his graphite eyes were sharp and seemed to have the ability to cut through her.

"Is it?" she asked, not quite sure how to respond.

He sat back, brows furrowed. "You look beautiful."

He didn't answer the question, but whatever. He gave her something better, a compliment. Her body temperature rose, going from slightly chilled to overheated.

"Um, thanks," she mumbled.

He continued to stare at her. Damn him and his gorgeous eyes. "I need to ask you a question."

"Yes." She smiled. "While this is nice, I'd much rather be at your place."

His lips twitched in amusement. Another failed attempt.

"Last night," he said quietly, "I helped you sleep."

Caught off guard, she let out a surprised laugh. Good to know her words had registered. "You've been thinking about this."

"All day," he admitted and shrugged. "I'm still a man."

Oh, she was well aware of how manly he was. The butterflies in her stomach flipped and started the Kid-n-Play kick step. Claire picked up the menu and gave it a cursory glance, mostly to torture him a little, but noted the fritters with four different kinds of what was described as light and zippy sauce. "Have you had the fritters?"

"They're delicious."

"Good. I will have them." She placed the menu down and looked straight at him. "By the way, the answer is yes."

His brows went up. "Yes?"

"You want me to say it?"

A genuine smile crinkled the corners of his eyes, making him even more handsome, if that was possible. "Humor me," he said.

She leaned forward, rested her chin on her palm, elbow on the table, and stared at him. "I touched myself thinking of you last night."

He let out a low groan, a sexy sound that caused that spot between her legs to go damp. Claire squeezed her thighs together. "How does that make you feel?" she asked, all hot and bothered.

Hooded eyes stayed on her for a beat, and when he spoke, his voice was low and raspy. "Tortured."

"You should explain that since we are only friends and all."

He laughed. "It means that image will be burning in my mind the whole evening. But at least we got one thing settled."

"What's that?"

"Good to know over the last ten years we've thought of each other."

Her whole body pulled for him, her blood thrumming through her veins to the rhythm of want. "You mean . . ."

He nodded. "I'm going to mentally recite the periodic table so I can calm down and we can go back to our non-date, date."

Well, that didn't help one bit. The idea of Forrest stroking the hardness of his arousal while thinking about her sent a shot of heat to the tip of her breasts, causing Claire to squirm in her seat. She was relieved when the waiter brought their wine and took their order.

The rest of the night flew by faster than a fighter jet. Time was a thief. They shared a basket of fries, drank too much wine and managed to catch up on ten years within a couple of hours. Laughter was shared. Here and there between the calm space of an old friendship rekindled, a touch of melancholy rested on them, but overall they stayed connected, in a trance. So much so they failed to notice the onlookers who glanced at them, or the sun dipping lower on the horizon as stygian darkness took over the sky, or when the street lights clicked on. When Forrest proposed they walk down two blocks to a nearby bakery for dessert, already half-delirious with pleasure and not wanting the night to end, Claire held on to him again and moved at a relaxed pace about the village the short distance down to the bakery.

A bell on the door rang when they entered the cozy gourmet boutique. The place was simple, high ceilings, wide plank floors, and wooden walls. Inside smelled of rising yeast, fresh cinnamon, and rich brewed coffee creating the feeling of a never ending warm embrace. Although she was full from the dinner and perhaps just a little tipsy from the wine, the delicious display of treats was too tempting to pass up. A staff member greeted them and exchanged a few friendly words with Forrest.

"What can I get for you, Doc?" a young man with shaggy blond hair asked.

"Hey, Tim," Forrest greeted warmly. "Two of your café au lait and one beignet."

"Make that two. Mine with chocolate filling." She elbowed Forrest's hip. "I don't share my sweets."

"Two chocolate beignets then," Forrest said, rubbing his hip with feigned pain. "We'll be by the fireplace."

"Excuse me." A girl with a blunt bob cut and pierced eyebrow appeared from the kitchen. Claire guessed she had to be in her late teens or early twenties. The girl looked at Forrest, but her eyes lingered on Claire. "You're Claire Peters."

Claire smiled. "Yes, I am."

The girl paled and for a second Claire thought she was going to pass out. Good thing her date was a doctor.

"I have all your records." She played with her apron pocket. "I just wanted to tell you that I think you're so talented and we're very proud you're one of our own." She smiled shyly. "I sing and one day would love to be like you."

Maybe it was the fact that she was sharing this magical night with the man she loved, or the fact she'd never lost sight of how much she had managed to achieve in the last ten years, but her heart softened to the girl. She'd always known part of it was due to a little bit of luck. Sure she worked her ass off and knew how to sing, but had James not discovered her that night, who knew where she'd be right now.

Her heart squeezed at the girl's nervous jabber. Once upon a time she'd been the somewhat timid girl with dreams to make it big. "What's your name?"

"Amber."

She shook the girl's hand. "Do you have anything recorded?"

"Um . . . No."

"Amber performs with a local band on the island sometimes," Forrest informed.

"Do you? That's awesome."

The girl smiled shyly.

"What's your favorite song of mine?" Claire asked with a smile.

"Oh, there are so many. I loved your last record though. All the re-makes with your own twist. Pure classic."

One of her favorites as well. A tribute of her love for eighties and nineties music. "Why don't you come to Vapor Friday night? I'm performing there. We'll sing a song together and . . ." The last words were lost as Claire found herself squeezed in a tight embrace.

"I'm so sorry," a flustered Amber apologized.

Claire chuckled. Hell, she still got star-struck. "It's okay."

"Thank you." Amber shoved her hand in the pocket of her apron. "I don't think I'll sleep tonight."

"You'll sleep. I'm just like you. Nothing special."

"Thank you, Ms. Peters." She hesitated then gave Claire another quick hug and disappeared into the kitchen.

"That was sweet and you're pretty special," Forrest said as he led her to a table. This time he slid into the seat right next to her.

"I was her at one time." Victoria's words replayed in her head. Claire shoved them away. "I caught a break."

"Don't sell yourself short. You're talented and you work your butt off." He tucked a wayward strand of hair behind her ear. "Did I tell you how beautiful you look tonight?"

Straight from doing the kick step, her heart performed a funny little beat in her chest. Claire tilted up her face to look at him. "You might have casually said something during dinner, but please don't let me stop you from speaking your mind."

"You're beautiful," he said, voice low.

Her breath hitched. "Be careful, Doc. The friend-zone line is getting blurry."

Forrest didn't seem to mind. He stilled, lowered his head, and brushed his lips against her bare shoulder, burning as they made contact. His sandpaper-rough stubble scratched her skin, stirring the all-consuming need to be in his arms, under him, over him. Claire moaned and would have devoured her date had he not pulled away and turned his attention to the young man with their desserts in his hands.

Picking up the freshly prepared pastry, she took a bite of the deep-fried dough sprinkled with confectioner's sugar and moaned. "Oh, my God!"

"Delicious," Forrest said as he drank his coffee.

"God, yes."

He laughed. "You said God twice. Sounds–"

"Orgasmic," she finished and enjoyed the way his jaw clenched. She licked chocolate from one finger, then another, her eyes on him the whole time. "Not quite." She took another bite. "But I love."

Their gazes held, his heavy-lidded with heat. "You're tempting, Claire." One rough thumb caressed her cheek. "Always have been."

Emotions swirled deep and strong inside her. "What are you going to do about it?"

"I don't know. For now, let's enjoy our desserts." Turning his attention to the plate in front of him, Forrest picked up the beignet and took a large bite. Then he closed his eyes and groaned. "You're right, this is good," he said, and took a sip of his coffee.

The sight of his mouth on the cup had her mind galloping off to X-rated scenarios, because those lips looked delicious. Soft and kissable, while the rest of him looked hard and strong. A tortured man in repose.

"Forrest," she said after a long beat of absolute silence.

Slowly his eyes opened and he looked at her again. "Yeah."

There probably would not be a goodnight kiss as she hoped, and that was okay. She wanted to claim that permanent spot in his heart again. But for now, this moment, the two of them, sitting side by side on the late winter night, drinking coffee and eating a sinful, calorie-filled dessert was more than enough. "I had fun on our non-date date."

"Me too." His voice revealed nothing, but then he smiled, it spread to his eyes, and happiness filled her belly.

CHAPTER SEVENTEEN

"The head never rules the heart but just becomes its partner in crime."
~ Michael Mclaughlin

FORREST SWORE UNDER his breath. His gut coiled into a tight knot as Claire continued to rake his brain. For starters, during their "non-date" date, as she referred to last night, he had to deal with the image of her on her back, eyes closed, and palm on her apex pleasuring herself with him in mind.

Pure fucking torture. He let out a deep breath. He'd gladly give away all of his possessions to watch next time.

Then there was her laughter, the kindness she'd shown to Amber. That side of her didn't surprise him. She'd always been kind, but it was good to learn Hollywood hadn't changed her much. Oh, the way she ate that fucking beignet. The whole time he had wanted to be the one in her mouth instead of that damn pastry. And when she was done with all the teasing, tasting, licking, and swallowing, he'd wrap his arms around her and do whatever floated his boat.

Fuck!

Yeah, he needed one of those. Only he'd sworn off the only person his body craved. Grabbing his coat, he stepped into the crisp cold air. Snow fell gently from the dark, cloudy sky. He drew a deep breath and exhaled, a frosty mist flowing from his mouth like smoke. But his body seemed impervious to the frigid weather. Ah hell, every inch of him simmered for Claire.

He should have kissed her. A month ago, their kiss, the sex, had been full of urgency, now he yearned for slow and deep, the feel of her mouth against his. Skin on skin. Maybe one more time to get her out of his system.

But he'd want more.

Nope. Not gonna happen. Foolish desire would not sweep him down that icy river to who knows where again.

Ever.

Something squeezed his gut and hit his heart. He'd always want her. He ached for her, probably would always ache for her.

Shit! Where Claire was concerned, maybe he needed to wave the white flag and accept he was an inmate for life. No chance for parole. His emotions forever fucked up.

He glanced at the clock in his Jeep. Six o'clock. Unlike him, she was probably still sleeping. He picked up the phone anyway, keyed in her name and stopped. He shouldn't. They had fun last night, but that's all it was. Claire was a runner. He'd been there, done that, even bought the T-shirt. He wasn't interested in a repeat performance, best to leave things as they were. Sure he understood why she reacted the way she did that night.

Kind of.

Not entirely.

If she trusted what they had, she would have come to him and let his love be her sanctuary. *She was eighteen.* Impressionable, easily bended. Still, ten years to finally come forward—and let's not forget she had a life in Los Angeles. Sooner or later, she'd leave again. Then what?

Always running. Just because she finally told him what drove her to bail on him didn't mean she was ready to stop. From the night she left, she'd rarely looked back. A day or two here and there for a wedding, Christmas–if her schedule allowed it, but her visits were always quick. In and out.

Until now. A month later, she was still here. But it was temporary. Just like she'd become.

Forrest massaged his temples to suppress the bitch of a headache he felt coming.

Besides, they were in the *F*-zone, well, maybe not quite the friend zone. Amiable was better suited–friendly, pleasant. In either case, friends didn't do lust. More importantly, he knew better than to act upon it.

He was logical, balanced, and his heart wasn't going there again. At this point, he'd lost track of how many times he'd reminded his heart it wasn't up for grabs.

He sounded like a broken record.

Still, he wished he'd kissed her. The brush of his mouth on her shoulder didn't count, and definitely wasn't enough. Hell, he probably shouldn't have done that either, but the temptation had overwhelmed him. Her skin, smooth brown and glowing by the fire, had begged for him to touch, to feel. Claire continued to squeeze at his brain, obliterating the thinking he needed to wheel-and-deal and shut her out. This middle ground between lust and logic was not good for his sanity. Neither was the semi-hard-on he was sporting.

Forrest stirred, aching. "Fuck, Claire," he swore and pressed the *TALK* button. Her name glowed on his smartphone. He was screwed.

"Hey," she greeted him in a melodious voice still heavy with sleep. "Why are you up so early?"

His mind shifted gears and accelerated to what she might look like right now. He knew she liked to sleep in those little short shorts and a tank, hair pulled in her usual ponytail. Her nipples were probably hard under the soft material. Removing his glasses, he scrubbed a hand over his face instead of banging his head on the steering wheel like he really wanted. "Heading to the farm," he answered, hoping that his tone didn't show how sexually wound up he was.

"Oh. Need help?"

"Aren't you in Chappy?"

"No. I stayed in town last night."

She was in Edgartown. Way too close. Within fifteen, twenty minutes tops, he could be at her door, get that kiss and be on his merry way back to Vineyard Haven. But he'd want more. A quickie would do too, up against the wall, on the sofa. Whatever, as long as he was buried in her. He groaned. His only savior was the fact she was staying at Charles' house and he had no desire to set foot there.

"Jason texted last night to let me know the boat couldn't cross over," she continued.

After they took the ferry back, he had driven off as soon as she entered her car. Leaving no crack in the window of opportunity for him to change his mind and drag her to his house. But he should have known she wouldn't be able to cross Norton Beach. Due to the crazy winter, it tended to freeze at night. She was so close.

"We stayed out too late, I should have thought of that." But everything about Claire, the evening, had been spellbinding.

"Not too late at all. I was having a ball." She let out a short laugh, then said, "I didn't want the night to end."

"Me neither." His balls just left the building. He was officially a sap. "Listen," he said, snapping the short silence between them. "I have to go." Better to end the call now. Who knew what he'd say next. Maybe, *I've been sporting a boner since you told me you were going to touch yourself and think of me.*

"Want me to meet you?" she asked quietly.

His heart stopped for a moment. He needed to get that annoying organ fixed. He blamed it on the unexpected offer. It was tempting and threw him off his axis a bit. "You're terrible at farming."

"Not true."

The stubbornness in her voice only made him want her more. "You can't even milk a cow."

"I don't like touching any other nipple but mine, and that's only when necessary."

He could almost see the teasing glint in her eyes and that made him laugh.

"And yours. Possibly between my teeth," she added in a soft, warm voice.

The semi-hard-on he'd been suppressing officially went into a full, massive erection.

"You taught me how to harvest beets. Do you remember that?" she continued, as if she hadn't intentionally put that image of his nipple between her teeth in his brain.

"I remember." He shifted slightly, adjusting himself.

"How old was I at that time, nine, ten?" she asked, laughter in her voice. The sound warmed his blood.

"Ten." He'd been thirteen and thought she was the most beautiful girl he'd ever seen. Almost two decades later, he still felt that way.

A short silence fell between them. Each lost in the time capsule of their youth to the day when he had found a clueless ten-year-old Claire practically covered under a large straw hat kneeling by the line of beets ready for harvest. Lowering next to her, he had removed the hat and shiny black hair fell to her waist. Her face scrunched into a scowl.

"Have you ever picked any vegetables or fruits?" he had asked.

She shot him a look as if he was a thirteen-year-old idiot. "Of course."

"On a tree?"

She looked blankly at him.

"You know, on a ladder?" he continued.

"Well, no. They were low so I just picked them."

Forrest nodded and chose not to go into details of what lay ahead for her. "You can pull the whole thing out like this." He demonstrated. "Don't remove the top. Beet greens have a delicious and distinctive flavor."

She giggled. "You're such a nerd."

"They also hold more nutrients than the roots," he continued, ignoring her comment. Most of the time he paid her very little attention anyway. They were only talking now because Jason had asked that he help her out. Wherever his best friend was, she was never too far behind. He long ago accepted hanging with Jason meant having Claire around. "At least that's what my parents tell me."

"I knew that," she responded, but the smile on her lips told him she was thankful for the explanation.

He returned the smile and placed the beet in the nearby basket.

"I fell in love with you that day," Claire said over the line, pulling Forrest away from the snapshot of something that happened almost twenty years ago, yet managed to stay so vivid in his mind.

"You were too young. Maybe a crush." At least that's what he and Jason had decided to call it after he'd confided in his friend and told him how his breath had caught at the sight of her like that. Of course he also promised to kill his best bud if he so much as breathed a word to Claire. Up until that moment in the garden, she had been a nuisance.

"No, it was love," she said firmly. "Just like when I was fifteen, seventeen, eighteen, all the years in between, after, and now."

Forrest's head fell back and he closed his eyes. After a second or two, he focused his gaze on the fallen snow. Everything around him was calm and quiet, nothing like the turmoil inside him.

"Claire, when you love someone, you don't run." His parents taught him that. Now he wondered how much of that pertained to their relationship. Had his father known about his mother's affair with Charles?

If so, when had he found out?

His gut clenched.

"I know," she said after a heavy sigh. "Back then, I was . . ."

"Eighteen," he finished.

"Impressionable. More so than I care to admit. I needed to come into my own."

"And you're there now?"

"Yes," she answered without any hesitation.

A thick silence fell between them. He glanced at the clock, twenty minutes had passed. "I have to get going."

"Forrest."

"Claire," he said in his best by-the-book voice.

"Have a great day," she said in a cheery voice then disconnected the call.

Less than fifteen minutes later, Forrest pulled his Jeep by the barn. Years of rain, sleet, and baking summer sun had taken its toll on the shed. He spotted a few stubborn patches of sun-bleached red paint clinging to the wooden sides and made a mental note to repaint it in the summer. Once inside, he hung his coat on the hook by the door and walked up the wooden ladder leading to the hayloft. He piled straw bales held tight by orange twine onto one another, then threw some over his shoulder to the lower level, the thumping noise caused the horses to stir.

"Time for breakfast," he said, jumping off the ladder's bottom step.

The horses hung their heads over their doors, ears perked, eagerly watching as he cut the twine off the straw bales. While they ate, Forrest moved about and inspected the rest of the area, making mental notes of what needed retouching. He thought of the day he found Claire kissing that stupid plum. It had taken all the strength an angst-driven eighteen–year-old boy could muster not to kiss her then. All because he had promised Jason he wouldn't make a play for her until she was at least seventeen. For some unknown reason that had been the magical age they felt she'd be mature enough for a *serious* relationship. Boys were idiots. Why the hell he'd ever agreed to that was still a mystery.

Maybe it was because he saw how much Jason genuinely cared for

Claire. Not the *I'm aware you have tits* kind of way, more of *you're a fucking pain in the ass to have around, but if I had to have a sister, it'd be you* way. Out of respect for his friend he had honored Jason's wish. That decision cost him Claire's first kiss, making Tyler the lucky recipient. The fucking bastard. Of course it irked him, always had and probably would continue to do so for the rest of his life, not that he was jealous of Tyler or anything.

Yeah he was, just a tiny, itty-little bit.

Tyler knew that too and loved rubbing it in his face.

By the time he stepped out of the barn, Forrest was covered in dust and hay. As he tossed his coat inside the Jeep, his father's Labs came bounding through the freshly fallen snow, big chunk of flakes fell onto their fur. They jumped, tongues hanging out of their mouths, wet paws landing on his thighs. Laughing, he dug in his pocket and handed each of the dogs a cranberry oven-baked treat.

"Keeping Mom company?"

The dogs licked his hand. He scratched their chins and the tops of their heads. Once they seemed content with the amount of affection, he walked the couple of yards to the house with his father's four-legged friends by his side. He glanced around, snow covered land stretched before him. The trees stood still, a dust of powder on their bare limbs. With the exception of birds chirping warnings, everything was calm and quiet.

As he got closer to the house, the black S-class Mercedes sedan came into view, and the familiar clutching seized his gut, as it did every time he thought of his mother and Charles. Only a month since finding out Luc hadn't been his father, he was about to come face to face with his so-called father. Ignoring the sick feeling inside, Forrest pushed the door open, bringing in a blast of the cold air from outside with him.

Absolute stillness and quiet greeted him.

For a brief moment, he thought about walking out, but he trekked down the hall to the kitchen. With each closing step, his heartbeat quickened. Faint sound of Miles David *Blue in Green* drifted from his father's study. He paused. White knuckles gripped the handle and turned it. Other than the music, a dark empty room greeted him. His brain rattled inside his head, memories of his late father came splashing so fast that his heart rate went haywire. He pulled the door closed so fast, it almost slammed. Realizing he was shaking, he stood still for a beat, swallowed the emptiness residing in his hollow gut, and continued down the hall to the kitchen.

He pushed the door open. His mother and Charles sat facing each other, fresh brewed coffee on the table, hands laced together. Bile rose in Forrest's throat.

"Forrest," she said, quickly coming to her feet.

"Why is there music in Dad's office?"

"I was in there earlier," his mother explained.

He purposely kept his gaze on his mother. Her eyes were a bit puffy, like she'd been crying. Any other day, he might have tried to get to the root of her tears, but today he didn't give a fuck. "Were you two fucking while Dad was alive?"

"Forrest!" his mother bellowed.

Charles came to his feet and stared at him. "Don't be an asshole. There's nothing going on between your mother and me."

Forrest snorted.

"You stayed away for a month," Charles continued, disgust filling his voice. "Did you ever think she needed you to mourn with her?"

"I'd tell you to fuck off but being you're my father and all."

His mother grabbed the sleeve of his sweater. "Stop," she said firmly.

Forrest pulled away as if her touch burned. "However, since this is not your house, I can tell you to get the fuck out."

"Since you're my son, I'm going to tell you to get off your fucking high horse," Charles spat back.

The two men's gazes clashed. Forrest's jaw rooted. Burning rage hissed through his body like deathly poison, screeching a demanded release in the form of violence. He shoved his fingers through his hair, turned on his heels and walked out of the house, ignoring his mother's call after him.

Thirty minutes later, the snow now falling more quickly, Forrest steered the Jeep onto Main Street in Edgartown half in a daze. The opposite direction of his office, the last place he should be. A ball of anger sat on his chest, waiting to take over. Since he couldn't punch someone, he needed another form of release for all the shit boiling inside him.

Sex.

With Claire.

He was about to make a left on Bay Road where he knew she'd be, when he caught sight of the small figure crossing the street. Puffy long black coat, face hidden behind the hood, a cup, of what he assumed was coffee in her hands. He didn't need to see her face, the sudden stir in his pants was a clear indication he'd found the reason he'd driven to town.

Pulling the Jeep to a nearby space, he parked, slammed the door and bolted across the street. "Claire," he called after her.

She stopped dead in her tracks and turned to him, smiling. Her face makeup free and so fucking beautiful it made his chest ache.

"Hey," she said, "coffee?"

He pushed the hoodie off her head, cupped her face and kissed her with all the pent-up frustration buried inside him. She opened for him, pressing closer, harder, kissing him with everything she had, and obliterating every thought. The worries of the day evaporated like a summer shower onto a hot car. When he finally broke their connection, they staggered back, gasping for air.

"No complaints, Doc, but to what do I owe this honor?"

"Blame it on a case of insanity. It's going around." Drunk on endorphins, he captured her hand. "We're going to my house."

CHAPTER EIGHTEEN

"Having a broken heart is like having broken ribs.
On the outside you look fine, but every breath hurts."
~ Anonymous

"KISS ME AGAIN," Claire said, sitting in the Jeep.

Forrest pushed up his glasses, and answered without a glimpse in her direction. "Later."

"Wait a second." Her hand pressed on his arm as the Jeep ignition revved to life.

Beneath the thick wool sweater, the muscles in his shoulders tensed. Fingers still gripping the key, he glanced at her. She almost gasped at the swirls of emotion–anger, grief, sadness. Flames of hell danced in his dark eyes, very similar to the night she willingly gave herself to be used as a cushion. As good as that moment had been, the cheap feeling the morning after was not high on her list.

"Kiss me again," she said again and curled her fingers around the cup of coffee.

"What is this about, Claire?" he asked, voice strained.

She cleared her throat. "I want to see something."

Through those sexy glasses, he gave her a long, steely look, then took the cup from her death grip and placed it in the cup holder. "Come closer."

The thickness of his voice caused a shiver to run through her. Not the *oh man it's freezing* type. Nope. The good kind. The one that made her want to straddle him and take every inch of his length deep, deep inside.

She scooted in her seat to be as close as possible until the only thing separating them was the gearshift. Somewhere along the way, his glasses were removed and placed on the dashboard. He leaned in, his focus intense and unnerving. With one hand on the back of her neck, he drew her face to his until their noses touched and their lips were centimeters apart. Their breaths mingled. Her heart fluttered inside her chest. And then he was kissing her again, his mouth firm and hungry. Claire's senses spun as his tongue slipped in, licking over hers. She gasped at the sensation, and his tongue delved deeper.

She fell into his kiss. Nothing but tongue, teeth, and desperation. Lust stirred in the pit of her stomach. She moaned, arched closer only to have her hip crashed against the gearshift. Desperate, she dug her fingers into his sweater. But that wasn't enough. She wanted that connection where the only thing that separated them was absolutely nothing.

Realization dawned. This burning desire from Forrest had nothing to do with what they once had or what might be. That magic when they'd been connected body and soul. She wanted it–desperately so.

He was seeking shelter from his chaotic world. Her heart said to let him use her once more. But the voice of reason, the annoying know-it-all said, *Hang on. This is crazy. You want more.*

Slowly, she released her grip and withdrew to her own corner. "I can't have sex with you, not today."

He said nothing. Claire held her breath, waiting, wishing he wasn't going to shut her out. Then he retreated and rested his head against the leather trimmed headrest. A heavy silence settled over them. This time there was nothing comfortable about it.

"I can't be a substitute." Even as she said the words, her heart bled for him. This man sitting next to her, she cared for him so much.

"You're not. If I wanted someone else, I'd go to that person."

Of course he had options, why would she think he didn't? *Silly girl.* Look at him. Women loved him, young and old. He was flat-out sexy, even with the caveman attitude. Still, her stomach dropped over the thought of being anything but a physical asylum for him.

"Something upset you. What happened?"

His jaw ticked.

"You're only here with me because of whatever happened at the farm. Talk to me."

"I don't want to talk about it."

She peered at him. "I can't be a cushion again, Forrest. I played that role for you before."

He went rigid, as if he was consumed with too much to share with anyone, especially her. "Understood."

But she felt all of his anguish and sorrow so deeply that her heart twisted into a knot of pain. She palmed the side of his face. "Did you see Charles? My mom said he's due back on the island either today or tomorrow."

He stiffened under her touch. "Drop it, Claire," he said in a low voice, filled with warning.

"You're not talking to Jason. He's your best friend. Your brother," she added in a whisper.

Her words stewed in the silence that simmered between them.

"You're grieving."

He said nothing.

"We often assign blame for a loss in an effort . . ."

"Cut the psychological bullshit. I don't need it."

They sat knee-deep in silence. Tension rolled off of him in waves, a strange thing to see because he'd always been the calm one among the guys. Not that he was a pushover, but definitely the peacemaker, the rational one. But with all the logic and common sense, Forrest always held the people he loved to a high standard. His views had always been black or white with no gray area. Don't lie. Don't cheat. Don't leave.

She left him.

Tragedy struck and he lost Luc.

His mother cheated and lied.

She understood his anger and ached for him. "I love you."

He studied her face for a beat. "You want love."

Her heart pounded with futility against its cage. "Yes," she said faintly.

A muscle in his jaw ticked. "That's something I can't give you."

Six simple words, but they brought tears to her eyes. Pain erupted from every place on her body and slammed into her heart. Claire's hand fell from his face to her lap.

"You had it from me once," he continued, voice low and measured. "You threw it away. You gave up on us."

"I never stopped loving you."

"Then why did you stay away for so long?"

Like boxers they circled around each other. The kid gloves were off, confrontation time. They'd trade slur for slur, insult for insult, and dig for dig. She knew she should stay quiet and wait for the storm to abate, but she couldn't help sparring with him. "I told you."

"Tell me again."

"My mind kept telling me to give up." She struggled to shift her gaze but her eyes were locked on his. "But my heart won't let me."

"I can't give you my heart, Claire," he said after a full minute of silence. "Sex yes, but nothing else."

"Understood," she repeated his word.

"Do you?" His stunning, gray-blue eyes conveyed a despairing chill his face couldn't hide. It made her heartsick. Crushed with sorrow, she looked away.

For a beat, there was absolute stillness. All noises muted. The air was so brittle between them, it could snap. And if it didn't, she just might. "I can even do lust, but you see . . ." she said with a shaky smile. "Even if sex is all you can give me, I'd want all of you. Your skin against mine in your bed instead of your sofa. Whatever you give me, Forrest, I want all of it."

"You left and never looked back. I've been here." His cold fury burned with dangerous intensity. "For years I waited, pining for you and I was lucky if I got a smile." His words spat out with the ferocity and rapidity of machine gun fire. "I didn't exist. Now you've decided you want me to love you and I'm supposed to accept everything."

"I never stopped loving you." Her voice shook, tears threatened to flow. "I've already explained."

"You thought I hated you. You needed to accomplish more, to come into your own."

There was silence.

All that was true. But coming from him, it made her sound selfish as if she'd never taken his feelings into consideration. In a way, he was right, but it had been a form of pragmatism–a practical approach to problems and her heart.

"I didn't think you wanted me."

"That's bullshit." His gaze locked on hers. "You never looked hard enough to find out. Instead you kept on going. You're a runner." His voice was brutal, accusing.

She remained as still as a cadaver and just as pallid, unblinking against his onslaught.

"I'm right here, Claire. I've always been right here. You want my fucking heart now after ten years and I'm supposed to hand it over." He turned his attention to the storm outside. The shutters had come down. His emotion walled off behind a mask. "I can't give you that."

She winced. His words packed a powerful punch. Carefully spoken, without drama, but with an air of finality. No matter how hard she railed against them, nothing would change. Nothing would ever be the same. They'd hit their mark.

"You're the person who broke me," he continued, voice low and rough. "For the rest of my life, you'll always be the one who hurt me the most."

"I've apologized. You have to find it in your heart to let go."

"I can't do that."

Claire took refuge in the silence.

What was there to say?

Platitudes wouldn't cut it right now. Whatever that was left between them was shattered into glassy shards. A great sob escaped her throat. To fight away her tears no matter how hard they wanted to show, she buried her face in shaking hands for a second and gathered whatever strength she had left. She'd fought and lost.

Catching the door handle, she pushed it open, let out a small sniff and kept her head lowered. "Goodbye, Forrest."

"Goodbye, Claire," he said in a bleak voice, stripped of any emotion.

The Jeep sped off just as she reached the sidewalk. The snow hurled tiny pellets of pain at her cheeks as red-hot tears ran down her face, rubbing salt into her open wounds. Dread crept over the icy chill air, numbing her brain.

She walked in a daze, her footsteps moved soundlessly on the street. She turned on Bay Road and came to a screeching stop. Charles' black sedan parked in the driveway came into focus. He'd been traveling since the big fiasco at the repass, visiting here and there to check on Marjorie. Until today, their paths had not crossed.

For a minute, she pondered how to approach him and examined her feelings for the man who'd raised her like his own. Caught between her love for Forrest, and the reason for all of his anguish, the anger and betrayal she hoped for failed to ignite. Instead an ache settled in her chest for father and son. She loved them both. On different scale, but the emotion was equally strong.

Charles wasn't perfect, but who was?

Certainly not her. For ten years, she used the words practical, realistic, to stay away from Forrest. Running away that night had been a realistic reaction, so she told herself.

What eighteen-year-old wouldn't?

As for staying away, it was easier to relate to what was real rather than to what might be possible.

While their backgrounds were poles apart, in a strange way, she empathized with Charles. Like her, he was flawed. The only child of wealthy parents, he grew up with the world as his oyster. While giving, he was never apologetic for what he had. Nor did he ever hand everything over to Jason. At one time, their father-son relationship had been strained, to Claire's relief, they'd managed to patch things up.

A complete opposite to her relationship with the only man she ever considered a father figure. In her twenty-eight years, he'd never stopped being the father she never had, from removing the training wheels on her bike, to accompanying her to every father and daughter dance at school. When her mother purchased the used Cabriolet for her, it was Charles who'd checked the tire thread and air pressure before she drove off with her friends. Even now, he attended her concerts whenever he could, and was always available for business advice. Other than her mother, he'd been her hero, her keeper, the one who gave her cuddles and kept her safe.

Her gut clenched. While her own father had bailed, Charles had stepped in and filled the role, requesting nothing back from her. Exhaling, she entered the house. She found him sitting in the family room, on the phone with a folder open in front of him. Upon noticing her, he ended the call.

"You look a little beaten," he observed.

"I just saw Forrest."

He let out a long, deep breath. "I hope your encounter wasn't nearly as bad as mine."

"Maybe worse."

"For that I'm sorry." He examined her for a beat. "He hurt you."

Emotionally he had ripped her apart. "Nothing I can't handle." She fell into the seat like a weightless sack and stared out the window. The gloom of the wintry day crept into her, seeping into her pores and traveling to her heart. More tears, no surprise there. She sniffed them back. "I want to be mad at you."

"Then be mad. It's natural to want to protect the man you love."

Up to a month ago, she'd probably avoid any topic of Forrest and her feelings. Today, she didn't have the strength nor did she want to. Through blurred eyes, she turned to face Charles. "Why did you wait so long to tell him?"

"I didn't tell him." He ran a hand through his close-cropped hair. "Neither did I expect him to overhear my conversation with Marjorie. For thirty-one years, I watched on the sidelines. It got tiring."

"Why now?" Jason had asked the same question that night but Charles had never answered.

"Long story. Nothing to get into now. But to summarize, I ran out of what ifs."

She understood that. Wasn't she in the same situation with Forrest now? "You should at least explain everything to him."

"If he'll listen."

"He's hurt."

"I know. But he's acting like an ass."

In spite of the melancholy mood that hung over like a black cloud, she chuckled. "I agree."

He stood up and shoved his hands in his pockets. "I have a few contracts to look over that Blake sent over to me."

"It's okay. I'm going to wallow in my misery. How are things with Jason? I know he was upset at Luc's repass."

"I told Jason everything. While he's not happy, we are okay."

Walking over to the sofa, he placed a kiss on her head. "As for your relationship with Forrest, give him time. He gave you ten years to figure out what you wanted. Dinner later?"

She looked outside. The snow showed no indication of stopping. "Everything will be closed."

"Then let's do an early lunch. Give me a few hours."

She listened to Charles' footsteps until they faded as silent tears fell down her cheeks. She continued to watch the snow, like an empty jar on a shelf, still holding her form, but without anything left inside.

Her phone dinged. Reaching in her pocket, she read the notification someone had raised the bid on Forrest. *Fight or flight*, Jason's words replayed in her head. Claire exhaled, placed the phone next to her and ignored the message. She could continue to engage in the battle, but what was the point? It was a hopeless battle. All the tenacity she'd worked up to fight had been depleted.

Within seconds, her phone vibrated again. Picking it up, she read Lily's text.

> *Check out the hottest couple on the island. Luv U.*

She skimmed over the caption.

> *Claire Peters shacking up with her boyfriend in Martha's Vineyard. Doctor-farmer. A sexy combination. The man is H-O-T, y'all. See for yourself!*

First, there was no shacking up. Second, they'd been in Woods Hole. A forty-five minute ferry ride from the Vineyard. But hey, the tabloids were always right. Claire scrolled to the picture, her arm tangled in Forrest's, body leaning into his. Their faces were pictures of pure bliss. To think that was less than twenty-four hours ago. Her heart splintered into tiny pieces.

Her phone chirped. Not wanting to talk, she let it go to voice mail, until it started again. Wiping her face, she read James' name and answered the call.

"Your voice is sad," he remarked right away.

"It's nothing."

"Darling, I worry about you on that island of yours."

She sniffed and smiled back the tears. "I'm fine." She could feel James wanting to push, but he wouldn't. Their business relationship worked because there was trust.

"A little birdie told me you're throwing a concert on Friday."

"That little birdie would be me." She'd sent him and Ava a text to let them know after speaking with Tyler. "It's nothing big. I'm doing a friend a favor."

"Well, it's already trending on Twitter, so it's big."

"Ava's doing?"

"Nope. I'm calling to see if we needed to do some damage control since the whole world will be attending."

Claire chuckled. "Vapor is not a big place. It's big for the island but not huge. Can't hold more than one-hundred people and believe me, Jason and Adam are not afraid to pull their Alpha cards."

"What about that boyfriend of yours?"

She groaned. "You know I don't have a boyfriend."

"Tall, dark, with smoldering eyes in a black leather coat. Not your boyfriend?"

She sat straighter. "Not boyfriend. For once the gossips are not accurate."

James laughed. "Don't tell me you were reading the tabloids."

As a matter of fact, she hadn't. Unless someone brought something to her attention, Claire tended to avoid all the tabloids. She'd witnessed what they'd done to Jason and Adam. James knew that and often teased her about it as he was doing now.

"Let's see . . ." His voice trailed. She could envision him scrolling through the tweets. "According to the last tweet that was just posted two seconds ago, you and McDreamy are more popular than Jared Leto and Lupita."

"Forrest and I are not dating."

"Neither are Jared and Lupita. At least that's what my sources tell me. But it doesn't mean they're not hot together or don't have crazy chemistry."

Unable to conjure an argument over how hot she and Forrest looked together or their chemistry, she sighed. "We were in Woods Hole having dinner. Not a date at all."

"Too bad," he said, his voice filled with regret. "You looked pretty happy."

She had been. Unlike the heaviness now weighing her down.

"But your voice is very morose. Something happened?"

"Long story."

"Okay. I won't ask. But as your manager, I strongly advise that you peruse social media more often. From what I am looking at, it's totally love. I hope the two of you do work out. So hang in there."

Funny, everyone was telling her to hang in there. Except the one person she wanted to hear those words from the most.

"Anyhow," James continued, "I wanted to let you know to expect some media coverage on Friday. Even if they don't get in Vapor, they'll be outside. So . . ."

"I know. Watch what I do or who I leave with."

"You said it." He chuckled. "But do have fun."

The morning passed by in a blur. Her mood ricocheted between low and lower until Charles insisted they go out for lunch. The snow had tapered some, but was still falling at a steady pace. Vapor was closed, but Sharky, a diner based on the movie *Jaws*, was open. A tuna fish sandwich it was going to be.

She stepped out of the car and froze. Across the street, Forrest stood with Kerry, the woman he'd dated briefly last fall. He smiled, opened the passenger door to the Jeep for her, and Claire's heart flopped.

As he walked over to the driver side, he looked up suddenly and cast a look from Charles to her and held it. Then he removed his glasses, blurring the image in front of him—her. Then he entered the Jeep and drove off.

Claire stood still, her stomach nauseous. Her lungs hurt to breathe.

"Ready?" Charles asked with a hand on her shoulder.

She nodded, unable to speak or move. Nothing left to feel. Emotionally bankrupt, sorrow and misery consumed her. Small crystal beads trailed down her cheeks. She let them fall, not raising a hand to stop them.

"Let's go back to the house, Claire. You can cry as much as you want."

There was more where that came from, enough to cry for hours.

And what then?

Then she'd drink another glass of water and start all over again.

CHAPTER NINETEEN

"Sometimes the heart needs time to accept what the mind already knows."
~ Rosa Peters

SLOWLY CLAIRE'S BREATHING hollowed itself and a small intense pain shot straight to the top of her head. Emptiness, a maelstrom of turmoil filled her. Dried tears hardened on her cheeks. She didn't care to brush them away, let them stain her face. Maybe they could toughen her heart in the process. Time fast forwarded into night. She lost track of the hours, or how long she cried. Not that it mattered. She wasn't numb, in fact, quite the opposite. A plethora of emotions came crashing in.

She should go to Forrest now. But the storm had them stuck in their respective corners. Or maybe he was with Kerry. Bile bubbled in her stomach.

Broken and grieving, he came to her during his time of need. She turned him away, because she wanted love.

Selfish.

Pragmatic, her conscience argued, caught in a web of denial.

Selfish–with a capital S or maybe all seven letters in caps . . . for emphasis. Her distorted view slowly came into focus. The last ten years had been about Claire Yasō Peters, a wildflower–not intentionally seeded or planted. When Forrest needed oblivion and sought her for shelter from the hurricane that stormed his life, she should have been his haven.

Wasn't that part of loving someone?

But you want more, remember? her well-advised inner voice astutely pointed out.

She wanted love. Forrest offered sex.

Strong sexual desire versus that deep romantic attachment, the line between the two tended to smudge. One was the jangle down the neck when eyes locked across a crowded room, the feel that awakened the heart. The other consisted of warm smiles that spread across the face just by thinking about the other person. The entrapment of the heart.

Both had downfalls.

One came with the removal of the perfect mask, exposing a not-so-perfect personality. Along with all the flaws, arguments came acceptance and an understanding that moods and minds might vary. Most of all, an unconditional care for one another with an expiration date of infinity. The other–sex. Great sex, intense physical contact, late night calls, flirtatious texts, and nothing meaningful. The heart stood no chance of being affected or trampled.

But what was love without lust? Could one truly exist without the other?

She craved both. Call her greedy, but she wanted all the *crushy* feelings, all the potential, along with the happiness and the growing old part. But most importantly, she wanted Forrest to reciprocate her sentiments.

She'd bailed when the going got tough. To react that way at eighteen was understandable, but she hadn't been eighteen for the last ten years.

A runner. For a while, distance was all that mattered. Distance from the island, from Forrest. She kept on running, widening the gap as much as she could, and never stopped to think . . . maybe he still loved her. For years, whenever her heart tried to force a confrontation, force her to look at the truth, she purposely shut it down, concealed all the things she longed for. Instead she kept her eyes glued to the GPS display, tracking achievement after achievement while the world passed in a blur of red and white lights.

And now . . . she chose to follow her heart.

But had her decision come a decade too late? Forrest was so consumed with grief that needed to be dealt with first. She wondered if he had any room for her, even if it were just lust.

It's impossible, said pride.

It's risky, said experience.

It's pointless, said reason.

Give it a try, whispered the heart.

She'd taken her foot off the gas pedal and realized a future without Forrest, regardless of all of her achievements, was no future at all. For as long as her memory served, he'd been a part of her. He seeped into her skin and rested in her bones. No time spent apart could take that feeling away. Picking up her phone, she clicked on the auction link. Three additional bids had popped up for Forrest. She was officially in a bidding war with a bunch of women vying for a date with the doctor.

Claire scanned the names, none said Kerry. But then again, all the names were made up. Oh well, fight or flight, right? She keyed in five thousand dollars, making her once again the highest bidder.

Flopping on the bed, she reached for her phone and sent Minka a text.

How are you feeling?

Minka's response came quick.

Nauseous. Appointment has been postponed to tomorrow. You? Saw the pic.

A smile touched Claire's lips. She answered.

Night of pic was fun. My bid is now at 5 thousand. I better win.

No point in pointing out she was officially fighting this war alone. Not that Forrest had given her any hope. If anything he'd been pretty firm on his *friend* stance. Well . . . not really. He flirted. He kissed her naked shoulder. He told her he jacked off to her for Pete's sake. Friends didn't share that kind of information. Well, technically she had opened that Pandora's Box. Forrest just went along.

Minka answered.

You'll win. Well, time for sleep . . . again. Hope 2 see you all tomorrow. Luv U.

Claire picked up the remote and turned on the television. While flicking through the channels, she dialed her mother's number. One of the things she didn't like about Chappy was the separation on days like today from the rest of the island.

"There you are," her mother greeted, "Charles told me he baked you brownies." Her mother chuckled.

"He did."

"I hope you ate at least two."

She glanced at the empty plate at the nightstand. The brownies hadn't been that bad. Smiling, she nodded. "I ate a few."

"So you've hit a bump with Forrest."

"I'm trying to take away ten years of hurting him." She let out a deep breath. "I don't know if that's possible."

"He's grieving. Sometimes the heart needs time to accept what the mind already knows."

She understood that. "Mom, are you okay there all by yourself with the storm and all?"

Her mother managed a full staff, but mostly when the house was occupied. Winter months were quiet on the Vineyard and Charles had been traveling, which meant she was alone.

"I'm fine."

For years she tried to convince her mother to stop working but was always met with a stubborn *I will not live off my daughter.* "Still not going to stop working?" It didn't hurt to try once more.

The question was met with rich laughter. "This is my home, Claire. I'm happy. Remember it's your turn to be happy too. I have to go, love."

There was a slight pause. Claire strained her ear, sure she heard a muffled voice in the background. "Wait, are you . . . is there someone there with you?"

"As a matter of fact, yes," her mother responded. Her voice, cool as a cucumber.

What the hell! Her mother was dating and spending the night with someone. She'd been on the island for a month now, why was this news to her? "Mom," she started with caution.

"Claire, I have a life. I date and today my date is stranded here because of the storm. He wants to formally meet you soon."

"Formally?"

"I was dancing with him at the potluck."

She remembered her mother dancing with a handsome man that night. "Be careful."

Her mother laughed. "Shouldn't I be telling you that?"

"I'm not spending the night with a man."

"Good point. I love you."

After ending the call, she grabbed her journal and flipped to the page with the heading Tattooed Hearts and wrote, *Love is like a dagger. It cuts deep and brands the heart, marking you forever.* Her phone dinged a message alert. She glanced at the text from Forrest and gasped.

> *Not even close to what you thought you saw. I wanted you. After all this time, it's still you.*

Her heart tripped and came to a full stop, then everything restarted at once. Excitement wired her body, lungs pumping air, brain waves running amok. Bouncing off the bed, she slipped into her boots, zipped down the stairs, grabbed her coat in the process and made a beeline for the door.

"Going somewhere?" Charles asked as they walked past each other.

"Lake Tashmoo." There was no need to say his name, everyone knew that was Forrest's hideaway.

"Weather is bad." Charles sat on the sofa and picked up the remote.

She grabbed her keys and zipped up her coat. "I'll make it." Walking back to the sofa, she kissed his cheek. "Thanks for the brownies. I love you."

He smiled. "Send a text to let me know you arrived safely."

Almost one hour later, Claire gripped the steering wheel as the Audi sedan slid over the thick, fluffy white powder on the ground, crossing a mile every fifteen minutes through the mini-hurricane of snow and ice. In normal weather, driving to Forrest's was a challenge. During a blizzard, it was downright impossible. Slowing the SUV, she made a right turn onto Meadow Lane, where two unlit dirt roads sloped side by side and wound through acres of woodland. The snow hung in the air, and fogged the windshield, obscuring her vision. She switched her headlights from low beam to fog lamps and crept through the gray murk until she pulled alongside the orange Jeep.

She knocked on the door. No response. Nothing but a gaping silence. She knocked again, this time with her fist, matching the rhythm of her thumping heart. Nervous twitter bubbled in her stomach. Then the door opened and brought her face to face with Forrest. His hair was damp and wavier than normal and looked as if he threw a sweater and jeans on at the last minute. He followed her gaze to his half-zipped jeans, giving her a peek of fine dark hair, and quickly pulled up the zipper.

"I was about to shower," he said.

She cleared her throat, ignoring the rush of heat that coursed through her and told herself to calm down for a minute. "Can I come in?"

Without a word, he stepped back. They stood staring at each other for a beat, sexual tension electrifying the space between them.

"Driving here was not prudent," he said in a gravelly voice. "There's a blizzard outside."

The act was a completely reckless one, but the heart had a way of throwing caution to the wind. "I read your text."

Something flared in his eyes—desire. Her heart picked up pace again.

"That could have waited," he said, voice calm.

A tiny burst of panic kicked the air out of her lungs. The man was so controlled. Here she stood, the cleft between her thighs moist and desperate, and he was telling her they could have waited to have sex. Definitely not. She would have driven through a tsunami tonight.

"No, it couldn't." There was a pause, then she added, "I'm sorry."

He ran a hand through his hair. "Me too."

She shook her head. "Your words hurt, but they were the truth." She released a small sigh. "I'm sorry for earlier. I'm sorry for walking away from you that night." Just thinking about Forrest sitting in his room waiting made her heart ache all over again. "I should have come to you. I shouldn't have ignored your attempts to talk to me, but . . ." she sucked in a breath, choking and fighting back tears. "You're the last person I ever wanted to hurt." Her uncaring attitude went on for too long. "I was so . . . selfish. I'm sorry."

She held her breath, waiting, hoping. She loved him, always had, and always would.

"Claire . . ." he started in a gravel voice.

"You still want me." It wasn't a question, but her stomach still tightened a little with angst.

"Always," he said without any hesitation, causing a pulse to run from the tips of her breasts to her core.

The air snapped and crackled. "I can do lust."

He closed the door and looked at her for a beat. Warning flashed in those beautiful eyes of his, a very serious warning. One that said, *In about thirty seconds, we are having wild animal sex.* She moved in closer just as he took a step forward, the space between them ceased to exist.

He gripped her hips and pressed her against the hardness of his arousal. "I can share my bed."

CHAPTER TWENTY

"Grab my hair like you grabbed my heart."
~ Anonymous

FORREST STUDIED CLAIRE. Her palms placed flat over his chest. Brown eyes hazy with lust looked up and drew him in. The fire she started in him over a decade ago flared, the ache for her tight and hard in his gut.

Torn by the urge to strip her naked and maybe . . . just maybe make it to the couch, or keep his balls in check for the slow, deep penetration he craved most. Desire rumbled through his chest. But he'd set the pace. He liked control. More importantly he wanted to know how she felt melting against him. Their first time after a decade of longing, yearning, had been purely physical, straight out, unadulterated blatant sex . . . for him.

Emotions tugged at his stomach. This time he'd reciprocate. This was Claire pressing against him. The woman he'd never gotten over.

He wanted to touch, kiss, and wrap his arms around her. Not just for the sake of the physical connection. That would never be enough. He yearned for something deeper–to lose himself in her. The need was so fierce it made his heart ache.

"Kerry's car broke down," he said for no particular reason, except it was important she knew he'd never go to someone else to spite her. No matter how he fought the longing, the warnings to not go back to what broke him, it'd always come down to her. "I gave a friend a ride."

"To her house," she said in a quavering voice.

"Then I went to Mrs. Kane to shovel snow."

At that she smiled. His gaze dropped to her mouth, bare and tantalizing. He trailed his lips along her jawline to her ear. She shivered against him. His mouth slid to the corner of hers and was rewarded by the clutch of her hands on his sweater. Having her cling on to him like . . . he was her only anchor, sent a leap of tangled emotions straight through him.

"No substitute, Claire," he murmured, just before their lips came crashing together. Hard, passionate, the kind of kiss that would make anyone weak at the knees, foggy in the head, and leave them not only wanting, but desperately needing more.

He wasn't immune. He was in deep, deep shit.

Slanting his mouth against hers for more, she moved with him, into him, making the connection all the more satisfying. He heard a heavy groan. His. Clearly he was out of his mind. Satisfying wasn't the right word. Not even close.

Hot. She was so hot he struggled to sustain control. And then she made one of those soft, mewling sounds from the back of her throat, silently telling him she had capitulated and was now at his mercy. The sound wrecked his equilibrium.

He kissed her more, sinking deeper into her taste. Their hands bumped into each other as they moved, grappling for control, something to grab, touch. Hers ran over his chest and arms. His fumbled with the buttons of her coat until it fell onto the floor.

She angled her body closer, her breasts pressed against his chest. Their bodies became magnets, crashing into their opposite charge, smashing, pushing, and discovering each other once more. Their tongues moved together in a hot duet. The temperature rose as they clawed their way through the kiss, desperate for more. Teeth, lips, mouth, tongue–all furious and fevered heat as their hands tore at sweaters and pants to get to that skin-on-skin contact.

It was then they broke the kiss and stared at each other, chest heaving, trying to catch their breath. Then she did what he least expected. She caught his hand and brought her lips to the black ink on his forearm. The act hit him square in the chest, and air whooshed out of his lungs.

"I've missed you," she whispered in a trembling voice, before continuing the onslaught by moving to his chest. She grasped a nipple between her teeth and ran her tongue over it.

His heartbeat sped up. "I need to shower," he said, pebbles in his throat.

"I like you sweaty."

Bending down, he scooped her in his arms. She let out a little giggle, wrapped her hand around his neck and didn't let go until he dropped her on the bed. "First shower, I'll be quick."

She arched a brow.

"In the shower," he said, and sucked on her lower lip.

AFTER WAITING IMPATIENTLY for what seemed like eternity, but was really less than five minutes, Claire bounced off the bed and headed to the closed door. She stood outside of the bathroom, listening to the sound of the water running. She bit her lower lip, envisioning Forrest naked, dripping wet. Sensations exploded in various parts of her body from all the emotions locked up in her heart.

Desire.

Need.

Love.

Lust.

Lust, the sudden, powerful, almost overwhelming desire for something that was definitely bad for you.

Bah! It was Forrest standing on the other side of the door. Her first and only love, they had given their virginity to each other. Even then, when they were inexperienced and discovering together, they'd been good together.

Lust was definitely not a bad thing. On the contrary, the hot doctor she was lusting after would be very good for her . . . without a doubt.

Stripping out of her boots and jeans, she pushed the door open and walked into the steam-filled room. Her eyes immediately went to the fogged glass door and fixated on Forrest's faint outline.

He stood motionless, one hand braced on the wall in front of him. His head hanging low as splash of water pounded between his shoulder blades, rippling over his body, from his sleek back to the perfect, mouth-watering curve of his ass. Every muscle in her body tensed. The first time she saw him naked a decade ago, she'd thought he was beautiful and never imagined he could get better. She'd been wrong. He'd filled out in all the right places and then some.

He was gorgeous.

Her heart jumped and a heightened awareness prickled every part of her body. She stood staring, enthralled by his sheer beauty. She forced herself to take a deep breath, to just breathe. Air in. Air out. He must have felt her presence because he glanced over, swiped at the glass, squinted and held her gaze. Then the door slid open. Claire stared. One finger signaled her to come forward.

She took a step and stopped, not sure if she should remove her bra and panties first. Eyes locked on hers, he wrapped his hand around his hard length and held. Her breath hitched. The juncture of her thighs throbbed and swelled.

"Keep coming," he said, voice gruff.

Her legs took over and moved forward, and then she was in the shower. He stepped back to give her room under the spraying jet stream. At first contact, the warm temperature of the water made her suck in a breath, causing her hardened nipples to rise. Forrest groaned, hooked an arm around her waist and pulled her to him. "You're so beautiful."

She slid her fingers into his wet hair and pulled him down. "Kiss me."

Catching her chin with his thumb, he tilted her face up and gave in to her request. Claire opened for him. His tongue delved into her mouth, seeking and demanding. His hands moved along her back and unsnapped her bra. He kissed her harder, garnering a little whimper out of her.

At the sound, Forrest pulled back just a fraction and looked into her eyes, hot wild lust in his gaze. It mirrored what she felt inside. She tugged him in, needing to feel him, wanting no space between them.

"Don't stop kissing me."

"Just slowing the pace," he said, running the pad of his thumb against her cheek.

She shook her head. "Don't ever stop."

"Never?" With his other hand, he caught one peaked nipple between his thumb and index finger, squeezed and rolled it gently.

Claire sucked in a breath. "Never ever."

His mouth smirked in this smile that made her know he was

thinking of something. Lowering his head, his lips grazed her jaw, her throat, across her collarbone. Before she knew it, he dropped to his knees and peeled off her panties. He let out a guttural sound at the sight of her bared in front of him, then he cupped her ass and squeezed.

"Open for me," he said, hands on her thighs.

She spread her feet and found herself wide open in every possible way. He slipped his hand between her legs, sliding a finger, then another, through her slick flesh. He teased and stroked until her core tightened, ready to unravel.

Then his mouth. *Oh God, his mouth . . .*

He licked her once, ran his tongue against her bare flesh and groaned. "You taste so fucking delicious." Then kissed the most sensitive spot, this time he took his sweet time–stroking, touching, kissing every inch of her so that she was worked up into a near frenzy.

His hands tightened around her thighs, spread her open even more, and let her wetness flood his mouth.

Her head swam.

Her hips rolled with abandon.

Her whole body pulsed for him, blood thrumming through her veins to the rhythm of want, a pounding in her ears that blotted out everything but the feelings that charged through her. And when he rolled his fingers over the bundle of nerves, she went over the edge, crying out his name.

His hands steadied her thighs, holding her while her body trembled. He didn't rise to his feet until her breathing was somewhat steady.

"Hold on to me," he said, leaning her against the wall.

"But . . . I want . . ." Her hands moved below his waist, skimmed his hardness and held.

Nuzzling his face in her neck, he shook his head. "Not now." He turned off the water, grabbed a towel, and soaked up each glittering droplet from her skin.

The intimacy behind the act of Forrest drying her caused her heart rate to kick up. When he was finished, he discarded the towel to the floor. Grabbing her ass, he scooped her up, bringing them at eye level, her breasts smashed against his chest. Her legs acted on instinct and wrapped around his waist. A wave of heat licked her veins, scorching her. She welcomed it.

"Bed," he said and ran his tongue along the outer edge of her ear.

Claire shuddered. He kissed her again, and she moaned with pleasure at the taste of herself in his mouth.

She needed to have him.

He had to take her.

He was hot as sin, smelled like lust, and radiated sexuality.

Wrapping her arms around his neck, she held on and didn't let go until they fell together on the bed.

He kissed her breasts, suckled and nipped until they felt heavy and swollen. He touched and licked every inch of her skin as if seeking to memorize her body or claim it. Either way, she was his. He could do it for eternity.

Intense heat built in her stomach and spread lower until she tightened and unraveled as she exploded. She was still shaking when he grabbed her hips and slid between her thighs, his steely length resting along her sex, hitting her clit.

Ahhh.

Her eyes fluttered closed. She arched to take him in. But he pulled back, and brushed wet locks of hair away from her face.

"Look at me, Claire."

Half-crazed with need, she obliged. His gaze was intently fierce, so much so she trembled. "Now . . . Please," she breathed, full of longing and untamed desire.

In one long, torturously delicious thrust, he slid into her, until every millimeter was buried deep inside, filling her all the way.

Home.

She gasped and screamed his name.

"Give yourself to me," he said, voice rough.

She knew what he wanted. Control. Complete control of her body. "I'm yours." She raised her ass and handed herself over to him.

Letting out a low, very male sound of satisfaction, he cradled her hips and thrust deeper. Claire's head spun. She gripped his hair and wrapped her legs around his waist so they touched in every way, bringing him deeper, skin on skin. He moved over her, in her, the intensity increasing until it became a feverish pace.

He kissed her hard and then pulled back to look at her before kissing her again.

And then again.

Each time harder, and rougher, tongue delving into her mouth as he moved faster. Each thrust deeper and harder, hips grinding.

The exquisite friction sent her flying. Her body clenched, and shattered, sensations rolled through her in a sinful chaos of bliss. She threw her head back and cried out in pleasure, spasms rocking her body in tight, sensual waves.

"Claire," he grunted her name, burying his head in her shoulder. With two quick thrusts, he came as the last tremors rippled through her. "So fucking good."

The heat of his voice on her skin sent another ripple through her, making her shudder against him. They lay stock-still, hearts pounding against one another. For a long moment, neither spoke. Words were not needed. The moment was incredible.

When he finally lifted his head, he brushed a kiss over her damp temple, and studied her. "You drive me crazy."

"Hopefully in a good way."

Rolling to his back, he hauled her in tight against him. "Insanity is never good."

"Say that to the heart."

He tightened his grip. She curled up in his arms and let the beat of his heart soothe her to sleep.

CHAPTER TWENTY-ONE

"Love doesn't need wisdom. It speaks from the irrational wisdom of the heart."
~ Deepak Chopra

FOR THE FIRST time in a decade, Claire woke up in Forrest's bed, in a pretzel position—skin on skin, legs tangled, fingers intertwined, and her head on his chest.

The sex had been great, but to be curled up in his arms, sharing body heat, the beat of his heart whispering softly in her ear, that feeling was primal.

With her body and mind relaxed, she felt . . .

Safe.

Peaceful.

At home.

Tidal waves of emotion hit her. The knot once rooted deep inside her chest disentangled and set her free. Overflowing with joy, her lips spread into a smile, all the years of anguish and sorrow slipping away. She scooted closer, practically on top of him at this point, and let the happiness soak in.

"Finally awake," he said, voice still rough with sleep.

She nodded, still floating.

"Feeling okay?" As if needing reassurance he didn't break her, his calloused fingers ran over her arm, making her skin prickle at the touch.

"Why do you always ask me that?" she asked, still listening to his heartbeat.

"Ask you what?"

Barely lifting her head from his chest, she peered at him. His eyes were still closed. His chin covered in days old stubble that was not quite a full beard. His thick hair all mussed up. Her heart stuttered. *God, he was handsome.*

"If I'm okay or good after we have sex."

He shifted, but not far enough for their bodies to stop touching. "For one, I'm much bigger than you."

She chuckled. "You're definitely big." The sore spot between her thighs was a sure indication of it. Not that she minded. Quite the opposite, she craved it.

"You're hopeless." He shook his head and smiled, the kind of smile that lit up his face and made the butterflies flutter in her belly. "I was referring to my physical size versus your build."

Just so there wasn't any misunderstanding, she released his hand, slid hers under the comforter and grabbed his thickness. "So was I."

With a groan, Forrest tightened his grip on her and swore beneath his breath. "I ask because I care. I don't want to hurt you physically or in any other way."

Her heart skipped a beat. Not the love declaration she longed for, but this was good, a step in the right direction. She understood the significance of the text that led to last night. How far he'd come to let her in even this close. Forrest didn't love casually. When he loved, it was fierce, wide open, and raw. His whole heart on display, that's who he'd always been.

Now he was guarded. Maybe a little less so than a month ago, but she had no reason to think he wasn't still trapped within the walls of his guarded heart. She understood his reluctance to risk his and accepted it.

"The feeling is mutual," she said against his chest. He had her whole heart for his whole life. "Do you have to go to the office or the hospital today?"

"I have some paper work to finish, but that can be done here," he said, chin resting on top of her head.

"Going to the farm?"

"No."

The one word answer spoke volumes and told her the farm was not a topic for discussion. As always the havoc in his life pinched her chest.

"By the way, did I happen to tell you how crazy you are for driving in that storm last night?" he asked in his typical calm voice.

"Yeah, but look how great things turned out." She nestled even closer to him, not quite ready to go. Change that, she never wanted to let go. But it was inevitable. Night had fled. The sun, an unwanted guest, streamed in through the windows. He laughed and squeezed her ass. "Speaking of that, from what I remember, our morning sex tends to be pretty awesome."

"We only had morning sex once." The words slipped off her tongue before she realized what she had just said. Another reminder she had left him waiting that night. Dread knotted her stomach. His body tensed next to hers and Claire silently cursed herself over her thoughtless act.

"Right," he said, and her heart ached at the hint of bitterness in his voice.

"Forrest . . ."

"Sshh . . ."

Her breath hitched. She swallowed the pain tugging in her heart. After a long silence, he rolled over and pinned her beneath him. His hands stretched her arms above her head. A strong, muscled thigh spread her legs, opening her for him.

He stared at her, his expression the usual composed and collected. One of these days, she'd have to ruffle him a bit.

"Another round?" She arched her back and tried to free one hand from his grasp. With a little push of his ass forward, he'd be inside her.

"In a minute," he said and gently squeezed her hands, telling her to stay that way.

The control. It frustrated and drove her wild all at once. "Now."

"Let me look at you."

He took his time too, letting his eyes move from her face down to her breasts. Claire sucked in a breath, feeling her nipples straining under his stare. Then his gaze flicked to her face, intense and unwavering.

They lay together like that for a moment. When he spoke, his voice was a little hoarse, but filled with conviction. "No more discussion of the past. No more apologies. It's about here and now. Good?"

She wanted to touch him so badly, but her hands were still stretched over her head. "Let me touch you."

Something flickered in those mesmerizing eyes of his. "Are we good?"

"We're good, Doc."

Dropping his head to her neck, his mouth blazed a path over her throat and collarbone. She tilted her waist so that his erection pressed right against her core. Forrest let out a low groan and rubbed his jaw to hers before finding his way to her breasts. In the next moment he was inside her, sliding in and out and making her want to weep with ecstasy.

A while later, Claire sat on the walnut-colored leather barstool in Forrest's kitchen, scrolling through her emails and text messages while lingering over that first cup of morning coffee.

"Anything important?" he asked while mixing the pancake batter.

"Minka sent a group text asking to meet for lunch."

"Great. Have fun."

"You're on the text as well," she said carefully. "They go for the ultrasound today."

He nodded. His face, hard as nails, revealed nothing. "I'll reach out to Minka."

Crestfallen, her head sagged down to her chest. She sent a quick text responding she'd be there.

"Anything else?" he asked.

Feeling his gaze on her, Claire rearranged her face into something she hoped was nonchalant and casual-looking and answered, "Other than that, my schedule is all clear."

After a long stare, he focused his attention back on the stove. She pressed back the nagging thoughts that sooner or later, the topic of Jason would have to be discussed. Both men meant a lot to her. Once upon a time they'd been best friends.

She watched Forrest move with efficiency between the stove and the pantry. He was immaculately proportioned, part sculpture, part human—a man set apart by the alignment of muscle and bone beneath skin. All of her life, she watched people edge around his walls as if mindful of the signs, do not touch. But she'd touched and kissed every inch of him. Well, there was one part of him she wanted in her mouth, that'd make him lose all that imperturbable calm.

They had time. Possibly forever.

For now, she'd savor this moment. There was something incredibly sexy about the whole thing. From the fact her morning outfit consisted only of one of his well-worn alma mater tees, to the hiss of the boiling teapot, and Forrest barefoot, in worn jeans and a navy blue Boston Red Sox World Series Champions tee, preparing breakfast.

She leaned forward and rested her elbows on the oak kitchen island, totally caught in a trance. He placed a stack of freshly made blueberry pancakes oozing with butter in front of her, then poured hot maple syrup over it. She inhaled the rich, invigorating aroma, tempting her tummy.

"I know you said you can drive to town," he said, sliding on to the stool next to her, "but I'd like to drive you."

She glanced out the window to see a white valley under blue, sunlit skies leading to Lake Tashmoo. The storm left at least eight inches of snow behind, covering every tree, rock, or leaf in sugary frost. The view was wondrous, calm, and quiet. Exactly how she felt inside. As for the drive out of the acres of woodland to the main road, that should be interesting.

"What about my car? I'd have to get it sooner or later."

He forked a piece of pancake. "I can pick you up wherever you are."

Not wanting to jump to conclusion, Claire pressed her palm against her stomach, silencing the butterflies batting their fragile wings. "You want me to stay the night?"

He met her questioning gaze. "Yes."

And her belly flipped.

"When do you leave for L.A.?" he asked, his attention back to his plate.

"I'm here until next week," she answered, her mind still reeling from the overnight invitation.

He glanced at her. "You're hoping you win the auction this weekend."

She smiled. "I'm going to win." That she had no doubt about. It was everything that came after that left her a little on the uneasy side. "We are going to have a date and a few more after."

His jaw bunched and ticked. "Stay here with me until then," he said after a long beat.

* * *

HE SAW THE surprise register on her face before a small smile played on her lips. He shocked the hell out of her with the proposition. That was okay because he nearly toppled over the second the words left his mouth.

She looked at him. Her brown eyes warm and sweet, like hot chocolate on a cold night at a football game. "I'd love to," she said in a whisper.

He nodded and focused on the stack of pancakes, ignoring the way his heart kicked a little. Okay a lot, over the knowledge for the next ten days or so, it was all about Claire.

Fucking heart.

No need wasting any effort of telling the stupid muscle not to confuse good sex, really good sex, great sex actually, with anything else. Not when it came to Claire, with her, sex was always more than just the physical connection.

And Forrest thought he'd been in total control. Well, the joke was on him. In spite of his best efforts to hold back, he fell in love all over again. Let's be honest, he never fell out of love.

Whatever happened to caution?

He had no idea what the hell had come over him. Or why he had a lump the size of a football stuck in his throat.

Scratch that.

He knew exactly what came over him. He shouldn't have gone there. He'd built a wall around his heart, a ten-foot thick, fifty-foot-tall fortress around it with no way in and no way out. For added precaution, he'd built a treacherous moat, ready to swallow any person who dared to try to cross it.

Over and over he told himself he'd never go through what he'd been through again.

Ever.

But then he looked down at his guarded heart and it whispered, *too late*. He'd gone down that slippery road again.

A completely illogical move on his part.

She was going to leave. She had a life in Los Angeles.

He got that. He'd always known Martha's Vineyard was no longer her home. That was the second reason he never pressed for an explanation or pursued anything more.

What would be the point?

She was temporary.

He knew that.

He was a sucker.

He walked right into this one by asking her to stay in his house with him, sharing his bed, every night.

His head spun with confusion. No way in hell should he have suggested something as crazy as sharing the same bed, breathing the same air for the next few days. It was one thing to spend a night here and there until she waved *sayonara*, but instead he threw caution to the wind and jumped into the chasm that was Claire.

The logic of the heart was absurd, but it still took over.

Fuck!

Pressure quickly built in his chest. Claustrophobia reached and grabbed him by the throat. Rising to his feet, he staggered back. "I'm going for a walk."

She quickly stood up. "Oh, let me put on my jeans and–"

"No," he said, a bit too quickly. Her brown eyes widened and he caught hurt in them. Now he felt like a douche. Exhaling, he raked a hand through his hair and tried to calm the fuck down. "I just need . . ." His voice trailed.

What exactly did he need?

Air?

Not the best thing to say to someone who drove in the snow storm twice to be with him, and it showed on her face. "Listen, Claire . . ."

Her hands went up. "It's okay."

But it wasn't. He asked her to stay, and then hurt her.

This was Claire. He loved her. She loved him. It was all over her beautiful face. They managed to touch happiness once more. It might even last for a long while this time around, maybe even forever, or it may pelt them with brief flashes. In either case, they should hold on to it. He shouldn't be freaking out right now. But he'd learned happiness was like water. It always slipped through the hands.

In about ten days she was going to leave again.

And then what?

See her three months from now maybe. Hook up whenever their schedule allowed it. Eventually that would get tiring. With Claire he always wanted that forever . . . infinity.

Meaningless. He'd have to keep things light and not think about possibilities.

It would work.

It would have to.

Otherwise he was fucked.

"I'll be back," he said in a low voice. "And Claire." Their eyes met. "Don't run."

She gave him a slight smile. "I'm not running."

Right. He was. He shoved a hand through his hair and walked out of the kitchen.

CHAPTER TWENTY-TWO

"Follow your heart, but be quiet for a while first.
Ask questions, then feel the answer. Learn to trust your heart."
~ Anonymous

AFTER WAITING ABOUT half an hour for Forrest to return, Claire picked up her phone and sent him a text.

I'm going to Chappy.

Her phone chirped. Forrest's text gleamed on the screen.

Take my truck.

Her hopes dashed. The good feeling from earlier dissipated. Her mind cycled with options of what to do. She could go to him. Finding him wouldn't be a mystery. He'd be by the lake. That was his spot. His serenity. Only she'd been down that road called denial. His mind needed time to accept and understand what his heart already knew.

He loved her. She loved him.

Now fully dressed, she grabbed the key to the Jeep and trudged down the narrow road banked with giant drifts of snow.

The drive to Edgartown was rough and relentless, which made the going slow. Even the ferries to Chappy were working on a late schedule. It didn't matter. Today she was full of patience. There'd be no running on her part.

"I didn't think you'd make it over," her mother greeted with a smile.

Walking into the living room, Claire tried not to make too much of her mother's skin radiating with happiness.

"Is your um . . ." Her voice trailed, not quite sure how to refer to her mother's . . . friend? She looked around the cottage, anything not to focus on her mother's happy smile and luminous skin.

"His name is Ralph."

"Ralph," Claire said, mentally appraising the name. It wasn't bad. From what she remembered, at the potluck the two had danced together most of the night.

"Ralph Parker. So what brought you here? Charles mentioned you stayed in Lake Tashmoo last night. I figure you'd still be there."

"I came to get my bag. I'm going to stay with Forrest."

Her mother arched a brow, a pleased look on her face. "Charles said the two of you might have worked things out."

Claire thought of Forrest's reaction during breakfast. More like they'd merely taken a step in the right direction. "Is there anything Charles doesn't tell you?"

Her mother gave her a coy smile. Something hit Claire. Her mother always had a close relationship with the Montgomery's, especially Charles.

"Mom," Claire started, still processing where her mind was going. "Did you know?"

Her mother busied herself moving around the cottage, picking up two empty wine glasses. "Know what?"

Two physical signs gave Claire her answer. The slight way in which her mother's shoulders went up—her sign of tension, and the fact she kept her gaze focused anywhere but on Claire. Like mother, like daughter, they were both terrible liars.

She slumped on the sofa. "Oh. My. God."

"Now, Claire," her mother started, face serious.

"Please." She put up a hand. "Give me a minute to process this."

After a short silence, her mother cleared her throat and lowered her weight next to Claire. "I've known Forrest was Charles' son from the first day I accepted the job offer to manage this place. It was part of the confidentiality contract."

As a person who lived by the laws of contracts, Claire was all too familiar with confidentiality agreements. At least she knew going in that fame would bring a certain loss of privacy, but the Montgomery's never had a choice. They were born privileged, under the microscope.

The general public harbored no sympathy for the rich and famous. One false move and the tabloids would have had a field day, just as they did with Jason after his mother's death. Except he'd been twenty-five, even then it hadn't been easy for him to understand and process the intrusion. Had the truth about Forrest's parentage become public knowledge while Jason and Forrest were too young and innocent to understand the implications, the effects would have been much more devastating.

Her stomach twisted over the possible circus. On the Vineyard, as locals, they were protected amongst their own–like the Vegas rule. *What happens here stays here.* But that commandment didn't apply off the island.

"Victoria knew?"

"Yes," her mother confirmed in a low voice.

Claire let out a long deep breath, her thoughts on Victoria's troubles. Behind the smiles, the mood swings, laid secrets darker and deeper than the mysterious sea. She struggled with an eating disorder, an unfaithful husband, who fathered a son with his best friend's wife. Jason mentioned his parents argued a lot. Now it all made sense.

Her heart ached for all of them.

"You never told me," she said in a subdued tone, not out of anger or betrayal but more of sadness for everyone involved.

"Darling, first and foremost, this is not my story to tell. Second . . ." She looked intently at her daughter. "Would that have made you love Charles, Jason, and Forrest any less?"

There was no need to answer that. She'd loved all of them, including Victoria. As for Forrest, she'd love him no matter what his last name was.

"I just feel bad for everyone. Those four were so close," Claire said, thinking of the relationship between Forrest's and Jason's parents. "To think they had this secret between them the whole time."

Her mother squeezed her hand. "Forrest needs to speak to Charles and his mother. He can't go on avoiding them." She stood up and walked over to the kitchen. Claire followed. "In the meantime, I'm really glad the two of you have finally decided to open your hearts to each other."

Forrest's heart was still locked up, but no need to get into that. "Baby steps, Mom. I'm going to pack."

"You almost look happy." A smile touched her mother's lips. "Almost there."

Claire's heart squeezed. She was lucky to have an open relationship with her mother. Leaning in, she gave her a hug. "Thank you for all you've given me. I love you."

"I love you too." Her mother pulled her into a hug. "By the way, Ralph is coming to Vapor with me on Friday."

"If he makes you happy then I'm happy. Looking forward to meeting him."

A little before noon, Claire pulled the Jeep into the parking area by the pier. She quickly found a spot alongside the few vehicles of other brave ones who dared to venture out. Other than her squeaky footsteps compressing the crystals beneath her feet, the streets were quiet and deserted. For so long she convinced herself the winter months on the island were dreadful, too dark and desolate, all the shops closed. No life. Unlike the everyday hustle in Los Angeles, Martha's Vineyard had always been too . . . calm. But today, the hush of the town lulled her into a comfort zone.

The little lies we tell ourselves in order to get by. On the island she could be herself, surrounded by friends and family. She was happy here.

She entered Vapor and took a quick inventory of the cramped space. In spite of the pile of snow lining the roads, the bar was nearly packed. This of course was ridiculous because had Minka not sent that group text, Claire wouldn't be out or at Vapor. As much as she loved the owners of the place, she'd much prefer to be back in bed with Forrest right now. But this was the Vineyard. Vapor and the island were salt and pepper, beer and pretzels. One didn't exist without the other. She spotted Adam working the bar, oozing his typical badass vibe. Any hot-blooded woman would see a tall, dark-haired, muscular guy like him and take a second look. But for Claire, Adam, similar to Jason and Blake, had always been in the brother zone.

For all the years she'd known him, he always projected an easy-going, laid-back attitude. Until a few months ago, she never knew how deep his scars ran. But today, he looked genuinely happy and relaxed, an exact opposite of the last image she had of Forrest. His brows pulled together as he struggled with a roller coaster of emotions. In the end he gave into avoidance and walked away. Funny, how the table had turned. Fate had a thousand wiles.

"You look a little . . ." His golden eyes carefully examined her as she grabbed a seat. "Happy and sad at the same time."

"That pretty much sums it up." No point denying the truth, Adam held a Ph.D. in personal struggles. She glanced at her watch. The others would arrive soon, reuniting the group of friends for the first time since Luc's funeral. Except for Forrest, he'd chosen to opt out. The rift in his friendship with Jason, imposed by Forrest, traveled to her heart, crushing her chest.

"Forrest is not coming," she announced. Adam didn't look surprised.

"And I thought I could be an ass."

Asses or not, she loved them all, and this gap in the circle and the origin of it made her queasy. "You can be." She chuckled. "How are you doing?"

"I'm well."

"Still going to counseling?"

He nodded. "Yep. Liliana attends once in a while. It's good."

Like Jason and Blake, Adam had found happiness. It made Claire happy. The circle, though a little larger now with the addition of all of their wives, was still tight . . . somewhat. "I'm so glad you decided to deal with your past."

"Some things we can only avoid for so long. Seltzer?"

"Please."

He filled the glass and stood back. "So why the sad face?"

"I'm in love with him." She had that kind of friendship with all of them where she could bare her soul with no reservation. There was never any judgment, only support and maybe a kick in the ass when necessary, but never judgment.

"Tell me something I don't know."

"I went to his house last night."

His lips twitched into a smile. "In the storm?"

She nodded and gulped down some of the seltzer water.

"What is it about you driving in the storm to be with Forrest?"

She couldn't help but chuckle. "That's funny."

"How's Mr. Crank the Wank doing anyway?"

Claire rolled her eyes.

Adam uncorked a bottle of white wine and grinned. "What? He was jacking the johnson instead of getting laid. Do you know why?" He filled two wine glasses then peered at her. "Because of you. I didn't realize it until the funeral. But it has always been you."

The words made her happy and sad all at the same time. He still loved her—happy. He didn't want to love her—sad. "Good to know."

"So what happened?"

She wrinkled her nose and made a face, to which Adam chuckled.

"Besides the obvious," he added. "Did he pull a switcheroo on you this morning? I can kick his ass."

"He asked me to stay with him until I leave for L.A."

Adam gave her one slow, surprised blink. "That's huge for the big goof."

"I thought so too, but then he basically ran out of the house."

"Good to see he can actually lose his cool." He refilled her glass. "He loves you, Claire. He's had it bad for so long."

"So why the freaking out? I'm thinking we are finally on the same page."

"He just had one of his nuts ripped off, be gentle."

"I know, and I'm trying."

"Daddy issue is a bitch. His is a bit different than mine, but it doesn't make it any less painful. I get it."

"So do I." With the exception of the one picture her mother showed her a long time ago, she had no clue who her father was. It took years for her to accept the abandonment, and probably would take just as long for Forrest to accept the lies, the secrets, and eventually the truth.

Elbows on the bar, Adam leaned forward and looked at her with serious eyes. "Also you're within reach. He can't avoid you anymore." He signaled the waitress to the bar, then focused back on Claire. "In case you haven't noticed, he's big at avoiding shit."

"Like dealing with his mom, Charles, Jason."

"Bingo. And you."

"I'm here."

Adam gave her a sad smile. "You're also leaving."

Leaving the island wouldn't be leaving Forrest, they'd find a way to make things work. Eventually they'd make a decision, but that was down the road. Right now was about the here and now. They'd make it work.

Wouldn't they?

Hope stretched wide.

Forrest's words months ago echoed in her head. *You are temporary.*

A pang hit her right in the center of her chest at the thought of walking away . . . again.

The front door opened, Jason and Minka walked in, arm-in-arm. While Minka appeared visibly shaken, Jason looked completely at ease. Claire's heart clutched and hoped it wasn't bad news. In either case, Forrest's absence dug a little deeper. She wanted him here, with her, with them.

"Hey," Jason greeted and pulled Claire into a hug. "You're filling our bar in two days."

"Sorry about that," Claire replied then gave Minka a hug.

Jason waved her off. "It's for a good cause. We are only giving access to Vineyard Gazette inside though. I hope that's okay."

"Works for me." She turned to Minka. "How did the appointment go?"

Minka and Jason exchanged a look, Jason's face revealed nothing. Why were men so hard to read? The front door opened. Lily, Keely, and Blake entered the bar and joined them. After hugs were exchanged and fist bumps by the guys, they huddled together. She was surrounded by love. A lonely, hollow gnawing gripped at her. Not out of jealousy, these people were under the family label in her life, and she was happy for all of them. She just wanted her own with Forrest.

Slow down, one step at a time. That should be her next tattoo.

"All right, here we are," Blake said, one arm casually slung over Keely's shoulder.

"So," Minka started and pulled at her curls. "We had an ultrasound to confirm our suspicions. We heard the heartbeats."

"Beats?" Keely said with a frown.

Minka handed the sonogram picture to Blake who took one look at it, frowned and passed it around. With the exception of Lily who squealed with glee and pulled Minka in a tight embrace, everyone looked and nodded with a blank look on their faces as if they were looking at an abstract piece of art.

Jason shook his head. "Can you guys read an ultrasound?"

"Nope," Keely responded. "I just see fuzz and two black holes with two dots inside." She grabbed the picture again and her mouth fell open. "Oh, my goodness!"

"Twins!" Lily shrieked, pure delight in her voice.

Adam took the photo and examined it carefully then looked at Lily. "You see two babies there?"

"Of course," Lily responded, then added, "There's two black holes here as Keely mentioned, and . . ." She pointed at the pea size dots in the middle. "These are the little munchkins."

"That's their placenta," Minka informed. "Keely and Lily are right, we're having twins. They are fraternal twins." She glanced at Keely. "I'm not sure if I should cry or laugh."

Keely was the first to move in and hug her sister. "Hey, we were great as children. Mom and Dad said we were ideal twins."

Minka sighed. "I'm a little nervous."

"Right now we celebrate. This is fantastic news," Adam suggested, already filling glasses with each man's drink of choice, wine for Keely and Claire and water for the two pregnant women.

"Says the man who never wanted to have children," Blake reminded his friend. In response, Adam flipped him the bird.

Jason squeezed his wife's shoulder and placed a kiss on her lips. Claire sensed her friend's concern ran a little deeper. Until recently, Minka and Keely's relationship had been tension-filled, more so on Minka's part. The sisters had made great progress but Claire would still put them in the WIP category—Work-in-Progress.

"You have us, Minx," Blake said to his longtime friend. Without Minka, Blake and Keely would have never existed. "As Adam said, this is a time for celebration." He looked around then met Jason's eyes. "Isn't that Forrest's Jeep parked by the pier?"

"I drove it here," Claire answered.

Blake's handsome face fell with disappointment. "Tell him next time we spar, it's a guaranteed ass whooping."

Jason waved it off. "Let him be a dick."

But Claire knew Jason well enough to know he was ticked off by

Forrest's attitude.

By the time she stepped inside Forrest's home, her head was heavy with muddled thoughts. She had to return to her life in Los Angeles. There was a crack in their circle. Dropping her bag in the hallway, she headed to the only room with a television and found Forrest typing away in his MacBook, an opened beer bottle on the coffee table. The television was on but muted. The only audible sound was the crackling of lively flames in the ample fireplace.

He tipped his head in her direction and patted the spot next to him, one hand still typing as he did so. She plopped on the sofa as close as possible so their hips touched.

"You okay?"

"Yeah," she answered, voice low.

His fingers continued to tap on the keyboard. She glanced at the medical jargon on the screen. *In addition to causing arthritis, Lyme disease can also cause heart, brain, and nerve problems.* A silence, neither comfortable nor heavy hung in the air. Then he clicked *save*, powered off the computer, and kissed her, a long, sweet, simmering kiss that left her wanting more.

"Minka and Jason are having twins," she said when they finally broke for air.

"Wow. How is Minka?"

"She's a little shaken."

Forrest nodded in comprehension. The drama between the sisters was well documented within the circle.

"What about Jason? You didn't ask about how he's doing," she asked and held her breath. The room grew still like a cemetery. With a sea of anxiety rocking her belly, she rose from the couch, dusted imaginary lint off her pants and walked across the room. A clear head was essential for this conversation, and sitting next to Forrest, hips touching, no way in hell could she not be sidetracked. "Jason is . . ."

"Let's not go there," he cut her off.

Thoughtfully, she examined his face. His dark hollow eyes showed what he'd been working on—to extract the human from inside of him. "We have to," she whispered.

"Why?"

Their gazes locked. Her frazzled nerves jumped all together, and in different directions. "Because he's your brother. The two of you were brothers even before you knew about Charles."

His gray eyes roved over her, then back to her face, and waited her out with a pointed look.

She drew in as deep a breath as she could and said, "You can't take your anger out on him."

"I'm not angry at Jason. I just don't want to have anything to do with the Montgomery men."

Funny, he was a Montgomery, right down to the stubbornness. "Jason has never done anything to you. He's guilty by association and that's wrong."

Silent as stone. Absolutely nothing.

"You should talk to your mother and Charles."

He shoved a hand into his hair, holding it off his forehead. "Now you're pushing it."

"Don't you want to know the whole story?" There had to be more. She'd seen Luc, Marjorie, Charles, and Victoria together. Something had to happen to bring Marjorie and Charles together.

"I know all I need to know. My mother cheated and Charles is a fucking scumbag."

"You should at least allow yourself a chance to find out the truth." She waited, but he said nothing. Wise thing to do here was probably remain quiet and force him to fill the silence, but her heart was hurting and once in a while everyone needed a good kick in the ass. "Does that mean you're not coming to my show on Friday?"

Forrest slowly stood up from the couch, walked over to where she stood and crowded her both physically and mentally. He put a finger under her chin and brought her face to his.

"Do you want me there?" he asked.

"You know I do."

He leaned in so that his upper body hovered over hers. "Then I'll be there."

For her, Claire noted, he was willing to put everything aside. The nest of butterflies were back in her stomach, trying to make their way out. "Jason will be there."

"I'm bigger than him." A smile lit up his face. "I can handle him."

"You just made me happy."

"I can make you happier."

She arched a brow, daring him to do whatever he wanted. Wrapping an arm around her waist, he dipped and lifted her off her feet.

Claire laughed. "You keep carrying me off to your bed."

His mouth was on the nape of her neck when he let out a low groan and slowly slid her body down against his, inch by inch, allowing her to feel every inch of him. Confused as to why they were not heading to his bedroom, she stared at him.

"Someone is at the door," he explained, voice gruff. "Don't move."

"I'm not going anywhere."

He leaned in for a deep, lingering kiss, muttered, "Give me two minutes." And disappeared. Claire flopped on the couch. Deep in her stomach, her muscles coiled, the tips of her breasts tightened and between her thighs tingled with need. After counting to twenty and no sign of Forrest, she headed to the foyer and came to a screeching halt. Forrest stood, feet planted wide in an aggressive stance that screamed pissed off, his eyes locked in a stare showdown with Charles.

CHAPTER TWENTY-THREE

"Love is of all passions the strongest, for it
attacks simultaneously the head, the heart and the senses."
~ Lao Tzu

CLAIRE FROZE, HER stomach churning over the thick tension bouncing between the two men. She looked at Forrest's stiff posture, so brittle as if one snap would shatter him into thousand pieces. His eyebrows knitted, jaw rooted, seemingly alone with his thoughts while his brain tried to organize the chaos in his life.

He hadn't had time to prepare for his father's death. His mother's confession catapulted him from shock to anger, and it gave him a convenient venue to direct his vexation at the injustice of it all.

They lied to him. Both of them and robbed his father of his place in Forrest's memory.

"I'll go upstairs," she said, wanting nothing more than to wrap her arms around him and give him solace.

"Stay." Forrest said, his eyes never leaving the spot where Charles stood. "Charles is not staying."

"Actually, I am," Charles responded in a surprisingly calm tone. "You're going to listen."

No sign of anger from Charles, but Claire knew him well enough to know his mood was just as pissy as his son's.

"You're not welcome here."

Forrest's voice was stone-hard, it forced Claire to take a step backward. Her eyes flickered back and forth between the two men, the atmosphere becoming more and more tight. A feeling of dread crept from her deepest inside.

"Get off your high horse, son."

"I'm not your son."

Charles walked past Forrest and gave Claire a long, calculating look. "Are you happy with him?"

The question caught her off guard. Of course she was happy. She was finally reunited with the man who owned her heart. They loved each other. Forrest just needed to accept that. But in a few days she'd be back in L.A. dealing with a crazy schedule promoting *Tattooed Hearts* set to release in the summer. Anxiety, the sleeping beast, awakened and filled her mind with uncertainty over their pending separation.

Distance didn't always break relationships. *Right?*

They'd make it work. More importantly she'd come back more frequently.

"Yes," she responded, but she hesitated. Forrest noticed, so did Charles. He glared at his son with cold, steady eyes.

"All your life, you've only cared about two women," Charles said, "You're going to lose them both."

"I don't need advice from you."

Father scoffed.

Son sneered.

They stood in their grandeur, angular jawlines hard as rocks. The resemblance wasn't striking, but it was there. Claire's stomach bubbled with uneasiness.

"Starting tomorrow you need to go to Herring Creek on a regular basis to check on your mother," Charles said, his voice filled with the authority he exuded as soon as he walked in a room. Another trait his son inherited from him.

"Don't you do that?" Forrest asked.

"You are her son! Her only child. Stop being a fucking asshole!" Charles' booming voice bounced off the walls and echoed down the hall.

Claire winced. Forrest's eyes narrowed at the man in front of him, and she knew from the dark, burning glare in his graphite depths that he was very, very angry, and ready to take on his biggest foe. A total shift, because he used to love Charles. He still did. Otherwise, the cut wouldn't run so deep. But she knew from experience Forrest's world had no grayscale, only polar extremes.

"Seriously . . ." Forrest shoved a hand through his hair. "You're the last person to call someone an asshole."

"I came here to talk to you. But you have this way of irritating the crap out of me."

"The feeling is mutual."

"I slept with your mother once. It's not something I'm proud of, but I don't regret it either because I care about Marjorie." He paused, shoved a hand through his hair.

Like father like son.

"We created you in the process," Charles said in a gentler tone.

"Fate is a bitch."

Claire stared at the floor.

"Are you still with her?" Forrest asked.

"What is it about once that you don't understand?" Charles challenged in rushed speech, his frustration on full display.

An awful, massive silence hung in the air. It made Claire's blood as cold as the wintry air that crept through the open door. She walked past the two men, still locked in a staring duel. Other than the rhythmic *thunk-tap* of her boots striking wood and the creak of the door closing, there was absolute stillness.

"When it comes to you and Jason, at times I feel as if I'm speaking to five-year-olds," Charles said, snapping the silence.

"It could be because you're such a great role model," Forrest spat in disgust. "Let's see, you slept with your supposedly best friend's wife and cheated on your wife twice."

Charles' jaw clenched. "Leave Victoria out of this. In spite of everything, I loved my wife."

"You cheated on her with her best friend," Forrest countered, disdain filled his voice. "Did she know?"

The room fell into a deafening silence.

"She committed suicide because of you," Forrest continued, his voice brutal and accusing.

Charles clenched and unclenched his fist.

Claire's heart froze and her stomach turned icy. "Forrest, stop!"

"Stay out of this, Claire." Forrest took a step forward to Charles.

"This is between us, isn't it *Dad*?" His voice grated on the *Dad* part.

She sucked in a breath and stepped in between the two men. "No." Her eyes darted between them, rage and frustration on full display. The sight made her heartsick.

"What are you doing?" She ran a hand over Forrest's uncompromising jaw. "You're not a cold, ruthless person. You've never been. Don't let anger change you into someone you're not."

Charles let out an impatient snort, drew in a breath and released it before speaking. "That day your mother came to the house to speak to Victoria but she wasn't home. I noticed how upset Marjorie was so we started talking." He stared at his son. "That's when I learned Luc couldn't have children."

"So you stepped in. Very honorable of you."

Frustrated, Claire threw her hands up and stepped back.

"Your father was a brother to me," Charles said in a heavy voice, ignoring Forrest's snarky comment. "I never meant to betray him. When I found out your mother was pregnant of course we told Luc the truth, but he asked that I let him raise you as his son." Charles let out a deep breath. "And so I did."

Luc knew all along Forrest had not been his son.

The news passed through her like a hurricane, its scythe blade tearing down everything in its path including Forrest. She watched the rapid rise and fall of his chest as he processed the information. His hands clenched and unclenched.

Charles, with all of his flaws, had always shown love to the boys and her. To step aside and let someone else raise the son he obviously wanted. The thought made her shudder.

"Not because I didn't want you," Charles said delicately. "I sacrificed what I wanted so I could give my friend, my brother, what he wanted most and couldn't have." His voice thick with emotion. "You made him happy. So I gave you up, but for thirty-one years, every second, I wanted to be a part of your life. I wanted to be your father."

* * *

CHARLES' WORDS RAINED down on Forrest with the fury of a hail storm. Waves of deep, stabbing agony forced his abdominal muscles to contract painfully. He deliberately kept his gaze off Charles, couldn't bear to look his way, because if they made eye contact Forrest's esophagus might close with disgust. Total disgust. And denial.

His once-sunny childhood memories forever tarred, disfigured into something grotesque. His brain, a violent whirl of stupidity, sought to discover a way to control the capriciousness of the situation.

Forrest's immediate reaction was to flee, and forget the pain that crushed and claimed his body for its own. He looked at Claire. She heaved a sigh. A frown settled between her brow, and regret came to him in this quiet moment. He now understood all the reasons why she ran that night. The saddest thing about betrayal was that it never came from those perceived as enemies. And though his brain knew all of this, his subconscious remained stubborn in its attempt to protect and ensure survival.

"You should leave," he said to Charles.

"You don't need to take over the farm. Your father . . ." Charles started and stopped. "Luc," he corrected, silently claiming his rightful place. "He had workers. They still come around, but your mother misses you. Talk to her," he said gently, his voice filled with emotion. "And when you're ready to speak to me, you know where I live." He headed to the door and stopped. "I want to build a relationship with you, but I won't force it. I understand your anger." He glanced over at Claire then back at Forrest. "Take care of her. She loves you."

It wasn't until Charles closed the door behind himself that Forrest drew in a steadying breath, then slowly let the air out of his lungs. "I'm going to do some work."

Claire took a few steps forward and closed the space between them. "I love you," she whispered and lit a spark in his dark and empty heart.

Her chestnut eyes blazed down to his mouth, then back up and locked with his. A feeling surged through him that felt startlingly like relief. And need.

So much fucking need.

"You should go upstairs and lock that door," he said because no way in hell was he going to manhandle her again.

"Why?" she asked in a way too sexy voice.

"Because I'm one pissed-off asshole right now. And if we do

anything, it will be pure fucking." He raked a hand through his hair. "But I get it. I know how that makes you feel, so—"

She caught his hand. Her eyes told him she understood and she was here for him, but he refused to take her pity, or worse, make her feel she was his cushion. She was so much more. Standing on her toes, she pressed her lips to his neck, making him suck in a breath.

"God, Claire."

"I'm here for you."

"You're not a cushion."

She didn't speak. Instead she captured his hand and led them back to the family room. She took the remote and turned off the television, then threw some wood in the fireplace. Orange flames celebrated with a wild, flickering dance. She stepped back and kicked off her boots. Her jeans and sweater followed. Forrest stood motionless, powerless, watching as she slipped off her underwear and then stood naked in front of him.

Sparks flared. The infinite love he carried in his heart leaped into a fiery blaze.

"Tell me what you need," she said, voice low.

"You," he said without a beat.

A smile touched the corners of her lips. "Good thing." She tugged on his shirt and pulled it off. Her fingers ran down the center of his chest and lower abdomen to the waist of his jeans and snapped them open. Sliding her hand inside the waistband of his briefs, she wrapped her fingers around his raging erection and squeezed. "I need you too, Doc."

This evoked a rough sound from him. "Kiss me," he almost begged.

"Anywhere?" she asked and dropped to her knees. Her lips were so close to his hardness, he felt the warmth of her breath caressing him.

He was practically vibrating in pure ecstasy. She ran her tongue from the root of his length all the way up in a slow, torturous lick. The act drew out another rough sound from the back of his throat.

Then she took him in her mouth.

Her lips tightly encircled his throbbing erection. All the blood from his body rushed to his cock, thick in her mouth.

His hands automatically fisted in her hair and held. "Fuck, Claire."

She started slowly with the onslaught, teasing, stroking him with her tongue before taking him deep in her mouth.

He hissed, teeth bared.

His body jerked as a tremor rolled down his spine. Hands tangled tight in her hair, his hips bucked, control slipping. Blood pounded in his head. Breath ripped out of his lungs.

He wanted.

He craved.

He needed to be—

In her.

"Not like this." His words came out muffled. His body was tense and ready to explode. "Damn it," he swore and roughly hauled her up.

"What's wrong?" she asked, and licked her swollen lips.

That image didn't help his brain one bit. He groaned and kissed her. "Inside," he said against her lips. "I want to be inside you when I come. When we both come." He broke away to strip out of the rest of his clothes, which he did in less than five seconds.

"But . . ."

"No buts." Dropping to his knees, he brought her down with him and gently pushed her back against the rug before him. He stared down at her in nothing except for the glowing embers licking her skin. Beautiful. So fucking beautiful.

His heart clenched. They grew up together. He'd been her protector, her friend, but his favorite had always been what they were now. Lovers. Owning her heart.

Arms stretched out at her sides, she gave him a smile, her brown eyes melting away all of his defenses. "You said something about fucking."

He removed his glasses and closed his eyes for a second, then brought her into focus. One finger trailed down her stomach to between her thighs and found her warm and wet. She arched her back, already making those noises he loved. When he slid a finger inside her delicate spot, she gasped and opened her legs wider for him.

Pulling him to her, she kissed him, and he let himself sink into the kiss, into her, willingly drowning in her heat.

"This is beyond fucking," he said against her lips. Cradled by her open thighs, he lost himself inside her. "So much more."

She moaned his name and nothing had ever turned him on more than this woman, and how she was with him. His. Their chemistry staggered him. It stole his breath and annihilated his heart. She was de-signed for him, and he for her. Cupping her sweet ass, he thrust into her slow and steady, and for the first time in over a month his world started to make sense.

Everything felt right. It wasn't about regrets, the years lost, or any of the other shit going on around him.

It all came down to Claire. As it always would.

He wanted their infinity. He wanted to be with her. Talking, touch-ing, fucking—whatever—a home, family, love—anything. He wanted it all with her. She'd become his sanctuary. His . . . *everything.*

"More," she said in a soft, throaty voice. "Please." Accompanying this sexy little please, she made a restless circular motion and lifted her hips so that he could sink in deeper.

Shit! That felt good. He groaned. "Do that again."

She writhed against him and he lost the tenuous grip on his control.

He could run for miles, spar with Blake for hours and not feel the exertion much. Now in her arms, buried in her body, his breath was coming in ragged pants. He reared up on his hands, back arched to get as deep as he could as he began to move. When she cried out his name, begging for more, he gave it.

"So good." His mouth found hers, swallowing her cries as he thrust into her. A little gasp escaped her lips. He loved it. Running a hand under her knee, he lifted her leg up to wrap around him so he could get even deeper. She stayed right with him as he claimed her.

He moved harder and faster inside her. Their ragged breathing melded. Their bodies molded, becoming one, her hips moved with his, urging him on. She felt so fucking good.

"Oh, Forrest," she cried and clenched around him, nails digging into his shoulders as she exploded.

Watching her in her throes sent him spiraling. A rush of hot pleasure raced through his body so fiercely that his arms trembled. He dropped his head with a rough groan, burying his face in the curve of her neck as he completely lost himself.

In her.

So good. That was his only thought as he went flying higher than he'd ever been. *So good, so damn fucking good . . .*

CHAPTER TWENTY-FOUR

"To hide the key to your heart is to risk forgetting where you placed it."
~ Timothy Childers

TWO DAYS LATER after basking in the essence of Claire, Forrest entered his parents' house and headed down the hall to his father's office. Not that he actually listened to Charles. He was here because no matter what, Marjorie was his mother.

On top of that, he had questions.

He needed answers.

Avoidance, the maladaptive coping mechanism that worked so well for him after Claire left, wouldn't provide a solution. Learning that his father had known all along about the details of his mother's pregnancy and asked two people to make an immeasurable sacrifice plagued his mind.

He pushed the office door open and flipped the light switch, bringing life to the otherwise noiseless room. He glanced around. Everything was still untouched. Several stacks of paperwork, pens in a tin on the mahogany desk, floor-to-ceiling bookshelves with books leaning against one another in the same direction.

Everything was neat. In order. Just like Luc had been.

His gut tightened. Memories awakened, echoes of his youth jarred his mind. Suddenly swimming once more in the tide waters of the past, he took urgent strides toward his father's library bursting with books and photo albums, and scanned the collection. Luc had been one of the last ones standing who still loved the touch and feel of a picture instead of storing them in the cloud where they eventually became an afterthought. He passed that appreciation on to Forrest.

Right now, he desperately needed memories of the man he loved and admired to stay with him, to soothe him, because the bad ones threatened to erase all traces of the things he held dear. Snatching three photo albums in no particular order, he walked over to the pristine desk with the attitude of a soldier returning to the battlefield. He sat on the swivel chair, gave his glasses a little push up his nose, and opened the first book.

He flipped through the first album and stopped at a picture of his mother cradling him, a smile of joy on her lips. He couldn't have been more than two, his head covered with a thick mass of dark, wavy hair. Luc and Charles were by her side, their index fingers clutched in Forrest's chubby hands, faces beaming with delight. No sign of tension, jealousy, or betrayal.

Sorrow reached inside and pulled his guts out with bare hands. The cadence of his heart picked up momentum.

Ignoring the palpitations, he turned the page. Another picture caught his eyes, this one he remembered as if it was taken yesterday. He'd been six at a family vacation with the Montgomery's in Majorca with the Mediterranean Sea in the background. Subconsciously, he wiggled his toes in his boots. He could still hear the waves of the ocean and feel the sand coating his toes. Once again, his eyes were drawn to the picture of Jason and him sitting between Charles and Luc, staring at the sea. Unbeknownst to them, his mother had captured the shot. Victoria had stayed behind in the house.

Clear, episodic memories flashed in his mind, kindling mental images of a time gone. He pressed on and flipped through each album, closely analyzing each print. Kindergarten graduation, birthday parties, all the major events of his formative years, Charles was always within his peripheral vision. Forrest never made much of it since Jason and he were the same age, attended the same school until college, it made sense to always have both of their fathers around. But there were those moments, his college graduation, medical school graduation, his time at the Montgomery compound at Charles' request.

Vivid, clear-edged memories of his life spiraled in pattern. Each one consisted of minute details of Charles in some form or another. Even when he thought of Claire, it came back to Charles, all the way down to his middle name.

Everything in his life came back to Charles Montgomery.

His godfather.

He chuckled at the irony. The lie of the role.

In retrospect Charles was always around, in the shadows, looking furtively through a narrow opening. Close but never close enough.

Pain throbbed violently around his skull, like a toothache in his brain, right between his eyes. Forrest took off his glasses and rubbed the middle of his forehead. His mind running wild with *What ifs*.

What if his father had left his mother?

What if Charles had left Victoria?

What if his mother had married Charles?

What if they had told him the truth from the get go?

What if . . .

His head hurt.

"This is for you." His mother's voice interrupted his thoughts.

He looked up at her. She appeared better than last time he saw her. Her gray eyes had a little more life, almost as if she had accepted fate and was finally moving forward.

He took the envelope she held out to him. "Thanks."

"Rosa told me Claire has been staying with you."

He nodded. "She has."

His mother smiled. "You've forgiven her. Perhaps one day you can forgive me."

"I understand why she left. I don't understand all of this."

She glanced at the envelope in his hand. "It's from your father. Luc," she added for clarification.

None was needed. In his heart, Luc would always be his father.

"I've wanted to give this to you, but you've been so angry."

Discovering your life was filled with lies and secrets tended to do that to a person. But he pursed his lips and kept his temper in check He watched her walk to the door. She had the posture of a ballet dancer—strong, erect, and graceful. At the door, she stopped and turned to look at him once more. The residue of regret flickered in her eyes. It made his heart ache because as Charles said, there were two women he'd loved unconditionally. One was at Vapor practicing for her event tonight and the other was staring at him. "Do you need help with anything?"

A smile touched her lips. "No. Everything is in order."

He almost laughed at the contradiction of the word, because nothing in their lives was in order. "I'm going to start coming here every day if you need anything."

She nodded. "Yes, Charles told me about that."

"He did, huh?" The man was full of himself, a trait that always annoyed the hell out of Forrest.

"Forrest . . ." she started in a pleading voice.

He put up a hand. "No need to explain."

She nodded. "Should I make us a late lunch?"

He had a lunch date with Claire, but he studied his mother, and decided if things went right, he'd have a lifetime with Claire. All the pieces once scattered seemed to have glued back together. Except the *she's leaving again* bit, but he was still trying to figure out where that piece might fit in the puzzle.

Could he ask her to stay?

Would that be selfish on his part?

What if she said no?

His stomach tightened into a series of rolling knots. Not wanting to examine his situation with Claire too closely, he decided they had time. A full week.

The anger he'd carried was weighing him down. That he needed to deal with immediately. For starters, work on mending the broken relationship with his mother. "I'll be there in a little." Once alone, he sent a text to Claire.

Have to cancel lunch. Still at the farm. See you back at Lake Tashmoo.

Her response came quick.

Everything okay? Need me?

A smile touched his lips. He'd always need her.

All's well. See you at home.

After a minute of silence to garner his strength, Forrest opened the envelope and pulled out the folded paper. He put on his glasses, and brought the words into focus.

Dear Forrest,

My mouth tastes of sadness as I write this note. My eyes are full of tears because the day you read this means I am no longer around. It also means you have found out I am not your biological father.

First and foremost, please accept my most sincere apology for withholding something like this from you for so long. You're my son. I love you. I carry you in my heart. I am so proud of the man you've become.

I hope you can continue to love me, carry me in your heart, and stay proud of me.

Like everyone else, I wasn't perfect. Actually, I could be inconsiderate and when it comes to you, my only concern was my own personal pleasure. Call me selfish because no matter from which angle you look at it, I robbed a man, a friend, of a chance to raise his son. I didn't even do it out of spite. While I was angry over what occurred, I learned to forgive . . . because of love. I love Charles like a brother. I love my wife. They both love me.

'To err is human; to forgive, divine.'

It is natural to make mistakes and it is important to forgive people when they do. We made a mistake by not telling you everything, but alas we are only humans.

Charles loves you. He always has. Your mother loves you. I love you.

Quite a conundrum, don't you think? For one person to be surrounded by so much love, to have two fathers, a best friend who happens to be his brother.

From what I know of my son, I am sure your world has been rocked. Like me, you like order and control. I ask that you let go. Stop overthinking. You can't control everything. Sometimes not being in control is the most beautiful thing in the world.

It was selfish of me to ask Charles to let me raise you as my own and never gave him a chance to be the father he wanted to be to you. From time to time I'd catch the longing in his eyes, but you know Charles. He's a man of steel.

The greatest sacrifice is when someone forfeits his own happiness for the sake of someone else. Giving up a child he obviously wanted was the ultimate offering to cheer my heart. I know he did it out of guilt over what happened with Marjorie, but he also wanted to give me the one thing I desired most and could never have on my own. A child. That my son is the ultimate gift.

I ask that you eventually forgive each one of us. Remember forgiveness doesn't excuse our behavior, but it will prevent our behavior from destroying your heart.

I love you . . .

Aujourd'hui, Demain, Toujours.

Your father.

Since his whole body was shaking, he dropped the letter on the desk and stared at it until he couldn't anymore. Then in choked desolation, he buried his face in his hands.

CHAPTER TWENTY-FIVE

*"When confronted with a challenge, the committed heart will
search for a solution. The undecided heart searches for an escape."*
~ Forrest Montgomery Desvareaux

FORREST PUSHED AND shoved through the endless sea of people
to the back of the room where his friends stood watching the madness.
Leaning on the wall next to Adam, he scanned the cramped space. The
atmosphere was one of elation—infectious grins, longtime friends and
strangers shaking hands, patting one another on the back.

"This is crazy," he said, not speaking to any one in particular.

Adam laughed and tightened his grip around his very pregnant wife.
"Your girlfriend is a star. People love her."

"Is this your first time seeing Claire in action?" Lily asked, tucked
safely in Adam's arms.

Forrest started to shake his head, but other than the few highlights
he caught on television, this was his first time getting an intimate view of
Claire's world. "I guess it is."

Keely leaned into him so that she could be heard over the strident
timbre of voices. "You're in for a treat. She's awesome live."

Jason appeared on the stage. Palpable excitement zapped through
the air, electrified buzz of voices charged the room. His friend raised a
hand, commanding attention. A hush fell over the crowd.

"This is a great night, not only for Vapor, but for Martha's Vineyard,"
Jason said into the microphone. "For the first time Claire Peters is performing on the island. Let's show her some love and welcome her
home."

A cacophony of applause burst forth.

"Ladies and gentleman, I give to you my friend, my sister, the talented and beautiful Claire." Jason's voice thundered over the crowd.

Anticipation hung in the air. The lights dimmed. Cheers erupted like an auditory volcano. Smoke twisted on the stage, forming wispy curls in the half-lit room. Forrest's eyes glued to the podium. She appeared, illuminated only by speckled lights from the ceiling. All quieted. Forrest's heart smashed around in his chest.

She took a step forward, hypnotizing the crowd in a deep, plunging dress that barely covered her ass. She looked sexy hot and every bit the star she was. Head high, she scanned the crowd then gave a slight bow. Another round of acclamation started and the crowd began to chant her name.

She owned the room.

Hard to believe this was the same woman who had her hands pressed on the floor-to-ceiling window in his living room less than one hour ago. With the ocean as their view, he had scraped her thong to the side for quick access and dived home. *Heaven on earth.* Forrest shifted and told his other head to calm down. This was going to be a long night.

"Thanks, Jay!" Claire and Jason hugged before he walked off the stage and gave her the full spotlight. She turned to the jubilant crowd and let out a little laugh. The sound was sweet and joyful. It echoed through the room and into everyone's heart. "What a welcome. A big thank you to Tyler for asking me to do this."

The audience cheered, as if they were forever grateful to Tyler for bestowing such a gift upon them. Forrest told himself Tyler had nothing on him when it came to Claire.

"It's so good to be here. I have no words." Her right hand went to her heart. She closed her eyes for a second, taking it all in. A spontaneous outpouring of emotion etched on her face. She looked happy.

The sight made the hair on the back of his neck prickle. Overwhelmed with emotion, he stood rooted to the spot and took in Claire, the famous singer.

"As some of you may know, I have this thing for eighties and nineties music."

Whooping and hollering followed.

She laughed.

The sound was so sweet.

"My last album was a nod to those two decades. I'm going to do a few numbers for you tonight."

She was forced to pause again by another round of clapping.

She raised her index finger and leaned into the microphone. The room went still. "And give you a glimpse of the theme song for my movie *Tattooed Hearts* coming out this summer. It's still rough." She wrinkled her nose. "But I love it and would love to share it with you all."

They waved and shouted like maniacs.

"It will have to be acoustic though, just me and a guitar," she continued. "Think you can handle that?"

Another massive round of applause. They were hungry for excitement and were putty in her hands, him included. She had this quality about her that mesmerized people. Even during their youth, she hadn't been aware of it, but it had always been there. Now a woman filled with confidence, it was more transparent. From the way she kissed him after reading Luc's letter, to how she gave all of herself to him in every way.

"Watch this," Blake said to him. "You're going to fall in love."

Too late. Already there, neck-deep in love.

Her fingers wrapped around the microphone, a smile appeared on her lips and then she started belting out the lyrics to *Hopeless* by Dionne Farris. Her voice was smooth, clear, quiet yet powerful as she sang each word. It carried a level of sadness, a longing, drugging everyone. She sang her own cover of *Iris* by Goo Goo Dolls, *Don't You Forget About Me* by Simple Minds, and *Ordinary Love* by Sade. All without a crack or flaw. Then she brought Amber on stage as promised and they sang *I Feel for You* by Chaka Khan and two of her own songs. The tempo to those songs was a bit more upbeat. An excitement rushed through the room, like liquid adrenaline being injected right into everyone's bloodstream–not strong enough to freak them out, but an adequate amount to make them feel the vibe of the music and let their body go free.

When Claire requested, they joined in the fun and sang along. The few faces Forrest was able to see grinned like idiots. They sang a few of their favorite lines completely out of tune but in joyful harmony. No one cared how they sounded, they were happy. And so was Claire.

She laughed, moved rhythmically to the music and played along. She looked pumped, excited, and more alive than he'd ever seen her.

It was as if all the mundane worries of her life had been muted and all there was to know about was . . . this moment. No worrying about the past, no anxiety about the future. Eyes wide, grin wider, in one adrenaline-fueled warrior yell, she jumped off the stage into the crowd.

Forrest's body automatically moved in the direction of the stage, his brain fast forwarded to protective mode, needed to be sure she would not be crushed. But Jason grabbed his shoulder and held him still.

"She's fine. This is what she does. This is who she is. Relax."

She gave herself to the crowd and the crowd gave back to her. Forrest took it all in.

It was magical. One moment, one brilliant feeling of togetherness between Claire and her fans suspended in time. Ten years or a lifetime from now, he'd remember tonight and the way she looked in her element. It was a circuit of energy—music, friends, good times, dance.

This side of her didn't belong on the island.

"All right! Are we having fun?" she asked the pumped crowd. Her voice pulled Forrest's attention back to the stage.

"Claire! Claire! Claire!" They roared.

"I love you!" Someone declared.

"Have my baby!" Another one proposed.

Claire laughed. "We're going to take a quick ten. Be right back."

Adam, the asshole that he'd always been, leaned into him and said, "They want your girl. You better do something about it."

The fucker. "Shut up," he replied without a glance at his friend.

Adam laughed, clearly enjoying his distress.

During the intermission, Jason managed to join them. He took one look at Forrest and shook his head. "Still got a stick up your ass?"

"Probably forever," he responded. No point in lying. His mind was still surging with perplexity. But his friendship with Jason should have never been tested . . . on his part. Anger was a powerful tool. "Congrats on the babies," he offered, man-code for saying *I'm sorry, I've been a dick.*

Jason nodded, seeming to accept the apology. "Ready to play uncle?"

"Do I have a choice?"

"Not from where I'm looking."

"Then I'm ready." They stared at each other for a second or two, neither willing to put their Alpha card away. "How's Minka?" he asked, initiating a conversation, silently folding. Since he'd been the asshole, it was only right.

"Nauseous."

"That will pass in a month or two."

Jason shoved a hand through his hair. "You should tell her that."

"Ah, the Wolf Pack all together again."

All heads turned to Claire. She was still smiling and so fucking beautiful that Forrest pulled her into his arms and kissed her. When he finally let her go, she let out one of her little laughs and touched her lips.

"Claiming her?" That came from Adam.

Since Adam's favorite display of affection was to give one of them the finger, Forrest flipped him the bird. "You're awesome live." He pulled her in and hugged her, pressing his jaw to the top of her head.

"Thanks. I have to go back for the big finale." She tiptoed in for a kiss. "I love you, Doc." The words slipped out of her mouth as a whisper.

He opened his mouth to reciprocate, but he tensed. A ball slammed against his chest. To feel and know you love someone is one thing. To give it life and utter the words was another. Especially after realizing there was a whole side of Claire Peters that neither of them had brought up. Like the elephant in the room–an obvious truth they'd shimmied around and ignored.

She was leaving.

She was a star.

She belonged on the road.

She was temporary.

The realization sank deep in his hollow gut.

His lungs screamed for air, then she kissed him again and gave him air before slipping back into the throng of people waiting to touch Claire Peters, the one that belonged to the world.

Blake gave him a shove, snapping him back to reality.

"What was that for?"

Blake chuckled. "You look like a lost puppy. Man up."

"Fuck off. All of you." Not in the mood to deal with his friends' shit, he slid them a look then squared his shoulders a little more to keep them at bay. After they choked out a low laugh, they retreated and refocused their attention on the woman responsible for all of his angst.

Somehow she managed to make her way through the crowd and back to the stage. One of the musicians handed her a guitar. Even before she spoke, everyone went quiet, as if they knew what was coming next.

"You see, I came back to the Vineyard for two reasons." She addressed the starving spectators. "One was because I couldn't write this song to save my life. My creativity well was dry. And the other . . ." She exhaled.

Forrest could see her eyes searching for him. When their gazes entwined, she smiled. A smile just for him. His heart swelled. His friends, brother included, chuckled.

"The other . . ." She broke their connection and dragged her attention away and focused on her fans. "Well . . ." She smiled again. "Love is a funny thing. Wouldn't you say?" His heart pounded fiercely in his chest. She sat on a stool and grabbed the guitar. The musicians faded in the background. "Ladies and gentlemen, *Tattooed Hearts*."

The lights dimmed for the second time in the night, and a bright spotlight was put on her face. Smoke danced in the bottom of the floor to the stage, tricking the eyes to believe she was nothing but a shadowy figure. Like everyone one in the room, Forrest stood still in an altered state of consciousness.

She inhaled deeply, savoring the moment, and started to sing.

In the arithmetic of love, one plus one equals everything,
And two minus one equals nothing.

Front and center was Claire's primal voice. A mixture of soul and blues, it was dark, guttural, and romantic.

It is a cruelty of life that a heart can keep on beating even after it has been broken in two.

Her voice trailed . . . weak and defenseless. Her fingers moved along the strings and produced a sweet refrain that spoke a musical language to the soul. Forrest stood a little straighter, her words flowing through him.

It can feel as though it is being gripped in an ice-cold vise,
and ache as if it will implode in your chest,
but still the boom-boom continues.

The strumming sound had a hypnotic soothing quality that Forrest craved.

I never said what I wanted to say, but I fell for you harder than a slip on
black ice.
I wish I could turn the clock,
I would have never left and would have loved you longer.
It was always you . . . Can't fight these feelings for you.
I came back for you,

She looked emotionally wounded. Her voice turned from delicate to fierce in an instant. Dark and painful. It sent goosebumps down his spine.

I opened my mouth . . . nervous about what would come out,
But then I saw your face and all of my worries escaped me . . . because . . .
Well . . . your name is tattooed in my heart.

Her voice carried around the room in waves, feathery as she sang the lyrics. Each word framed in vulnerability but strong, at the same time. There were no victims in the song. It was a metaphor for first love, in all its intensities.

When she stopped singing, there was a brief silence, like an indrawn breath, as if everyone could still hear the last vocal her lips touched. Then there was a massive round of applause, praising and raising the roof a few inches.

"Looks like you're seeing Claire for the first time." Jason patted him on the back then headed back to the stage.

Once there, Jason pulled Claire into a bear hug, a proud smile on his face. The sight did something to Forrest's heart. Not out of jealousy or envy, but admiration of the depth of their friendship.

"Isn't she awesome?" Jason asked into the microphone when he finally stepped away from Claire. A rhetorical question of course, but the spectators hailed their approval.

"And a big thank you to Amber for helping us rock the house," Claire added, a reminder she had a special guest. "I convinced Jay and Adam to give me a few minutes to sign autographs, take pictures and all of that stuff. So come on over, but don't trample me. I have a big bodyguard in the back of the room. Right, Forrest?"

She called him out, which had his heart go into a funny little beat in his chest. Her minions turned, followed her gaze and appraised him. Even the fuckers he'd known all of his life seemed to be pondering if he was good enough for their Claire.

It took longer than Forrest anticipated to exit Vapor. Everyone wanted a piece of the woman he couldn't wait to get in his bed, under him, on top of him. Whatever—he desperately needed to touch and kiss every inch of her. Maybe it was because a part of him tonight felt her slipping away once more, only this time she wasn't running. She had become so much more than the girl he fell in love with eons ago.

Hands weaved together, they made their way to his Jeep. Camera flashes popped from every angle, almost blinding him. Questions were thrown at them.

Is this your boyfriend, Claire?
Are you Mr. Peters?
Is it true the two of you are getting married soon?
A close source said you're pregnant. How far along are you?

She felt small around him, but not from fear or vulnerability. Quite the opposite, she seemed in total control. He squeezed her hand, more so for his own reassurance, and opened the door for her. They drove in silence. Her head thrown back, eyes closed.

"You were great tonight," he said, much more mildly than he felt.

In his peripheral, he caught her turn to face him. Taking his eyes off the road for a second, he allowed himself to drink her beauty. She took one of his hands and pressed her face into it. "Do you ever wish you could freeze a moment?"

Them. Forever. Forrest clenched his jaw. "Yes."

"What's yours?"

He had so many, most of them involved her. "Tonight, watching you perform."

"Having you there made it special. You made me high."

She closed her eyes again. She appeared content, at peace. Something buzzed. From the corner of his eye, he watched her fumble through her tiny purse and pull out her phone. A little gasp escaped her lips.

"What's going on?"

"I need to go back to L.A."

He glanced at her pinched brow. A heavy weight settled in the pit of his stomach. This was ridiculous. He knew she eventually had to leave. "When?"

"Tomorrow. As soon as I can," she whispered.

He nodded. He understood. She was temporary. He knew that all along.

"I'm getting a humanitarian award," she explained. "I need to be there."

He nodded again.

"Forrest."

A muscle twitched involuntarily at the corner of his right eye. "Claire."

"Come with me."

The sound of her voice, almost pleading, made his heart squeeze hard. He glanced at her for a quick second. "What?"

She shifted her body so that she was looking at him. "I have to attend this event. I can't skip this. Just for the weekend. We go tomorrow and return Sunday night." She let out a deep breath. "Come with me. I'm not ready to let you go."

"The weekend," he said, mentally giving consideration to her invitation. What could go wrong with spending a night in her world? Of course, this would only delay the inevitable. But his heart, locked up for so long, now high on Claire wanted a little more.

"Yes."

Emotions tugged at his heartstrings. A little voice told him to bolt, to run, to get the fuck away. They had an expiration date and this trip might be it. Instead, he took her hand and brought it to his lips. "All right.

I'll get a ticket when I get home."

"No need. I'll have my assistant arrange everything. Thank you."

He peered at her again. A faint smile touched her lips. She looked relieved as her fingers texted away. So was he, at least for now because with a grim sinking feeling in his gut, he also wasn't ready to let her go.

CHAPTER TWENTY-SIX

"Keep some room in your heart for the unimaginable."
~ Anonymous

CLAIRE STEPPED INSIDE the chic lounge. And just like that, she was back to the life she walked away from a month ago. It felt strange being here after so long, as if she no longer belonged in the city of dreams, the City of Angels. A city blessed and cursed with a glorious dream and façade of hopes.

Her place of residence for the last six years.

While she liked living here, she hadn't missed it. Thoughts of her life here surfaced once or twice, but nothing that sent her spiraling or wishing she'd been here instead of the Vineyard with friends, family, but most of all with the man standing quietly by her side.

She glanced at Forrest. His face revealed nothing. If ever there was such a thing as a fairy godmother, she'd wish for the ability to penetrate his thoughts. Maybe obtain the superpowers of Jean Gray or Professor X just so she could get a peek of his mind.

Dressed in dark denims, a white button down, and a navy blue blazer, he appeared relax and in total control. But she knew he was taking in every detail of the environment. The luxury four-story apartment house was the epitome of L.A. living. The Wetherly House featured stunning interiors with sophisticated open spaces and clean contemporary lines, theme-centric artwork everywhere. The sixty-five exclusive residences were complimented by stunning views to L.A. Basin, close access to trendy hot spots when one wanted to see or be seen. The building was living elevated to an art.

"Ready?" she asked. The question wasn't particularly addressed to Forrest. If anything, it was an attempt to break the silence between them.

"Let's go." He offered her the typical Forrest smile, captured her hand in his and gave it a light squeeze.

They headed to the concierge to retrieve her mail. On most days, she blended well with everyone. The complex was small, private, and other well-established entertainers either lived there permanently or kept a temporary place for when they were in L.A. But today, a few glances, from men and women, lingered longer than necessary. When they pulled away, it was with obvious reluctance, especially the women. Not that she blamed them. For as long as she could remember Forrest always attracted attention. Why should today be any different?

If anything, she should have expected it. He fit right in and could easily pass for someone in the entertainment industry. Yet, his composure indicated this wasn't his world. Not that he gave any hint of uneasiness. Nope. Not Forrest.

He just . . . well . . . stood out.

Everything about him screamed confidence and in total control.

"Ms. Peters," the attractive clerk said with a smile. Her gaze flicked over to Forrest for a beat too long, then back to Claire. "Your assistant," she stared, stopped to clear her throat. "Your assistant asked us to hold some communications here for you," she continued and handed a thick yellow envelope to Claire.

"Thanks, Julie."

"Welcome home. We missed you here," she said, visibly struggling not to stare at Forrest.

She smiled, but inside her heart faltered. The Wetherly House had never been home, but it was her reality. Forrest had officially entered her world. He got a peek of who she'd become during the performance at Vapor, but to be here fully immersed in her element meant he was about to get a full view. Not that she had anything to hide, but insecurities crept. What if *Claire Peters the Star* was too much to be with?

Last night had been a glimpse of her lifestyle, not even close to the high-speed pace of her daily grind. She stopped mid-stride and scraped a hand through her hair, suddenly nervous. Forrest didn't hesitate. There was an ease in everything he did. His hand stroked up and down the curves of her back, an attempt to ease away her worries.

"You're nervous," he said, lowering his head so that his lips brushed her ear.

Funny, she shouldn't be. This was her territory. She should feel at ease . . . *at home*. But even the salty air and sand here failed to come close to life on the Vineyard. As for her condo here, it was best classified as a place of refuge after the stress of the day. But her heart—that always longed to be with Forrest. Now he was by her side, taking in everything . . . well, yeah, nervous didn't come close to what she was feeling.

She took a deep breath, and forced herself to move forward. "Um, no . . ." Never mind she visibly jumped at the touch.

"Yeah, you are," he continued. "No need to be. Come on," he nudged her forward. "I want to know all you've become. I love what I've seen so far."

With his words, she felt the heavy weight of tension lift. As soon as she closed the door of her two-bedroom, he put his bag down and dropped his jacket on top of the leather bag. Then he stepped further into the living room and into her world, causing a fleet of nerves to settle in her belly once again.

His gaze swept over the open kitchen sea pearl counters, the custom oak cabinetry with polished chrome. He paused and inspected the vase of fresh yellow flowers James sent over to welcome her back.

"From James."

He nodded. "Your manager?"

"Yes. He plays Charles' role here for me."

A muscle in his jaw ticked, but he said nothing. He took a few steps further inside the living room, lingering over the decorative details fabricated from natural materials carefully chosen by Claire that helped contributed to the understated elegance.

"Your place is beautiful," Forrest noted.

"Thanks. I like it here." That wasn't a lie. It might not be *home*, but a true home was a feeling, not a place.

His eyes stayed on her for a bit. "It suits you."

She pursed her lips, the tone of his voice revealed nothing, but the words failed to come across as a compliment. Her stomach shifted uneasily, anxiety smashed around her inside. She watched Forrest as he walked to the strut bookcase and scanned her pictures. A few highlighted her career, events she attended, there was one with her mother with Charles, another with Keely and the others, and one of her at the farm surrounded with the four of guys. He picked up a picture. A photo of the two of them together at her eighteenth birthday party, her arms linked behind his neck, her face tilted up to his, a smile on their lips. Jason had mailed her the frame picture after she left with a note that simply read: *I hope you don't ever forget what you left behind.*

"Claire," he said turning to look at her. "How did your other boyfriends feel seeing this picture here? I know there were at least two after me."

The thought never crossed her mind. It had been natural to keep the picture on display, a reminder of what she once had and lost. "I never gave it much consideration. Selfish of me."

Nonetheless, it felt good to know he somewhat kept track of her life. The two serious boyfriends he referred to had been nice, kind, and wanted to give her the world. But they failed to emerge and take over the spot Forrest had in her heart. The picture probably sealed her fate with them from the word go.

"Any regrets?"

"No." The only regret she had was the time they'd lost.

After he placed the picture back, he closed the space between them. "I'm sorry. I was so caught up in my hurt that I avoided all you've become. I'm proud and happy for you."

She smiled. "I grew up."

"I've noticed." His eyes were fixed on her. "I've always noticed even when I acted like I didn't," he said, and his voice was deep, with the slightest rasp to it, like velvet that had a rough edge.

That edge sent a charge through her. Or maybe it was his words. "I'm glad you're here with me."

He cupped the back of her neck and pulled her to him. "How much time do we have before the gala?"

Looping her arms around his neck, she pressed against him, loving how strong and hard he felt against her. "I have to get my hair and makeup done. You're coming with?"

"Not to the makeup part, but I have every intention of coming with you," he said with a sexy glint in his eyes.

She laughed, the residual tension of the day easing away. "Then that gives us a couple of hours. How much time do you need?"

"A lifetime," he said, and brushed his lips against hers.

Claire's heart kicked. She told the stupid muscle to calm down. *It's just an expression, not a proposal.*

"But," he continued, his lips now trailing down her neck. "For now a couple of hours will do."

"Bedroom is . . . whoa!" She laughed as he swept her off her feet and into his arms again. "I might get used to this."

He kissed her again. "Not might. You should. Bedroom."

She gestured with one arm then quickly held on to him again and told the angst in her stomach to get the hell out of town. They were going to work out and find their happily ever after. They had to.

HOURS LATER, AFTER spending most of the day in bed with Claire, Forrest's steady gaze stayed on her as she moved about her bedroom. To the naked eye, she appeared so prim and proper in a lacy, knee-length navy dress. Only the sensuously cut silhouettes gave gawkers like him a hint of skin to admire, adding an understated sexiness to the outfit. Her hair, pinned in a French twist, adding a flair of elegance.

She looked sexy and classy in that *I'm-a-Superstar, you can look but can't touch* kind of way.

But he'd touched and he wanted to keep touching, again, and again, until they were exhausted. She slipped into a pair of black pumps with a strap across the top of her feet. He examined the heels; they had to be at least four inches. He never understood why women put themselves through hours in these barely-there stilts, but even he had to admit they made her kick-ass legs look so fucking amazing it made him ache for physical contact once more. When she lowered to fasten the strap, he caught her hand. Her brown eyes smiled at him.

She looked like pure sex.

"Let me do that," he said, and dropped to his knees in front of her. But first his hands skimmed over her hips down her toned legs. As he secured her shoes, she raked her hand through his hair, forcing him to look at her.

"This is pretty sexy," she said in a feathery voice, her eyes now intense and serious.

His heart galloped. Need coursed through his veins. All he wanted was to bury his face between her legs again. But restraint was the most powerful aphrodisiac of all. Slowly his hands glided down her legs and back up again, beneath the skirt of her dress. He squeezed her ass, then rose to his feet.

Forrest blew out a long stream of air. He was officially addicted. Hell, when it came to Claire, he'd been a junkie since puberty hit him. Putting some distance between them, he swore under his breath.

"You said something?"

"No." His voice came out hoarse, making him sound like a backed-up teenager.

She peered at him from over her shoulder, a slight frown furrowed her forehead.

"What?" he asked, buttoning his shirt.

She smiled. "You're nervous."

"I am?" If only she knew where his mind actually was, she'd stay right across the room or risked getting bent over, or maybe lay her on the bed and spread her open. As much as he loved her ass, having her fully exposed for his viewing was by far his favorite. They didn't have much time. The limo was due to arrive soon. Fifteen minutes tops was all he needed and *voila* . . . home sweet home.

She nodded. "About tonight."

He couldn't help but smile. "I'm not nervous."

"Do you want to take two separate cars?"

He knotted his tie then slipped on his jacket. "No. Why are you asking?" Shit. What the hell was he missing here? "Would you rather we take separate cars?"

"No. I just thought maybe . . . you might not want all the tabloids stuff like last night at Vapor. I know that's not who you are," she said, referring to the frenzy the two of them photographed together had apparently caused on social media. Apparently they'd become the latest media darlings.

Neither had checked, but their friends had texted pictures. She was right, he wasn't into any of that. But that was part of who she was. He was familiar enough with the paparazzi from Jason and Adam to know how to handle it. Most of all, that was part of the Claire Peters package.

"I don't mind the media."

"They will dig into your past." There was a careful note in her voice. "About Luc."

He didn't like the idea, but something told him Claire or not, there was no avoiding that hump in his life. That came with being a Montgomery. "I think you might rush the process, but it's unavoidable."

"And you're okay with that?"

He nodded.

She bit her lower lip and didn't look convinced one bit. "So then what's bothering you?"

"I was thinking of how we could have sex again," he admitted.

She arched a brow, her gorgeous lips formed into an *oh*. Then a smile touched her mouth. "So you're okay with us being officially photographed tonight?"

The thought never crossed his mind. "I haven't thought about it. What's the big deal? Someone took a picture of us at the funeral, at Woods Hole, and last night."

He obviously was clueless when it came to the rules of dating someone in the public eye because she gave him that *Oh-you-idiot* smile, and then closed the distance in the room between them in those four-inch heels. He had no choice but to curl his hand around her waist, pull her to him and let her feel the evidence of his nervousness.

"Oh." She blinked. "And I thought you were getting cold feet."

"I'm warm all over."

She cleared her throat. "So you're good with all of this."

As evidence of how good he was with whatever she was talking about, he pressed her a little closer. A little whimper escaped the back of her throat. It pleased him. But he released his grip. "I have a feeling you're trying to tell me something. So explain."

"Well, a picture of you and me together knowing there are going to be tabloids outside in Hollywood terms, it means we're official."

That worked for him. "What's wrong with official?"

"It means we're dating."

"Okay."

"So you're okay with the world knowing you're dating me?"

He pulled her into him again. "While it may crush my playboy status, I think you're worth it and so much more. As a matter of fact, I'll show you how much tonight."

"Promise?" she purred, her eyes twinkling with mischief.

He stepped back just enough to look into her eyes. "I promise." He grabbed her hand. "Come on, let's go. By the way, you look beautiful."

She nuzzled against him. "Thanks, Doc. You look pretty hot in a suit."

He swore. "The word hot or hottie should be expunged from the English language."

She laughed and pinched his ass. "I love you and I'm happy."

"Me too." For the first time in a long time, he meant it.

CHAPTER TWENTY-SEVEN

"My heart waits."
~ Claire Yasō Peters

HER HEART WAS flying and the world seemed to stop. The night had been grand, especially with Forrest by her side. After the award ceremony, they attended the after party–danced and flirted the whole time. A part of her hadn't wanted this dream to end. On the other hand, that meant they'd be on the first flight to Boston tomorrow then catch the ferry back to the island. One more week with Forrest without any interruptions, then time to dance to the rhythm of reality. Claire plopped on the sofa and stared at Forrest as he made his way to her open kitchen. He looked amazing in a suit and tie.

"Have I told you how beautiful you look in a suit?" she asked, her voice doing that breathless thing whenever she was around him.

He shook his head as he poured a glass of water and brought it over to her. "Men aren't beautiful."

She laughed. "Thanks. You don't like hottie, so beautiful it is. And so thoughtful and considerate."

"You make me sound like you have me by the balls."

"Oh, I don't think I can ever have you by the balls, Forrest Montgomery Desvareaux." She took a sip of the water. See, he brought her water, which was thoughtful. A thoughtful man was sexy. "But I know where I'd like to have your balls."

Her phone buzzed. She glanced at the notification and smiled. "I won the bid."

"I owe you a date." He took her feet in his hands and just when

Claire thought nothing could top the night, he started massaging her tired tendons.

Heaven.

Thoughtful. Considerate. Intelligent. A body to die for. A sexy combination of brains and brawn. The glasses were an added oomph. While he could wear contacts or afford LASIK surgery, he chose to wear the spectacles as a badge of honor, with no care whether he was perceived as nerdy. Others' opinions never meant much to him. "God, that feels good." She hadn't realized how bad her muscles ached until he started applying the gentle pressure.

"I know what I'm doing," he said, that sexy gravel in his voice sending a charge through her. "I have trained hands."

"Ah, yes, being a doctor and all."

He laughed. His eyes crinkled in the corners, and the laugh lines on either side of his mouth deepened, stealing her breath. She loved the sound of his voice, fully animated and relaxed. This was the Forrest she'd known and loved all of her life. She closed her eyes and settled into the wonderful way Forrest was loosening her muscles when her phone went off.

An unsettling feeling began welling inside her. It was well past midnight. Unless it was a dire situation, her friends never called her this late, which left the only other person who had free range to contact her at any time. Calls at this time from him always meant drop everything and let's go.

Picking up the phone, she took James' call. "Hi," she greeted her manager in a cheerful voice. Positive energy attracted positive things. Maybe he wanted to tease her again about how she was trending on Twitter. Hope coiled tight inside her.

"You can't return to Martha's Vineyard tomorrow."

Well, talk about straight to the point. Her breath hitched. Before answering the phone, she knew the shrieking sound had reality check written all over it. But her stomach still clenched. "James–"

At the mention of her manager's name, Forrest met her gaze. Something flickered in his, it made her gut clench.

"What's so urgent?" she asked into the phone.

James exhaled on the other end. A sign this wasn't fun for him either. "Production company for *Tattooed Hearts* is on my ass now that you're back. It's almost the end of March, they want their song. Did you write it?"

"Yes," she answered in a choked voice.

"Great. Now you have to record it and Claire, don't forget you were on a promotional tour. You have obligations."

Legal binding obligations that could get her into a prodigious mess, she knew that and had every intention of fulfilling them. It just that. her heart needed to find its home. She peeked at Forrest still rubbing the sole of her feet. He met her gaze and held. His features were blank, but his eyes as always spoke to her. There was something in his—like he knew this would happen. She wouldn't go back with him. Her stomach had dropped to her feet.

"When does my schedule clear?" In the past, she always worked on auto-pilot. Never cared. She never had to.

"End of June."

Claire rubbed her eyes, breaking the contact with Forrest. "That's over three months." Without Forrest.

"I'm sorry," James offered gently. "I caught the highlights on TV. You looked happy tonight."

She had been. A sigh of surrender left her mouth. "I need tomorrow's itinerary. Ava can send everything in the morning."

"Should already be in your inbox."

She shifted uncomfortably on the sofa and pulled herself straighter, inadvertently dragging her legs from Forrest's grasp. He looked on, but made no effort to hold her. Claire's shoulders stiffened with tension. "Thanks," she said into the phone.

"Claire, I'm sorry. I know you're trying . . ."

"It's okay. Thanks, James," she said and disconnected the call.

A heavy silence hung over them. She glanced unceremoniously around the room until her gaze landed on Forrest. Their eyes intertwined. Realization whirled around them. The big elephant they managed to avoid for the little bit of time was fully awake. She sagged back on the sofa and stared at the ceiling.

"You have a life here." He spoke first. His voice was calm as always, but there was an undercurrent now, the slightest tension. Which, coming from Forrest was monumental. "I knew that was part of the deal."

"What does that mean?" she asked and held her breath. A jolt of panic immediately rifled through her entire body.

"It means this is where you belong." He looked at her for a beat. His eyes were pensive, his mouth grim. "I love who you've become, but . . ."

"I belong with you," she interjected, knowing where this was going. But he had it all wrong.

He gave her a long look, then removed his glasses and scrubbed a hand over his eyes. "You belong here."

There was finality in his voice that chilled her bones. He rose from the couch, distancing himself from her—from them. Desperate to hold on, she flung to her feet and grabbed his arm.

"I love you, Forrest. If I have to choose, I'd choose you."

He stepped closer, cupped her face and kissed her long and deep. "You shouldn't have to choose," he said against her lips. "I can never make you choose. I love you too much." He smiled; a joyless smile. "I fell in love with you that day I helped you in the garden. I didn't even know what the hell it was . . ." His voice trailed. "But it smacked me hard in the chest. Almost twenty years later, I'm still in love with you."

The revelation should have her in rapture, walking on air. Instead she felt flat, dejected. Because even though he'd just declared his love for her, he didn't look happy. On the contrary, the man she loved looked like his heart was breaking into a million pieces.

"I'm glad you invited me to L.A. and let me in the part of you that I shut out for so long," he continued in a low voice, filled with regrets. "And for that I'm truly sorry."

She pressed her face in his hand and kissed his palm. "Come with me. It's only three months. Stay with me."

He stepped back and shoved his hands in his pockets. "Where are you going?" he asked, but his voice gave her no sign he was actually considering the idea.

"I don't know." She really didn't. One day she could be in Atlanta, New York next, and Utah after.

"You have a tour to finish," he said in a perfectly calm voice. "I know. You put it off long enough. Don't you think?"

"We can make us work. I know I'll be on the road a lot, but I'll come back to the island as much as I can."

"How often?"

"I don't know," she answered, heart hammering in her chest. "Whenever–"

"Your schedule allows," he finished, no trace of bitterness in his voice. "I'm willing to go anywhere with you, but I want permanence. My home is the Vineyard."

"We can make it work." She wanted to point out couples like Angelina Jolie and Brad Pitt, Will Smith and Jada Pinkett. They found a way. But her shoulders slumped because even in her ears, they sounded doomed. She was temporary. Although she'd stopped running, she was still lost in the torrid vortex of the past.

Her stomach churned with a cocktail of emotions. A tear slid down her cheek. He wiped it away with his thumb, and brought the salty streak to his lips. "Don't cry," he whispered.

She shook her head, unable to speak. They stood staring at each other. When she couldn't take it anymore, emptied, like a collapsed balloon she let herself fall back on the couch. In a busy silence, she watched as Forrest removed his jacket, unknotted his tie and sat next to her. Then he reached his hand behind her head and unclipped her hair.

With a gentle tug, he turned her face so she was looking at him. Removing his glasses, he placed them on the other end of the sofa before focusing back on her, a dark edgy expression on his face. "Make love to me," he said, and then kissed her. Tender at first. Then not so tender.

Her arms reached up and tangled around his neck. Wanting to be as intimate with him as she could, she kissed him back. She swept her tongue across his lips and garnered a low, guttural sound deep in his throat. It was a soulful, hungry sound that consumed her. His mouth opened on hers, igniting flames all the way to her toes.

His hands were swift on her dress, going straight to the delicate buttons. Nimble fingers snapped one button loose. "Is this your dress?" he asked, kissing his way to the outer shell of her ear.

"Yes."

"I owe you a dress."

A pop snapping sound followed, she broke off a startled gasp when the front of her dress came apart. With a flick of a finger, her bra fell from her shoulders, bearing her breasts. He groaned, dipped his head and kissed her collarbone. Then lower. When he licked the tip of a nipple as if she were a sinful dessert, Claire sighed in sheer pleasure.

"I want to touch you," she said in a hurried voice, unbuttoning his shirt. In her impatience, she tore off a few buttons.

"Touch me."

She tugged off his shirt and ran her fingers over the firm ridges of abs, it generated a slight trembling movement from him.

His mouth was on her breast. He sucked then took it between his teeth and gave it a quick bite. She moaned at the sharp, sweet sting of pain mingled with pleasure. Quivering from head to toe, she arched her back, giving him more access. He repeated the same motion on the other.

That sweet ache between her legs throbbed, and Forrest was the one and only who could soothe her agony. Grateful to be wearing a dress, which was pretty much a belt around her waist now, she straddled him, and unzipped his pants. His fingers slid her panties to the side and stroked the spot between her thighs that was burning for him.

"So wet," he said hoarsely. "Now."

She sank onto him, and gasped silently. He filled her so completely, and held her like she was all he ever wanted.

"So fucking sweet," he whispered in that sexy, gravel-filled voice. She cupped his face and he gripped her waist, and she made love to him in her living room.

"Claire," he whispered, his eyes locked on hers.

"Forrest."

"I love you," he said, holding tight to her.

His words melted her. That deepest connection was her greatest wish. This was everything she'd ever wanted—to love and to be loved back by this man.

Overwhelmed with emotions, she looked away once to catch their hazy reflections in the dark of the window. They looked like two people who couldn't get enough of each other. His eyes squeezed shut, his breath came fast and harsh, and he moved deeper into her. She watched for another moment, thrilling inside at all that the window revealed about him, and how he felt about her. She turned back to him, their bodies colliding, their lips connecting, her arms wrapped around him as they came together.

Then he carried her to the bedroom, turned on the shower and washed her down. In desperation, they reached for each other again. With her hands on the shower wall, Forrest plunged into her as the water beat against the tile floor. Steam rolling over them. Their cries reverberated, blending with the running water.

Once in bed, they made love again, a little slower this time. He kissed her deep, moving in an unhurried motion as she writhed beneath him, lost, completely gone.

"Tell me something beautiful," she murmured.

Pushing her hair away from her face, he looked into her eyes. "Claire."

Her heart toppled over. Tears threatened to spill. She blinked and cried out his name as they rode the wave.

She wasn't sure how long they stayed like that—tangled, holding tight to each other. As if they disconnected, they might never find their way back. She held on until he brought his weight to his arms and slowly withdrew from her body. He sat on the edge of the bed, hair rumpled, as his unguarded eyes swept over her.

She had the oddest feeling that he was cataloging her—from her hair, lips, breasts, and then her eyes, as if this was their last time. This time she didn't hold back and let her pain roll down her cheeks in silent tears.

"Don't cry," he whispered, running a hand over her arm.

"I'm not."

He smiled.

"You'll wait for me," she repeated the words she'd uttered to him so many times in their lives.

He kissed her. "Forever."

"I'm coming back to you when I'm done."

"I know."

CHAPTER TWENTY-EIGHT

"A committed heart does not wait for conditions
to be exactly right. Conditions are never exactly right."
~ Charles Montgomery

AS SOON AS Forrest arrived in Vineyard Haven, he drove to downtown Edgartown and caught the *On Time* ferry to Chappaquiddick. While being shuttled over he pulled his phone, swiped the screen to send Claire a text. She beat him to it. In his inbox was her picture. Wide, luminous eyes, a bit puffy from lack of sleep and tears shed stared back at him. His heart swelled. Pain in the back of his mind came forward by the slightest reminder.

He read the text.

Order of travel for this week. Seattle. Wisconsin, Utah and New York.
Where do you want to meet? Missing you so much.

His fingers brushed across the screen of the smartphone, tracing her full lips and the smile meant only for his eyes. He tapped a response.

When New York and for how long? A day, can't do. You'll be busy. Two
days? Second day just you and me. Otherwise, next time. Heading to
Chappy. Thinking of you.

Since he didn't expect an immediate response, he shoved the phone in his jeans pocket and focus straight ahead of Norton Point for the two-mile ride to the peninsula. Best thing to do was not to think about her or the fact less than twenty-four ago he'd been soaking in everything Claire.

He failed.

Thoughts of her flooded his brain. Pulling his phone, he examined his text again and stopped at the one day, can't do words. In actuality, he'd take thirty seconds of her day, if that was all she was able to give, but he knew the next few months were going to be insane. It was best to let her be, give her space to focus and not be a distraction. And maybe, just maybe, she'd find a way back home.

Emptiness settled in his chest. He exhaled and was relieved when the privately owned and operated ferry docked. Although winter was on its way out, a chill lingered. Cold air brought salt to his lips. Cry of the gulls that wheeled overhead in their lazy arcs filled his ears.

He drove through the isolated island. The actual landmass of Chappy was small, only about thirty-eight hundred acres with a population of less than two hundred people. Forrest turned on the radio, John Legend's *Shelter* played at a low volume. The singer's voice didn't intrude or disturb him. Fingers tapping lightly to the melody, he stayed focused on his mission to the Montgomery compound He slowed his pace as he drove over Dike Bridge and glanced at the fishing boats scattered over the harbor like fall leaves in a pond. The colors were engaging, random, bringing forth echoing memories from his childhood spent in the tight-knit community.

One of his most perfect memories he clung to was fishing here with his father, Jason, and Charles. That snapshot was golden and sacred, something to keep it in his heart forever. Hence the reason he was here.

Minutes later, he drove past My Toi Gardens, the small Japanese garden where he'd spent a fair amount of time with Claire.

He steered left, off the dirt road, and entered the Montgomery compound. Suddenly his stomach burned. He didn't have to be here. As a matter of fact, he'd told himself many times hell would freeze over first before he acknowledged the man. But Luc had always been a persistent man. Even in death.

It was more than that though. Charles' sacrifice gnawed at his conscience. Forrest made another left, drove to the large oak tree and parked under the tree house. He stepped out of the Jeep, but didn't head to the estate. For a beat, he surveyed the thickness of the tree. With its great boughs, it strived to touch the sky, and with its noble roots, it strengthened its hold on the ground.

He glanced up at the tree house. It stood mute in the winter air and impressively large. Like Charles, he thought.

He pressed one hand against the oak, his fingertips traced along the crevices that ran through the bark. His eyes came to rest on the sign nailed to the tree. Its once-vibrant red paint now blistered with rust. The wood grain ridged from the soaking in of the icy droplets, the relentless freeze-thaw taking its toll. But the words held on and were still legible. He glanced over them. *Girls Not Allowed. This means U CLAIRE!*

A smile touched his lips as he remembered the time she snuck out of the cottage to see him. That night they shared their first kiss. Felt like yesterday. He could still taste her mouth against his. She'd been hesitant at first, then curious.

Claire at seventeen had tortured him. So much so that even during a simple game of pool, he'd made sure their hips stayed pasted together just to feel her. Eleven years later, nothing had changed.

Forrest shoved a hand through his hair, chuckled and gently kicked the seat of the swing Charles had built for Claire once he learned she was banned from the man-cave.

Everything came back to Charles. Even Claire.

Not that he detested the older Montgomery. Up until recently, he loved the man and admired his dedication to Jason and his son's friends. All of them had always been welcome at the compound, not just Forrest. Some of the memories he held dear were time spent with Charles and his family.

As he crossed the immaculate lawn, a vision of Charles holding his wrist and ankle spinning him like a shot-sputter blazed through his mind's eye. Forrest lifted his glasses and dug the heel of his fingers in his eyes in an attempt to bury the memory. The mental image stayed vivid in his reverie. The happy wails as Charles spun him, the garden turning into a green blur, as he flew-flew, until they could spin no more. Even the finest details of Charles' face, creased with love and joy as Forrest laughed were crystal clear.

He entered the house. Immediately his pace increased. Each footfall clip-clopping down the hallway, shattering the silence. Deep in thoughts, he almost bumped into Charles. Forrest quickly came to a halt. A brief look of surprise crossed the older man's face, but disappeared as fast as it came.

For the first time in a long time he looked Charles over. Tall, broad, powerful shoulders, blue eyes as vivid as Jason's, dark hair sprinkled with gray. But what caught Forrest's attention was Charles' arrogant, masculine nose. It was slightly crooked and a bit too large. They had similar noses.

His breath caught in his chest, and his heart stopped for a moment. Forrest removed his glasses and took a step back. "Expecting someone else?"

"Where's Claire?" Charles asked.

"On her way to Seattle, I believe."

Charles looked at him.

"She has to finish the promotional tour for her movie."

Charles nodded. "Are the two of you finally in a good place?"

"I think so. But . . ." Forrest let his voice trail. Not going there. No need to discuss Claire's career and their relationship, that's not why he was here.

"Both of you will figure things out. She loves you. Always has." Charles walked past him down the hall into his office.

Forrest followed. For a moment neither spoke. "I read Dad's letter."

"Good."

Charles Montgomery, a man of few words. Forrest watched him, completely unreadable.

"What are your expectations going forward?" he asked his father.

Charles looked at him. "A relationship."

"We already had one."

"Then it should continue as it used to be."

Forrest walked over and stood by the large window, put on his glasses and focused on the garden filled with flowering quince and mock rush. "To me you'll always be Charles. Luc was my dad," he said while watching a cardinal poke for seeds at the tall flower's spike.

"Understood," Charles responded in a dry voice. "You're thirty-one years old. I never expected otherwise." He paused. "I just wanted you to know that you're my son and I love you."

Forrest's heart rattled around his ribcage. He turned and met Charles' gaze. "I've always known you love me. I've always felt it."

Charles nodded. "Good. Then we're good."

Neither made an attempt to move. They stood in the quiet room, Forrest lost in thoughts, memories, time lost, and his second chance with Claire. "I need some time to process everything," he said into the room, snapping the silence. "I'm working on it."

"I was thinking you, Jason, and I can maybe have a drink soon," Charles said.

"Let me know when."

Charles found his phone and seemed to check his calendar. "How's next week?" he asked, meeting Forrest's gaze.

"That works." Forrest's scratched the back of his head. "I should be going," he said and headed for the door.

"Forrest," Charles called to him.

Forrest stopped, hands on the door knob.

"I'm glad to see you've reunited with Claire. She loves you."

"I love her." He opened the door and came face to face with his mother.

Her hand flew to her mouth, eyes widened in obvious surprise. Forest's gut twisted.

"Forrest," she whispered.

He studied his mother. Her cheeks flushed, eyes bright. "How come you and Charles are always together?"

She smiled, walked past him into Charles' office. "Because we're friends."

"Were you ever in love with Dad? Luc?" He said his father's name for the first time.

A soft laugh escaped his mother's lips. Charles shoved his hands in his pockets. "I loved your father." His mother's voice shook a bit with sadness. She swung around, glanced at Charles then back to Forrest. "Charles and I have history. We are friends."

Right. He took a closer look at them standing side by side. Maybe for now friendship was all it was, but under all the layers, he also picked up an attraction. "When and if you ever decide to move on to the next phase, tell me. Don't wait until one of you is dead for me to find out." He started to walk away, then paused and turned to face the room and focused on Charles. "I'll see you next week."

He didn't breathe until he was in his Jeep. He dug in his pocket for his phone, tapped the name of the three men he considered brothers and texted.

Meet at Vapor in one hour.

Jason responded.

Already here. All three of us. Bring your sorry ass over.

Brows furrowed, he continued to study his phone. No text from Claire. Not that he was expecting one. Still his heart sank. Yeah, she had him by the balls. He threw the phone on the passenger seat and drove to catch the ferry over to the mainland. He had one more stop to make.

DEATH WELCOMED FORREST as he entered the cemetery. Aside from the whispering wind amongst the trees, screeching silence awaited a trespasser. Moving further in, a fresh chill ran anew along his spine. He stuffed his hands in his sailor jacket as he passed people standing, crying and talking to departed loved ones.

He was here to the same thing.

He needed to talk to Luc and this was the only way. While his mind was still processing the turns his life had taken, the anger had subsided. He was here to let go. The proximity to his father's frigid bones would close the gap between them for a moment. Ignoring the raw emotions that swelled inside him, he walked up to a slab of black granite and bent down to read the gold lettering at eye level. "For a while I was angry because I couldn't accept you didn't give me life, but you did. So did Charles and Mom. I'm lucky. I'm not angry anymore," he said to the gravestone.

It stood there with its youthful glow, strong, erect, ready to last a hundred years or more. Yet his father had already perished and begun his inevitable decay. Something so permanent to mark something so transient.

"If anything," Forrest continued. "I'm sad for you." He ran a hand through his hair. "For Mom, Victoria, and Charles." He exhaled. "But I've learned something from all of this. I am learning to let go. You're right, it's freeing." He lifted his glasses and rubbed his eyes. "I will love and cherish you always, and I thank you for the unconditional love. I'll be back to visit."

Sucking in a deep breath, he rose to his feet and walked over to his Jeep.

About twenty minutes later, Forrest entered Vapor. He spotted the other three guys right away and headed to the table. Blake shoved a beer in front of him.

"Here," he said, "We figured you were pissy."

"Why am I pissy?"

"Claire dumped you." This came from Adam.

"Claire didn't dump me."

"So why isn't she back with you?" Blake asked then took a sip of his beer. "According to the tweet Keely sent to me, it turned out she's dating her co-star."

"I thought it was Rafa," Adam added.

Rafa was Lily's brother who flirted openly with Claire when they met. Forrest groaned. "Claire is in Seattle for work."

Blake slid his phone in front of Forrest. "We know. You haven't seen this picture."

Forrest glanced at the screen and was greeted by a picture of Claire with her co-star's arm around her waist, a smile on her lips. Not the smile she had for him, he thought. He pushed the phone back to Blake. "So you guys decided to make me feel better."

Jason who had been silent took a chug of his beer. "Did you guys break up?"

"No." He swallowed a gulp of the beer and shook his head. "I really didn't think men have these sessions." He tilted his head in Adam's direction. "Well, he needed one a few months ago."

Adam flipped him the bird.

"You all cornered me when I became a pothead," Jason added.

"And drank too much," Blake added.

"And slept with too many women," Forrest reminded his friend, his brother.

All three of them looked at him.

"Yes, that is wrong too," Forrest said. "If a woman does the same thing, it . . ."

Adam put his hands up. "Oh please stop we know . . . no need for the fucking lecture."

Forrest shrugged, but smiled. "Just sayin'."

"Duly noted." Adam groaned.

Forrest laughed because Adam had morals, strong family values, and worshiped Lily. Good to see with all of that his friend's edge hadn't diminished.

"So what's the issue?" Jason asked. "Why are you here and not wherever the hell she is?"

"You seem to forget I work."

His friends scoffed.

"I have patients to see," he said firmly.

"I'm sure your list of sick patients," Blake said, quoting the word *sick* with his fingers, "will dwindle now that you are in a serious relationship."

"How many appointments do you have tomorrow or this week?" Jason continued to barrage him with questions.

Maybe two, but to answer them would be wasted breath. "And the farm," he said instead.

"You have a full-time staff," Jason pointed out.

Forrest really wished they weren't brothers. And for fuck's sake, he was older by three whole months. "I think I'm smart enough to get your point."

Adam chuckled, clearly enjoying the fact the tables had turned and he was no longer the one getting cannonade.

"Claire will balance her schedule once this madness is over," Jason continued, as if he hadn't heard a word spoken by Forrest. "These obligations were made before you." He looked at Forrest. "You know that's how she dealt with not having you in her life."

Forrest placed his glasses on the table and scrubbed his face. "I got it."

"So you'll wait for her?" Jason asked.

"What the fuck. Who is more invested in this, you or me?"

Blake and Adam snickered.

"You and I both know how long I've loved her."

"Good. I'm glad you remembered." Jason smiled, seeming pleased. "Now don't fuck it up."

"When am I known to fuck up?"

All three fuckers stayed mute.

Okay, so he kind of messed shit up with Jason, and maybe he could have gone after Claire after she left and demanded an explanation, but that one could go either way. "I fucked up once and now we are talking again."

Jason snorted. "I'm sure there's more. I'll think about it."

Blake's phone dinged on the table. He looked at it and frowned.

"What's up?" Forrest asked his friend.

"My parents."

All three men sat a little straighter.

"It's time to send them money again," Blake continued and picked up his phone.

"Where are they nowadays?" Adam asked.

"England," Blake answered casually.

"Do they know you're back on the island?" Adam asked, chugging his beer.

"Nope."

Forrest wasn't fooled by his friend's unconcerned tone, and he guessed none of the others were either. Hell the whole island was well-versed on Blake's parents, but this was one of the few topics on the *Do Not Discuss* list. "Because . . ." Forrest said carefully.

"Because if they find out, they'll be here breathing down my neck and driving me bat shit crazy. You all know I ran off as soon as I was able to. I don't want them here."

Neither of them said a word. They picked up their beer and quietly drank.

By the time Forrest entered his house, it was dark. And he was tired . . . a good thing because that meant it'd be easy for him to pass out.

After he showered, he realized he had two text messages from Claire.

Doc, thought you might be available to chat. Heading to Wisconsin tomorrow for three days. Say you'll meet me. Miss those sexy glasses of yours. BTW, check your suit pocket. Left you a key. Come by whenever.

The other text was shorter and to the point.

I love you.

CHAPTER TWENTY-NINE

"Home is where the heart is."
~ Anonymous

FOR A DECADE happiness had been an elusive shadow for Claire. Now finally within reach, she had no intention of letting it slip through her fingers. Sitting on the terrace of the open air Japanese restaurant on Rodeo Drive, she examined the crowd. Everyone looked to be in good spirits. Excitement radiated from their faces. They smiled and laughed with ease. They hugged hello and again for goodbye. They talked rapidly, gesturing with their hands while drinking wine or a cocktail.

Why not her?

Until the night of her eighteenth birthday, her childhood had been happy. Her life on the island had been happy. Her relationship with Forrest had made her happy.

She breathed in the early spring air and welcomed the relaxed atmosphere. Just in time. Two weeks of non-stop action had taken its toll on her physically and mentally. The only reason she made this one-day pit stop in L.A. was to meet with her manager before flying on to New York.

She needed sleep. Desperately so. Not a power nap either. Only the state where her nervous system was relatively inactive, postural muscles relaxed, and consciousness practically suspended could possibly get rid of her deep despondency.

Maybe in her own bed, she'd be able to get a good night's rest. It had evaded her so far. In the inkiness, she'd tossed and turned, never able to find the right position. A lingering haze of sleep hovered somewhere at the back of her mind but always too far away to reach, floating in the pool of memories.

She missed her family. She missed her friends. She missed the island. But most of all, she missed Forrest, his kisses, his face, the way he smiled.

They talked regularly, even managed a routine. They called, sent text messages, and emails. But what she craved the most remained out of reach–that deep physical and emotional union that only happened when two people touched. It didn't even have to be sexual. Holding hands, tucked in his arms. Whatever. Anything. She ached for it.

Here and there during a late night conversation, they talked about possibly connecting midway or at one of the places she was scheduled to make an appearance. Those plans fell into a yawning black hole and never came to fruition. Mostly on her part, because her daily itinerary barely left room to sit down and enjoy a decent meal.

To think, the grueling schedule was not even at its end. After the promotional tour came the movie premiere in the U.S. and overseas. That in itself consisted of another whirlwind of traveling. But the madness should be shorter. By the end of the month or maybe summer, she should be free to go back to the island.

Back home.

Back to Forrest.

The movie had already garnered a positive buzz. Her fans were eager to see her stretch her wings. This was her big break as an actress. She should be walking on air instead of feeling so down in the dumps. Problem was what once filled her with excitement now left a void in her life.

She waved at James as he entered the restaurant. After hugs and a quick update on his children, he slid a thick envelope across the table to her. She eyed the package then her manager. "What's this?"

"Another script for you to read to see if you're interested." His tone was casual and warm, without any pressure. "If yes, then you'd start filming in the fall."

She took a sip of her wine, sat there and listened to her manager go on about meetings and filming sessions. Something shriveled inside and her stomach knotted. "I'm not interested, James."

He stopped, leaned back in his chair and appraised her. Then he smiled. "It's time?"

She had everything she ever wanted. A thriving career. A big bank account. Fame. For ten years she told herself those things, although superficial, were sufficient. They validated her. She should be ecstatic. Actually, for a while she'd managed to persuade herself she had been. But after returning to the island and reconnecting with Forrest, everything had shifted.

She yearned to be someone's permanence. And that person was back on the Vineyard. It took ten years to stop running and accept what her heart wished for. Family, friends, and Forrest.

Always Forrest.

He was her home.

"All of this means nothing if Forrest is not in my life."

"As your manager, I'm supposed to make you aware of any opportunity that is presented to you."

James had always looked out for her. She had no reservation he'd continue to do so. "I know and I love you for that."

He took the envelope and put it back in his messenger bag. "But I'm glad you've decided to pass on this."

The waiter approached their table. After a quick polite exchange ensuring their needs were met, he took their order and left.

"For now," she went back to the reason she'd requested to meet with James. "I'd like to only focus on my music. That's my passion."

"What about the touring?"

That part she hadn't figured out yet. "I don't want to spend months on the road anymore." That piece she was sure of. "Maybe a few concerts here and there."

Concern touched James' face. She understood it. Out of sight meant out of mind. Fans were fickle that way. To stay relevant she had to stay current and worth seeing. Once upon a time consumed by the need to prove her self-worth to the Victorias of the world, *and even to herself, might have steered her decision, but not anymore.*

Luckily, that Claire, the person with the doubts, and daddy issues had found peace of mind. "I love my career," she said with conviction because it was true. "But I don't really care if I become yesterday's news. There are other things I want and a man I want those things with."

"Listen, Claire," James said after a long, hard stare. "You're allowed to take a break or slow down. For ten years you've been going non-stop. You don't need the money." He signed the check and pushed his chair back. "I know Ava is stopping by later to bring some documents to you. Should I have her bring your flight information?"

"I already have it."

James arched a brow. He knew her well enough to know she had something up her sleeve.

"I take it you're stopping somewhere."

A smile touched her lips. "I'm going home."

CLAIRE ZIPPED HER overnight bag while humming the tune of *Tattooed Hearts*. It was recently released for air play, and climbing several charts, even sitting at number one in several categories. The tune was catchy in that elegantly minimalist approach with only her vocals, the guitar and the piano. It made sense that her best song yet was written about Forrest. The thought made her grin.

Tomorrow they'd reunite. Her insides vibrated with joy. Unable to stand still, she moved about the bedroom and picked up her phone. She started formulating a text to share her pending arrival with Forrest then stopped.

To surprise or not to surprise? Forrest hated to be caught off guard. She could see his handsome face. Pinched brow, eyes sharp behind his glasses, the chiseled lines of his mouth edged up in a half-smile.

Surprise him it was going to be.

A buzzing sound came from the speaker announcing she had a guest arriving. She checked her watch. Ava was due to arrive. Claire threw the phone on the bed, bit down a smile and headed to the living room and came to a screeching halt. Her heartbeat raged out of control at the sight before her.

Forrest.

He stood still for her inspection. His intense stare allowed her to take him in before a full-face smile deepened the creases around his eyes. "I owe you a date."

Surprised into speechlessness, she watched as he stepped inside her apartment. All six-foot-three of him in a relaxed wardrobe that never renounced his elegance. Faded jeans, black crew neck tee and a black bomber jacket, his dark hair tucked under a low crown, torn and tattered Boston Red Sox baseball cap, and an overnight bag slung over his shoulder.

He looked so delicious.

Her heart ached suddenly because she'd miss seeing him every day and every night. Unable to contain herself, she ran to him. He dropped the bag and wrapped his arms around her waist. He pulled her tight as if she were the most precious thing in his life, as if he couldn't wait another day, another second, to touch her.

She loved the feeling.

She held on. Butterflies did a crazy bounced low in her belly. *He feels so good.* "I love you," she breathed, the air from her lungs stolen by the moment.

"Forever," he said, his mouth touching her earlobe.

It wasn't a question, but she answered anyway. "Yes. Infinitely."

He gave her one last squeeze and then he kissed her with a passion that took her breath away. When they finally broke for air, he led her to the sofa.

"I was going to come to you tomorrow," she said, heart still pounding so fast it threatened to burst out from her chest.

"Oh yeah?" He looked surprised. Pleased.

Claire nodded. "A quick stop on my way to New York."

There was a slight quirk at the corners of his mouth. "Now you don't have to." He smoothed back her hair and held her gaze. "I'm going with you." He wasn't asking for permission. He was letting her know his intention.

She blinked. Martha's Vineyard was his home. He loved his house, the lake. "That's three months on the road."

Forrest smiled. His thumbs caressed her cheeks. "You're my base."

Her heart was officially at stroke level. To make sure, she didn't pass out, she held on to him. "What?"

"I know I said the island was my home before I left, but I was wrong. You're my home, Claire."

Goosebumps covered her skin. Her heart squeezed tight, so damn tight she was bereft of speech.

A wrinkle appeared between his brows as he studied her for a beat. "This is a bit sudden," he said quietly. "I understand if you need time."

Time.

For what?

She blinked again, forcing her head out of the clouds and focused. He looked . . . susceptible to being wounded. "I need you." She could have sworn he let out a breath. "I want you." She kissed the dark shadow of stubble along his angular jaw line "God, Forrest–" Unable to continue, she buried her face in his chest and clutched tightly to him.

At times, love needed no language. With his arms holding her, they sat in a beautiful silence for a beat. When he stood, he stepped away, her gaze immediately followed him.

"I would have come sooner," he said, voice coiled with emotion. "But I needed to find someone to cover the clinic."

"I'm your home." The thought made her heart melt. Tears ran unchecked down her face.

"Yes." He extended a hand, which she gladly took. "Don't cry."

"Tears of happiness." She sighed in pleasure as his strong arms closed around her. "You're my home too. You always have been."

"Good to know." His voice was strong and undisguised with relief as he pressed his lips against her forehead. Then he buried his face in her hair and released a long, rough breath that seemed to come from the deepest part of his heart and soul. "Claire."

"Forrest."

"I love you."

EPILOGUE

"And at the heart of mathematics lies the concept of infinity."
~ Anonymous

THE SUMMER BREEZE rustled Claire's blouse and hair. Laughing, she tilted her head back and inhaled a lungful of the salty ocean air.

"We're here." Forrest's mouth brushed against her ear.

Moaning, she pressed her back against the wall of his chest, and listened to the sea crashing against the side of the ferry as its engine stopped.

"Ready?"

She turned to face him, as always her breath caught by his sheer beauty. Tiptoeing, she placed a lingering kiss on his lips then slipped her hand in his. "Let's go."

With fingers threaded together, they stepped off the ferry in Vineyard Haven and were greeted by blue skies, and the sweet air of the island. There was something about the Vineyard that automatically relaxed her body.

Perhaps that was why she loved it here so much—it stabilized the rapidity of her thoughts, grounded her in a place where ticking of clocks did not govern a lifestyle.

"Did I tell you Chappy and the rest of the island have reconnected?" Forrest asked as they walked off the pier.

Chappaquiddick, a peninsula of Martha's Vineyard, stood as a truly separated island after its bay broke through the beach and joined the ocean. For almost a decade, Chappy and the rest of the Vineyard had remained separated.

Until now.

It had to be an omen. A good one for sure. Her worlds were merging, joining. Seagulls wheeled over their heads and cried, welcoming them home. "No more gap between our worlds."

"None."

She pulled out her phone to send a text to her family and friends and realized she had no phone signal. Oh well, cell phone was officially off, a fortunate stroke of serendipity. Just her, the island, her family, friends, and Forrest.

Free therapy.

Reboot. Reset.

Home.

Lily had given birth to a beautiful girl. Claire was looking forward to playing auntie. She slid into Forrest's parked Jeep that Blake dropped off earlier in the day. "How does it feel to be back after months on the road?"

He revved up the engine. "It feels nice. But I'd walk away from here to be with you. Don't ever forget that."

She knew that. He'd spent the last three months following her around the globe, not once mentioning the need to be back on the island. Her heart did that funny little dance reserved for the man sitting beside her. The last time she'd been this happy had been . . . *here* with Forrest. His love was infinite and without limits, as was hers. She understood that.

"I want to be here with you," she reassured him.

"I never want to be the reason you walk away from your career. You were meant to sing."

When she informed Forrest she would be taking a break and not focus on recording another record until a year or two, he had been adamant about her not choosing between him and her career. This wasn't about two possibilities. She'd continue to sing and travel, just not the grueling schedule she maintained for so long. Living became more important. "I'm not walking away from my career. I've readjusted my priorities. Do you know how I coped with you not being in my life the last decade?

"Tell me."

"I worked until I couldn't think. Whenever James brought up a project, I did it as long as it didn't interfere with my singing." She turned to face him and slid her fingers into his hair just for the sheer pleasure of touching him. "I love to sing, I won't give that up. But I don't want to be a full-time actress. As for designing, I'll design a wedding gown when and if I feel like doing it." She smiled and said, "I want us."

His eyes darkened behind the glasses as if he was contemplating something then he turned his attention to the road. "I want to take you home but everyone is waiting for us at Vapor."

Brisk wind ruffled her hair. Tucking a few strands behind her ear, she sat back and put on her shades. "Let's go."

As they drove down Main Street, Claire took in the scenery of the island now fully awake with tourism and those who always departed for the winter months. A bicycle bell rang from the bike path and Forrest waved at Mrs. Kane. The streets with no traffic lights were busy but flowed smoothly. After a short drive, Forrest pulled the Jeep into the parking area at the pier across from Seafood Shanty.

As always, Downtown Edgartown, the heart of the island, was full of life and energy. The restaurants, ice cream parlors, and bike shops were all open for business. With her hand encased in Forrest's, they walked the short distance to Vapor.

To Claire's surprise, the place was quiet. A rarity. The only people inside the island's favorite hangout spot were their friends, her mother, Ralph, Charles, and Marjorie.

Confused, she looked at Forrest. "Why is Vapor empty? Did something happen to Adam and Jason?" She spoke to everyone often, but her time had been limited, she might have missed something.

"Vapor is closed for a few hours." He released his hand from hers to place it on the small of her back and led her to their family. Hugs were quickly exchanged, welcoming her back.

"Welcome home," Jason whispered in her ear. "And thanks for making the big guy whole again."

"How are you, Minka?" she asked her friend, now three months pregnant.

"Other than I keep snapping at my husband." Minka gave Jason a secret smile. "I'm well. But I can't wait to give birth and hold these babies."

Claire grinned and turned to Adam standing next to Lily with a tri-blue colored wraparound baby carrier on his chest. A gift she'd personally picked out and sent to the happy couple after receiving a text with the picture of their newborn. "She's tucked in there somewhere."

Adam nodded and pulled back the cotton material to reveal a cozy, sleeping baby with a mass of dark hair and tanned skin like her father. "Meet your niece, Christina Sofia Aquilani."

Claire's heart squeezed. The name was a nod to his parents. "Can I hold her?"

"Of course." Very gently he removed the sleeping baby from the safety of his chest and handed his daughter to Claire.

The newborn opened a set of big brown eyes and gripped Claire's thumb. She let out one of those soothing baby sounds and gave Claire what she thought looked like a smile, then let out a sharp, high-pitched sound that went straight through Claire's head.

"I'll take her." The proud papa took his daughter and rocked her on his chest, whispering to her in Italian.

"She's all about daddy right now," Lily said. For proof, the cry had subsided and Christina was once again safely pressed against her father's heart.

"Daddy's little girl," Blake pointed out. "It's only fair." He lowered his head and placed a kiss on Keely's lips.

Claire glanced over at a smiling Lily as she watched her husband and their daughter bonding. So much love in the room, this time there was no hollow space in her gut.

Charles walked over to Forrest and placed a hand on his son's shoulder. Aware the two had been working on mending their relationship, she was glad to see the tension that was once so thick between them had dissipated. Not that Forrest would ever be ready to refer to the other man as his father, but she knew in his heart he had accepted the role Charles played in his life.

"Go ahead," Charles said to Forrest. "You made those two shut down Vapor for you."

Forrest slid his father a look. Charles shrugged his broad shoulders and looked amused. She was utterly confused about what was just said between the two men. She peered at Forrest. He stared at her, his expression faded from relaxed to serious.

"Claire." Forrest pulled a small velvet box from the pocket of his jacket and crouched before her.

Someone let out a smothered laugh. She couldn't tell which of the guys it came from. It didn't matter. The vicious thumping of her heart made her forget about everything except what was happening at the moment.

"I asked everyone to meet us here," Forrest said, voice thick and gruff. "Because I thought it was fitting for us to be surrounded by the people we love the most when I ask you to marry me."

He opened the box and revealed a stunning ring with an open curved diamond band in the shape of the infinity symbol. There was a huge gap of silence, not even a sound from baby Christina. Then Claire's lips parted and released a breath.

"Marry you," she said, and her voice made a funny noise as it cracked with emotion.

Forrest smiled. "You're crying again."

"I am?" Oh God. She'd been doing that a lot lately. She quickly swiped her cheeks. "Happy tears."

"I love you. I want to be your home as you are mine. Say yes so those jerks can stop staring at me with those silly grins on their faces."

She stared down at Forrest, the big, calm man, who always knew what he wanted. She'd loved him forever. "Yes." She blinked to stifle in-coming tears and looked into his beautiful eyes. He was a man of few words, but his eyes . . . they always spoke to her. And he meant every word. She cupped his scruffy face as he rose to his feet.

"Yes," he repeated her word, his voice raw with relief.

Claire let out a chuckle. She went up on her tiptoes and wrapped her arms around his neck. "Yes," she whispered once more against his lips. "I've loved you for so long."

He kissed her again. In the back of her consciousness, she heard a few cheers and clapping. Forrest scooped her up in his arms. Claire let out a scream filled with delight and held on tight. "I'm officially spoiled."

"Good," Forrest muffled against her lips.

"Hey," Charles said, his voice echoing the happiness inside Claire. "Are we celebrating?"

"Tomorrow," Forrest answered. "Claire and I are going home."

Then he was kissing her again as he carried her away. She lost Forrest and found him again. The second time, guided by not only their hearts, but with maturity, things made more sense. Timing had a lot to do with everything in life. Sometimes regardless of what the heart desired, love continued to run away and escape . . . because ten years ago, they hadn't been ready for each other yet.

Now, they were in a suitable mindset and primed for their infinite journey together.

Everything within her flooded with happiness, need, lust . . . love. "Thank you for waiting for me."

"Forever, Claire. I'd wait for you forever."

She loved him.

She loved life.

She was happy.

She was home.

The End

ABOUT THE AUTHOR

MIKA LIVES IN New Jersey with her Happy Chaos—her husband and their two energizer bunnies. She's addicted to Spotify, a cute scarf, football, tennis, soccer. Yep. She loves sports.

When she does have time to breathe, and isn't behind her computer, you can find her working on her garden, reading, hiking with her camera slung over her shoulder, or practicing her knitting skills.

She loves to hear from readers. Connect with her on Facebook, Twitter, and Goodreads, or drop her an email.

Email: *mikajolie2@gmail.com*

For latest news on her current works-in-progress, interviews with fellow authors, or just to see what she's up to, check out *www.mikajolie.com* While there, sign up for her newsletter, where you can hear her latest news and enjoy giveaways.

BOOKS BY MIKA JOLIE

MARTHA'S WAY SERIES
The Scale—Book One
Need You Now—Book Two
Tattooed Hearts—Book Three

PLAYLIST

Nightcall – by London Grammar

Gods & Monsters – by Lana Del Rey

Breaking The Rules – by Jack Savoretti

Renegade – by X Ambassadors

Mr. Brightside – by The Killers

Stay – by Thirty Seconds To Mars

Take Me To Church – by Hozier

Feel Good Inc – by Gorillaz

Summertime – by DJ Jazzy Jeff & The Fresh Prince

Blue In Green – by Miles Davis

DARK 'N' STORMY RECIPE
from Tattooed Hearts—Book Three of Martha's Way

This awesome drink only takes two ingredients—dark rum and ginger beer—to create this easy-drinking, refreshing classic cocktail from Bermuda. If you can't find it Gosling's Black Seal rum, substitute another dark rum such as Myers's. This is one of my faves. Enjoy!

Ingredients
Ice
2 ounces Gosling's Black Seal rum
6 ounces ginger beer
1 lime wedge

Made in the USA
Columbia, SC
03 May 2023

16053478R00150